NEVER WRAITH

NEVER WRAITH

SHAKIR RASHAAN

Entangled Publishing, LLC
644 Shrewsbury Commons Ave., STE 181
Shrewsbury, PA 17361
rights@entangledpublishing.com

Entangled Teen is an imprint of Entangled Publishing, LLC.

Visit our website at www.entangledpublishing.com.

Cover art and design by Bree Archer
Cover images by
Ople Witsanu/Shutterstock
Interior design by Toni Kerr

ISBN 978-1-64937-334-2
Ebook ISBN 978-1-64937-335-9

Manufactured in the United States of America

First Edition August 2023

10 9 8 7 6 5 4 3 2 1

entangled teen
an imprint of Entangled Publishing LLC

To babygyrl,
It took a while, but I kept my promise. I love you.

At Entangled, we want our readers to be well-informed. If you would like to know if this book contains any elements that might be of concern for you, please check the back of the book for details.

CHAPTER ONE

Right. Left. Right cross. Left hook.

I'm up at damn near four in the morning in the basement of my uncle Xavion's house, waiting for my alarm to tell me it's time to go to school. I run through the sequences in my head, remembering what Unk has been teaching me since I was little, burning off the negativity I built up over the past couple of days.

Sweat soaks my shirt, but I don't care right now. I just need to get rid of as much of this aggression as possible.

Left hook. Left hook. Right. Right. Left. Right. Uppercut. Just like that.

If I had a choice, I would've gone and done something that, technically, Unk wouldn't approve of, mainly because I'm not exactly *old* enough to go by myself to do what I'd prefer to do to blow off some steam. Too many questions to answer. I don't have the connects here that I have in the A, so I have to settle for taping up my hands, pulling on the sparring gloves, and taking out as much frustration on the heavy bag as I possibly can.

I need this anger to go away, but it only grows with every jab.

My life has been upended. Again. *What did I do to deserve this?*

I mean, my uncle is cool as hell, and I love spending the summers with him, but there's a huge difference between coming down here for a couple of months and living here for the rest of the school year.

No one has told me why I had to move. I shouldn't be here, and I sure as hell didn't do anything wrong.

I had a whole life in the A, and my nana—God bless her—did everything she could to raise me. The SWATs—Southwest Atlanta—can either make or break a person, and I don't break easy. Nana made sure of that.

Hearing the heartbreak in her voice when she said I had to move was more than I could bear. She was vague about the why of it all, but she kept saying that it was for my own protection.

The jabs come faster and harder now, and the impacts echo against the walls. My vision blurs as I blink away sweat and tears.

Right. Uppercut. Left hook. Hook. Keep hooking. Overhand right. Faster, bro. *Faster*.

The alarm on my phone blares, shaking me from my thoughts. I stand still and clear my vision, and *whoa*, I've left a sizable dent in one spot on the heavy bag, nearly ripping the fabric. I let out a low whistle. A few more punches and that would've torn for sure.

My arms feel like someone tied kettle bells to my wrists. The exhaustion and soreness, though? That's exactly what I need, and I focus on the soothing, burning sensation coursing through my body. I rest my forehead against the bag and take as many breaths as I can to cool down, then stagger toward the stairs to take a shower and get ready for school.

"If you keep that up, I might have to seriously consider getting you into Golden Gloves."

I flinch, mouth, "What the—" and look up. Then blow out a breath. It's just Unk. I guess he decided that scaring the hell out of me needed to be checked off his morning to-do list.

"Yo, how are you able to move around this house and I can't hear you coming?"

Unk gives me this grin like he knows some ancient secret or something. "Don't worry about all that. I might teach you when you're older." He makes his way down the stairs, then glances at the bag. "You okay? Is there anything we need to chop it up about?"

I shrug. "I feel like the reset button got pressed on me again. Sorry about the heavy bag. I'll fix it when I get home later."

He walks toward me, nodding, then finds the scissors and cuts the tape off my hands.

"You've been through a lot," he says, "and I know this feels like another bump in a road full of roadblocks and potholes, but tough times don't last. Tough people do. You're one of the toughest I know, and I am wowed every day by what you can handle."

Man, does he have to break out the monologue?

"I hear you, and spending summers down here with you was always lit, but on a full-time basis? No disrespect, but this ain't it."

Unk throws away the tape he cut, does a quick check of my hands for bruises, and sighs. "All I ask is to give it a chance. We have to make the best of things for now. Who knows? You might actually like something about Oakwood Grove."

That's debatable, but now isn't the time to argue. I'm gonna be late for school if I don't hurry up.

"Yeah… Who knows?" I put the gloves away and then start trudging up the stairs. I don't realize how dead my legs are until I take the first step. *Arggghhh.*

As I head to my room, I avoid any and all mirrors. I know what I'll see. My emotions are still there. Raw. Edgy. Volatile.

Once in my room, I start the shower, praying for relief as the steam rises, hoping my thoughts are clearer by the time I finish. I step inside to scrub the weird energy off of me, then close my eyes and allow the soothing sandalwood scent from my handmade soaps to transport me anywhere but here.

I swear, this town better not be a total snooze fest, or I'll be putting a lot of miles on my Jeep on the weekends.

As I pull up on the Oakwood Grove High campus, I start going through my long list of stress-relief techniques. The 4-7-8 trick should quell the rising anxiety I normally feel when I enter a new environment.

Inhale. Out. Close your mouth and hold. Finally, exhale…

"Yeah. Nope," I say out loud. And trying it a second time doesn't do a thing for me, either.

I switch to the 3-3-3 method. First, I have to pick three things I see around me. I scan the immediate area to get a good look at the massive building, noticing the crimson-and-gray dome that accentuates the front entrance to the school, with the words OAKWOOD GROVE HIGH SCHOOL emblazoned across the overhang. The brick surrounding the entrance gives way to long columns that flare out and make the building appear V-shaped. And what's with all the huge windows? I can see right into the classrooms.

Students are making their way into the building, and the sheer number of them pumps up my anxiety again.

I don't even want to get out now, and I'm not rolling down the windows so I can hear three things around me. I just wanna stay in my bubble.

No. Scrap that plan.

I rub the amethyst teardrop pendant laying on my chest—a gift from my nana meant to center my energy—to ground me for at least a few minutes, as a last resort, but my anxiety levels have shot through the roof.

When I slow-roll into the parking lot in my black Jeep Wrangler Rubicon—I named her Storm, after the baddest and prettiest of the X-Men—I notice all eyes on me, which triggers more anxiety. I know my Storm stands out, and real talk, how can she not? The lift kit and thirty-five-inch oversize tires with glossed black matte twenty-six-inch wheels alone turn heads, not to mention the neon purple lights that glow underneath at night.

I notice the eclectic mix of vehicles spread out over the space, from the sports cars grouped together in one corner to the pickup trucks that take up most of the spaces, and I even see other Jeeps. At least Storm won't be the only one. They're nowhere as dope as mine, which is why all the attention is so laser focused on me until I get out.

Still, I *really* don't want the spotlight right now. Maybe once I get my bearings, I'll be all right, but today ain't it.

I'm planning to make the best of a bad situation, though. Like Unk said, maybe this town isn't as bad as I think. My plan is simple: Get in. Take the damn classes. Get out. Rinse. Repeat. Pray that graduation day comes faster than it takes a hot knife to cut through butter and get the hell out of this town on the first thing smoking.

When I pass by one of the benches, I notice they're splashed in the crimson and gray school colors, with the phrase "GHSA AAA State Champions 2019" painted in bold lettering across the back.

Yep. Football is religion in the South, and this is undeniable proof.

At the center of the courtyard stands a massive oak tree that takes over the entire area. Okay, so massive doesn't quite cover it, but from the width of the trunk alone, the school had to be built around it, because that tree was here first. I snap a pic on my phone for later, for inspiration. There's a landscape painting in my mind, and this would fit in perfectly.

When I pull my phone away, I spot a group of girls sitting at the base of the tree. I hadn't noticed they were there.

But…wait a minute… Who's *she*?

I don't mean to stare, but even from this distance, her hazel-green eyes capture me, making me want to stay there in the moment. The other girls aren't all that pressed, and they seem to fade into the background, leaving just *her* sitting there, trading glances with me.

She narrows her gaze while we stare for what seems like forever as her honey-bronzed braids frame her heart-shaped face. Her golden-brown skin makes her eyes stand out that much more. I'm already lost in whatever dream I've accidentally slipped into, and I don't want to leave any time soon.

She touches her face with her hand for a moment, and I follow with my eyes as it moves from her cheek to rest in her lap.

Her legs are tucked under her, perched on a blanket she shares with the other girls around her.

What in the world have I gotten myself into already? I haven't been here three seconds, and I'm standing here looking like I'm lovestruck.

Settle down, bro. We're not here for all that.

Then she grins, and my defenses have almost disappeared. I return a smile of my own and consider motioning for her to come and say hello.

Maybe this town won't be so bad after all.

But I think better of it; I don't know anything about her, regardless of the way she's managed to turn my whole attitude around with a simple glance. I shake out of whatever trance she put me in and head for the front doors.

Inside, I find the front office, and I'm pleasantly surprised at how helpful they are with everything I need to get started. That's a plus. It's definitely the opposite of what I've dealt with at the other high schools. Still, I'm guarded.

Ms. Tyler, a petite woman with an oval-shaped face and flawless beige skin, gives me my schedule, flashes a smile. "You're all set, Mr. Salah. If you hurry, you can make it to your first class before the late bell rings. Welcome to Oakwood Grove," she says.

"Thank you, ma'am. I'm looking forward to being here." Okay, so I'm lying, but I don't want to be rude, either. I turn into the hallway, look down at the schedule and the location of the first class, and… Where's a tour guide when I need one?

I move through the crowd as everyone rushes to their classes, trying to temper my anxiety over the weird glances and all the whispers. I turn around the corner, frustrated over heading down another wrong hallway, and this one's decorated a lot more than the others, with large signs and bold lettering all over the place. One banner sums up the reason why everyone is still in the halls— it's Rivalry Week. I don't have time for this mess. And then I see something about a Bicentennial event or whatever, and I know I'm over it all.

It's bad enough I have to transfer in the middle of the semester. Now I gotta deal with school spirit on steroids?

I spin to head back in the other direction and accidentally bump into another kid. I put my hands up to show I'm not there for any pressure. The last thing I need is to get caught up in something for no reason.

From the irritated look on this guy's face, though?

I'm gonna need to buckle up and get ready for whatever heat he's gonna bring.

CHAPTER TWO

"My bad, I was trying to find my history class," I say, backing up to give us more space.

"Yeah, it is your bad, new kid," he spits at me, then grits his teeth. "The history classes are on the second floor."

Why does he have all this heat on him, and why is it directed at me? I barely grazed him. "Thanks, I'll remember that."

I sidestep him, but he steps in my path. "Whoa, not so fast, New Kid."

So...he's gonna be *that guy*.

"My name is Yasir Salah, my boy," I say. "Not New Kid."

"I don't care, and I didn't ask." He cracks his knuckles in front of me like he's trying to make a point, keeping up pressure that doesn't need to be applied.

If he thinks I'm gonna flow with—I don't even know what to call this—he's gonna find out the hard way that I don't follow rules very well.

"Look, let's keep this simple," I say. "If you can just slide left for me, I'll slide to the right, and we can move on. Sound like a plan?"

I make my move to the right, brushing against his shoulder, because he still wants to block my path. Nah, not feeling this already. I walk down the hallway, and I almost make it to the corner before I hear this dude yell my name.

"I know you can hear me, 'ya-seer say-lah.' Don't ignore me. You won't like how that goes down."

The energy shifts in the hallway, and I feel every bit of the aggression coming at me. I turn around to step toward him and the rest of the group around him. He meant to rile me by saying my name loudly and pronouncing it wrong, and now everyone in this hall has stopped to watch, holding their phones out pointed at me. Like, really…what's with people and their early morning drama?

I already feel the anger coursing through me, like an avalanche ready to rumble down at the slightest disturbance. I dare this dude to go ahead and be the trigger so I can let loose with every bit of icy fury I have. He needs to learn a lesson, and I'm ready to teach and then some.

Just as I start to see nothing but black, I hear my nana's voice ringing loudly in my ears. *There is more than one way to handle bullies, my child. Promise me you will find another way. If there is no other way, decimate all in your path.*

I run a silent count to turn down the rage I'm still feeling, remembering my promise to her.

Fine. I'll have to do this another way.

I step toward whatever-his-name-is so I can deal with this quick, and I come face-to-face with one of the other guys in the group.

He's the runt of the litter, but he's built like a bulldog, with a chihuahua's attitude, and he looks like he spends more time getting groomed than a poodle. Half of his hair is an odd shade of red, and the other half has been dyed dark gray. School colors? This must be a football thing.

I pull back a few feet, but this dude closes the distance on me. "You heard my ace calling you, right? Do I need to shake the wax loose from your ears or something?"

Why is it always the short ones that have all the attitude?

I glare down into his ice-blue eyes, clenching my fists as I consider my options. It doesn't look good, even with my skills. There's too many of them. "Look, I need a few feet, all right? I don't do well with people in my personal space."

Whatever-his-name-is, the one who started it all, speaks up again. "I can understand why." He sniffs the air. "What is that funky-smelling cologne? Like, damn, bro, you couldn't wear something that wouldn't have everybody running for cover?" There he goes with the low-hanging insults. Typical.

"Yeah, Ian," Bulldog Boy chimes in. "He smells like someone dipped him in some burned wood and God knows what else that is... Whew." At least I know what the ringleader's name is now. He called him Ian. "If you wanted to make a first impression, you did that. I don't think that's what you wanted to do, but go off, bro."

Okay, shots fired. Nothing I haven't dealt with before, though. "You're worried about my cologne, Ian, but what I'm wondering is whether you used a crowbar to get into them skinny jeans. Who told you that was a good idea? Do you need to see a doctor about your blood circulation? I can recommend a few good ones."

Ian frowns as laughter bounces off the walls. I guess he doesn't like it when someone comes for him.

"And for the record," I growl, "my last name is pronounced 'sah-lah.' I know you heard me when I said it the first time. I knew some of y'all football players were slow, but if I have to remind you again, it's gonna be a problem."

To my amusement, Ian retreats to his crew. A few of them stare at me, trying to keep from laughing, and a couple of the others nod at something else being said between them. Ian turns back with this look like he has me checkmated. "So you got pressure? We can relieve that, for real. I'm gonna let you ride since you're new and all, but you need a lesson on how things flow around here."

Big bark from a little bitch who has goons backing him up. "And I suppose you're the one who's providing that lesson, huh? Look, bro, can we deal with that, like, next week or something? How about I pencil you in for, let's say, next Tuesday after school?"

Someone walks up from my right side, which surprises me. I usually have a knack for sensing if someone comes close, but I get distracted by the scent of jasmine and honeysuckle. I whip my head in the direction of such sweetness, and what my eyes land on are the most exquisite pair of hazel-green eyes I've ever seen in my life.

The same eyes I'd gotten caught staring at in the courtyard.

"Don't you know it's not polite to harass new kids on their first day?" Her voice is almost as soothing as her gaze. Damn, I'm in trouble. "He hasn't been on campus an hour and you're already starting up. I know you have something better to do."

Ian glares at her, making me feel some type of way. I want to drop a punch to his gut for the way he looks.

"Zahra, shouldn't you be off somewhere designing another crappy electric engine or something? Move along. This doesn't concern you."

Someone else pops up behind me, only this time I see him coming. Now, anyone who can make me feel short has my respect off break. This guy towers over everyone, but he stands behind Zahra like he's her bodyguard or something.

"You're funny, Ian," he says. "I'm trying to understand what makes you think you're supposed to be a part of this unwelcoming committee."

Ian rubs his hand over his face, looking all kinds of annoyed. "Kyle, don't think that because we ball together I won't give you the business, either." He turns his attention back to me. "It's our job to make sure these kids know how things work at Oakwood."

"Nah, you *want* things to flow a certain way, and I've told you before, the rules have changed," Kyle retorts. He moves to stand in front of Zahra, getting in Ian's face. "You still think you're the dude at the top of the stairs, and I'm telling you that you ain't it no more."

I shake my head. After watching all this go down in front of me, I can't decide whether I want to laugh or take pity on them. I turn toward Zahra, playfully elbowing her as I figure out what I need to say. "Okay, I think I got it now. This was part of the lesson I'm supposed to learn, so let me see if I have it… You're supposed to be the resident 'god on campus,' is that how this works? I'm supposed to do whatever you say or else, is that right?"

"That's exactly what's up, bro." Ian grits his teeth, glaring at me like he wants to fire off a punch or three. "Either you roll with it, or you get rolled over. I don't know where you're from, but you better head back there before something bad happens to you."

Is this man serious right now? "I see you need to get your life, for real. This ain't no real-life version of *All-American*, okay? I flow how I want to flow, and I meet people on their level. Whatever energy you give, I'm returning it, with interest. It's up to you to figure out how I treat you, got it? If you bring the smoke, don't be shocked when I bring the hellfire."

Zahra giggles, winking at me before she turns her attention to Ian. "I think he's made himself clear that your 'rules' don't apply to him. Maybe you should take that cue and try something that isn't so, I don't know, stupid?"

Before anyone else can get a word in, a resource officer who could pass for Thor shows up, startling everyone still waiting for more drama.

"Okay, everyone, you can head to class," the officer commands. As expected, everyone scatters, including Zahra and Kyle, finding the closest hallway they can find. "Ian Lance, I don't remember whether you and your minions are supposed to be on this side of the building, but I suggest you get to where you're supposed to be before I check for myself."

Ian glares at me, nostrils flaring, despite Thor's stunt double being close enough to rip us both in half. I refuse to back down, feeling so heated I think my skin is burning. He's not ready to catch a fade from me, I promise. We can put the gloves on and keep it clean, and he won't last a round.

Ian backs off, turning on his heel as he walks away from me and the officer. "You're lucky Sarge was here."

I don't care if Sarge is there. I lunge at Ian with every ounce of energy I have. What I'm not prepared for is how *strong* Sarge is. I know I said he reminds me of the God of Thunder, but I didn't expect him to actually live up to the moniker. He's literally holding me in place with nothing more than his outstretched arm. I give him a glance, and the look in his eyes lets me know that if I push my luck, he's gonna have to put me down, and I've been through enough of those to know I don't want that pain.

Message received, good sir. I'm not trying you any time soon.

"I can't wait," I yell at Ian as he finally turns the corner. I'm trying to save face more than anything now. I've never been held in check like this by an officer before. "I'm sure we'll have lots to discuss."

The faint scent that kept my attention — and calmed me down — has me searching for where Zahra had gone while my bravado was on full display. I can't find her right away, but I finally see her and Kyle making their way down the opposite end of the hall with the other students.

I try to call out to her, but nothing comes out of my mouth. I try a second time, and still nothing. Wait a damn minute. Why can't I say something? What in the world is going on? I can't be that nervous around her already, can I? I just met her, and I can't even say that we really *met*, met.

Zahra turns before she disappears around the corner, and she stares long enough to make me uncomfortable, but in the best way. Then she smiles the way she did when I saw her in the courtyard, and…by the gods, her smile shines brighter than the sun and melts me in seconds. Next thing I know, she winks and mouths, "See you later, cutie," before I lose sight of her.

Sarge cuts through the haze quick, grabbing my shoulder to get my attention. "Are you okay? You're new around here, right? What's your name? I'm Sargent Bolton, but the kids call me Sarge."

I still can't speak. Between not really hearing a single word he's said and clearing my head from Zahra's sweet scent being in my space all of five minutes, I need to get my head together quick. "Yasir Salah, sir. I'm good, Sarge, but you might want to see why Ian had problems with me. All I did was bump into him, and I apologized for it."

Sarge nods as he checks me over. "If anything gets to be more than you can handle, let me know. None of the other students want to challenge him because of his father, the mayor. Based on what I've witnessed, you might be an exception."

"I won't let things get out of control," I reply, then make my way to the stairs to head to class. Yeah, I won't let things get too wild — but if he tries me again, things could end differently.

CHAPTER THREE

After my first week at Oakwood High, I'm seriously not in the mood to deal with people anymore. I'm in classes with Ian and at least one of his crew. The subtle shots and digs at me while the teachers weren't looking took their toll. My promise to Nana to not retaliate is working against me, and it's making me look weak because I'm not fighting back.

I keep my promises, but they're making it extremely hard.

"Hey, Yasir, what's new with you?" Hearing Zahra's voice calling out to me as I make my way to Storm throws me off balance a bit. I don't even know this girl, and the fact that she affects me like this is not a good look.

I drop my bookbag in the backseat, then close the door. "Things are okay, I guess. You good?"

She blushes. "I'm doing okay. How are you adjusting to Oakwood?"

I shrug. "I'm doing the best I can, under the circumstances. I'm trying not to think about it right now. What's on your mind?"

"I'm sorry. I'm a good listener if you need an ear to bend. Maybe we can figure out a way to help you. Word on campus is that you moved here from Atlanta, right?"

I offer up a nod, but I'm still not willing to bare my soul. "I'd rather not dwell on that, either. I just wanna get home and relax this weekend. I haven't had a real moment to myself since I got down here."

"So does that mean you won't be at the game tonight?" Zahra blurts out before she places her fingers against her lips. She fumbles with her hands, and I'm wondering for the first time if I make her nervous. "I mean, it's Rivalry Week, and I'm sure everyone will be there."

Oh, for the love of… Is she kidding me right now? I rub the back of my head, jumping on the defensive before I realize what's happening. "I have this thing about… I'm not sure… It's probably pretty crowded and packed at the stadium, I assume, and I don't know anyone."

I fight every urge inside me to push her away as she reaches for my hand. I'm uncomfortable around her, but I'm craving her touch at the same time. What the hell is wrong with me? She stops for a moment, staring into my eyes with a curiosity that I don't know how to describe. As she slips further inside my space, suddenly I'm as trapped in the moment as she is, and I don't want her to go.

I pull away, snapping us out of our shared haze, but she still has this hopeful expression on her face. "I would love to see you there if you're still not sure about going. Is there anything I can do to convince you to come through?"

Maybe it's the way she says it, or maybe I just want to switch things up a bit, I don't know, but I nod in response. "I'll try to make it out there tonight, but only because *you* asked me."

Zahra smiles and slips one of her fingers inside her honey-bronzed braids. "Great! I'll be looking for you in the stands. We can even sit together if you'd like."

"You don't have to do that, Zahra."

"Please, my friends call me Z."

In that moment, I freeze. Okay, just like that, and she wants to be friends? Who is she trying to convince? Because it can't possibly be me. It's only the first week of school, and I haven't been all that friendly around anyone. I still have to get a vibe and a rhythm, and it ain't gonna happen in a few days.

I tilt my head toward my left shoulder and try not to frown, but I guess the tone of my voice gives me away. "Are we friends, Zahra? Like, deadass."

I don't mean to sound so rough, but I can't help myself. She gives me a curious glance, biting her lip. "Um, well, would you like to be friends? I guess I shouldn't have assumed."

I'm stuck between giving her a hard time and wanting to apologize for being so edgy. Yeah, on second thought, I'm not ready to give in like that, not yet. "Okay, let's not pretend here, because whatever this is between us and how fast it seems to have happened has me a bit confused. The way you look at me... It's like you feel like you've known me, even though we've never laid eyes on each other before. I don't know you."

"Would you like to get to know me? As friends, Yasir? No cap." She's still leaning against my Jeep, allowing the question to linger between us. I open my mouth to say something else but stop myself the moment she gazes into my eyes again.

I can't afford to let my guard down, but she's not making it easy.

She leans in closer, almost like she doesn't want to intrude any more than she has already. "May I?"

I nod as she places her hand against my cheek. She takes a deep breath, slowly exhaling as her gaze never leaves mine. "Tell me what's on your mind, for real."

What's really on my mind, she asks? How about how I'm vibrating so intensely that I could start an earthquake? Or maybe why I feel so drawn to her, like there's some mystical force that's binding us together? I'm not supposed to be feeling this way, so why in the hell am I feeling this way?

And why can't I tell her to remove her hand from my face?

"I'm sorry, I'm just on edge, and I shouldn't have taken it out on you." I sigh and close my eyes for a moment before opening them. I'm still stumped by one simple question. "Why are you being so nice to me? What makes me so special?"

She's grinning now, keeping her hand steady. "I can't explain what's happening, either, but I know that, for some reason, I've developed strong feelings for you already... I hope they're positive, because something tells me it would be a shame to not have the chance to get to know you better."

When I pull her hand from my cheek and hold it, her eyes light up. I hold her hand a few more seconds longer than I'd planned, a smirk spreading across my face. Then, without warning, I'm taken prisoner inside of her stare again, but I'm willing to be captured this time. I feel warm, welcomed… I can't wrap my head around the why, but I need to feel this again. The sooner, the better.

Then I check my watch and realize if I don't get moving, I won't be able to do much of anything later. I pull my key fob out to start the engine. "I hate to cut this short, but I have a few things to take care of at home so I can go to the game."

She jumps as the rumble of the engine startles her, but she moves into my path to Storm's hood, cutting me off from the driver's side. "So you promise you'll be there, right?"

For the first time since we started talking, I give a genuine smile. I almost forgot what that feels like. Maybe getting to know her—as a *friend*—might not be such a bad thing.

I hop in the driver's seat, then roll down the window and pull out of the parking space. "I'll see you later tonight."

She's grinning wide, and I try not to focus on the way her nose wrinkles up when she does that. She keeps playing with her braids, and now I'm really wondering if "just friends" is all she might be interested in.

Only one thing crosses my mind the moment I step through the door: I need to get everything done quick, fast, and in a hurry.

Where all this energy came from as I speed around the house acting like I want to break the sound barrier or get into the *Guinness Book of World Records*, I'll never know.

Dishes. Done. Trash cleared throughout the house. Done. Bathroom cleaned. Done. Room cleaned. Done.

Wait a damn minute.

This can't be life right now.

Yeah, I better come up with an explanation that Unk will believe, or I'll end up in a question-and-answer session that could last hours. Ain't nobody got time for that.

How in the world did I get here? I'm working through everything in my head, weighing the good and bad of heading out to the stadium tonight. I don't want to admit that Zahra has some influence over my decisions, but look at me. The whole house got cleaned, including my room, so I can sit next to her at a football game. Who does that?

I glance down at the clock sitting next to my Black Panther replica helmet—Wakanda Forever!—doing my best to keep track of my timing to make sure I'm not rushing. I need to take a shower, get dressed and freshen up, then make it to the game. One look in the closet and I want to scream; I didn't realize how much my nana's paranoia affected my wardrobe. I mean, I know I can't be *flashy*, flashy, but I'm not trying to go out looking all basic.

Maybe giving Storm a bath and wax will make me feel better.

I catch a rhythm, getting into a zone, thanks to the music piping through my AirPods, and the next thing I know, I burn through the wash in less than thirty minutes, and I still have time to put on a fresh coat of wax.

I immerse myself, watching Storm shine before my eyes against the waning sunlight. She's gonna turn heads tonight. I can't wait.

"Whoa, based on what I've seen inside, do we need to have a conversation?" Unk asks from the front porch.

I shake my head as I continue working. "Yo, how do you manage to pop up when I least expect it? And how did you get home without me seeing you? Is there a secret entrance I don't know about?"

Unk strokes his goatee, and from the grin on his face, I see the punchline coming. "You probably got so lost in babying your ride and didn't notice me drive right past you. I wonder if I should ask you to wash my truck, since you're being so charitable. You got your Jeep looking *niiiiccceee.*"

I've got to do better about zoning out when I'm listening to my music. I give up a shrug, stretching my arm out to keep it loose. "Charitable, Unk? Nah, I just wanted to make sure I got her right before I get dressed and head out tonight."

He tilts his head, a surprised expression on his face. "Oh really? And where are you heading, considering you *never* go out, even when I suggested it?"

I pause for a moment, squeezing the wax on the applicator, scrambling for a reason to give him. "I'm going to the football game tonight. I figure I might as well, since it's Rivalry Week with Baytown High and all."

Unk makes his way down the stairs from the porch, giving me a long glance. He raises his left eyebrow, then grins like he knows why I want to go out, but he doesn't say anything. "So go and enjoy the game. You need to be a teenager for once instead of being caught up in whatever has been going on in your head."

"Unk, I—"

"Hear me out, kiddo," he interrupts, placing a hand on my shoulder. "For the past decade, we've been trying to play by your nana's rules, presumably for your protection. In that time, thankfully, no one has come for you, which is a good thing. That means, as much as I bought into her paranoia, I have to admit that maybe we can loosen things up a bit."

I'd be lying if I said I didn't want to find out what life looked like with the shackles off. "I'm trying to figure it all out, and some things are easier than others. Just…I don't know."

"Speak on it, Ya-Ya. You know I got you."

I scratch the back of my head. I hate going against my grandmother. She took me in when no one else could. Even the thought of it makes the hairs on my arms stand up. "You're right; I'm not feeling whatever Nana was talking about, either. But maybe we can wait a little longer before I feel comfortable cutting loose?"

He gives my shoulder a squeeze, smiling the entire time. "I can understand that. I'm good with whatever you decide. Now, finish your wax and get moving. I have a few things to do myself."

"Whoa, and what kind of plans do you think you have?" I tease. "Who told you it was okay to get a life?"

Unk laughs, and I laugh along with him. He leans against the front grill, it tickled him so much. "Oh my God, too funny, I swear. Okay, how about this: you tell me your real reason for heading to the game, and I'll tell you what my real plans are."

I put my hands up in mock surrender. "Nah, I'm not that curious. Have fun tonight, and I promise I'll be home by curfew. Bright and early for the usual ride?"

"As always, kiddo. See you in the morning."

"So you ain't got time for your Day One no more, bro?"

Hearing Dante's voice and seeing his face on the FaceTime feed while making the drive to the stadium is just what I need. Dante is my Day One; I've known him since I first came to the A. He is as close to a brother as I could get, and my nana treated him as such.

"Hey, what's good, my boy? I've been trying to get my life down here. I feel like I'm in another country with all the madness going on." I settle the phone on the hands-free car mount, rolling along at a steady pace to keep from bouncing the connection around too much.

"If I remember correctly, it wasn't much of a life to get." Dante chuckles. "At least Unk is good with all this. That whole deal with you getting bounced to live with him was foul. Squad been asking about you, though."

Mentioning Squad…he had to know it would trigger me.

I didn't have a chance to really get together with them to at least let them know where I was headed. I left that to Dante to explain it, which I guess wasn't the best thing to do, now that I think about it. Everything happened so fast. All I can do now is move forward and hope they understood.

Most of them would. *She* probably didn't.

"I'm planning to get back up there soon… I have some things I need to talk to Nana about," I reply, avoiding the mention of Squad on purpose. "Once I'm up there, I'll hit you so I can catch you up."

"Where you rolling? And you got the top off, too? You trying to flex a bit, huh?" Dante asks. "Good thing we got that neon on there before you left. Otherwise you would have been better off just staying at home."

"You'll be all right, my boy. I'm always on my game, even if I have to play hide and seek," I answer back, trying to watch the road and pay attention to the call at the same time. "I still have a few more tweaks to the engine to make, too. I've been scouting the comp, and there's not too many that can keep up with Storm."

"Well, with that hybrid HEMI we put together, what did you think was supposed to happen?" Dante boasts through the connection. "We knew she could decimate everything in her path outside of supercars once we got the proper calculations down. Enough of all that, though… I need to know if the girls are as hot as they say, bro. And don't say you ain't been peeping game, either."

His focus on girls takes me straight to Zahra. I don't know whether I want to be upset or happy about it, either. Even when I was at Douglass—my last school before I "transferred"—there was only one girl who had a shot at keeping my attention, and she had to work to even get me to look her way.

No wonder I'm so heated about what Zahra is doing to me. She hasn't had to put in a second of work, and I'm already into her. "Yeah, there are some baddies in the mix down here, for real. That's why I'm rolling to the game tonight. Oakwood has some rivalry game, and it's supposed to bring out the cream of the crop, according to the boys I heard talking."

"Good, because I have no intentions of bringing sand to the beach, you feel me?" His laughter is so infectious that I can't resist jumping in with him. "I mean, you my boy and all, but you know the drill. It makes no sense to bring girls when there will be girls to holla at while we're down there."

"I got you. I'll holla once I'm done with the game. I know you'll be up, so make sure you got the line clear, all right?"

"All right, bet." Dante moves with his phone to head out of the house. "I gotta head out, too. We heading to the Langston Hughes game; they playing Douglas County tonight. It's gonna be fire!"

I shake my head. When we were rolling deep, Squad never did go to a game at the school we actually attended. I shouldn't be surprised they wouldn't be going to one of Douglass' games…until they started winning again. "Just stay out of trouble, bro. I ain't there to pull you out if things go left."

"You make sure you do the same, little bro," Dante tells me, his face growing serious. "Make sure you find backup down there, all right? We're all a bit tight that you're down there with no one outside of Unk to cover."

"I'm good for now. Ain't like I'm really trying to get into anything down here." I roll my eyes as I think about it. "I'm not built for this small-town life. I'll head down to Jax or something to see what's popping down there if it gets too boring."

"Okay… I'll tell Squad we linked up by FaceTime. I'll get at you later. One."

"One." I close the call, enjoying the breeze. I do my best to calm the rising anxiety, but I have a hard time focusing on the road. With the call from Dante and these reminders of the past, all I can think about is my mom. Today was a lot, and I'm feeling a little overwhelmed by it all. "I miss you so much. I wish you and Dad were here. I need you."

I keep driving down the road, and I don't know whether there's something in the wind or if I want my wish to come true so badly that my mind's playing tricks on me, but I feel a pair of lips kiss my cheek and something like a hand touch my shoulder.

We are always here with you, Ya-Ya. Mommy loves you so much. We are here with you, my son…I promise.

I hit the brakes so hard the tires squeal against the street. My heart races as I swerve to find parking. The minute I cut the engine, I reach for the spot where I felt the kiss, blinking hard and fast as I'm struggling to make sense of what happened.

"Okay, that was… Did that really…" I shut my eyes tight to bring that feeling, that familiar presence back. But I can't feel it anymore. I bang my hands against the steering wheel, then take a deep breath and wipe away a stray tear, start the engine, and finish my drive to the stadium. I'm already late to the game, and I don't want to disappoint Zahra.

And I'm not sure why, but I just know that I won't be right until I see her face.

CHAPTER FOUR

I hear the roar of the crowd, and I'm in instant panic mode. There are too many people in the stands. No space to breathe. What the hell was I thinking, telling Zahra I'd be here?

I sit in the driver's seat for more than twenty minutes while in the parking lot of the football stadium, changing my mind at least a half-dozen times over whether to stay or leave.

I sigh deeply. It doesn't matter what rages inside me. I can't escape the way my body vibrates every time I have a passing thought about her. She has my attention on a level that excites and scares the hell out of me at the same time. I need to find out why she affects me like this and why I can't shake it off.

I cast my eyes skyward, whispering a prayer for strength before opening the door and getting out of the car. Each step feels like my feet are encased in cement, but I finally make it to the front entrance. I can't even answer a simple question from the lady I purchase the ticket from, nearly freaking out over the sensory overload.

This would have been easier to deal with if Squad had my back, but they're in the A, probably acting a fool as usual. *Get your life, bro. You can do this.*

My senses heighten at the sounds of the marching band and the cheerleaders. I move through the people standing around in the breezeway leading up to the concrete seating. The crowd is already on their feet as one of the Oakwood receivers catches a long pass and races to the end zone for a touchdown.

"Taylor Ricks for the touchdown!" the announcer booms. "The

Grove is now up 28–7!"

The roar of the crowd has my senses overwhelmed. I clap my hands over my ears to muffle the noise, but that doesn't work *at all*. I stand in place for a few minutes, closing my eyes to calm my heartbeat, which has ramped up like I've been running for miles.

I breathe in through my nose, then breathe out through my mouth. There's a group of kids to my left who are jumping around and vibing with the band, and that's throwing me off all over again. I squeeze my hands tighter over my ears to try to silence things for a few fucking seconds so I can calm down.

I feel my heart rate slowing down and breathe a sigh of relief. Now I can get back to the why of it all tonight—if I can get my feet to move.

I have no idea where to begin looking for Zahra, so I head toward an open section near the bottom of the stands, doing my best to duck around the "Cougar Pride" banner that's in my way, close to where the cheerleaders are set up on the track encircling the football field.

I keep searching, losing hope that I can find her as I hop down each section of seats to get to the open section I found. I almost give up until I see her sitting near where I'm headed. Zahra's sitting with the cheerleaders, but I get the feeling that she's not a cheerleader. The "Team Manager" emblazoned in dark-gray lettering across the back of her crimson zip-up hoodie is a dead giveaway, now that I've paid enough attention to notice. Or maybe she's borrowing someone else's hoodie, who knows? Okay, I may be overthinking things a bit. I need to settle my nerves before I bring on a panic attack, and I haven't had one of those in a couple of years.

I stop for a few seconds, completely focused on her, unable to move. She's so pretty, no wonder I have so much trouble talking to her. I mean, *look* at her.

The torture I'm putting myself through for someone who hasn't yet proven whether their connection was a figment of my imagination or not…I'm better than this nonsense. The more I try to free myself from the negative thoughts in my head, the more a pronounced rage makes itself clear and present from somewhere deep within my core.

I don't know how to explain what's going on with me, but whatever this is rumbling deep, it's confusing, and I'm low-key irritated. It's like something—or someone—is trying to rise from the back of my mind and influence what I'm thinking and how to react. It's weird, and I don't like the temporary loss of control.

I'm angry with myself for even putting myself in this position. I was good with the whole loner routine, but then I had to go and get caught up in a pretty girl who has me twisted. I don't wanna be here, but I wanna be here. This constant back and forth is wearing me out, and I wanna yell just to ease the pressure building inside me.

I look to my right, noticing a few of the kids from school staring at me. I pay too much attention to their hand motions and body language, making it plain that my being in their space is not wanted. I ignore as much of it as I can, choosing to focus on suppressing my fight-or-flight instincts. Lashing out, even if I'm in self-defense mode, would be worse...way worse.

My senses are on tilt now, and it's only a matter of time before I need to figure out how to get out of here. What throws me off even more is this constant vibrating and rumbling from deep inside my body. It's growing more and more this time, as though it is preparing for something, like an eruption.

I freak out for a moment; my skin feels hot, and I swear there's a deep crimson glow surrounding my body, brightest on my hands and arms. Even when I close my eyes to will it away, the moment I open them, it looks like it's only intensified its brilliance.

I have to get my emotions under control, but all my senses become more sensitive by the minute. I'm close to panicking. I try to force the vibrations to stop, convince myself that no one around me means any harm. I take deeper breaths, relying on what my nana taught me to calm down and focus. The last thing I need is to let my anxiety turn to anger.

The conversations around me grow louder, but I don't see anyone moving closer to me to be able to hear things so clearly.

The negative comments are coming more frequently, aggravating me to the point where things almost overwhelm me. I want to get away from it, to silence the noise for a few moments, long enough to settle down.

I close my eyes, deciding that finding Zahra would be my main focus. When I search the last area that I remember finding her, I don't see her there anymore. Irritation over not being able to keep up with her has me amped up, and I scold myself over not simply moving closer to her so she can see I was there. Now, I have no clue where she could have gone, and I'm stuck dealing with these jackasses who haven't moved and whose voices I can hear as though they are sitting next to me.

"Hi, Yasir, I'm glad you didn't abandon me after all. I almost gave up on you."

I jump out of my skin, annoyed over how I didn't feel her walking over and sitting down next to me. All the other distractions must have caused me to lose focus, and I make a mental note to do something about it. The jeggings she's wearing and a graphic T-shirt peeking from inside her hoodie that depicts RiRi Williams catches my attention first. She has her braids swept up in a messy ponytail, and she's wearing a peach lip gloss that brings out her bronzed skin tone, but the stadium lights play tricks on me. I'm convinced it's an intoxicating mix between bronze and amber, almost matching my eye color. She's been kissed by Ra, the Egyptian sun god, and I'm willing to go blind staring at the glow surrounding her.

I blink a few times, praying I'm not dreaming, checking around us to notice that the crowd in the immediate area around us has suddenly disappeared. It must be halftime. "Um, hi, Zahra."

"Are you okay? You looked like you needed rescuing." She moves closer to me, and my heart is beating faster than it takes the Flash to go from zero to Mach 1. *Keep it together, bro.* "I should've come and found you. This stadium can be a bit much for people who haven't been here before."

I turn to meet her concerned gaze, and I swear everything melts away in seconds. I want to get lost inside her eyes, and I have a harder time forming words than usual. "Yeah, I don't do well in large crowds, but I try to manage. Having you here helps. Thank you for finding me. It means a lot."

We keep shifting around each other like we're trying to figure out if we want to be close to each other or if we want to act like we don't. I catch her blushing as our eyes meet for a few seconds, and I sweep a stray braid out of her face, grateful for the excuse to touch her. I don't even care that the crowd is as large as it is anymore. As long as she's sitting next to me, none of that even matters.

"I don't know if I'm actually helping or not, but I'm really glad you didn't ghost me," Zahra replies, putting her hand on top of my arm. I feel an instant spark the moment she touches me. "I'd really like to finish our convo from earlier, if that's okay?"

All of this is happening too fast. There's no way she can be this into me in such a short amount of time. As much as I don't want my insecurities to rise to the surface, I can't help myself. I stare at her, ignoring her surprised expression. "Can I ask a question?"

"Sure, ask me anything."

"Have you figured out whether your feelings toward me are positive or negative yet?" I avoid her gaze, choosing to focus on the field and the game. I'm a bit scared that I ask the question, but I fear the answer even more. "I realize actions speak louder, but I guess I want to know… I *need* to know…"

She leans in and wraps her arm through mine, and my whole body ignites against my will. I turn toward her, and she blushes. "Yes, I've figured it out, but I still want to get to know you better to make sure you are who I think you are."

"And when will we have time to get to know each other better so you can let me in on the answer to my question?"

Her eyes never leave mine. I can't take my eyes off her, either. I just don't want her to leave. "Soon, I promise. I don't want to keep you waiting too long, but I said what I said. I need to see you, and I plan to do just that."

Zahra leans in closer. Her smile takes down any walls I'd built up to keep her from getting in deeper. I don't press my luck, though;

I've been down this road one other time, and that ended badly. I don't want to mess this one up; something feels different, and I need to find out what it might be.

The minute I sink into Storm's leather seats and push the ignition button to hear the engine roar to life, I release a long, relieved sigh. I made it through the game without any other issues. That alone is a victory I have no problems claiming.

I need to recharge badly because whatever energy I expended has me tired and then some. I have no problems going home, pulling the covers over my head, and crashing out until early morning when it's time to head out with Unk.

I take a moment to reminisce over what turned out to be a wonderful night. The highlight came when I escorted Zahra and her best friend, Kendyl, to Zahra's car. Kendyl is on the cheerleading squad, and while Zahra isn't squad, she does function as a team equipment manager—thank goodness I was right—which gives her access to the field, which makes her cheer-adjacent in my book.

Kendyl's a little taller than Zahra, and she struck me as Afro-Latina from the hint of a sing-song cadence in her voice, and her saddle-brown skin shined under the lighting in the parking lot. Her hair was pulled back into a naturally wavy ponytail, and her striking hazel eyes and pouty lips attracted attention from the boys all the way to the car. Still, she kept a close eye on me the entire time, something I expected a best friend to do, so it didn't bother me all that much. Sooner or later, I'm gonna have to handle the third-degree questioning from her. I'll just have to be ready.

I tried to hide how impressed I was that Zahra drove an Audi RS. It was silver and gleamed against the moonlight, and Raiden—Zahra's nickname for this pretty piece of machinery—was part of her master plan to eventually design electric motors and jet engines. I made a mental note to have a longer convo about what she knows about engines in general and a few other things that have my imagination in overdrive.

Still, there's something about a STEM girl. If you know, you know.

I watched as she gushed about naming her prized machine after the lightning god from the *Mortal Kombat* games and movies. She even races, which made me wonder if she really had skills like that. I'm not gonna lie, though: I honestly thought it belonged to one of the groups of boys who were bragging about their cars when I first got to the stadium. That's what I get for assuming too much, huh?

While I want to settle down a little bit, the truth is I'm amped up. I'm not feeling hip-hop tonight, so I connect my phone and scroll through my playlist. I smile when Burna Boy pops up; this is what I need for real! The bass in the speakers syncs with my heartbeat, influencing the aggression in my driving as I cruise down the road. I make it a few miles into my drive when I notice a group of boys off to my right. I check in that direction, focusing on the one in the middle of the group. As I get closer, I see Ian nearly getting his face bashed in by one of the other boys while another holds him down to keep him from protecting himself. They're all wearing Baytown colors, and it doesn't take long to figure out that Ian is in a world of trouble.

My instinct takes over as I slam the brakes, then hop out of my Jeep to confront the group. Things might be complicated between us, but he doesn't deserve to go out bad like this.

"Let him go, right now, and you can walk away without a noticeable limp."

All eyes are on me as they snap their glances in my direction, and the one throwing the punches steps away from Ian and heads toward me. "Who the hell is this? Do you know this man, Ian?" he barks, balling his fists. "Maybe you need to help him catch these bows for costing us the game, huh? You Oakwood, too, my guy?"

"I don't know him, Jordin," Ian replies. He glares at me, tilting his head toward my car. I know what he wants me to do, but that's not an option. "Just some rando who has a savior complex. He needs to learn not to stick his nose in business that doesn't pay him."

"It's obvi that I don't learn lessons, but I'm not about to stand by and watch while you beat someone down without making it a fair fight." The other two boys close a circle around me, each with a problem that they feel needs to be handled. I keep my cool, still talking big, whether we are outnumbered or not. "Step away now, and no one will get hurt. Last warning. You won't like how this is gonna end, trust."

My nerves are on edge all over again, and I'm scared that I've broken off more than I can handle. One on three, with Ian held down and unable to help—the odds are definitely not in my favor.

"Are you kidding me?" Jordin scoffs, looking at the boy standing next to him before he turns his attention on me. "You're out of your depth on this one. Just take the L and go home."

I grit my teeth as I try to keep a line of sight on the other three boys who are circling me. He might have a point, but I'm not about to let him know that. "Can't do that, bro. If I have to catch a fade, then bring it. Let Ian go so it can be a fair fight. I thought you South Georgia boys were supposed to be nice with your hands."

Jordin looks at the other boys, then shakes his head as he stares at me. "Reggie, Mark, drop this fool, please. Larry, keep Ian steady. This won't take long at all. This one needs his mouth shut."

"Why don't you come and shut it, huh? Big talk when you got back up, yo." Yeah, fear is controlling my mouth, and it's wrapping itself in a swagger that I don't have the greatest confidence in right now. To put it in Unk's terms, I'm writing checks that I'm not sure my fists can cash. "Or maybe you ain't got it in you to do it?"

Mark and Reggie rush me from behind, trying to grab at me and pull me down. I turn to confront them, ducking one wild swing from Mark at my head and dropping him to the ground with a swift left hook to his jaw. I'm already in motion, staying on my toes to keep my movements as random as possible. I stay in the view of my headlights, keeping the fight from shifting into the darkness.

Reggie steps in, getting a punch into my ribs, causing me to yell out in pain. He gets me good, and the power behind that punch worries me. I sidestep a couple more swings from him, landing a left hook to his rib cage that causes him to wince, holding his side for a moment before he comes at me again. He manages to get another punch across my jaw as I try to get in to crack a few bones, drawing blood with the strike and causing me to fall back against the front of my car.

"You got some pop, I'll give you that. I'm gonna need to put you down quick," Reggie yells as he continues to swing at me, going for the knockout punch. "Hold still. You're making this hard on yourself."

I keep weaving and ducking; the adrenaline has me on edge and unable to focus. I feel like I'm gonna pass out if I don't end this quick.

The way I feel right now is strange, and I can't make sense of it. I feel faster, stronger, and like I can't run out of energy, no matter how much I burn. Everything is moving in slow motion, like I'm a part of an anime battle sequence and I can see every move as it happens and move to avoid getting hit while landing bone-crunching hits to my adversary. I've never moved like this, and it has me confused and a bit scared of what's happening to me, but not to where I can't make short work of Reggie.

He feels another punch to his jaw, and the way he screams in pain almost takes me out of my zone. I can't make out what he's trying to say, and from the way he's flinching as he tries to move his mouth, it's easy to figure out that I broke it. He yells out as he rushes at me in anger, ready to do whatever it takes to end me.

I finally find the opening I need, landing three or four hits to his ribs and chest, hitting him hard enough to make him drop his right hand to protect his body. From there, it's easy: a right-handed uppercut to his chin and a couple more to finish him off as Reggie falls unconscious to the pavement.

Two down, two to go.

I'm still a bit disoriented from whatever I'm feeling, almost like I'm coming down from the most intense adrenaline rush ever. I stare at my hands and arms, and I swear they look like they're...

glowing? I blink a few times to figure out if I'm hallucinating, and the crimson glow is still there, almost causing me to panic. Am I on fire? What's happening to me?

I try to focus on the immediate threat, and that's the other two boys that are still upright and probably coming for me. I close my eyes to try to focus for a few seconds. I need to not get damaged too badly or, worse, unalived. That's not part of my plans, either, dammit.

Before I can turn around to deal with Jordin, I feel a blow to my lower back, dropping me to the pavement. I stare into Jordin's eyes before noticing the metal bat in his hand, and in that moment, I know I'm in real trouble. I have no way of protecting myself if he decides to start swinging, and I'm trying my best to scramble to my feet. I can't get my footing, and fear quickly turns to panic now.

"That's it, that's the look I was waiting for. Sooner or later, you were gonna get got." Jordin spits on the ground as he crouches over me. "You got heart, my guy, but that's over with now. Time to put you to sleep."

"Nah, bro, it's time to sing *you* a lullaby," Ian interjects as he throws a punch to the side of Jordin's face, watching him drop to the concrete like a sack of potatoes. "Night-night, bitch."

He comes face-to-face with me in the next instant, both of us checking the unconscious bodies around us. I study Ian's irritated expression. "What's got you looking like I stole your favorite chain?"

"I told you to stay out of it," Ian shouts. "I had it under control. What do you want, a 'thank you' or something?"

"Oh yeah, you had it all under control, my boy," I point out, stepping deeper into his personal space. Fear is still driving the adrenaline rushing through me, and I don't care that I'm on the verge of talking reckless. I just covered him, and he wants to sound ungrateful? "And nah, you don't need to say thank you, but you're welcome, anyway."

As the sirens blare in the distance, Ian pushes me toward my car. I don't know how they knew to come. Someone must have seen us fighting and called 911. I keep resisting, confused over what he's doing. "What the hell is going on? You need a witness to deal with this mess."

"You don't know how Oakwood Grove works. Just get out of here and let me deal with this," Ian roars before opening my door and pushing me inside. "I won't repeat myself. Get the hell out of here. Right now! Go!"

CHAPTER FIVE

I t takes a lot for me to get out of Storm and drag myself through the garage door. I can't remember the last time I hurt this badly. I gave as much as I got, but I'm gonna feel every bit of that blow to my back for at least the next couple of days.

I hope Unk isn't sticking to his usual routine whenever I go out. He doesn't go to sleep until he knows I've made it through the door safely, regardless of the time of night. It's always been a comfort, but I need him to be asleep tonight. I really don't feel like explaining why I'm moving so slow, and I know he's gonna notice and ask questions I don't want to answer.

I'm dragging so badly that I don't realize that I've bumped the end table by the door, which disturbed the statue of Nyati, the Divine Mother of Kindara. Unk keeps a lot of them around each of the entrances into the house as an otherworldly layer of protection. I'm groaning as I stretch out to keep the figurine from falling to the floor. I secure her back in her space and breathe a sigh of relief, leaning against the wall to steady myself before I move again.

I don't want that smoke. Nope. If he doesn't kill me, Nana will have a whole meltdown if she were to find out I broke one.

My phone vibrates in my pocket on a rapid-fire kick, and I ignore it for the time being. It's probably Dante and Squad rubbing it in about the Langston Hughes score. They've been lighting everybody up this year. I'm not trying to hear any of that right now. I have my own issues to sort out.

The great room is dark, which is a good sign that I might get to my room without too much fuss. I stop through the kitchen to grab a bottled water so I can trudge up the stairs as quietly as possible.

My phone is going off for real now, which is irritating me big time. I'm already kicking myself for not getting Zahra's phone number while we were vibing, so I know it's not her.

I'm fumbling with my phone to just turn it off or something, so I don't make myself so freaking obvious that I'm home. The house is already quiet, so any noise is liable to alert Unk that something's going on and he needs to see about it. He's already gonna be awake in a few hours to get ready to head out to the boat so we can work on the day's catch—he owns a seafood shop in downtown Oakwood Grove—so interrupting his sleep is a sitch I don't want.

Hearing the light switch flip is a dead giveaway that Unk stuck to his normal routine after all. Dammit. "How was the game, kiddo?"

Okay, two options.

First option: come clean and drop everything on the table and be up all night fleshing out the good and the bad of it all.

Second option: hold some cards close to the chest until I can figure out what else I need to tell him later, which will be a shorter convo and I can get some sleep.

Considering everything I've gone through in the past few days, and I went to a whole football game after being at school, wanna guess which option I'm about to take?

"The game was lit, no cap." Well, I'm not lying about that. The football team is pretty nice, for real. "I guess Oakwood might not be so bad, but I'm still not sure yet."

"Well, it's a start." Unk leans against the wall, and I can feel him studying me further, like he's looking for something. He pauses for what feels like forever before he says, "Are you gonna be good to roll in the morning? You look like you got into the game a bit more than what you're letting on."

I grip my ribcage as I flinch over his question about going out on the boat. Playing this chess game in my head is wearing me out more than trying to hide legit injuries I took earlier dealing with Ian and his drama. I can only hope to be sore in the morning so

I can roll out and avoid more questions I'm not ready to answer.

So instead of taking the out my uncle is giving me, I tell him, "Yeah, I'll be ready to go in the morning. You know I can't leave you out bad like that."

Unk furrows his brow, and I know he's not buying it, but I gotta sell it so he can rock with it. I'll make it up to him another time, but for now, I'm putting on as good of a performance as I can pull off. I breathe a sigh of relief when I see him nod. "All right, Ya-Ya, get some sleep. Wheels spin at four in the morning."

As he walks back to his bedroom and closes the door, I shake my head and wonder how in the world did I get myself into another fine mess. I get to my room, drop my keys on the desk, and groan as I pull my hoodie over my head, leaving a trail of discarded clothing to the bathroom so I can get a nice, hot shower going. It's been a hell of a first week, and I pray I'll have as much of a dreamless sleep as humanly possible.

I'm playing out the whole night from start to finish, and I'm already critical of the moves I should've made and the ones I was better off not making. I don't like doing this to myself, but I can't help it sometimes. Nana's always said I should never be my own worst enemy, but I don't see it that way. Still, I'm trying to find the silver lining through all of the doom and gloom I'm insisting on bringing to the surface all over again.

That silver lining is about five foot six and I swear is made of brown sugar, cocoa, honey, and gold.

I just wish I'd at least swapped numbers with her or something.

Okay, Yasir, chill. Focus on the positive. She rocked with you the whole game. The vibe was fire. That's gotta count for something, you know?

I let the water cascade over me, pretending that it's washing all the negativity off me and circling down the drain. The heat feels good against my bruises, and I stand in place for a few more minutes until I don't wince every time I move.

I'm still trying to make sense of what happened with Ian and that whole incident. More to the point, where in the world did that crimson glow come from? I know I was running a little hot, but for it to manifest itself like I was about to catch fire doesn't make any sense. I felt like I could've broken more than Reggie's jaw. As angry as I was, his jaw would've been the least of his problems.

Paralysis was on my mind.

It shouldn't have been, but he pissed me off.

Since I have a moment to myself to think about it, where did all that seemingly endless supply of energy and strength come from?

And where did it all go like it never happened in the first place?

So many questions to answer, but I'm not about to lose sleep over it tonight. I have to shut things down and be ready to go in a few hours.

I turn off the shower, grabbing the towel off the bathroom counter, stretching across my bed to scroll through the messages I ignored when I was trying to keep Unk from ripping off the third-degree questioning. Sure enough, it's Dante giving me the updates on the Langston Hughes blowout. I do my best not to get upset, knowing I'm supposed to be up there with my people instead of down here hitting the reset button, but with each picture I see, it gets more difficult to keep from raging.

I decide it's better to head up to the studio and get some painting done or do some sketching. I'm not in a violent mood, well, not anymore, so going downstairs to work that off isn't necessarily what's needed right now. I want to feed into the vibe I felt with Zahra earlier. I think that'll help ease me into a better headspace so I can sleep.

The top level of Unk's house is split into two large spaces, one for him and his hobbies, and the other one for me and my creative energy. He had my space designed and crafted in such a way that I can see the stars at night or bask in the warmth of the sun during the day. It's airy and has a lot of windows, including the skylight.

I keep all my paints, pencils, chalks, everything in separate bins against the wall opposite the large window on the other side of the studio. The skylight shows the clear and starry night sky, and I admire the beauty and darkness being shown before me. An inspiration with a pretty girl at its center takes hold of me.

All the easels are covered except for one, since I have a thing about not wanting to see the pieces as I'm creating them. I move to the bins, take out the pencils, then slide over to the chair in front of the easel with the blank canvas and get to work.

I focus on her face first, capturing the contours of her cheeks, the oval shapes of her eyes, and before I know it, my fingers act on their own. It's like they have as much of a memory of what she looks like as my subconscious, and I don't question how my hands move. I sit back and let the magic happen.

I capture the intricacies of her face and hair with a precision that scares me at first. I feel like I'm invading her privacy with the way I pay attention to the perfect shape of her eyebrows or the way she bites her bottom lip when she wants to keep from grinning. Before long, I've added a headdress that wraps through her hair, and I imagine her on a beach, wearing a maxi dress, walking barefoot along the edge of the surf.

I'm sketching so fast I feel like the lead is going to break from the pressure and speed.

I just don't want to lose the image that's forming in my mind's eye before I'm finished with the capture.

As I'm putting the finishing touches on the piece, I hear my phone vibrating against the table next to me. I pick up the phone to see what the notification is about.

I almost stop breathing the minute I see the message coming from my IG.

Hi, Yasir, I hope you're awake. I just wanted to say I had fun tonight.

CHAPTER SIX

My anxiety shot through the roof the minute I responded to her message. After I ask for her number so we can move this out of DMs, I end up playing the "what if" game the rest of the night and into the morning. My head swirls when I try to sleep, bordering on a full-on headache, and the walls close in on me at home.

Never mind the *other* incident that happened…and the unanswered questions that came with it.

That inhuman strength…bodies lying on the ground.

The bruising on my hands, and my body, with no way to explain it to Unk, which was especially awkward when I pulled up the nets from our fishing trip. He pretty much kept quiet about what he saw, but that lasted about two-point-five seconds, and I ended up spinning a tale about how I helped someone change out a tire to try and gloss over the fact that I was in a full-tilt melee and barely escaped with more serious injuries.

At least we were able to pull a large catch for him to pick through, which would keep his attention off me for the rest of the day. It was a better day than normal, which has me questioning whether what happened to me last night had anything to do with it. It's like I knew exactly where to find the premium seafood and stopped right on top of that spot. Normally, it takes a couple of tries to figure it out.

All right, focus, Yasir. One sitch at a time. That can wait.

I've never been in a situation where I had to fight more than one person at once. If I didn't know any better, I'd swear it felt like

I'd blacked out and my body took over for a few seconds. Except I was there, in the fight, the whole time.

And the thing that puzzled me the most: why did Ian make me leave the scene before the police arrived?

I could've used a self-defense argument, but since I'm new in town, maybe Ian was right to get me out of there. I still had no clue of whether the other boys would say something to the cops, nor could I really trust Ian, but sticking around to find out wasn't the best option, either. Perfect definition of a no-win situation.

I do recall being in the fight with Reggie and Mark, two of the boys in the situation, and I remember Larry holding Ian down when I first got there. I was so involved in the fight that I have no clue how Ian even got loose to be able to save me from having my bones broken. What's most confusing is the severe state that all the boys were in once it was only me and Ian left standing. It looked bad, seriously speaking, and I'm wondering if he called the police himself trying to cover for me.

None of this adds up.

The not knowing kept me awake, which is why I took Storm out and am now rolling down the highway, my speed nearly matching the I-95 South signs. I'm on the verge of erupting—a desperate urge to release the tension is the only solution I could see—but it had to happen somewhere other than at home.

That's not an option.

Thankfully, I already have a place in mind where I can cut loose a bit without anyone being too nosy. I found it while scouting other locations for me and Unk to find more seafood for the shop. Considering tonight is a full moon and the tides would rise, the seclusion would be both expected and welcomed. The change of location would do wonders for my psyche, that's for sure.

That location is called Driftwood Beach.

An iconic location known for its driftwood speckled throughout the beachfront, a result of decades of erosion, according to historians. What used to be a maritime forest is now a sandy shore lined with weathered tree trunks and branches, creating an enchanting, or spooky—depending on the perspective—sight unlike any in the country. It's a haunting and mystical locale I need to sort things out in my head, and it would also give me the much-needed inspiration for, well, who knew what may come from it.

I already have a spot picked out, ready to see the night sky. I have to sort out so much in such a short amount of time, it's overwhelming me. I should talk with Nana or Unk, but my head isn't there yet. The clarity I need, I want to find it from within first, and then I can find the courage to speak my heart as clearly as possible.

I put the doubts out of my mind while parking Storm as close to my favorite spot as possible. It's not where I'm supposed to park, but no one came looking after the operating hours, and her off-road capabilities make it easier to slip away in the unlikely event that someone does happen to stop by.

I step out of the driver's seat, sauntering toward the shore while witnessing the shades of purple and orange framing the evening sky as the sun makes its descent toward the horizon. It's a stunning display, one I capture on my smartphone as inspiration for something I might want to create later.

I close my eyes to bask in the warmth of the waning heat of the sinking sun. Nothing else matters. Not the insanity of being in yet another new high school, not the anger of being away from the A, not even my rising angst over whether Zahra would hit me up to talk. The sunset provides a simple lesson: Don't rush. Stressing won't change its outcome. Things have a way of working themselves out.

The moment I find the set of driftwood that forms a weird series of jagged edges on the far side of the beach where no one would dare travel, I plant my feet into the sand in the center of it and stare into the darkness. I savor the brief period of isolation, both inside my mind and within my temporary surroundings. These times are rare, and I want to indulge in them for as long as possible.

I search for some kindling and rocks to build a fire, digging a small circle in the sand to start the burn. After the flames roar to life, I drop to my knees to enjoy the flickering light, delighting in the brilliance and the various colors, watching as it dances against the breeze. The oranges and yellows provide a lovely contrast against the blackness of the night, except for the stars speckled throughout the sky.

I purposely lose myself in the fire, asking for guidance as I continue playing out the incident with Jordin and the group of boys who tried to take me and Ian out. I go through every minute, frame by frame in my mind, trying to figure out if I missed anything, any detail that would answer at least one of the questions I had.

My phone rings, breaking through my thoughts. I don't mean to react like someone shocked me with a taser, but I'm so far inside my head that the disturbance jolts me. I reach to grab it before the ringing stops, not bothering to check the caller ID. Then it hits me: what if it's Zahra? I'm not ready.

"Hello?"

"Hi, baby, how is your weekend going?" Nana's voice pops through my earpiece, sounding like sweet syrup over a hot stack of pancakes. "I wanted to check in on you to see if you are doing okay. I had not had a chance to talk to you since you moved."

"Yeah, I'm a bit better. I'm glad to hear your voice," I tell her, hoping my tone sounds upbeat enough that she won't ask any questions. "I just headed out of town to unwind a bit. I needed the exercise and the isolation to clear my head."

I think I hear her say something, but the words come out choppy. "Where are you now? The connection is spotty, and I couldn't hear what you just said. I got something I wanna ask you."

"I am at home, as usual, but I am in the backyard. You know how bad reception gets out here. Let me see if I can move to a better spot." The sound is muted for a few moments before she pops back on the line again. "Okay, hopefully, that is better. What is on your mind, my child?"

"Well, Nana…there's this girl, and…"

"Whoa, whoa, and whoa," she interrupts. "Nana needs to make sure she heard that right. You know my hearing is not what it used to be. There is…a…*girl*?"

I feel the headache coming on again just that quickly. *Oh my*

God, bro. Don't go overboard, please? "Yeah, there's this girl, and she wants to link up, and I was hoping to get some quick shopping done for a new outfit or two. Like, I wanna impress her."

"Yes, sure, I will send some money over, and you get whatever you need," she says to me. I hear the excitement in her voice, but I don't want her to get her hopes up yet. "And while you're at it, you should do something special for her."

"Pause. I didn't say it was a *date*, date, Nana," I caution as I try to calm the excitement. That fails as soon as I see the large deposit notification come through on my phone. "Whoa, I thought you said some money, not two stacks? I still can't do a lot on the wardrobe. I have to keep a low profile, remember? Isn't that what you told me and Unk?"

"You have one shot at this, and I do not want you to blow it," she warns. Her whole tone worries me. Why the change of heart now? "Besides, it will give you a reason to come see me. You can bring her up here so I can get a good look at her."

I glance up at the sky, trying to gather what little patience I have left to keep my emotions in check. Sure, I want things to go well with Zahra, but not at the risk of my mental health. "We're just spending time talking… I think there's something there, but I don't know where things will go from here."

"Trust your gut, Ya-Ya. That is all I am trying to tell you. Now, is there anything else I need to know about?"

An incoming call saves me from having to answer that question. I pull the phone up so I can see the number. I nearly panic when I see Zahra's name pop up on the screen. "Nana, I'll call you back. I need to take this."

I switch calls with the quickness. "Hello?"

"Hi, Yasir? Um, it's Z. I'm sorry I didn't call earlier. I was working on some songs and lost track of time. Is it too late to talk?"

Hearing her voice stops my world as I know it. I keep my composure as best I can, grabbing some water to help clear my throat so I sound like I have some sense. "Hi, Zahra. No, it's cool to talk. I'm just relaxing down near Jekyll Island. I wanted to get some inspiration for a few new pieces."

"That's dope. Maybe you can take me down there one day," she replies, throwing me off balance. Did she just suggest…? "Can we link tomorrow so we can talk?"

I check around the beach real quick, battling with the negative thoughts in my head. *You're not being punked, bro. This isn't a dream. Just be cool.*

"Um, can we meet up after school on Monday? There are some things my uncle wants me to do, and I can't get out of it." Yeah, that's it, throw Unk under the bus to buy some time. He'll be all right. "I mean, if it's okay with you."

"It's fine. I'm good with Monday after school." I hear a giggle come across the earpiece that makes my heart thump through my chest. "It will give me some time to get myself together for you, especially since I won't have anything going on."

"I don't know why. You're perfect. You've always looked pretty every time I've seen you," I blurt out before I have a chance to stop myself. "Um, I mean…cool, it's a date. Maybe you can show me some of the motor designs you've been working on. Who knows? Maybe you might convince me that EVs are the way to go. I doubt it, of course. My engine might not be fully electric, but she burns clean and fast…probably faster than yours."

"And what makes you think you can beat me?" she scoffs. "Wait a minute… How did you know I worked on electric motors?"

"You're not the only one with sources." I can't contain my smirk. Thank the gods we aren't on a video call. "I may be new, but I'm not without my methods. Besides, *maybe* I signed up for the engineering club when I first got to Oakwood. I mean, you probably know I'm into IT and information systems. Maybe we can teach each other a few things."

"Hmmm, maybe, if you show me some of your designs, then I might be willing to show you mine. It's only fair, right?" she coos. "See you at school on Monday. I'm looking forward to our chat in person."

I disconnect the call, grinning so hard my cheeks hurt. For the first time since I could remember, I can't wait to get to school.

CHAPTER SEVEN

I sketch away on my notepad, chilling in my studio after suffering through yet another nightmare. The piece I immerse myself in serves as a distraction from whatever's going on in my head, but I'm not sure if I really want to create it, either. This newest sketch centers around a subject I'm hoping to avoid, but with tomorrow on lock, there's no way I can keep my mind off her.

Ever since our brief conversation yesterday, I've been shaking over the implications. The meaning of our potential chat hits with the force of a bullet train, and I have no way of slowing it down or changing its direction. I'm not gonna lie, she has the ability to derail everything I've planned, and I don't know if I want her to or not. I'll choose to face a firing squad instead of laying my feelings out in front of her.

What has me curious...and baffled...is this focus, this clarity that I don't remember having before. It doesn't freak me out, but now I'm noticing things that I haven't paid attention to before. I can't explain it, but the connection between us seems to be intense, despite it only being a few days.

Still, I can't stop the voices from suggesting it might be all a dream. Is there more between us? Do I even affect her the same way?

I put the questions out of my mind, heading downstairs to my bedroom to get dressed and ready for the daily drive out to the harbor. Unk's already waiting on me—he's consistent like that—so we can take the boat out to the prime spots to capture as many crabs and shrimp as possible. The better the catch in the morning, the better the sales at Unk's shop in the afternoon.

Unk already has the engine running when I come out through the garage, so I open the passenger door, stretching before I settle into the seat. I glance at him, trying to make sense of the concerned expression on his face. "Morning, kiddo. You were up earlier than usual. Sketching and painting again? Did you get some speed-bag work in, too?"

"Yeah, but how did you know I was awake?" I ask, snapping the seatbelt in place as he turns up the heat in the cabin. "I needed to give my hands a break on the bags for another week. My wrists were getting a bit sore."

"Well, I heard the humming while you were sketching. Hard to ignore it. Your nana used to hum that song to you when you were little," Unk tells me as he puts the truck in gear and pulls out of the driveway.

"Dang, you heard that? I thought I was insulated up there."

Unk chuckles as we roll through the neighborhood. "You're insulated, yes, but the rooms aren't soundproof…you know, in case you get any bright ideas this year."

I recoil, embarrassed that he's bringing *that* subject up for a possible discussion. Just the idea of him hearing me getting physical with a girl…yeah, nah. "Okay, that's a visual I didn't need this early in the morning, for real. Consider it noted, and do we need to have a code or something, in case one of us has company?"

"Hmmm, I think we do need to have a conversation, and it starts with the question, 'Who is she?' Oh, and don't say there isn't anyone, either. Nana called me asking about it."

I want to hide my face to shield the grin creeping up on me, but I change my mind. No need in hiding it now, but I can't jinx it, either. "Well, there's someone… I mean, I'm linking with her tomorrow to talk, but I'm not sure how that will turn out."

"And why won't it?"

I shake my head, wondering if Unk has been hiding in a cave for the last few years. "Are you kidding me right now? Have you forgotten the things I've had to do to 'hide' from people who are still *supposedly* trying to kill me, according to Nana? You know, the same warning she'd been drilling in my head since I was seven? If I have to hide from whoever 'they' are, then how am I supposed to be real with her?"

To let my nana tell it, when I was seven years old, I was brought to her to raise because my parents were involved in a tragic event that took their lives. She was vague on the details, but there was one thing that was repeated over and over and over again—those same people wouldn't stop until my entire family was erased.

The problem? I can't remember a single thing about what happened that night.

Unk exhales slow and easy while he waits for the traffic light to turn green. "I get it. This wasn't the best of circumstances for either of us. You lost your parents. We lost the safety and warmth of family. Outside of your nana, there's no one connected to your past...at least no one we've been able to find yet."

I remain silent for a few minutes, letting his statement sink in, realizing how true his words are. I blink away the dread that threatens to overtake me, intent on changing the subject to something more pleasant. "You are my family, Unk, and that's all that matters at this point. I mean, outside of Nana, but... You know what? I don't want to talk about that right now."

"Okay, what do you want to discuss?"

"How about the woman who's been trying to holla at you in the shop in the afternoons?" I raise my eyebrow.

He smirks. But a few seconds later, he flashes a smile, then slides out of the truck to head toward the boat. "Boy, get the gear so we can get this catch for the day."

"Hey, you, how was your weekend?" Zahra asks at school on Monday.

"Hi, yourself." I flash her a smile. "Crazy weekend, but nothing

I couldn't handle. I like your outfit. And you changed your hair, too. It's a good look."

I bet she wasn't expecting me to notice, from the way she's blushing. She changed from the honey-bronze braids to dark-brown faux locs with a hint of purple, and she has the nerve to show off with the same peach makeup combo that had me under her spell Friday night. The denim skirt is a nice touch, too, and the collared shirt she's wearing over the top of a T-shirt that says "STEM Girls Get Things Done" really catches my attention.

I put my own fit game together, too. I decided one of my navy-blue hoodies that has "Don't Sweat the Technique" emblazoned on the front in gold lettering pretty much says what I'm thinking today. The khaki cargos and the matching Timbs are working their magic, too. Oh, and I may have changed my oils to give off a different scent that, from what I can tell, hasn't had anyone reacting like there's a skunk in the building like normal.

Zahra leans against the locker, glancing at me like she's trying to figure out what to make of my new look, then she winks at me. "I have a feeling you can handle a lot more than you let on." She pauses. "Are we still good for later?"

I place the books in my locker, then close it and reset the combination lock. "Yeah, we're still good, but I'm not gonna lie and say I'm not nervous. You make me nervous, Z. It's a good nervous, but damn... I can't even figure out the words to say to you right now."

She grins like I just let her in on a whole cheat code or something. She slides her hand against my shoulder and gazes into my eyes. "Oh, and you don't make me nervous?"

"I would have never guessed that I did, for real." I lean against the lockers, matching her body language. I can't stop staring at her. "I mean, who am I to make anyone nervous or anything? I'm not that dude. I just do what I do, you know?"

"You have more power than you realize," she points out, closing the distance between us and then lowering her voice. "I know things have been a bit new and weird for you, but I sense a shift in the winds. Don't ask me how. I just have a really good feeling about it."

"I'm sure Nyati will have the final say, but I'll trust your 'feeling' on things, too." I don't know what made me evoke the Divine Mother, but should I let it go or try to explain? No way she knows who I'm referring to, right? Or maybe she doesn't care and I'm making more out of this than I should be.

Zahra doesn't say anything, though. She just... I don't know, she sort of looks through me like I'm not there. After a few more seconds of silence, I've lost my nerve. "Z, are you all right? Hey, talk to me. You're spacing out."

The bell rings, alerting everyone to get to their classes, but I can't leave her completely off balance. She finally snaps out of it and looks at me like it's the first time she's ever seen me. "I'll explain when I see you later today," she says. "We have a lot to talk about."

She places her hand against the left side of my face. I'm caught off guard, but it feels natural, too. For the next several moments, no one and nothing else exists, and I notice a curious expression on her face, like she sees something weird.

"Is there something wrong with my face?" I say, half teasing but also wondering what exactly is going through her mind.

She smirks. "We both need to get to class now. I'll see you later."

For the most part, I manage to get through and make it to Storm in one piece at the end of the day. I place my bookbag on the backseat so I can get home, when I get a quick reminder that the more things change, the more they stay the same.

"I see someone just upped their profile a bit today. You must be riding high after the campus caught your buzz, huh?" Ian approaches me, with Eric—Bulldog Boy—in tow, flanking him. "Well, enjoy it while it lasts, buster, because I'm gonna dim that shine the best way I know how."

I look skyward, sending a silent prayer to Nyati for strength and patience. The last thing I want is to get suspended over nonsense. "By the gods, bro, I need you to get a hobby or something. This is getting to be a bit more than I'm willing to deal with right now. Say what you need to say so we can get on about our days, please? I got things to do that don't include you and your minion."

Ian looks back at Eric and shrugs before he turns to face me. The smile on his face confuses me. What's his angle? "My bad, folk, I'm just messing with you. I actually wanted to say thanks for bailing me out of that sitch with those Baytown boys. Good looking out, even if I said I didn't want you there."

I flinch for a moment, trying to understand where this is coming from and why he decides to say something now. "Okay, pause, what's your angle, my boy? One minute you're applying pressure, and the next minute you're trying to squash it. Tell me what's really good because I don't know if this is it."

Ian shakes his head, and I lean against my car, waiting for him to figure out how he's gonna spin this one. "Okay, look, maybe I gave you a hard time to see if you could handle it, you feel me? The truth of the matter is I did some digging, and it turns out you had quite the following in the A. I should have respected that when you didn't try to come through acting like you were all that."

Is this man serious right now? And who the hell did he run through to check up on me? I make a mental to get at Dante, ASAP. In the meantime, I'm keeping this guy within arm's reach, because he's not telling it all. "I'm glad that you saw what you saw. All I'm trying to do is deal with my madness and do what I do. Whatever happens happens, but I'm not here for whatever you think I'm here for."

"And that's my point, Yasir. There's no reason why we have to have any beef, right? So I want to put you on and invite you to a party I'm hosting on my dad's yacht in a couple of weeks." Ian holds out his fist, waiting for me to tap up. "Consider it my effort to bury the hatchet between us, let you see how the other half of Oakwood rocks."

I consider the tense cease-fire for a few minutes, keeping my eyes trained on him and Eric the entire time. I wait for either of them to blink, twitch, anything that gives me the go-ahead to light them both up for trying to okie-doke me. A few more moments pass, and they're still acting like the invite was legit.

I raise my fist to tap Ian's, nodding at Eric as I slip into the driver's seat. I still feel like I'm being set up for something, but I can't see all the pieces on the board to be certain. "Bet. I'll catch up when we get closer to when you're hosting and get the deets from you."

CHAPTER EIGHT

'm lounging around the park for a few minutes, grateful for the time I have to myself before Zahra arrives. I wrack my brain, trying to understand how things have gotten to this point in such a short amount of time. I need to get my life together with the quickness. Once we're in each other's space, anything can happen.

My stomach knots up in every way imaginable, my thoughts racing through my head at speeds that would have made Usain Bolt jealous. Weeks ago, I was still at my nana's, settling into a rhythm and figuring out what to do about my junior year. Now, I'm in a new town, new high school, and might be barreling headfirst into a full-blown… I don't know what to call this thing between me and Zahra.

No matter how much I try to rationalize it, I'm at a complete loss over how I managed to capture her attention. Hell, I'm not anyone special. I'm simply doing me.

I glance around the spot I've chosen, Palmetto Square Park. I don't know Oakwood Grove all that well; I literally googled somewhere to meet up. She lit up when I suggested it, so I guess I got something right.

I stroll around the park until I find an empty bench in a row of them, surrounded by the ever-present Southern Live Oaks that lead to the iconic fountain in the center of the park. At least, that's what the article I found said. Did I go too far in choosing a location to have a first conversation? What if she takes this the wrong way? Ugh, I have half a mind to text her and suggest somewhere else.

The way the trees frame the fountain to near perfection calms me a little bit. The pattern of the water spraying from the statues adorning the fountain provides a quick inspiration to sketch. The branches offer an eerie yet beautiful and mysterious intimacy that lends a glimpse into what's on my mind and heart.

The waning sunlight gives way to the ambiance of the evening. By Nyati, I'm starting to sound like a whole sappy romance movie. I mean, who says words like "ambiance?" Am I overthinking all of this? It's only a conversation, right? But, like, what if I read this the wrong way? What if I'm making this more than it is?

I almost decide to text her to meet me somewhere else... anywhere that doesn't feel so over the top. The last thing I need is for her to give me a glance like this isn't supposed to be what I think it is. That would kill me on the spot. Now, do I want to do something like this for her that includes a location like this? Absolutely. But right now? The more I think about it, the more anxious I become.

Then something strange happens.

A warmth I haven't felt since I heard my mother's voice radiates through my body, calming things down within minutes. It doesn't last too long, since my emotions insist on ruling instead of logic, but I sense everything at this point. I need to get it under control.

I check my watch, realizing that Zahra's at least twenty minutes late. I shake my head, willing every negative thought out. I have to keep it together. There are too many people in the area for me to lose it.

I think about texting her, but I don't want to look clingy, either. I should have known she wouldn't show. Maybe it's all an act in the first place. Why does she want to bother with me, anyway? I figure I'll chill here for a few more minutes before I head home.

Before I can make a move to stand, I hear something rumbling. It sounds...I don't know, like a growl, to the point where I check around me, thinking there's a wild animal in the area. The growling continues, low and rumbling, and before long, I hear a voice.

"Relax, be patient, kiddo. She will arrive soon."

I panic, my eyes widening as I scan the area around me. Why am I hearing a voice that doesn't belong to me, and why is it telling me to stay and wait for Zahra?

"Trust me, Ya-Ya. This one is special," the voice continues, sending the familiar warmth to calm me. *"I promise, you won't regret it."*

"Dad, is that you?" I whisper into the air, wanting desperately for it to be him.

"Hi, Yasir, sorry I'm late. There was an engineer's club meeting that got called at the last minute—" Zahra stops in front of me, a worried expression splashed across her face. "Are you okay?"

I close my eyes, cursing under my breath. "Sorry, I was trying to settle my nerves. I wasn't ignoring you, promise. I've been looking forward to this all day, but I wasn't sure if you would show or not."

Zahra scratches her head. "Um, did you check your phone? I sent you a text, like, twenty minutes ago."

Nah, I can't be that clueless, right? I pull my phone from my pocket, and to my shock, the message she mentioned pops onto the screen. I don't have the guts to meet her gaze. I feel like an idiot for not doing something so damned simple. "I'm sorry, I guess I zoned out a little too deep."

Zahra sits on the bench, turning her body toward me. "It's okay. You can make it up to me in the future."

I grin, thankful she's letting me off the hook. I take a deep breath, running my hands through my twists before I think about what I want to say. I come up with absolutely…nothing. "I feel like I have all these questions, and now that you're here in front of me… I don't know where to start."

"I think we're in the same boat," she admits. "I'm still trying to figure out how we got here, too. It feels so wild, but it's been that kind of a week."

You have no idea, girl. I steel myself before I gaze into her eyes, hoping I won't fall victim to the way she looks at me. Nope, doesn't work. Her eyes leave me so enchanted, it should be illegal. I can't stop staring, no matter how badly I want to stop.

I focus on her, watching as her eyes widen, feeling my heart skip a beat when she winks at me, wanting desperately to know

what's on her mind and petrified over the answers. Her eyes are
so clear, the most brilliant shade of jade I've ever seen in my life.

Wait…weren't her eyes hazel-green? How are they so much
greener right now?

I place my hand on top of her thigh, feeling her tremble
beneath my fingers. I sigh, happy and freaked out over her reaction
all at the same time. I finally have a real idea that I'm not in this
alone. Maybe she's as nervous as I am, too.

"How…how did we get here, Z? I'm trying to understand, and
I can't come up with any realistic reason. I haven't been here long,
and the next thing I know, we're…well, *here*."

She slips her hand on top of mine, sending an electrical surge
through me. How in the entire hell did that happen? "Well, to be
honest…you sorta had my attention the minute you stepped on
campus."

"Wait…*what*?"

Zahra averts her gaze for a few moments before facing me
again. She slides closer into my space, staring into my eyes. "I can't
explain why you're on my mind so much, and to be honest, I don't
know if I like it or not."

I inch away from her when she says that, flinching when she
tries to reach for my hand. I don't want to react that way—every
fiber in my being rebels against it—but the confusion I feel over
what I think and what she just admitted to has me stuck. "So what
exactly is this, then?"

I start to pull away, but she grabs my hands, and I freeze. Her
hands feel sweaty, or maybe I imagine they are to keep from
thinking about how wet my palms are to the touch. I don't have
the heart to face her after what I said seconds ago, not wanting to
see the disappointed expression I assume will be on her face.

Instead, I feel her fingers caressing my cheek. I close my eyes,
leaning into the sensation, surrendering to my selfish desires to not
have her hand leave my skin. I hold on to the thoughts in my head,
hoping her small gesture leads to something more… Only I don't
know what *more* I want, much less what I can handle.

"Yasir…I know it might not mean a lot right now, but I hope that things are getting easier," she says to me. "I've been in Oakwood Grove since I was a little girl, so I can't imagine what it must be like for you. Can you forgive me for not understanding?"

I clasp my hand over hers, even as it still lies on my face. I hear the mysterious voice in my head, urging me to get my genuine feelings out. "I'd be lying if I said that I want to be living here… but I do know one thing. I have feelings for you. It's made being here a little easier."

Zahra stares into my eyes, making me melt instantly. "So does that mean you forgive me?"

I study her face, taking special notice of the way her lip quivers. Her hand hasn't left my face the entire time; if anything, she presses it deeper into my skin, playing with the area where my dimple normally shows. I take my hand and caress her cheek, lighting up the minute I see the smile spread across her lips. I can forgive anything if I get to see that smile every chance I get.

I break the silence between us, giving a subtle nod I hope she doesn't see. "I forgive you, Z."

Her smile widens, her face glowing under the waning light giving way to the sunset. "Thank you. I was worried there for a minute."

"So, now that we've gotten that out of the way, what's on your mind?" I ask as my gaze lingers over her face. "I mean, we were supposed to be getting to know each other, right?"

"Now that you mention it…" she ponders. "Where are you from? I know you came here from Atlanta, but where were you born?"

I scratch my head, trying to pull the answer out of my head to respond to her question. The more I think about it, the more frustrated I become. "I wish I knew. My nana said that I was brought to her when I was little, after my parents died, and my birth records had to be manufactured so I could live with her in Atlanta."

"I'm really sorry. If you don't want to talk about it…"

"No, I mean…they've been gone a long time, and as much as I

miss them, all I can do is keep them in my thoughts and my heart as best I can," I try to explain. "All I've known...all I can remember... is growing up in the A."

"So tell me about your nana."

The mere mention of her warms me up and sparks a curious grin from Zahra. "My nana is the strongest woman I know. The neighborhood I grew up in, they protected her like she was some sort of sacred treasure. The kids I grew up with swore she was a witch, but like a good witch."

She leans in closer; interest lights up her eyes. "Do you know where your nana is from? Did she ever tell you? Maybe that might help you understand where you're from."

She has a point there.

I shrug, unsure of what I want to say. "It never really came up in conversation, to be real. I had questions about my parents while growing up, but she always said that we would have a conversation about it when I was old enough to understand."

"Well, you're almost seventeen. I would say that kinda qualifies, right?" she points out. "My daddy always told me that if a person can't embrace their past, they can't possibly have a future. Maybe we can talk to your grandmother, see if she might be willing to have that talk, now that you're 'old enough'?"

"You...you would do that for me?" I arch my right eyebrow, studying her face. "I don't know what to say. No one has really ever wanted to... I don't know where to start. Should I get, like, one of those DNA testing sites or something? I heard they're really vague."

She giggles, shaking her head. "We can find another way, starting with your grandmother."

"Okay and thank you for wanting to help... For real, it means a lot to me."

I look into her eyes, placing my hands on top of hers. I move closer, almost hoping she would give a clue that she wants me there. I notice her eyes dart from left to right as my lips are so close to hers that I can feel the air as she exhales. I want to kiss her, but I don't want it to be weird. I lean in to press my lips against hers, closing my eyes to focus on how soft her lips are…until I feel a kiss on my cheek.

"Um, okay, that was awkward." I hide my disappointment as best I can, but I can't help wondering if I read the situation wrong after all. "Did I do something wrong?"

Zahra plays in her hair as she avoids my gaze. "Yasir…okay, so I wanted to…but it feels like things are moving so fast right now. We haven't had a chance to really catch a vibe, and…"

"And *what*, Z?" I cut her off. A few seconds later, I stop myself, shaking my head several times. I'm not gonna be "that" guy. "You know what? Never mind, I get it. I read this wrong, and I shouldn't have tried to kiss you. I feel so stupid right now."

"No, Yasir, it's not like that at all, it's just…"

I hold up my index finger, causing her to stop mid-sentence. I shift my body away from her, focusing on one of the trees to keep from looking at her as I search for words. "I'm sorry, I guess I'm kinda… I really like you, Zahra, but I don't want to make you feel weird around me. I'm still kinda figuring things out here, and there's something about you that makes me feel safe. Does that make sense at all?"

She grabs my hand, keeping me close to her. She takes her finger and turns my head to face her. "I like you, too, but I don't think we should rush things. I know it might sound weird, but I feel like I've known you forever, and we haven't been around each other enough for me to feel that way."

I turn my head away from her, and it's taking everything within me to suppress the frustration I'm feeling. I want to scream because I can't understand the mixed signals that I'm getting from her. At the same time, there's a part of me that feels like things are moving too fast. I mean what I say that I feel safe when I'm around her, probably more than I've ever felt around any girl.

I brace myself as I turn to face her again and pray to the gods that I don't give in the minute I continue the convo.

"So what do we do about this?" I ask, staring into her eyes. "There's something between us, and I know you feel it, too. I don't know about you, but I can't go around acting like we're good as friends for much longer."

"How about we just let things flow the way they're supposed to, and whatever happens happens, and we don't fight it," she replies with a shrug. "I don't know, it sounds like something my mom would say, but it's a whole other thing to do it for real."

"All right, I guess we can try that."

I rise from the bench, pulling her up with me, and escort her back to our cars. I open the door to her car, leaning inside once she settles into the driver's seat. My gaze widens as I take note of all the tech she has inside her car. From the dashboard to the middle console, I wonder how deeply connected everything is inside. "Um, we need to talk about the IT security upgrades you're gonna need in your car, for real. I wouldn't want something this pretty to get hacked."

"Oh, I don't think I have to worry about that." She winks as she presses the ignition button. "I made sure to take all the precautions to keep that from happening."

I smirk as I pull out my smartphone, open an app, and click a few buttons as Zahra looks on. A few minutes later, I press and hold a button down, and the accelerator pushes down about halfway to the floor.

"What are you— How are you—" she stutters in shock.

I keep clicking on the button, revving the engine without Zahra applying any pressure to it. I continue pressing the button, mimicking her shocked expression before giving a satisfied nod that I've proven my point.

"Like I said, we might need to talk. I'm kinda good at what I do," I tell her as I disengage the app and place my phone back in my pocket. "I enjoyed our talk, and I look forward to the next one. I'll see you at school tomorrow."

She gives me a little wave, and I close the door, waiting for her to pull out of her parking space. Once she leaves, I hop in the driver's seat of my Jeep before I burst into laughter. It takes the slight pain of the sting out of what happened with that almost-kiss, but I know it's only temporary. I hope I can recover from that L because that was embarrassing.

So she wants to take it slow. I guess we'll just have to be friends…for now.

CHAPTER NINE

The next morning isn't total chaos, but it hasn't been a walk in the park, either.

I've gotten to the point where I've reached my limit dealing with Ian's crew and their constant focus on making my life at the Grove miserable. I'd hoped that Ian had gotten the word out about how I bailed him out with that Baytown crew, but I guess they either didn't get the memo or they decided to ignore it.

After the confusion with Zahra last night, I have some extra aggression I need to get rid of, and I want all the smoke they're giving so I can apply as much pressure on them as possible.

And I promise, *pressure* got applied.

By the time I'm done with them, there's nothing but crickets and whispers in class over how I'm not the one to play with anymore. No cap, it feels good to give what I've been getting, and the only way to handle bullies is to match their energy. I'm SWATS-certified, which means it's gonna take a lot more than what they've been bringing to break me.

Now that that's done, my hope is that they run back to the fort and tell their leader to clear up all this confusion so we can finish up the semester in one piece. The whole point of me being down here is to keep a low profile, and they're making sure that doesn't happen.

The downside of expending all that energy is that it leaves me in a weird headspace, and I'm not always strategic in my attacks. That's where having my Squad helps the most. One of them would've been able to at least get me to calm down before things got out of hand.

It's probably why I don't pull punches when I see Kyle approaching. I'm not in the mood to deal with whatever he wants to discuss, and as much as I don't want to admit it, I'm feeling isolated and attacked from damn near every angle. Having a friend would be a good look right now. "I'm not in the mood to put up a fight today, my boy, so say what you came to say and be done with it."

The weird part about how I'm feeling after seeing Kyle at my locker this morning boils down to one thing: he's the textbook definition of an enigma. One minute he acts like a barrier between me and Ian and the rest of his crew, and the next minute, he looks completely unbothered by it all. It keeps me on edge, second-guessing whether I should be on guard whenever we're around each other.

I should've seen him coming. He and Zahra are tight, so it was only a matter of time before I got a visit from him. I'm expecting her bestie Kendyl to start up sometime soon, too. It's just a matter of time before she comes for me once she's done her investigative work. Best friends are funny that way.

"Bro, this ain't what you think. I didn't come here to fight." He keeps his palms open, which really doesn't faze me. It's giving Trojan horse vibes and then some.

"So what do you want? Make it quick. I ain't got all day." I shoot back. "I'm late for work with my uncle."

Kyle breathes deep, closing his eyes for a few moments before he focuses on me again. "Look, yo, I get it, trauma response and all that from them coming at you all the time. I'm probably gonna have to work to keep from triggering you, but I'm not your enemy. I don't rock with Ian like that."

"Could've fooled me," I reply, trying to figure out his angle. I flex my fingers like I'm waiting for an ambush.

"Okay, look, let's keep it a buck." Kyle steps to me, his palms still open and hands held up. "You have every right to feel how you feel, but I promised your girl and my girl that I would make sure there's no pressure between us."

Hearing Zahra and Kendyl mentioned in the same breath causes me to narrow my gaze at him. "Z isn't my girl, at least… Wait a minute, you and Kenni are a thing? If that's true, then that means…"

"Yeah, bro, it means sooner or later, we're gonna have to deal with being in each other's spaces. And you two can play games all you want about being 'friends,' but I know my bestie," Kyle replies. "For what it's worth, I'm sorry about my part in not helping to block what you've gone through and not doing more to make you feel more comfortable. It's not right, but for some reason, Ian's zoned in on you now. He only does that with people he sees as a threat."

Dealing with the noise is nothing I haven't handled before, but I'm getting tired of proving that I can rise above it all, especially when I didn't do anything to deserve all this pressure.

"I'm not a threat to anything or anyone. I just got here. All I wanted to do was get through high school in one piece so I could do what I wanted when I graduated." I shrug, at a loss over what I could've done. "I mean, what the hell could possibly be on his mind?"

"I don't know, but the one thing I do know is that we all try to figure out how to fit in," Kyle points out, shaking his head over where his conclusions lead him. "That amps up a few levels when you're playing for Oakwood."

"I can't relate. I'm not an athlete, and I don't have any designs to ball here."

"Could have fooled me. Rumor has it you're real nice with your hands."

I scoff at that take. "I'm only boxing to keep from really getting my ass kicked. I figure if I can get a few good shots in, it might take the heat off me."

Kyle stares at me, tilting his head to his right shoulder. "Yeah, but rumor has it you put two of those Baytown boys to sleep… If that's not nice with your hands, I don't know what to tell you."

I'm a little disturbed by what Kyle just said. If Ian's telling people that I helped him, it could get to ears that don't need to hear about, or know, where I am. I've got to find a way to shut down that noise before it causes more trouble than it's worth.

"Good, maybe I can enjoy my school year a little more if that word keeps going around." I feel that familiar twitch that throws me off, and I close my eyes to calm down. I return my attention to my new…acquaintance? Calling him a friend feels way premature. "I appreciate you wanting to ease the pressure. It's a start, but we're not cool, at least not yet. That's gonna take time to build trust. I get that you and Z are close, but that means nothing to me."

Kyle extends his fist, tapping mine as a sign of good faith. "That's fair. How about this? I'm hosting a party this weekend; my birthday is Saturday. Come through with Z, and we can hang some more, build up some more good will."

I'm hesitant, trying to figure out how best to explain myself. "I don't handle crowds well, for real. And I don't know if Z and I are a thing to be coming to a party as a couple."

"Look, you gotta start somewhere, and whether you want to believe it or not, my best friend is feeling you. She may not show it, but trust me, I know her," Kyle says to me. "And as far as my party is concerned, I got your back if any outside pressure comes through. You have my word."

"I'm still not sure…" I want to protest. This is going in a direction I'm not comfortable with, and I need to put a stop to it quick.

Kyle puts his hand up to cut me off. "I'm not trying to hear it. If you like her, and it's obvi you do, then I'll see you this weekend."

I rub my hand over my face. He's right. I can't sit on the sidelines anymore. "Fine, I'll ask Z and then let you know if we'll be there."

"All right, bet. And tomorrow, I'll introduce you to some of the others who don't roll with Ian if you're up to it. Meet us in the courtyard after school."

• • •

"**W**hat's good, kiddo? How was school?" Unk asks.

I have so many ways to respond to that question, and for the first time that I can remember in the past three weeks or so, there are some positives. I nailed my English paper. I didn't have to deal with too much drama... Even the convo with Kyle turned into something good.

So why do I still feel so anxious? "I feel like I'm trapped in a new alternate universe, Unk, for real. I know yesterday was Monday, but it feels like somebody's trying to play games and forgot to tell me."

I catch him in the living room, in the middle of a binge-watch on Netflix, when I come in and stretch out on the microfiber sectional. We only have about five minutes before the current episode ends, so I'm content to relax until it's over before he picks up the convo.

Unk sits up, lowering the recliner back to a seated position, and pauses the stream before he turns to face me. "Lay it on me, Ya-Ya. It sounds serious."

I try to manage my nerves as the answer to his initial question probably turns into a whole other gamechanger for me. "I have a...well, I think, I don't know. The one I was talking about before? Anyway, her name is Zahra."

"And Zahra is?"

"A friend."

He strokes his beard, processing my answer. "Hmmm, sounds complicated."

"Yeah, at least...it kinda is complicated, I guess." I shrug, interlacing my fingers and tapping my thumbs together. "Or maybe it isn't and I'm just making more of it than I should."

He narrows his gaze. Yep, here comes the investigative session. "Why do I feel like you're dreading this more than you need to be? This is an exciting time."

"Okay, maybe it should be, but I don't know what to think right now."

He points toward the recliner in the other corner of the room. I feel like the only things missing are cigars and his single-malt bourbon. I get up from the sectional and move to sit in the recliner. He leans forward, making sure I have his full attention. "So enlighten me, youngster. What have you been dealing with?"

After settling into the plush leather cushioning, I take a deep breath to get my thoughts together. I realize I have been keeping a lot of things close to the vest, so to finally unleash some of it feels like a weight is lifting from my shoulders. "So I was kinda rocking with this girl when I was in the A. When I left, I didn't really close things out with her."

"Okay, and what does that have to do with this new…friend?"

"Yeah, I don't know, it probably doesn't, but I'm not sure," I start to say. "I told Nana about her, and she's kinda expecting me to bring Z to see her."

"Now I see why you're hesitant. Things don't need to be messy if you do that," he advises. "So tell me about Zahra. She must be something if you're going through all these chess moves."

I light up the minute he asks the question. "She's… There's something about her that's enchanting, and the things she brings out of me, I can't explain it. She has me under her spell without even trying. And she's smart…like, *smart*, smart. She can teach me a thing or two."

"That's the way it's supposed to be, kiddo." He grins. "So… when am *I* gonna meet her?"

Um, pause…what?

I don't know how to answer that question. I mean, she's not my girl or anything like that, but… "If she's game, I can ask her to come over tomorrow night," I offer. It sounds good, but now I'm freaking out. "I know she's not the first girl I've felt *this* way about, but there's something special about her. I mean, it's like… I don't know how to explain it."

"Don't try to. Just enjoy the ride," Unk replies. "Now, since we're dropping bombs and such, I guess I should tell you about Lennox, the woman I'm seeing."

Whoa, and whoa… Now this I gotta hear. I sit up in the recliner with this silly, surprised expression on my face. "Pause… You mean, it's getting serious? And her name is Lennox?"

"Yep, we've been out on a couple of dates since you and I last talked. I like her a lot, and I think the feeling is mutual." He tilts his head toward his left shoulder, studying my reaction. "It's a vibe, that's for sure."

"Then we need to have them both over for lunch or something, right?" I inquire. "I mean, if it's a vibe, then I need to see what's up with her, too."

"Do you think it's a good idea? I don't want to move too fast."

Is he kidding? What is it that he loves to say? "It's nothing until it's something." Well, it's something. "Man, yes, why not?"

"Okay, we can keep it light, no expectations. Just enjoy things out in the backyard until you and…?"

"Zahra."

"You and Zahra have somewhere else you need to be."

I smile as I get up from the recliner. Today's turned out to be a good day after all. "Good talk, Unk. Thanks for not making this weird. I was kinda stressing about it. It's gonna be an interesting time, for sure."

"Yeah, but I'm sure we'll figure it out," he says. "This is new territory for both of us."

CHAPTER TEN

I finally have a chance to crash in my room for a few minutes, taking a moment to close my eyes and breathe. I'm doing everything I can to keep my mind off the convo with Kyle earlier, and let's face it, there's someone who's probably waiting for one of us to give up the details over what happened.

I mean, it's not like we were gonna get to scrapping or anything like that, but even if it did, I'd hold my own. Kyle's tall and built solid as hell, which is saying a lot for a seventeen-year-old boy. He doesn't strike me as the type to fire off just for the hell of it, and I didn't ignore his attempts to stay civil, despite giving him every chance not to do it.

I lay on my bed to get my head together before I FaceTime Zahra, doing a silent count before her face pops up on my screen. I'm still wondering why I get so nervous and so calm at the same time, but I don't think about it anymore. She makes me smile, and that's all I care about right now.

"Hi, Yasir, how did it go with Kyle?"

"Well, damn, Z, hello to you, too. It went…well. I mean, we both have our limbs, so I guess that counts as progress." I chuckle for a minute as I think about how things eventually smoothed out. "I'm still trying to trust people, but it's not a walk in the park."

"Okay, so, I was low-key trying not to let this be the first thing I wanted to talk about, but when I didn't hear from either of you, I started freaking out," Zahra confesses as she bites her bottom lip. "I'm glad things didn't go left, but part of me kinda wanted something to happen. It would've given me a reason to see about you."

The convo between us feels like we're out of sync, which has me concerned. I'm not used to her sounding so unsure of herself. Any plans I had to get any homework done have been pushed off to later tonight. I need to make sure she's okay first.

"Yeah, he said something about hitting me up about his birthday party this weekend, so it's a start," I tell her. "Your bestie seems to be cool people, and I'm hoping I'm right about that."

Zahra's sitting there just bouncing on her bed, and it's not hard to see she's excited, but she's trying to keep it in check. Now, that's the girl I'm used to vibing with. "Yay, at least neither of you is in the hospital. I was checking TikTok to make sure you weren't on the feed. I'm relieved, for real."

I hesitate for a moment, unsure if I want to say anything, but I change my mind at the last minute. "So quick subject change… I kinda told my uncle about you earlier."

She blushes so hard she turns the camera away. I hear her say something under her breath, but I can't make it out. She finally turns the camera back to continue the chat. "Oh, wow, I really must be special now. So when's dinner, and should I wear something subtle or just be me?"

"Actually, it's lunch, and how the hell did you know?" I raise my right eyebrow, wondering how she managed to guess almost right. "Are you psychic or something? Do we need to have a different conversation right now?"

She shakes her head, placing an index finger to her lips. "Hmm, just a wild guess, pretty boy. Now that I think about it, I can't wait to tell my mom about you. She's been curious about my good mood lately."

I don't know how I get triggered or even why her mention of her mother causes it, but my mood changes in seconds. I ignore her confused expression so I can turn the focus away from me. "Tell me about her, if you don't mind? Where are your parents from?"

She gives me a curious look, and I know I sort of changed the tone of the convo, but I just don't want to think about my parents right now. "My parents are from the Island Republic of Kindara. What about your parents?"

Yeah, this isn't going all that well. I don't want to talk about them. "I don't remember a lot about my parents. They died when I was really young, but…" Nah, I can't talk about this anymore. I need to find a way to change the subject. "You know what, tell me more about your parents and Kindara. Where is it? I'd love to know more about it. Sounds like an amazing place."

Zahra's eyes light up, and I'm equal parts jealous and relieved. I can't help but wonder where I come from myself, and the fact that she revels in her homeland is something I would love to have. "Kindara is so many different things to me, but even the word paradise doesn't cover it for me," she expresses to me, tapping her index finger against her left temple as she continues to think about what she wants to say. "As far as where Kindara is, it's not far from the West African coastline, and we can get to anywhere from Senegal to Ghana."

I lean back against the wall to get comfortable as she grins while thinking about the other things she wants to tell me about her home country. "Now, what Kindara is? Oh em gee, we might be here all night if I start up."

"Well, I'm not going anywhere," I reply, matching her excitement to keep her talking. "What is Kindara to you?"

"Paradise." Zahra beams as she considers her words. "Everything that makes me fall in love with the island is there: the white sand beaches, the crystal-clear blue water that makes you feel like you can see almost to the bottom of the ocean, the lush tree line that surrounds the inside of the island. It's the food. Her people. The animals that live in harmony with us there. The twin volcanoes that are named for the Vodaran fire goddess, Nahara. The River Ko, where you can float on a boat from the north side of the island to the south. Mount Kindara with its mysticism and legends that are said to be housed inside. Kindara is probably the most magical place on earth for me."

"And what about your parents?" I continue to keep the focus

off me for as long as I can, trying to find anything that will keep her talking and not asking questions. "Did they grow up on the island? I remember you said you've been here in Oakwood Grove since you were little."

"Yes, but we spend the summers out there, and just about every spare moment we can. My parents are from the Kua village, on the southwest corner of the island. There are several different villages that make up Kindara, too. Kua is where the farmers grow the food and distribute it throughout the island. Then there's the Mipaku. They protect the island's perimeter and borders." Zahra gets comfortable in her bed, and I breathe a sigh of relief, at least for a few moments. "The Wahunza, they forge the metals that are needed for construction in Drana Trini, the capital city, and all the larger cities on the island. The Sayansi village is the science and technology area of the island, where I hope to settle once I'm done with school. Then there's Solara, which is the academics and scribes and the educators, and finally the Serykala, which is the government and politicians, and the Kabula la Maji, which is the Water village."

She tilts her head toward her left shoulder, and I immediately feel a shift in the focus in the convo. "Do you know anything about Kindara?"

I shrug. That's a nope from me. "Nana's mentioned it, and she didn't give up much information—at least, not enough for me to be curious. I've never really been outside of the States. Boring, huh? I mean, I'm sure you've been back to Kindara a few times, right?"

"Yes, I have. Maybe I can find a way to show you one day. It's a beautiful island paradise," she says to me, but all I can give up is a nod that's not all that convincing. "Don't worry. If you're willing to learn, I would love to tell you everything I know."

"I'd like that, I really would," I reply. I'm serious, too. I love the way her eyes light up when we talk about her home country. "Maybe it might be somewhere I can put on my bucket list after we graduate."

"Well, now that we've gotten that out of the way." Her smile turns into a subtle smirk. "Um, so, I wanted to talk about what happened last night when we talked."

I close my eyes before I say another word. I don't want to say the wrong thing. "I guess it's my turn to keep from looking like I'm out of sorts. Honestly, I don't know how to explain what happened. I was so nervous that I guess I read the situation wrong."

She waves her hand in a dismissive manner. "I want you to know that you didn't do anything wrong, okay? It was…bad timing, maybe? I'm not really all that good at these types of things, either."

I tilt my head toward my left shoulder, matching her curious pose. Why is she trying to take some of the blame? "That makes two of us. I was scared that I really messed things up."

"No, not at all, I'm just loving the way things are flowing between us right now," she reassures me.

I smile, like really smile, and I feel my dimples sinking deeper into my cheeks. "I guess I need to go. I have to create my oils for the next few weeks."

"About those oils, though." She closes her eyes for a moment, and I wish I could see inside her head to know what she's thinking right now. "Why do you need to wear them? I mean, I love the way they smell on you, but I can sense something beneath the oils. It's hypnotic, if that makes sense."

"I guess that's something else we can find out." I get up and walk into the bathroom, carrying my phone with me so we can keep talking. "All I have been told is that I need to use them because there are people who would be able to track me down and take me out."

She covers her mouth to stifle a gasp, and I instantly regret letting that information slip out. "Why would anyone want to kill you? Did your parents do something to someone?"

"Yeah, I'm starting to wonder if it's all a shell game, to be honest. Whatever happened, it has nothing to do with me, but my nana is convinced that I need to be careful. Anyway, I made a few changes, so we'll see how that goes." I glance at the time and realize there's some things that need to get done or I'll be up way later than I want to be. "Enough of all that, I need to get busy and get some homework done, too. Can I check on you before bed? I still have to tell you about Kyle's birthday party invite."

"You better, or I'll be coming for you," she counters. "I can't wait to hear about it. Sounds like it will be fun."

CHAPTER ELEVEN

"**W**hoa, is that Yasir? He looks like a whole different person."

"And he's not wearing that God-awful cologne anymore. It's a good look on him."

"And he's changed his hair, too. He trying to get *fine*, fine."

I can't stop chuckling as I make my way through the halls this morning. Everywhere I go, all eyes are on me, with a few of the girls turning into insta-groupies when I swear to the gods they didn't know I existed. Last night while I was FaceTiming with Z, some clothes and oils I ordered finally arrived. No disrespect to my nana, but the things she cosigned on were not it. My fit game was in desperate need of an upgrade, and I'm low-key grateful that all it took was an interest in a girl to get her to loosen up.

By the time I stop at my locker, the halls are buzzing. Whether I want the attention or not, the spotlight is focused on me and bright as hell.

While the attention is both appreciated and anxiety-inducing at the same time, I don't care about the newfound crowds who did what they could to find out what the fuss is about. Only one matters, and as long as *she* approves of the new look and the subtle changes I made to my "signature" scent, it's worth all the trouble.

I soon find out what the price of instant fame after being shunned looks like, as Amber Waters, one of the girls on the cheerleading squad with Kendyl, and a couple of her friends, Tori and Jenna, all descend on my locker. I don't see them while I pull my books to prepare for my first classes of the day, but the moment I turn around, they enclose in a circle around me.

"Well, damn, Yasir, we'd heard that you'd leveled up a bit, but I didn't know it was like *this*, though." Amber licks her lips as she does the head-to-toe check. The look in her eyes lets me know I need to get out of there before she gets the wrong idea. "If this is how you're gonna rock your fits from now on, a girl might have to see about you."

I search for anyone or any opening that can get me out of this situation. She's been eyeing me since I got on campus but never said two words to me until today. Like my nana loves to say, "Something in the milk ain't clean."

"Um, Amber, I appreciate the compliment, but I need to get to class."

"Oh, I'm sure you can spare a few minutes for me, cutie," Amber retorts as she moves closer into my personal space. "I mean, you can't be smelling all delicious like this and not expect someone to want to get a taste of it, right?"

"Okay, Amber, I get that you appreciate the fit and the new look and all but…" I lean against the lockers, resigning myself to the fact that the only way I'm gonna get out of this mess would be to ask the question I don't want the answer to. "Why are you applying pressure now? I'm not understanding how you and your girls are all up on me when I wasn't the flavor of the week last week, anyway."

Amber looks at her girls, getting the nod from Tori and a smirk from Jenna, before she moves even closer, placing a palm on the locker above my shoulder. "Okay, so I know the buzz is that you're trying to get with Zahra, and I'm feeling that, so do you. But that doesn't mean we can't have a situation of our own, though. Y'all ain't together yet."

I shake my head, sliding away from Amber to create some distance between us. "All right, ease back a bit. I'm not feeling this sudden change of heart, deadass. The only reason you're getting this bold is simple: the buzz is hot on campus, and you're chasing the heat."

"What's past is past, pretty boy, and the only thing that's important right now is that I see you, and I like what I see."

"That's cap. Look elsewhere, shawty. I ain't going for it."

I can't decide whether I'm relieved or worried as I notice Zahra and Kendyl standing behind Tori and Jenna, grabbing everyone's attention in the hallway. I play it calm for a few moments, but inside I want to freak out over what happens next. Girls are wildcards in situations like this, and while Z and I aren't *together*, together, this ain't the type of drama I want to deal with first thing in the morning.

And then Zahra winks at me. When I say the relief that comes over me when I see her do that? I need the bailout, please and thank you.

I smirk as Amber turns around, caught off guard by Zahra being in her personal space. I stifle a chuckle, surprised over being involved in something out of *Riverdale*. The only thing missing… well, I don't want to think about that.

"Z, hey girl… I was just having a conversation with Yasir. What are you doing here?"

Zahra's answer to Amber's question shocks me to the point of wondering if I'm hallucinating. Things start happening in slow motion, and I'm powerless to stop it. Zahra slides Amber out of the way, then steps in front of me, wrapping her arms around my neck and pulling me down for a kiss that makes me forget anyone is in the immediate area.

What. The. Hell. Is. Happening?

Instinct takes over from there, and I straighten up to my full six-foot-three-inch height, taking Zahra a few inches off the ground as we create a spectacle with the unexpected PDA. While we kiss, my senses heighten, and I hear Kendyl being, well, not so polite in her "request" that Amber, Tori, and Jenna leave the area before something bad happens to them.

Well, damn, if I'd known it would be that easy, I'd have said something sooner.

I finally feel her break from our embrace, then gently set her down on the ground. I don't want to be rude to her bestie, so I make sure to acknowledge her first. "Hi, Kenni. At the risk of sounding cliché as hell, that wasn't what it looked like."

Zahra keeps her hands around my face, placing small kisses across my lips. "Don't worry, Kenni sort of saw this coming once word got out. I guess I need to worry about your expanding fan club now, huh?"

I blush, causing a giggle out of both girls. I shrug, truly at a loss over all the fuss, but I have a twinge of anxiety creeping up my spine, too. "I didn't do much of anything to get all this attention, Z. I mean, the outfit is a bit outside of what I normally wear, but I felt like it was time for a change."

Kendyl scoffs, tapping me on my shoulder. "Yeah, about that... whatever you decided to do, I'm gonna need you to keep that same energy. People were legit trying to find out who was wearing the new scent, and when they found out it was you—"

Zahra chimes in, almost finishing Kendyl's sentence, "Let's just say, we had to get to ground zero quick, because it was only a matter of time before someone would act on it." She leans in, then closes her eyes and lays her forehead against my chest. "I can sense the change in your oils and lotions, too, Yasir. You increased the sandalwood scent, didn't you?"

I'm grinning like I won the lottery, impressed that she noticed the difference. "Actually, I increased the sandalwood and the coriander, and it seemed to do the trick."

"Yeah, I'm gonna need you to keep that mixture from now on, okay?" Zahra bats her eyes, tapping her index finger against my lips. "And as for this fit...what are you doing after school, sir?"

Kendyl laughs out loud, checking the clock. "Chica, we need to get to it, and so does he. Love you, mean it."

I steal one last kiss and wave to Zahra as Kendyl pulls her around the corner. "Um, we're gonna need to talk about what just happened, Z. I thought we were, you know?"

"Um, friends can kiss, right?" she teases before she disappears.

I smile, wondering if things are starting to shift the way she mentioned the other day. I recover and make my way to class before the resource officers start making their sweeps of the halls.

I slip into English class and get to my seat, but I'm already causing a distraction the moment I sit down. By the time I figure out what's happening, the girls in the class, who had taken great pains to be in other areas of the room, all but encircle my seat, much to the chagrin of the other boys observing the situation.

Oh, boy, today's gonna be tough sledding.

I resolve to just get through the day, including the classes I have with Zahra, and figure out a way to, as my uncle loves to say, "govern myself accordingly."

CHAPTER TWELVE

Okay, Kyle's true to his word, and the way he's coming through in the clutch is impressive. That's all I can say about that right now.

Before I have a chance to even get out of the school parking lot, he literally pulls me into this crowd of kids and starts making the introductions before he turns them loose on me. For real, I feel like I'm in an impromptu initiation into a secret society with the way they are coming at me with all these questions. I don't remember the last time I went through something like this, but I'm not about to let them smell any type of weakness on me, either.

It's a rare extrovert energy burn for me. Normally, I'd have shied away from the rush of personalities, but after the quick convo Kyle and I had after I thought he was betraying the precarious trust between us, I feel like it's time to show them who I am.

Once I realize who they are, the walls disappear, and the flood gates are wide open.

And I'm not the only one who notices, either. "You're cooler than I thought you were, Yasir. It was fun chopping it up with you," Taylor Ricks, one of the boys Kyle told me about yesterday, mentions as I keep managing all the different chats happening around me. He's not as physically imposing as Kyle, but not many boys our age are, either. Taylor's maybe a couple of inches shorter than I am at six foot one, and considering he's the starting running back, he's well put together. I couldn't help noticing the girls gawking at him, but it's hard for them not to. His tawny skin, arresting light brown eyes, and wavy brown hair—I mean, it's giving runway model looks, for real. "It's too bad you're not on the squad. I think you'd be nice on the field."

Marco Grant, one of the basketball players in the group who looks like he's Kevin Durant's younger brother, height and all, jumps into the chat. "Nah, yo, he'd be nice on the court. We might need to run a pickup game, see if you got something."

Man, listen, the way the conversation is flowing while I'm chatting with most of the members of the football and basketball teams…well, the football players that aren't in Ian's circles, anyway. While I realize that there might be some on campus who associate on a limited basis when it comes to him, I'm not convinced that they would be a part of the same circles. Maybe I've been going about this the wrong way all this time.

Everyone in the group isn't an athlete, though. A few of the boys, and all the girls, are STEM kids who are very familiar with Zahra. The girls consider her the queen bee when it comes to that world, which shouldn't have surprised me. I got that vibe after a couple of the engineering club meetings I attended. It's cool to know that the larger world inside the school doesn't revolve around one group of kids, and it puts me at ease, at least a little bit, anyway.

Funny that the weather is as warm as it is for early October. The sun beaming down on us while we're vibing feels like this is supposed to happen. Even the breeze came through easy and low-key, adding to my good mood.

I can't resist peeking over at the girls as they observe the situation for themselves. I smirk as I zero in on Zahra, her grin giving me a boost of confidence to stay in the thick of the chatter happening around me. I ignore the anxiety—at least, I'm trying to— of being in larger groups where possible, but it doesn't take away from the fact that I'm not being shunned, and things are working out well, for real.

I shoot a text, asking Zahra to meet me where Storm is parked. While I had seen her in class earlier in the day, I hadn't *seen* her seen her.

I jog toward the parking lot with Kyle, beaming as I notice

the girls making their way in our direction. I elbow Kyle to give the heads up, watching him light up the minute Kendyl gets close enough for him to reach out and embrace her. I notice Zahra hesitate when we get close to each other, almost like she's not sure what to do.

That makes two of us. Especially after that kiss? Sheesh. This "just friends" thing is legit stressing me out.

"You look like you're in a good mood," Zahra remarks as she stands in my personal space with this slick grin on her face like she conspired with Kyle. "You looked comfortable hanging with the boys. If I didn't know any better, I'd swear you were starting to get acclimated to your new element."

"Don't get it twisted. I'm still trying to feel them out, but so far so good. I guess the real test is this weekend."

"Well, you know I have no issues figuring out how to calm things down," she coos in my ear. "Besides, it shouldn't be too busy in certain areas of the house. Kyle's parents have a pretty expansive estate, so it should keep drama to a minimum."

"And what makes you think I want you to calm things down?" I tease, leaning away when she tries to touch me. "Maybe there might be some other girls at the party who might wanna see about the kid."

The look she gives me could've pierced through steel, and I burst out laughing. She slaps my shoulder *hard*, crossing her arms over her chest. "And maybe a few of the fellas that will be coming with Kyle's cousin might wanna holla, too. I mean, they all play with him, you know."

I feign a heart attack like someone had just shot an arrow, which makes her giggle. "You ain't have to do me like that, though. I was just kidding."

"I don't know, pretty boy. We're just hanging out as friends. Why would I want to keep another girl from seeing about you?" She winks at me, biting her bottom lip. "Maybe it might make me want you more."

Kyle cracks up laughing as he wraps his hands around Kendyl's waist. "You two are funny as hell, for real. I'll bring the popcorn to see how this plays out, if you two are serious about this, of course."

"I guess we'll see." I brush off the gauntlet she's laid down, determined to not let her get to me. "So, according to the fellas, this party is gonna be huge?"

Kyle rubs the back of his neck, staring off in the distance for a few seconds before he lets out an annoyed sigh. "Despite what we might be able to do, you know Ian and that bunch may want to come through. They take the air out of any room they're in, and that's not gonna happen, not when I'm supposed to be front and center. I tried to tap dance around the subject all day today, but one of the other kids opened her mouth about seeing me at the birthday party, and the flood gates took over from there."

"So what's the backup plan, in case they do show up?" Zahra leans against me as they all continue to muse about what to expect. I try to act like the traces of her perfume aren't making me weak. "I mean, your parents usually contract security with these big parties. I'm sure this one will be no different, right?"

Kyle nods, but then he snaps his fingers, pointing his index finger against his temple. "Yeah, and that might calm some of it down, but Ian's pops and mine are... Well, they're cordial. My dad is on the city council, and there's some tension. There's a lot of other moving parts that make things complicated. They might not have a choice but to let him in."

"So we deal with him by icing him out," I say. Yeah, easier said than done, but I have an idea or two of how to pull that off. I've dealt with kids like him before, and some solutions are universal. "Look, you said it yourself: he loves the spotlight. The more we take it away from him, the more he will loathe it. Once he realizes it's all about the birthday boy, then they'll roll out on their own."

"Yo, that's not a bad plan." Kyle takes Kendyl by her hand to head toward his car, tapping fists with me as they walk. "Let's roll with that. I'll check up with y'all later. Kenni and I have some shopping to do, or so she keeps telling me."

I nod, tapping fists with him again before opening the passenger door for Zahra to hop inside. Once I ease into the driver's seat, I turn to Zahra… Wait a minute, what's this look on her face? I didn't do anything wrong, did I? "What is it? Was it something I said?"

"I'm literally trying to figure out where this version of Yasir Salah has been this entire time," she muses, caressing my face like she hadn't ever seen me before in her life. "It's a good look on you."

"Well, you're the one who's helped create this version. I guess you kinda have a say in how long I can stick around, huh? The question is, do you want to be a friend of this version, or do you want to be my girl?" I flash a grin that makes her blush. I'm not exactly being subtle, though. Blame it on the good mood I'm in. "You can't be all flirty and everything and then act like we're supposed to not be…you know…together."

Zahra pauses for a few moments as she ponders her response. "And if I want to be your girl? Not saying that I'm ready yet, but what if I do?"

"So I think the others had a pretty good idea. We might need to get the outfits together for the weekend. We can at least do that, until we figure out what *this* will finally be."

"I like the way you think. Pick me up in a couple of hours?" Zahra asks as she slides out of Storm and skips to her car. "I have a few spots we can go to get what we need, and there are a few things I wouldn't mind showing off just for you. You know, since we're figuring things out and all that?"

"Say less, pretty girl. I'll see you in a couple of hours."

"Yo, Unk, can I holla at you for a minute? It's kinda important."

The minute I get home, finding Unk tops the to-do list for the afternoon. I need to have "that" talk about girls, and he's the nearest source to use as a sounding board. I have questions—man, do I have questions—and this happens to be one of those times where I need the uncut version.

We head out to the back deck and sit in the wicker chairs,

enjoying the cooler weather. He pops open a Modelo, his usual wind-down beverage of choice, while I sip on a ginger ale. He leans back in his chair. "Okay, kiddo, what's on your mind?"

I rub my hands together while I figure out how to start things off. My nerves are on edge, which only seems to happen whenever Zahra is the topic. "How do you know when you're treating a girl right?"

Unk turns up the bottle, taking a gulp and drumming his fingers against his thigh. "Let's see. It might be as simple as seeing a smile on her face after you've done something for her. Sometimes, it's a matter of being consistent in your words and actions. Women are hard to figure out like that."

"Well, that's not much help at all." I laugh as he cuts his eyes at me, taking another sip of my drink. "Like, is there a way to not feel like you're messing up at every turn?"

"You know, if I had that figured out, I'd be on a Ted Talk tour right now, making millions." He chuckles at his joke before he glances over and realizes I'm serious about my follow-up question. "All right, here's the real, young'un. If you're comfortable with yourself, and you do the things that make her grin, keep that in your memory and repeat when necessary. Do you know what she likes?"

"Kinda."

"Then you're gonna need to find those things out through the times you just sit and talk."

I think about that for a minute, and I'm still drawing blanks. "I guess I really don't know, for real. All I know is I like seeing her smile when we're together."

"That's the new energy swirling around you. When that calms down, that's when the things you've found out become more important." He nods a few times, rubbing his goatee a few times. "Case in point: I know that Lennox enjoys when I cook for her at the shop after hours sometimes. When her birthday comes around, and that's soon, I'll put something together and we can lounge around in the back of the truck while she enjoys what I've created."

"But isn't that boring, though?" I'm starting to regret asking these questions. They aren't getting me anywhere. "I mean, I'm trying to impress her when we do go on a date."

"I can dig it, but it doesn't always have to be something big for a first date," he tells me as he studies my reaction. "If you really want to impress her, you can find somewhere that she hasn't been before, show her something new."

I sigh heavily, remembering some of the #couplegoals I'd been noticing on social media, both around Oakwood and back in the A…including one I shouldn't have checked up on. "But I can't get caught up doing something weak. The pressure is real, and if it don't give what it's supposed to give, I'm already starting out digging myself out of a hole."

Unk can't stop laughing, and I'm sitting there trying to figure out what the hell is so funny. "Man, where do y'all come up with these sayings? Look, nephew, if and when you and Zahra get together, just stick to the four simple words that have helped me."

"And what words are those?"

"Listen to your woman."

"Come on, Unk. For real?"

"It kept your parents together, and so far, it's keeping Lennox smiling, so yeah, I'm serious."

The thing I always love about my uncle is that, despite his methods sounding completely foreign to me, he's been spot-on almost my whole life. He was right about boxing. He was right about learning about computers. Why would he be off the mark when it comes to dealing with girls?

Never mind all of that, though. He gave me the perfect chance to switch subjects. "Speaking of keeping Ms. Lennox smiling, I think you need to keep doing what you're doing. I like her a lot. She fits you."

"And you'd be better off making sure you learn what makes Zahra smile. I'm just saying."

"Nope, not putting this back on me, that's not how this works."

He takes another sip of his beer, furrowing his brow. Yep, that's my cue to stay in my place. "I'm glad you like her, because I'm trying to see where that goes. She puts a smile on my face, too."

"Yeah, I've been noticing. You've had a lot more energy around the house and at the shop." I finish my ginger ale, getting up from the chair to grab another one. I come back with another beer while I'm up, sitting down to finish my thoughts. "Not gonna lie, she's a baddie, too. I didn't know you had that kinda pull."

"Yeah, I see I'm gonna have to learn you a few things, kiddo." He waves me off, giving up a slick grin that makes me crack up all over again. "All right, I think we've had enough for one night. You've still got homework to finish, and I have to work through my reports to make sure we're still able to live decently."

I give a thumbs-up, letting him know that, for once, he didn't have me dead to rights. "Actually, I handled homework before I got home. I'm meeting up with the fellas to get some shopping done. I'll be home before curfew, of course."

"That works for me. We can relax tomorrow morning, too. I'm good for the rest of the week."

Man, that's music to my ears! I tap fists with him as I move toward the front door. "Good talk as always, Unk. I'm sure it won't be the last one."

"Nah, I know it won't be," he says. "Whatever goes down, just be yourself."

CHAPTER THIRTEEN

How did Kyle and I get caught up in the girls' mini shopping spree like we didn't have our own outfits to figure out? I mean, some of the stores aren't a bad look—because reasons—but they are taking way too long to get things worked out.

I'm trying, and failing, to stop laughing at the outfits they keep trying on while inside one of the boutiques. While it's fun for the moment, my patience is running thin. I know what Unk said, but this is torture, for real.

Zahra doubles over in laughter over the ridiculous combo Kendyl comes up with. "Oh my God, where in the world did you come up with that? Did you just cover your eyes and pick or something?"

Kendyl can't keep a straight face as she holds up the outfit in the mirror. "I really tried to find something off color, I promise, but this is hideous. What do you think, baby?"

Kyle has this expression on his face that says, "I'm over it all."

"I know you can rock an outfit that's off the beaten path," he says, "but this ain't giving, seriously speaking."

"Do I need to check your closet again to make sure you're still the fashionista I know and love?" Zahra asks as they continue putting the wild combinations against their bodies. "I get you wanna be edgy, since Halloween is coming up, but that look is a nah from me, sis."

Kendyl's still a bit nervous as we continue to pick through pieces. "Love you, chica, but as much as I enjoy torturing the boys, I don't want to linger around in Beach Creek enemy territory. We play them tomorrow, and the last thing we need is to be caught out here."

Zahra dismisses her confused expression, and I'm a bit confused, real talk. "It wasn't all bad. There weren't any issues that couldn't be handled. I smoked that boy straight up...well, not entirely straight up. He had to use NOS to try and keep up, but he asked for it."

Wait. Pause. "You were racing, Z?" I lean closer to her.

Kendyl rubs her temples, reaching out to mock strangle Zahra's neck. "You have a damn gift for understatement. Things could've gone way left that day, sis. Come on, now."

I jump into the convo quick, almost demanding an answer to my question. "What happened, Zahra? What did you get caught up in?"

Zahra holds her index finger up to silence Kendyl quick before she turns to face me. "Nothing happened, for real. We got out of there without too much trouble, okay? Kenni's making a bigger deal out of this than it is, so I don't need you getting amped up about it, either."

Kendyl scoffs, frowning so much that I'm willing to believe her version of how things went down. "Right now, all I care about is getting out of here in one piece. It's bad enough we have to be in their place tomorrow night. If you thought the rivalry game with Baytown was bananas, Yasir, the game with Beach Creek will feel like a blood feud."

Kyle chimes in to add to her comments. "She's not wrong. Things got out of hand last year, and it almost took the game off the schedule for this year and beyond. Some things just aren't worth the trouble."

"So why did we come out this way if things are tense like that?" I ask. I don't know how the lines are drawn down here. "We could've jumped down to Jax if it was gonna be all this drama."

Zahra wraps her hands around my face. "Don't worry about them. They're overreacting."

"Nah, we're doing what has to be done to keep out of the line of fire," Kyle objects. "Let's get up outta here now while we're ahead. I gotta get back home and get things together for the party, too."

I don't like the warning bells sounding off in my head. Zahra's being a little too casual about whatever happened that has Kendyl spooked, and I'm not in a place to ask. Being in this in-between with her has my anxiety levels on tilt. I want to protect her—and I'm feeling something from deep within that almost compels me—but that's doing boyfriend things when I'm not her boyfriend.

As the girls head to the register to check out, I step out into the mall to try and get my head together. I feel a serious headache coming on, but I can't figure out why it's shooting through me so quickly.

Kyle presses his hand against my back, snapping me out of my discomfort. "Yo, you good? You look like things are a bit off."

Before I can answer him, we hear someone yelling at us, and next thing we know, we're surrounded by boys wearing Beach Creek lettermen jackets. By my count, it's at least six of them, and they have cut off every possible way to get out. In an instant, my headache goes away, and in its place, I feel a heat that I can't explain. I want to say it's a fight-or-flight response, but I know when I'm in a fight, and I don't run.

"Well, well, well, I didn't think anyone from Oakwood would show this close to the game, much less one of the superstars on squad," one of the Beach Creek players spits out. "Any other week and it wouldn't be a problem, but you just had to pick this week, huh?"

Kyle keeps his cool, cutting his eyes in my direction, placing his palms down in a silent cue to stay as calm as possible. *Easier said than done, my boy.* "Look, this ain't gotta get messy, all right? We were just rolling out, so just break up this circle and let us and our girls roll. Nobody has to get put on ice before the game tomorrow. We can settle that on the field."

I stare down one of the other boys who seems to be focused on me for some reason. "You got pressure, yo? You looking at me like I took your favorite toy or something."

"Yo, we got a problem, Vonte?" Ian cuts through the circle with force, facing the boy who started yelling at us. Where the hell did he come from? And I'm even more confused as Eric follows him into the mix. "You boys know better than to roll up on Oakwood players like this. I know y'all don't like to play fair, but this is just stupid."

I don't know what to make of this situation at all. Ian's acting like we're crew, but when we're on campus, we got issues. Make it make sense.

"Yeah, we got big problems, and we have no problems solving them, Ian." Vonte steps closer to me, tripping my protective instincts. "This dude is new, though, but he doesn't look like he's squad."

"Yeah, but he's Oakwood, and the Grove takes care of its own," Ian bites back, throwing me and Kyle completely off balance. This solidarity nonsense has got to be an act. "Now, run along now, before something bad happens to you."

I'm staring Vonte down as he continues to move closer inside my personal space. I don't have time to explain any of this to Unk, so I step back to create some space between us. "Bro, I don't know you, and you don't know me. Let's not do this tonight, all right? I'm not even from around here, so I don't know what this is all about."

"Doesn't matter to me, you rock with the Grove, then you have to be dealt with," Vonte sneers at me, balling his fists like he's ready to shoot a fade. "I don't know why I'm even bothering with you. You're not even in my weight class."

Shots fired. "That's all right, it just means it's gonna be more embarrassing for you when this is all over."

Vonte wastes no time, throwing a right hand that misses badly, followed by a left hand that I duck just as easily. He tries to throw another right hand, and I catch his fist in mid motion.

Something takes over...and the next thing I know, I'm squeezing his fist with every ounce of energy I have in my body, dropping him to his knees as he shouts in excruciating pain. I start to twist his arm as I keep his fist in my grip, gritting my teeth and applying more pressure.

The crimson glow shines over me, taking me out of my headspace for a few moments while I'm still focusing on doing as much damage as I can. I want him to suffer, and for a few seconds, I don't care if I do permanent harm.

"Yo, let me go! You're gonna break my arm!" he yells out, staring into my eyes.

"But I thought I wasn't in your weight class, my boy?" I hear myself say, but the accent that comes with it shocks me to my core.

Where did that come from, and when did I have the ability to speak like that? It sounds like I've picked up a sing-song cadence and something that sounds like a combination of a Jamaican Patois and Ghanaian Pidgin English dialect, and where the hell did the bass in my voice come from?

"If you want your arm back, all you have to do is ask. Not sure if I'll grant your request, but you can always ask and find out."

"Yasir, let him go! It's not worth it!" I hear Zahra's voice cutting through the crowd. "Please, Yasir, let him go so we can go home."

I drop Vonte like a switch has flipped inside me. I turn to face her, but I see her reacting to something happening behind me. I guess that Vonte is trying to get the drop on me while my back is turned, so I immediately turn on my heel to size him up for another fight.

Ian's yelling at the rest of the Beach Creek players, waving his index finger at them like they've broken some sort of code. "I should've known y'all were soft, coming at someone who can't be on the field to get some get-back. That's okay, we'll settle it for him tomorrow night."

Vonte continues to flex his fingers, glaring at me the whole time. "You won't be settling anything at all, bro. You're the ones who came through with all the noise. We're just making sure you get silenced. Tomorrow will take care of itself, I promise."

I hear Kendyl say something that trips my anger into another gear. "What are we supposed to do, Z? We can't just let them roll through like they own the building. I even recognize two of them. They were the ones you raced and got salty because you beat them and then tried to run us off the road."

Kyle reacts before I do. "They did *what*? Point these fools out, baby. Now."

I turn to Zahra again, and she buries her head in Kendyl's shoulder like she didn't want that part of things to get out. "Kyle, for real, let it go. This isn't worth it."

Nope. It absolutely is worth it now.

I close the distance on Vonte before he has a chance to react. "You tried to harm her," I say. My newfound accent is coming in full force now. "I can't let you see your next sunrise. You will feel pain tonight."

My hearing is dialed up to a thousand, and I pick up all sorts of conversations happening, even through the shouting happening around me.

That accent…he can talk like that to me anytime.

I wonder if that's his actual speaking voice because…goodness, it sounds like a soothing lullaby.

Yo, that Oakwood kid ain't playing around. He's got Vonte scrambling. I've never seen him look so shook.

Despite the distractions, I'm focused on Vonte, and I have no plans to stop until he submits to my will. The familiar otherworldly strength I felt when I was saving Ian from the beatdown of his life is back, and the surge feels so good that I don't want it to stop. Ever.

Zahra tries to get my attention again, but I'm not hearing her. All I can see is black. "Yasir, let it go, I'm begging you. We can deal with that later, okay? Let's not do this here."

Ian begs to differ, which is funny to me, because I want him to amp things up. "Nah, Z, let him handle that. Show these Beach bums how the Grove handles business. Let the champ do his thing. Those hands are lethal."

"Ian, you don't know what will happen if Yasir cuts loose," she cautions. "He needs to calm down. I'm serious, this isn't the time."

I'm too far gone to worry about consequences anymore. He needs to bleed.

I throw a left hand, hitting Vonte's ribs, causing him to bend over in pain. I grab Vonte's forearm while he's dealing with the punch, and the sheer strength of my grip has him repeating his plea for me to let him go. I don't know why he's screaming. It's not like I've broken a bone—at least, not yet.

On second thought, he hasn't suffered enough.

I continue my assault, holding Vonte's arm in place while I alternate between body punches to his ribs and stomach and tagging him a few times across his jaw. I'm not gonna lie, it feels good to really cut loose, and I'm oblivious to the spectacle I've made of myself. All I care about is making him pay for even considering harming Zahra.

Vonte's holding his free hand up in surrender, but I ignore his gestures to inflict more pain. He's gonna feel it well after I'm finished with him. I see the fear in his eyes, and it doesn't even move me to ease up on him, despite his desperate screams for me to stop. I cut my eyes in the direction of the other boys, and I grin as I notice they've stopped fighting to focus on my dismantling of one of their own. I shoot a quick glance at them, silently daring them to try to rescue him so I can give them a taste of the fury in my heart.

"Yo, he's had enough, Yasir!" Kyle's shouting at me, but he can forget about getting through to me. I don't want to stop, and I'm not gonna stop. "He's giving up, bro. Come on, let him go!"

I hear someone humming through the noise. It starts out low and soothing, and then the pitch changes, like it's coercing me, trying to get me to stop what I'm doing. I ignore the sounds, waving them off as an unwanted invasion of my mind, turning my attention back to the task at hand.

A few seconds later, I hear Zahra's voice, as clearly as though she's standing next to me, whispering in my ear. "I need you to hear me, Yasir, please. This isn't the time. There will be another opportunity. Just step away and come with me. I got you."

By Nyati, how is she able to bring me back from the edge? I close my eyes to tune her out, but I can still hear her humming, cutting through the darkness, almost willing me to snap out of it. Can't she see I'm trying to make this dude pay for what he tried to do to her?

"Just come with me, Yasir. Let him go and come with me."

I know the cliché "resistance is futile" can be a bit overblown, but I swear I can't say no to her. Fine! I'll delay the inevitable and deal with him later.

I release the grip on Vonte, but I never take my eyes off him as I back away. I feel Zahra's hand grasping mine, pulling me to her. I lean down as she continues to hum in my ear to settle me down.

"Z, I—" The words don't come out immediately as I try to come down from an adrenaline rush that leaves me trembling in her arms. "I'm sorry, I just—"

"Shh, it's okay, I promise. We weren't harmed, just a little rattled." She keeps her hand against the back of my head, and it's the most soothing feeling as she caresses my neck. "I know you wanted to handle that, but it will get handled, just not here, and not now. Do you hear me?"

"I hear you… I wanted to bury him so deep in the ground I saw black," I explain as I lean into our embrace, burying my face in her neck. "I can't let that ride, baby. He's gonna pay sooner rather than later."

By the time she lifts my head to get a better look, Savannah PD and mall security swarm into the area to handle the crowd. Kyle and Kendyl are heading for us, and I notice Ian and Eric walking off in a different direction now that the almost-fight has been broken up. I scowl at the smirk on Ian's face before he disappears into the crowd.

Once we have a chance to get to the parking lot to breathe a little, Kendyl and Zahra both are giving us the side-eye. Zahra glances up at me, a worried expression splashed all over her face. "What in the world just happened? We left y'all for two minutes and all hell nearly broke loose. I thought y'all were supposed to be the cooler heads."

"We were minding our own business when those Beach bums showed up and closed in around us," Kyle recounts. "One of them said something about trying to cancel our season before we even stepped on the field, and I wasn't about to step away from a threat like that. So we stood and made it clear that everybody's season was gonna get cancelled, since they wanted to play mind games like they wannabe gangsters."

"But we watched Yasir ducking punches when we got there," Zahra says. "How did they focus on him? He's not on the team."

Kyle grumbles, still flexing his hands to calm down. "They came for Yasir first, I guess they assumed he was a part of the team, and when dude tried to rush him, Ian and Eric popped up out of the blue. Next thing we know, things amped up a few notches. You know Ian, always down for the brawl if he can get away with it. Yasir dropped dude to his knees before we could react to the situation, and I was convinced he was gonna put him to sleep." Kyle looks over at me, shaking his head in disbelief. "If I hadn't seen it for myself, I wouldn't have believed it. That kid had you by at least fifty pounds, and you had him ready to tap out."

Kendyl slides into the convo, asking the question I think is on all our minds. "Why was Ian egging things on like he wanted things to escalate?"

Kyle shrugs as he continues to pace back and forth. "Who knows what's going through that boy's mind when things are happening around us? I knew we could handle things if they did crank up, but it didn't need to get to that point."

"Well, I'm just glad things didn't go too far," Kendyl announces as she slips her arm inside Kyle's. "I think it's time to head back to the Grove before something else happens."

Zahra grasps my hand to pull me toward the parking lot. "Let's get these boys home before something else goes left. We'll catch up with y'all later."

"Sounds good to me," Kendyl replies as she walks off with Kyle. "Later."

Once we're outside, Zahra slows the pace. I already have a clue of what's coming, but it doesn't mean I need to talk. "What really happened? It's not that I don't trust Kyle, but something's not adding up."

I gaze into her eyes, and I come up with the easiest answer I can say. "Ian saw us getting surrounded, and he and Eric jumped in, looking to get someone to fire off. He came in jawing, and no matter what we tried to settle things down, he kept the pressure coming."

She shakes her head and sort of huffs. "I saw you avoiding wild swings from that kid from Beach Creek before you took him down. Did Ian amp that up, too?"

"Can we talk about this later? I'm dealing with a ton of adrenaline that's still racing through me," I say. "I need to get you home before I crash, or you'll be the one having to drive. I promise, we can talk about the fine mess Ian almost got us into once I've had a chance to calm down."

I can tell she wants to push the issue, but the moment she places her hand against my chest, her expression changes. She can feel my heart racing, I know it. "Okay, but we have to figure this out. Something happened to you that I'm gonna have a hard time explaining to my bestie later. For now, just take me home. Tomorrow will be better."

"I know. It's been crazy, but maybe you're right. Tomorrow might be better…at least, I hope so."

She slips a kiss across my cheek, but she keeps staring. "Yasir, I need you to know, whatever it is that's going on with you, you can tell me. I'll understand. We'll get through it."

I rub the back of my head, avoiding eye contact. "Nothing is going on with me, I promise. My nana always said I had a bad temper, so I can chalk up tonight to needing to work on that."

It's a convenient excuse, and I stop the convo right there, hoping she gets the point.

I don't have time to make anything make sense right now, but the best thing I can do right now is focus on tomorrow.

And hope that tomorrow is better.

CHAPTER FOURTEEN

They will hunt you until you give them what they want…and they will kill you if you don't.

I stifle my screams to avoid waking Unk, covering my mouth to muffle the noise as best as possible. The walls in the house aren't exactly thick, and I don't want to have another conversation over why I can't sleep.

I haven't had a nightmare this bad for a few months. When they hit, they were bad, like *bad*, bad. Nana thought she would have to create batches of different herbal mixes just so I could sleep every night. They would start and stop without much of a heads-up, and whether I liked it or not, I'd have to deal with it. The suffering would continue until I could figure out whatever "they" wanted and, for that matter, who "they" were. Every time, the same demand was made, and every time, my refusal was absolute, despite my insistence that I didn't know what was demanded.

"I don't know what you want. I don't have what you want!" I say over and over again, each time more definitive than the last, but I can't escape reliving the same sequence of events. I have trouble making sense of why I keep saying those words. If I could have an out-of-body experience inside of my own dream, that's exactly where I am during this whole thing. I don't believe it's me, but somehow, it's me.

My clothes are stuck to my skin, dripping wet from the sweltering Georgia heat. Despite it being the last week of September, summers never really end here. I rub my face, wishing I could rip this horrific nightmare from my mind. At this point, any relief from the attack on my psyche would be welcomed.

I check the clock on my nightstand. The glowing red light shows the time as a little after midnight. Relieved I have a few hours before heading to the boating docks, I catch my breath. Only two places exist where I can purge that energy: either the studio upstairs or the boxing gear in the basement.

That inner voice from my dream continues its assault. *You know what they want. It's been inside you all along. Just give them what you possess, and this can all be over. You can live a normal life.*

I sit up and stretch as I shake the voice from my head. I want to get out of bed, but my mind and body aren't on the same page. I give myself a pep talk while drowning out the criticism. "Come on, bro, you have to get this out of your system. It'll be good to burn it off for a few hours."

A sudden burst of energy flows through me. A good creative session may just do the trick. I realize there won't be enough time to get things together once I finish working with Unk, so I prepare a batch of special colognes for the week. The process becomes one that I've come to enjoy, in a manner of speaking. The ritual keeps me close to my parents, even though it was my nana who taught me once I was old enough to learn to do it on my own. Not gonna lie, though…I hope that sooner or later, I won't have to do it anymore.

I sit in front of the sink, taking care to wipe the mirror that fogged up from the steam of the hot water pooling in the basin. I open the containers, which hold the ingredients I need. One by one, I retrieve the creams and oils I use to mask my unique "scent," as I was told. A scent that prevents those responsible for my parents' deaths from being able to track me down so they can kill me. Nana's quiet on the reason my life is in danger, though.

The peculiar mix of fragrances—a family recipe of myrrh, sandalwood, tonka bean, and coriander—is a part of my ritual. The original combination is supposed to be enough to repel human senses…like those who are on the hunt to find me…but not so overpowering that my teachers suggest I change my "cologne." Thank the gods the concoction isn't too offensive at first, but when

I found a way to tweak the mixture, it has quite the opposite effect on most of the girls at school.

Once I finish my routine with the scented oils, I stretch and make my way upstairs to my sanctuary on the top floor of the house.

Over the door of the studio, I read a phrase Unk had drilled in my head so many times, I want to throw up:

"Don't quit. Suffer now and live the rest of your life as a champion."

That quote from the greatest boxer of all time has held me together for the past few years. In fact, I'd taken up boxing, thanks to Unk, and as the rumors at school will have anyone believe, I'm that good—despite never fighting in a live match. I don't know how much longer I can last, but I do know that quitting is not an option. Muhammad Ali might have been talking about how much he hated training, but I'll take that over surviving high school any day.

Either the studio or the boxing equipment calls to me during times of stress or anxiety, and if I had my way, I'd stay lost in both spaces for the rest of the morning. After what I've just gone through, I need the release, but I still can't shake the nagging feeling inside of me. There's something there, in the nightmares, that I can't put my finger on, but it feels important. If I can break through the wall and find out, it might calm a lot of things down…at least, I hope it does.

The minute I step inside the dimly lit studio space, the familiar sea breeze scent from the candles I burn surrounds me, its remnants lingering in the air from the last session a few weeks ago. I take a deep breath, letting out a satisfied sigh as my mood changes in an instant.

I cultivated the space as my own over the years, a haven where I could fly free and travel wherever my heart desires…until I have the means and time to actually start checking off my bucket list. The places I've traveled always feel like home, and I paint each of them with the same passion and fervor, showing as much brilliance and detail as my creativity could muster. Egypt. Tanzania. South Africa. Ghana. Colombia. Barbados. Jamaica. Each locale holds some special meaning, whether they house a wondrous sight or the simple reasoning that I love the landscape.

They all, however, pale in comparison to a location I've placed above all others…Kindara, my nana's birthplace, and apparently, Zahra's family is from there, too.

I stare at the most recent image I sketched on the pad sitting on the easel—a palatial estate cradled in the cliffs of Mount Kindara. Sketching always grounds me; I connect to the places that resonate most with me through my art. Nana always told me that Kindara is full of mysticism and that magic flows through me with every stroke of the brush…or so she keeps telling me.

I wonder if Zahra knows anything about the magic of the island. It never hurts to ask, right?

I've never really been to the island, to be honest. All I have is my vivid imagination and the nightmares that I've suffered from for as long as I can remember to guide me with the imagery I create.

I carefully detach the paper from the sketchpad, rolling and taping it down to join the other completed artwork in a protective container sitting to the left of the easel. Grabbing my pencils and getting comfortable on the stool, I close my eyes and take a deeper breath. Moments later, I nod, satisfied with the next image I want to create.

I battle with the voice inside my head, staring at the blank page. Nana would never lie to me about what happened to my parents. I know it would have never existed, but the memories stay locked in the back of my mind, just beyond my reach, tormenting me.

As I keep myself busy with the outlines of the drawing, I hum a tune Nana frequently sang when I was a young boy to drown out the noise. The lullaby takes me away from the studio, bringing me to the shores of the massive Kindaran coastline in an instant. With each stroke, I envision the way the ocean's waves crash onto the beach before they recede. I can feel and taste the ocean breeze, tilting my head to embrace the warmth of the sun.

The beach gives way to a forest that provides a protective border that encircles the island, with thick, sharp branches and prickly shrubs that make it difficult to come out on the other side unscathed. The wildlife hidden within the vibrant, emerald foliage ranges from mesmerizing to deadly. The beautiful yet dangerous labyrinth comes with a simple message to strangers who dare to come ashore: enter at your own risk.

From there, I'm transported through the calming waters of River Ko, named for the Vodaran God of the Seas, as the ferry traverses into the Kabila la Maji, or the Water Tribes. I wave at the other children who are learning to keep their balance while inside the boats as they pull fish from the river. I dip my fingers into the cool waves, amazed at the aquatic life traveling alongside the watercraft as they swim toward the northern savannah.

Several ospreys are in formation above me, their expansive wingspans appearing to touch each other. Some already have fish in their talons, while others are in full dive before leveling off mere inches above the water, grabbing their dinner and then flying off over the trees framing the river. I continue sketching as I hum in sync with the pencil skating across the page.

Once we disembark from the ferry, a Jeep Gladiator truck takes me through the hilly terrain, the rough ride bringing me farther into the heart of Kindara. To my right, the majestic beauty of Mount Kindara up close causes me to gasp in awe. Just above where I remember creating an estate on the mountainside, the opening to the Nyati Temple lay hidden in plain sight…something Nana has told me about so many times I swear I've been there before. According to her stories, its walls house the true wealth and nature of Kindara: sacred Vodaran magick and another world beyond this one. Only those who are chosen by the Divine Mother could travel there.

At the top of the mountain, Kindaran sculptors are hard at work carving the images of Nyati and her seven children into its side. I've never fully committed them to memory, but in this dream, I can recall them as though they are second nature: Ko, Vodaran of the Sea; Zatara, Vodaran of the Earth; Adin, Vodaran of War; Abibatu, Vodaran of Magick; Nahara, Vodaran of Fire; Ubaka, Vodaran of Air; and Ashanti, Vodaran of Love.

To my left, off in the distance, the twin volcanoes, named for Nahara, rumble in a rare show of power during this specific trip. I marvel at the spectacle, taking the pair of binoculars in the middle compartment to get a closer look at the low roiling of the lava trickling above the lip of the basins. The direction of the flow faces toward the ocean on the west side of the island, building another difficult entry point into the countryside.

To the north, I observe the airplanes as they take off and land at the airport near Drana Tirin, the capital city, which is beyond my ability to see at that moment. I don't worry too much about it; I'll visit other parts of the island soon enough. I can't believe the splendor surrounding me and wish Nana had the ability to take me there, but I'm content with what she'd been able to do for me while I was growing up.

I'm still sitting in my studio, a little confused over how I'm able to dream walk—that's the only explanation for what's happening to me. I'm always asleep when I travel to Kindara, but I know I'm awake. I would've never been able to make it up here if I were asleep. The whole thing is disconcerting, and I'm struggling to maintain my balance on the stool. I take a deep breath and continue through to the end, but I have no idea how I'm supposed to wake out of this when I'm already awake.

The Jeep finally comes to a stop at the gates of a village called Solara, but instead of finding peace when I gaze upon the enclosure, goose bumps cover my skin, a telltale sign of my agitated state. Smoke rises above the twenty-foot-high stone walls. I move the pencil across the page at a feverish pace now, depicting the fires and explosions throughout the village. Despite the initial panic in my heart, I trudge forward in a desperate attempt to find out what was happening inside.

In the next moment, an alarm sounds, and no matter how hard I try to advance, an unknown force holds me still. My confusion turns to anger as I'm yanked away without warning from the village, from Kindara, and across the ocean at lightning speed, bringing me back to the studio. "No, don't take me away, please! I want to know what happened!"

I'm unable to get my bearings, and the blaring of the smartphone alarm threatens to cause a headache I don't need. I silence the device, slowing my breathing before focusing on the canvas and the picture I had been sketching during my "trip."

Despite the weird way I managed to travel while awake and then get ripped away during my latest journey back to Kindara, I'm ecstatic over the richness of the landscape captured in my latest creation. I love all the aspects I've captured, including the legendary Kindaran sunsets that, in Nana's opinion, eclipse anything I'll ever witness Stateside. I stroke my chin as I consider my options over how I want to complete the painting. "All I need is the right color combination to paint this, and it'll be perfect."

In a flash, a tune Zahra hummed when we were in the mall during the problems we had with Beach Creek seduces my ears. The faded sound of her voice hypnotizes me, raising my body temperature to a low-grade fever. I don't feel agitated, or overwhelmed, for that matter. I close my eyes to imagine her near me, continuing her welcomed assault on my senses. Her soothing tones...despite being miles away...warm me as nothing else has since I left the A.

The confusion threatens to overpower me, as I can't figure out where all of this is coming from...and how I'm able to vividly create a painting of a place I couldn't remember living? It's one thing to have it happen while I'm sleeping, but I was awake the entire time. How in the world did that happen?

It's time to get back to Atlanta, ASAP. I have to know if what is happening to me is being created with magic. It's the only way to explain what just happened to me. There are too many questions, and Nana may be the only one who can give me the answers I need.

CHAPTER FIFTEEN

I'd planned on having this convo sooner, but the way things have gone since I got here, time slipped away from me.

I've talked to Nana since I've been down here. I make it a point to call her at least every other day, but we don't video call all that much. Today, I need to see her face, and I'm sure she wants to see me, too.

Questions deserve answers, and I want her to be aware of what's happening to me. She's the only person who can tell me the truth.

I think about heading out to the back deck to talk to her, but I think better of it. The neighbors are nosy as hell, and I don't think a talk about the possible existence of magic is something regular people need to hear. I don't know how she'll react to what I have to tell her.

I wait for her to pick up the call, and I set the phone on top of my desk in my room so my hands can be free. I have a habit of moving my hands when I'm explaining something, and I don't want the phone moving around while we're talking.

She finally picks up, and seeing her smiling face puts me in an instant good mood. My nana is a stunning, beautiful woman, and no, I'm not biased. People question her age because they can't believe it. Like, she and Angela Bassett could pass for sisters, and we all still have a hard time believing the Queen Mother of Wakanda is as old as she is, too.

"Hello, my darling boy. This is a pleasant surprise." I can tell from the background that she is in her sitting room. She gives me a wide smile as she keeps herself busy crocheting another piece. "How are you doing down there with your uncle? Are you settling down pretty well?"

"Yes, ma'am, some things have been good. I'm trying to adjust." I take a sip of my water bottle, feeling my throat tighten up. "I've tried to stay out of trouble, but you know how that goes."

She laughs when I mention that, putting my mind at ease a bit. "You and that temper were a challenge, that is for certain. I thought the boxing was supposed to help give you the outlet you needed?"

"Yes, it has, and I haven't gotten into any trouble at school, I promise." I want to make it clear that she has nothing to worry about, even if I am kinda lying to her about it. Being away from me and not having any influence was one of her major concerns, and I don't want to add to them. "It's nothing that I haven't been able to handle, and Unk's been great. He's helped me a lot with how things flow down here."

"Well, that is a relief. Since he has not called to let me know anything, I can rest my mind knowing that you are doing well." She stops for a moment to get a sequence on the cloth locked in before she focuses on me again. "So when are you coming up to see me? I have not seen that handsome face of yours in a few weeks, and the last time we talked, there was a girl you were trying to impress. How is that coming along?"

Yeah, she has a gift for understatement at times, and I thought she'd forgotten about me mentioning Zahra. "It's going okay, so far. I told her about you and maybe her coming up with me to visit."

"Well, now, that would be very interesting, and I would be happy to welcome her when you come up."

"Nana, I need to ask you something, and it's kinda important."

"Sure, baby, what is on your mind?"

I take a deep breath as I choose my words carefully. "Well, while she and I were getting to know each other, she asked about my parents and where I come from, and I couldn't tell her because I honestly don't know anything outside of what you've told me."

Nana nods slow and easy, putting down her piece to give me

her undivided attention. "Okay, what questions do you have?"

"I'll get to that in a minute, but I need to explain something else," I tell her as I get comfortable in my chair. Okay, so I can't lie to my nana. It just doesn't ever feel right. "I had been caught up in a couple of fights away from school. Before you start, I didn't instigate any of them, but…it feels like something takes over when I fight."

She continues to nod at what I say to her, and I notice she doesn't freak out. She might not have been, but it causes a bit of anxiety for me. "Okay, go on, baby. Tell me everything."

"Well, after a convo with the new friends I've made down here, one of them said that my eyes glowed in a deep shade of crimson red." I keep purging, remembering that she's always been a safe space. "I didn't know what they were talking about, so I played it off like it was a camera filter. My eyes had never done that before, and I don't know what to make of it."

Nana reacts for the first time during our talk, and now I really want answers. She offers a smile as though she can feel the rising fear flowing through me. "Okay, first, I want you to know that there is nothing wrong with you. I need you to understand that. Do you hear me, Ya-Ya?"

"Yes, ma'am."

"This girl that you've been seeing, where is she from? Is she from Georgia, too?"

I don't understand why she asks the question, but I don't think it would cause any harm, either. "She and her family are from Kindara, Nana, same as you."

Her eyes widen, and she sits up in her chair, getting closer to the camera. "How soon can you and this young lady come up to see me? I would like to speak to her, too. I have a feeling, but I will not say anything until I see you two together."

"Nana, is there something I need to know about?"

"I promise, my darling grandson, if I see what I think I will see, and it matches the visions I have been having over the past couple of days, I will explain everything. It may mean more than we know." Nana gives up another warming smile, blowing kisses at the screen, causing me to blush. "When was the last time you had any nightmares?"

Last night. Almost every night.

But I hesitate to say much. "I had one earlier this week...but that aside, there's something else that happened," I say, quickly changing the subject. Now that she's willing to open the book on Mom and Dad, I figure, why not? "After my first day at school, I had a... I wish I could understand what happened."

"Go ahead, baby, you know Nana has seen a lot in her life."

Not like what I'm about to tell her, though. "I spoke into the air that I missed Mom and Dad, and a few moments later, I felt Mom kiss me on my cheek and Dad's hand on my shoulder."

When she doesn't bat an eyelash over my reveal, I sit there, stone-faced, with more questions than answers about my own grandmother. How is she taking all this in stride like she's done all this before? "Okay, baby, we need to sit down and handle everything that is coming at you. What I need for you to do is understand that this is normal for people like us."

"Pause, Nana...us?"

"Yes, baby, but this is not something that we need to talk about over a video call." She clasps her hands together and takes a deep breath. "I honestly thought I would have more time to prepare you, but I guess the gods had other plans. First things first, when you have a chance, and hopefully soon, please come see me, and bring your friend with you. I have a feeling this visit will change everything."

CHAPTER SIXTEEN

How is she gonna just drop something like that and then decide she needs to go?

Is she for real right now?

I'm stuck between calling her back and not calling her back, and the indecision has me completely out of sorts.

People like us.

That statement sits like a weight on my shoulders that I don't have the strength or the knowledge to carry. She knows more than she's letting on, and while I understand wanting to be with me when she explains it all, I don't know when I'll have the time to even make that trip. Now, I have no choice but to make the time, or this is going to eat me alive.

I feel the aggression racing through me, feeling my pulse through my fingertips. My body feels hot, almost feverish, and I'm vibrating so intensely that I'm pretty much at the point where I want to rip someone's head off. I know I'm frustrated, it's not hard to recognize it, but doing something about it is a whole other issue.

I don't even think about it. I'm in the basement in minutes. I need some of this, whatever this is, off me.

The gloves are on. The music is on this time around, too, and the more upbeat and raw, the better. I want to hurt tonight, or hurt something, it doesn't matter to me. I just don't want to think about what the hell my nana teased, and I don't want to rattle my brain trying to figure out the why of it all.

With each punch, I let out a grunt or a growl. Unk's not home tonight, so I'm taking advantage of getting every drop of negative energy out of my system so I can function as normally as possible. As the session continues, I feel stronger, which has me a little confused. Usually, when I burn this much energy at the beginning of the session, I'm done within minutes.

I can go all night, the way I'm feeling right now.

My phone rings, and I let out an exasperated yell. My music is interrupted, and I'm already not in the best of moods. Whoever it is, they're about to catch all the smoke. I tap my earbud to accept the call without looking at the screen. "What's up?"

There's silence on the other end, but I don't worry about it. The FaceTime connection is open, and all they can probably see is the ceiling. After a few more seconds, they finally speak. "Yasir, it's Z. Are you okay? I was a little worried about you."

Yeah, now that I know it's Zahra, I breathe a little, but I'm still not interrupting what I've got going on right here. I'm punching harder and faster now, grunting and yelling as the hits keep coming. "I don't know how to answer that question right now. I'm irritated, and I need to get some of this negative energy off me. I appreciate you being worried, for real, but I'm not about to start capping to make anyone feel better."

I hear her let out a sigh and mumble something to herself before she says another word. "Yasir, could you sit down for a moment for me, please? I have something I created that I want you to hear."

I'm still throwing jabs with everything I have in me, still confused, and now I'm a little worried over why I'm not anywhere near tired. In my mind, I'm willing myself to be in a better mood, but I don't have the energy to fake it until I make it. I wish she understood that I need to be by myself right now. I know I'll lose my nerve if I face her, even on a video call, and want to make sure she smiles.

She doesn't get the memo, though. "Pretty please, I promise it will be worth it. *Please*, Yasir."

The punching stops seconds later, and the next thing I notice when I pick up my phone is her pretty face on the screen. I have a hard time keeping the scowl on my face. Dammit, I knew this was gonna happen. I slow my breathing a bit, studying her facial expressions for a few minutes. She licks her lips as I sit there, looking dumb as hell for allowing her to soften me up. "It's not working, whatever you're trying to do," I lie, hoping it's somewhat convincing.

"Isn't it working, pretty boy?" she teases as we let more time pass without either of us saying much of anything. She winks at me, an easy smile spreading across her lips. "Can you sit there right now and say it's not working?"

I close my eyes and mumble something under my breath. I shake my head a few times before I open my eyes and stare at her. I offer up a half smile, my gaze zeroing in on that smirk she has when she thinks she has me wrapped around her finger. I mean, it's working, but I'm not gonna tell her that. "Nope, it's not working at all. So what do you have for me to listen to, cuteness?"

On cue, she pulls her guitar from where it rests on her right hip and starts strumming a few chords. The moment she hums the chorus, her gaze never leaves mine. Her voice takes over the moment, its tone cutting through the air as our eyes stay locked. The guitar riff is soft and suggestive, and as much as I hate to admit it, she has me under her spell.

Before long, I match her rocking motion, my smile easy and smooth, and she blows a kiss between lyrics, putting a little honey on the end. She stops playing, maintaining eye contact. "So how do you like it?"

"Beauty, brains, and a siren's voice. I think I'm in trouble." I can't stop staring at her. The spell still holds me right there with her. "I liked it a lot, just like the songstress. How am I only now finding out that you play the guitar? Are there any other surprises I need to know?"

She blushes, but then her expression turns a little more concerned. I brace for the questions I know are coming. "Can I ask why you needed to put some time on the bags?"

I tense up for a moment, but then I remember that she wants

me to trust her with my thoughts. Okay, let's test that hypothesis, shall we? "I'm trying to figure out where I fit at Oakwood, and how I fit in your world, for real. I'm still the new kid, and while I've managed to catch some attention, it hasn't been all good. I'm not comfortable, and it's had me on edge, especially the last few days."

"You've been fitting in just fine. What makes you think you haven't been?"

"I saw the way Kenni looked at me after the incident at the mall. And when I was on a FaceTime with Kyle a few days ago, he noticed something weird that I didn't know how to explain." My breathing intensifies, and I feel my pulse quicken. I swear I don't want to sound like I'm rambling, but it's all coming out, no matter if I think it makes sense or not. "I wish I could explain, but I don't know how to right now. I had a hard time explaining it to my grandmother, and by some miracle, she understood what I was saying."

"Yasir, just breathe with me, please?" The stress must be all over my face if she encourages me to slow down and not feel so nervous. Yeah, good luck with that. She matches the rise and fall of my shoulders as I do my best to take deeper breaths. "Kenni and I were concerned for your safety. Kyle's, too. Beach Creek can be a bit rough around the edges, and we didn't want y'all caught up in a fight with them."

"So neither one of you looked at me like I'd grown a third eye or something, huh?" I'm legit shaking on screen, and I don't know what I can do to come back from the edge. She's quiet—too quiet—and that tells me everything I need to know. "Yeah, that's what I thought. Let's be real—could you even rock with me, even as friends, knowing there's something off with me?"

She frowns, and I wonder if I took it too far. "I don't know who you were rocking with in the A, but that's not how this works, I promise. I would never step away from anyone once I've decided they're my friend."

"Z, I feel that, but there's something going on that I haven't even had a chance to get a real word from my nana. None of you signed up for whatever is going on with me, and I'm not sure I signed up for it, either." I don't want to show her how scared I am, but I can't hide from her for some reason. I take a towel to wipe my face, holding it a little longer as I compose myself. The minute I remove the towel, I flip my tone. "I know what you said, but—"

"I said what I said, and you're not about to step away like that." She's so pissed I can feel her heating up. Yep, I took things a bit too far. "If it means we go to see your nana and get the answers you need to figure it out, then that's what we do, okay? And I'm not taking no for an answer, either."

I take a few more deep breaths, pulling the gloves off and taking the safety scissors to cut the tape off my hands. "I get it, all right? I'm not used to people sticking with me when the mud gets thick. Only ones I've ever been able to count on was my Squad back home, and even they had to earn it."

"I'm here for you, Yasir, I'm serious." She leans into the camera in an attempt to make herself crystal clear. "When you're ready to roll up, I'll be riding shotgun inside of Storm."

I nod a few more times, grabbing an electrolyte water bottle and inhaling half the bottle in one gulp. I wait until I can clear my throat before I glance at the screen. "Thank you, Z, and I'm gonna hold you to it. I have no idea what to expect when I go back up there. There's so much unfinished business to take care of."

"Then we'll go take care of it, all right?"

"Say less, pretty girl."

"Good, now get some sleep. We still have school in the morning."

I chuckle, which eases the pressure I've been feeling all night. She's so wonderfully frustrating—I never know if I want to kiss her or wring her neck. She's lucky I like her. "Just so damn bossy, I swear. Good night. I'll see you in the morning."

CHAPTER SEVENTEEN

The next morning is intense. It doesn't take long for word to get out about the incident at the mall, according to texts from the group, but Ian's the only one talking and wants to whip everyone into a frenzy. I have a theory, and I don't like where it's leading me. I have a feeling Ian is trying to expose me and get me into something that is liable to get me into some real trouble.

I don't have any real proof, but I think he's gonna slip up sooner or later.

I also think it's way more personal than I'm aware of, and that scares me more than anything. The game he's playing—being in my corner one minute, then being my sworn enemy the next minute— there's something else going on, and I need to pay more attention to him when he's around me. If I play my cards right, he may give me the answers I'm looking for.

The game later in the evening comes with its own level of intensity, but me being thrust into the spotlight as the side show is not what I had in mind. I did what I could to manage my emotions, but it takes longer than usual to clear my head before I can even think about entering the building.

I get out of Storm and take a deep breath. The kids are already staring. Girls smile at me, while the boys give thumbs-up signals… Huh? What kind of information was shared overnight? Even the quick conversation with Zahra at my locker didn't provide much clarity, as she, Kyle, and Kendyl couldn't decipher much.

By the time I get to English and sit down with Kyle, the curtain has been raised on why everyone is buzzing.

"Uh, Yasir, you're gonna want to see this…" He holds his phone out to me, and I can almost see the sweat roll down his forehead.

A video that had gone viral on social media of me and Vonte going at it, with a lot of shares and comments comparing me to boxing champ Canelo Alvarez.

Fuck. This is not good.

Anyone could possibly have seen that video. What if I gave whoever-they-are a way to find me after Nana went through so much trouble to keep me hidden?

I bend forward and bang my head against the desk a few times, sighing deeply and breathing slowly despite freaking out on the inside. I mean, it's high praise to be compared to the undisputed Super Middleweight champ and best pound-for-pound boxer on the planet, but this isn't what I need in my life right now. If it goes viral, it's only a matter of time before word gets back to my people in the A…including Nana. "So the secret's out, huh?"

"Yeah, champ. You've been trending all morning," Kyle says, seeming relieved with my response. "I'm surprised a few boxing promoters haven't been lighting your phone up," he teases as he taps fists with one of the other boys in class. "I guess I need to see about having you as my bodyguard when I get to the next level. No one will want to mess with you after that performance."

"Bro, you don't understand. This is not good." I'm rubbing my hands together with every ounce of nervous energy I have in my body. I shake my head as more notifications rattle off faster than lightning, adding to my anxiety levels big time. "I'm trying to keep a low profile, and this is gonna blow things way out of proportion."

"Don't sweat it, bro. There are perks to being the 'it' thing. Ask Ian." Kyle chuckles. "Man, he's liable to be hotter than fish grease by the time he gets wind of this news."

I don't give a damn about that right now. I may have put a larger target on my back than I planned. All the fears that Nana had when I was growing up—what the hell have I done?

"Bro, I still don't get it. Why did he have our backs at the mall? He's been trying to bury me since I got here, and in the course of one night, we ended up on the same side?" I'm struggling to figure out what part of the high school survival manual I'm supposed to read that will explain how to deal with this. "Make it make sense, for real."

"Look, bro, it's like having a big brother growing up. He may give you the blues, teasing you at every corner, but the minute some of the boys from the neighborhood start bullying you, he and his boys will lay waste to everyone in sight. It doesn't exactly make sense, but that's the way it goes."

"You're right, it doesn't make sense, but I'm an only child, so it probably won't ever make sense to me," I say. "It's fine if Ian tries to take me down or whatever, but outside forces don't get the luxury. Got it."

"Yeah, but trust me, he's still not your biggest fan," Kyle advises. "Don't drop your guard around him, even if he's still trying to be civil. Besides, after last night, I think a lot of the boys are starting to get a little tired of always having to back him up when it isn't necessary. What we can't do is constantly clean up messes we didn't create."

"I'm not anyone's cleanup crew, so you don't have to worry about that out of me."

"Speaking of messes, I'm gonna need you to stay home for this next game, bro," Kyle leans in to whisper to me. "Those boys got embarrassed last night, and they're gonna want payback. We can't have your back when we're on the field and in the locker room during the game."

If he thinks I'm gonna sit on the sidelines, he has another thing coming. "That's not gonna fly, my boy. Who's gonna keep an eye on Zahra and Kendyl? They're exposed, too, and someone's gotta be there to handle that."

"You've got a target on your back, Yasir." Kyle checks his phone and nods at something on the screen.

Yeah, nah, that's not what's gonna happen. I look at my dawg, flexing my fists to calm down as best as I can. "Who else is going to look out for them? I promise, whoever you're thinking about, I trust them as far as I can throw them."

"Well, whether you like it or not, lover boy, who we have in mind is the better option, and they don't mind getting caught up if the need arises," Kyle remarks. "I know you took them down on your own, but they're gonna be out for blood, for real. We can't tell you what to do, but I'm just saying."

"I'm not leaving Z, not after what happened last night," I deadpan. "They know we're together, and I'm the only one who actually traded fists. The others will try to deal with you on the field, so you have to worry about that. Let me worry about the sidelines and the stands."

Kyle shrugs. I'm guessing he no longer wants to argue the point now. "I don't think anyone will be able to get past security to even get to the girls since they'll be on the sidelines with us. The Grove still takes care of their own. If you're so insistent on being there, then you're gonna need backup. I just got word my cousin Quentin and his boys will be in town early for my party to come to the game. They're in the League, so they definitely have a presence. Maybe those extra pairs of eyes will help settle you down."

I tap my fingers against the desk, considering Kyle's alternative. If he trusts his family, then I guess I can try to trust them. "Okay, let's rock with that. I'm good."

"Good, that settles it." Kyle checks his phone again as another notification comes through. He can't stop laughing at the reference he saw from the video. "We will have your back once we bury these boys again. Besides, superstar, me and some of the boys might have to be *your* bodyguards to keep the masses away."

I suppress my laughter at that remark, but I wonder whether things are getting too far out of my control. It's one thing to keep things self-contained at Oakwood Grove; it's quite another to deal with the outside variables. One thing I know for certain: no matter what, I'm not gonna miss the game tonight, under any circumstances. Zahra's going to support her friends, and I *will* be there to protect her.

• • •

Being a fan in the stands of either team during this game is torture, for real, considering the sheer number of big hits the players from each team are taking. Neither team wants to give an inch, and if any of the star players are injured, they never let on to any of the coaches or medical staff.

"Kyle Channing breaks away for another long gain!" the announcer's voice bellows from the press box. "Oakwood Grove is inside the twenty-yard line!"

The Oakwood Grove fans are roaring, hoping for another score to break the tie, and I'm blending in with the crowd to keep from drawing too much attention to myself. I'm sitting in the stands, looking on with the rest of the Oakwood Grove fans at the carnage on the field. The battle of attrition has claimed casualties on both sides, but it has somehow spared the most important pieces on the field to keep the contest heated and even. I have no choice but to remain as helpless as the rest of the spectators and hope that the clock winds down as fast as possible.

As Kyle promised, his cousin Quentin and his friends added an extra layer of protection in case anyone got a little aggressive away from the field. I nod in their direction, grateful that I won't have to handle things on my own, despite the bravado displayed earlier in the day with Kyle. He has enough to worry about out there.

I cringe at yet another hit on Kyle as he tries to break free into the open field. He manages to get closer to the goal line, but he has to be carried off the field as he holds his midsection. Several scuffles break out in the aftermath as the officials attempt to settle things down.

The announcer tries to be the voice of reason as I notice several people trying to jump the protection fence to get on the field. "Ladies and gentlemen, please refrain from entering the field and allow the officials and coaches to restore order or you will be removed from the stadium."

Yeah, this is gonna be a wild game, and it hasn't even gotten to halftime.

Zahra got pulled in for emergency duty to help with the medical equipment and hydration tents near the cheer section. I keep a closer eye on that than the field, making sure that Zahra and Kendyl are as safe as they can be. I also sit as close as allowable in the stands and rely on silent hand gestures between me and Zahra to maintain the connection despite the higher-than-normal crowd noise that has drowned out any other communication.

I want to enjoy the subtle flirting between us, but with the heightened animosity I sense in the immediate area, I'm focused more on trying not to alarm her with my facial expressions. My phone rings, and when I see it's Zahra, I look out on the sideline, noticing her making the hand gesture to pick up the phone. Her brow is furrowed, and she's bouncing her knee while she leans against the fence.

"I can feel you, Yasir. I need you to calm down, please," Zahra says, taking her hands and turning them palms down and pushing downward, giving me the cue that I need to settle down.

"How are you able to feel what's going on with me, Z?" I cock my head in disbelief. We need to have some deeper conversations so I can understand her intuitive nature. "I'm calm. I don't have a choice but to be. It's not like I can do anything at the moment but play sentry."

Zahra blows a kiss, flashing a smile that takes my anxiety levels down a few notches in mere moments. I maintain eye contact with her through the next few minutes in the quarter, ignoring the outside noise in the process.

"That's better, cuteness. You're much more relaxed now." I watch as her body relaxes, too. "Keep that energy until the half and I'll see if I can steal away to see about you." Zahra grins as she makes herself busy on the sideline.

I stand for a minute to stretch my legs. "I'm gonna grab something to drink, but I won't be long, promise. I don't want to leave you out of my sight."

"Hurry back, please. We'll be here." Zahra waves before she

gets the other girls together to reset the cups on the table.

I climb the stairs to make my way to the concession stand, passing by a group of boys I don't immediately recognize. The way they're staring at me, I wonder if I owe them money or something. Whatever, I'm gonna get something to drink, so I ignore them as I hit the breezeway to stand in line.

I stand in place for a good couple of minutes before I have the urge to hit the restroom. I check around to see if anyone from Beach Creek has been trailing me or not, then make the quick walk to the restroom to handle business and get out. Times like these I wish Dante and the Squad were here to have my back. Not that Kyle and the others don't, but they're on the field taking care of business. I sigh in relief as I enter an empty area, giving me the chance to slip in and out without any further issues.

I step over to the sink so I can clean my hands and get back to the concession stand and back to my spot. I don't want Zahra to worry. I peer into the mirror for a few moments, keeping my focus trained on anyone who would come into the restroom. Thank the gods I could finish and leave; I have a taste for some nachos that needs to be handled as soon as possible.

I saunter out and... Well, damn. The four boys I passed on the stairs are all leaning against the opposite wall, staring me down hard. They have menacing expressions on their faces, looking like they have nothing but pain on the menu, and I figure to be the main course.

That exit gate is looking really good right now, and I do a quick calculation in my head, wondering how fast I can get to Storm to at least get a tire iron, anything to make this a somewhat fair fight. My gaze darts from the exit to the group, back and forth as I continue to weigh my options. I have no way to get at Quentin or the rest of my backup, so I'm left with no choice but to go with door number one.

In the next second, I break for the gate, opting for a power walk to keep anyone from noticing I'm in danger. Out of the corner of my eye, I can see the other boys chasing me, matching my pace with the same energy and speed.

I make it to the curb that leads to the parking lot, scanning for anyone who might be in harm's way. Once the coast is clear, I switch up, going from power walk to a brisk jog, still trying to keep the chase as low-key as possible until the last possible moment. I continue to glance behind me, noticing my would-be attackers are still in pursuit.

I make it to Storm, unlocking the doors and jumping into the back seat to snatch anything I have in the cargo area to defend myself. I lose sight of the boys while scrambling, and by the time I find something to pull, two pairs of hands grip my ankles and yank me to the ground. I try to turn on my back to get into a defensive position, but I feel a fist to the back of my head and another fist to the small of my back.

I grab for my back first, the pain shooting through my legs with a severe tingling sensation that borders on the inability to feel anything. I manage to turn over, with my back against the ground, to get a good look at the boys. One of them tries to kick at my stomach, but someone pulls him away as the others laugh at my vulnerable state.

"So this is the one whose hands are supposed to be deadly? He don't look like much," one of the boys scoffs as he balls his fists. "How Vonte let this fool get the drop on him, I'll never know."

So these boys are linked up with Vonte? Yeah, I should have known he might have had something to do with it, but I'll have to deal with him later. Right now, I need to get out of this without having to go to the hospital.

While I want to keep loudmouth at bay, my fight-or-flight instincts are in full-tilt fight mode. I turn to face the group, scanning to figure out the best way to defend myself. I try to sound like I'm not panicking, dropping as much bass in my voice as I can muster. "I guess you're gonna have to find out for yourself if these hands work or not, huh, bro? Your boy couldn't handle the smoke, so I guess you need your own lesson."

"Say less. Come on, boys, time to have some fun."

I slip by one of the boys, ducking a swing from the second boy trying to double-team me, dropping an elbow on the center of his back with enough force to hear a crack and that boy yell out in pain. I circle back to the first boy who rushed me, but I catch a punch to the ribs before the boy drives me into the side of one of the nearby cars.

I take a few more shots to my ribs before I find an opening. A swift left hook to the boy's temple drops him to his knee. I look to my left, ducking another swing from the third boy but catching something hard and metal against my knee. I howl in pain as I crash to the ground, grabbing my leg while looking up at my attackers, wondering what they might try to do to me.

In the middle of the fight, I hear a gunshot ring out.

And then a couple more after that.

I freeze instantly. I don't feel any pain from being hit, but I can't figure out which one of them has a gun. I better figure it out fast before I do get shot.

Darkness overtakes my sight as I fight from getting overtaken. The only thing I can hear is the boys' muffled screams and a series of crashes. I attempt to push through the darkness so I can see what's going on, but the more I push, the darker the shroud becomes.

I shout against the confines of the shroud, but the silence that greets me is consuming. I continue to claw at it, but it doesn't help, and I scream out in utter frustration. I have no control, and it's pissing me off. I'm in the middle of a fight, but I'm not *in* the fight.

Before long, the shroud lifts, leaving me with a scene out of a horror film. I clasp my hand over my mouth as I take inventory of the four bodies on the ground. Blood is everywhere, and none of the bodies move. I'm too scared to check to see if any of them are still breathing, fearing that I'll leave fingerprints and the cops may try to pin the crimes on me. My first instinct is to leave quick before someone else enters and draws their own conclusions.

Then I come to my senses.

I can't leave them here like this, either.

I pull out my phone and call 911 to report the assault as I step over the bodies to get to Storm. I do my best not to sound calm, insistent on making it clear to the operator that the people I see on the ground need immediate help.

I know I finished what was started, but that doesn't mean that I can't have a heart.

But I'm not gonna stick around to make a statement, either. That's begging for trouble.

I open the driver's door and check around before I sit in the seat. It takes every ounce of energy I have to look like I'm not freaked out over what just happened...and I have no way of knowing what I did. Going back to the game is a no-go, so I push the ignition button and head out of there, determined to put as much distance between me and that stadium as I can. I send a text to Zahra, praying she gets it before she realizes I haven't gotten back from the concession stand.

I check the rearview mirror once I reach the exit to the parking lot, stopping long enough to wipe the remnants of blood from my cheek with the towelettes I have in the middle compartment. I bang my hands against the steering wheel instead of screaming at the top of my lungs. Fear mixes with confusion, and I still can't figure out what happened.

My senses are on overdrive from the fight, and I hear the distinct screams of the people who'd happened upon the boys. I...I'm not sure if I killed them or caused critical damage. I block out the frantic voices and continued screams as I push the accelerator and peel out of the parking lot. I need to get home and get myself together before I go back to campus to pick Zahra up.

I wish I could chalk this night up to a horrible nightmare, but...I was awake for every second of it, and I was helpless to stop it.

Even more terrifying? I didn't want to stop it.

CHAPTER EIGHTEEN

Panic is coming close to consuming me.

I'm posted up in the parking lot, thoughts racing through my mind as my heart pounds through my chest. I struggle to keep calm, but can you blame me? I mean, after the scene I left about a half hour ago, I'm surprised I remembered how to breathe.

I've never felt more alone.

What have I done?

The wind blowing through the trees sends a shiver up my spine, lending to the uncertainty of the moment. I keep Storm running, since the weather decided to turn colder than usual, and I need to keep warm. Or maybe I feel cold because I don't know what happened at the stadium and I'm left to my vivid and overactive imagination.

I don't know who I can trust. There's no way to know if those kids are dead or alive without… I can't take the chance to go back and find out. I'll give myself away in a heartbeat. I'm not a criminal, but I would've acted like I was guilty.

I play the whole thing out in my head over and over, or as much as I can recall, anyway. The howl of the wind sounds so judgmental, almost condemning me for not sticking around. I convinced myself that not checking the bodies was the right move; my fingerprints would have been all over the place.

Man, I've been watching too many episodes of *Law & Order: Organized Crime* with Unk. At least I called for help before I left the area. If anything, someone will have heard something and relayed the message that those boys aren't unalive.

Even the campus rattles my nerves a bit. The forest that surrounds the school seems to roil and sway as the wind whips through it. Maybe it's my own paranoia playing all sorts of tricks on my psyche, but I swear I hear the trees talking among themselves, judging me.

A series of rapid-fire pops causes a fight-or-flight response as I duck down into the middle console to avoid whatever is being shot. But after hearing a few more pops against the hood of my Jeep and then on the ground, I realize it's nothing more than pecans being shaken from the trees. I grip the steering wheel tight, upset with myself that I've gotten so skittish. I need to get my life, quick.

I dial Dante on instinct. I'm not sure if I wanted to call him or not, but I have to get this off my chest. He knows where the other secrets are buried, and I need him to bury one more. I close my eyes as the phone trills, half expecting him to not answer. They're at a rivalry game, and the noise level has to be ridiculous.

I hear the background noise and know he's still at the game. "What's good, little bro? I didn't expect to hear from you until sometime tomorrow."

I hesitate in that instant. Do I tell him? Squad will find out the minute I do, and that might create more problems.

"Yo, you good, my boy?"

I'm stuck in my head now, playing a quick game of chess to make sure this is the right move to make. If I tell him, then it gets back to...*her*. I'm not prepared for that at all, but this has the potential to crush me if I keep it bottled up. Every time I close my eyes, all I see are the bodies lying around me in such unnatural positions that I can't deny what I've done. I have to accept the fact that I might have taken a life.

I want to throw up.

"Diablo."

That gets my attention. Full stop.

He only uses my nickname when he needs me to focus and get things done. It's obvious he wants me to focus. Consider me focused. "Hades."

"Good, you're hearing me. Now tell me what's happened."

I hate when he could read me like that. "I might have gotten hemmed up. I might have caught a few bodies."

Dead silence on the line for several minutes, except for the shouting and screaming of the crowd in the stands. I don't freak out yet; this is the routine between me and my "big brother." I wait for him to sort through his thoughts before I think about saying something.

The background noise dies down, leading me to guess that he's headed away from the stands so he can hear me clearer. "You might have caught bodies? It's only been a month. What have you been doing down there?"

I hear a call coming through, and I pull the phone away from my ear and notice it's Zahra calling me. The game must be over, and they can't find me. Dammit. Not good. I send the call to voicemail so I can focus on Dante.

"Nothing," I snap back before I catch myself. "These boys play by a different set of rules down here, Te. All I've been doing is keeping my head down and doing me."

"Yeah, I feel you, but when you're just doing you, people get salty. You that dude." Dante starts talking to someone, but I can't make out the convo between them. He comes back to the phone to make a simple statement that's not so simple. "Let me move some things around, and we'll be down there in a couple of weeks."

"That's not necessary."

"It's obvi to me that it is necessary." I hear a tone out of Dante that I haven't heard since someone tried to come for Nana a couple of years ago. "I knew better than to let you talk me out of having someone watch your back down there."

"Aye, look, I can handle myself," I bark, this time not caring about how he will respond. "You got me twisted if you're gonna treat me like some rookie on the block. If you're coming down here, it's because you and Squad wanna come through."

"This isn't up for discussion. I promised Nana that I would keep you safe."

"Nope, it isn't. Leave the heat at home if you come through. I mean it."

The line goes quiet again, agitating me. I have no intention of backing down this time. I start to get a grip on how things work down here, and the last thing I need is my old life colliding head on with my current one. I'm not ashamed of it, not by a long shot, but I've slowly come to the realization that some things don't need to follow me.

"I got you, Ya-Ya. We'll wait things out up here…for now."

I exhale slow and easy, looking skyward, shaking my head over dodging that bullet. "Thanks, big bro. I mean that. I need time to work through things down here. Once I'm good, I'll make a trip to the A. I miss my people."

"Yeah, your presence is missed, too…by some more than others."

Another call comes through from Zahra. I send it to voicemail again, but I know she's gonna keep calling until I answer my phone. I've got to answer it before she panics and gets the rest of the crew involved.

That veiled comment freezes me. "I know what you're doing, but there's nothing I can do about that now. I'm iced out, and I can't get around that."

"I feel you, and I'll do what I can on my end. You need to make that right, and you know it."

"Say less. When I'm up there next. Promise." I hear the next call from Zahra beeping in my ear, followed by a series of text message notifications. I close my eyes so I can settle myself and not sound so unnerved. "Got another call coming through. I'll holla at you."

The call drops before I can switch over, and I almost lose my nerve to call her back. What the hell do I tell her? I still don't know what I've left back there, and I can't let her know what I know, either.

I take a deep breath and call her before I lose my nerve.

As the line trills, I figure out the best way to handle her the minute she answers the phone. Based on how she reacts, I can adjust from there. I just have to make sure I don't react to the worry in her voice.

The minute I hear her voice, all those plans fly out the window. "Yasir, tell me you're okay, please. We heard about what happened in the parking lot outside the stadium. Were you caught up in that?"

Yeah, I better come up with a lie real quick, or this call will go left. "I'm…I'm okay, I promise. I'm on campus waiting for you as we speak. I'm sorry it took so long to get back with you. Something weird happened at the harbor with my uncle's boat, and we went to check it out."

I hear nothing but silence for a few seconds, and now it's my turn to nearly lose my mind. "There was an attack of some sort at the game… Some kids from Beach Creek were hurt, or maybe worse. I was scared that you were caught up with them."

Thank the gods she doesn't think I had something to do with it. I breathe a sigh of relief as I get back into the vibe with her the best way I can. "I kept my head on a swivel the whole night. Besides, I can't get caught up in anything. We have more than a few things to do this weekend. The last thing I want is to add a hospital stay to the itinerary. I don't look all that good in hospital gowns."

Zahra stifles a laugh, and I feel a little better. "I can't wait to see you back at campus."

"Neither can I…but I have to admit, I may need to be a good boy tonight and take you straight home." Police lights and sirens pass by me, clearly in a rush to the stadium. I need to keep talking to distract her. "Also, uh…we do have brunch with my uncle and his new girlfriend in the morning."

There's a pause. "Um, so when did you plan on telling me about that?"

The accusing tone of her voice throws me off. "I promise, it's not an ambush. Remember when I told you that once I trusted you, I had no problems telling you things as I learn them? Well… about that."

"I want to choke you right now," she stresses to me. "I still might when I see you for making me worry, but you could've set that up a little better, Yasir."

"I know, but it's been a crazy night. Did we win, at least?" I try to steer the convo away from her being irritated with me, but I have a feeling that won't happen.

"We did, but what's going on that the extra guest is invited to witness?" Zahra inquires, throwing a bit of extra syrup on top of that request. "I mean, I want to make sure that I'm properly dressed for the occasion."

"Nah, cuteness, it doesn't work like that," I tease. She's not gonna get over on me that easily. "I promise it isn't anything too fancy."

"You're lucky I like you, or I'd cancel on you without a second thought." I hear her giggle, and it immediately makes me smile. "We can talk about all that the minute I slide into my Jeep."

"*Your* Jeep? When did we come to that agreement?"

"When *you* decided to spring some epic secret on me with less than twenty-four hours' notice."

"Excuse me?" I hear her speakers get muffled by something.

"Yeah, that's a best friend code violation, which means Storm is now half mine as penance for your oversight. Isn't that right, bestie?"

Wait. Kendyl's on the phone? What in the… Hold on a second. "Best friend code? Pause, I didn't even—"

Kendyl doesn't even miss a beat. "Yep! So when are you picking me up in *your* Jeep, sis? And he better make sure it's gassed up and cleaned out, too. We have things to do this weekend!"

"Oh, so we're playing those games now." I know she's playing— or is she? "You're lucky you have me on speaker, I swear."

"Yeah, whatever, you heard my bestie. You can't disrespect the code." I hear a couple of clicks and then more silence before Zahra says another word.

"I really am glad you're not hurt, Yasir. I wouldn't have been able to function, and I probably would've gone hunting for whoever harmed you."

I'm not sure if I should be flattered or worried over what Zahra just said. "Hopefully, it won't have to come to that, *best friend*. It's okay, though. I'll see you when you get back on campus. I'll be posted up with Storm, and I'll have the neon glowing, so you'll know where to find me."

"You won't be hard to miss. I'll see you in a few."

I can't be sure that what happened tonight won't come back to bite me, but I can't worry about it right now. Even though I do my best to make Zahra believe that I'm okay.

I'm *not* okay.

CHAPTER NINETEEN

Zahra saunters toward me as I lean against Storm's hood, basking in her amethyst-tinged glory, the neon glow making it easy to find me. I can't avoid a mischievous grin as she gets closer, my heart racing as I'm unable to sit still. Every bit of me wants to wrap her up in the tightest hug possible, if for nothing else than to release some of my frustration.

Storm's engine rumbles as she approaches, and Zahra gives me a glance that should have melted me where I stand, regardless of how cold it is out here. By Nyati, I have to find a way to build up a tolerance to what she's doing to me.

I keep my hands inside the pockets of my Miles Morales–inspired airbrushed hoodie, and I avoid eye contact so she can't see how worn down I feel. I still have a smile plastered on my face as I wait until the last minute to take them out to wrap my arms around her. I flinch as her tight squeeze pushes in on my bruises, and then I try my best to keep a straight face to escort her to the passenger side.

I smile as she sinks into the leather seats, taking comfort in the heat inside the cabin. I wave at Kendyl as she hops into Kyle's truck, making the hand gesture for Zahra to call her when she gets home. I have no idea what that might be about, but that's none of my business, either. I open the driver's-side door and quickly jump in just before a shiver runs up my spine. The wind is disrespectful tonight. "Let's get you home."

We pull out onto the street, heading away from campus to make the short drive home. I have the usual Afrobeat rocking, bumping Ladipoe and Burna Boy as usual, but then I put Zahra into shock when the tracks switch over to Ayra Starr and Tems and then come back to the States with H.E.R. and Dua Lipa, Doja Cat, Chloe Bailey, and Megan Thee Stallion. I'm vibing for more than one reason, but the main one is that I really don't wanna talk about what happened earlier. The look on her face lets me know I'm not getting off the hook all that easily.

Especially when the bruises on my hands are exposed—and on my face, too.

I didn't have a lot of time to clean up, so I did the best I could. To think that she would ignore any of it, now that I think on it, is a whole stupid move on my part. All I can do now is wait for her to find a spot to jump in and start the inquisition.

She picks up the phone to pause the music and turns her body toward me. She then grabs my hand before I can jerk it away, reaching into the middle console to grab some wet wipes and napkins to clean the area.

"Careful! Still driving here." I wince at the sting.

She frowns at the reaction to the alcohol stings on my open wounds. "Do you want to tell me what happened?"

"Do you really wanna know?"

"I never ask questions I don't want the answers to."

I nod, still jerking as she finishes cleaning my right hand. I switch to give her my left hand, which doesn't look as bad, but that's not my main concern. "I don't know if I want to tell you or not. It will keep you out of the mix in case something else happens."

"Do you mean the madness at the game tonight?" She gives me a look that I don't know how to read. I'm not sure if she's scolding me or trying to protect me. "The officials said that the Beach Creek kids were taken to the hospital with really bad injuries. There were reports of gunshots and some other things."

"I'm surprised it wasn't worse."

"You're *what*?" She blinks a few times like she wants to make sure she heard what she heard. "Were you there? Tell me what happened."

I glare at her, but she's not backing down from her questions. To make her point crystal clear, she presses into my cuts, causing me to scream out in pain. "All right, damn, you don't have to torture me, Z."

"If that's what it takes to find out, then yep, it's gonna happen."

I take a sharp breath and exhale hard. "Those boys Kyle and I ran into at the mall had some friends in the stands. They followed me out to the concession area, and when I tried to make a run for Storm, they cornered me and tried to inflict some major damage."

"So it's safe to say that didn't happen." She finds some cloths to wrap my right hand so it doesn't get infected. "How did you manage to get out of there and they caught the worse of it? I'm so confused…and low-key feeling safe at the same time."

"I didn't plan for any of that to happen, Z." My hand trembles beneath hers, and I groan when I squeeze my hand again. "I don't even know if I killed any of them or not, but they weren't moving, and I got scared and ran before anyone could find out I was there."

"Well, for now, I don't think they're gonna worry about looking for anyone. They're calling it an animal attack."

Maybe she thinks it would calm me down to know what's going on, but I end up closing my eyes, battling every urge in my core to scream out in frustration. I stop Storm for a few seconds so I can compose myself, and in seconds I feel her hand caressing my cheek. "It might give us some time to figure things out."

"There's nothing to figure out."

"It was self-defense, Yasir."

I don't say much of anything for a couple of miles, waiting until I turn into her subdivision before I break my silence. "I'm sorry I lied to you about where I was, Zahra. I have a hard time trusting people."

"You can trust me, okay? But I need you to keep it a buck." She turns my head as soon as I pull into the driveway and park. "Between me, Kyle, and Kenni, we'll figure out something, if and when the time comes. Now, tell me about this brunch thing tomorrow. Is there anything I need to prepare myself for?"

"Well, you get to meet my uncle, so there's that." I give up a genuine smile, even though it hurts to do it. "And his new girlfriend, too… Okay, wait, before you say anything, it really wasn't my idea."

"Mhm, you sure about that?" She narrows her eyes, then studies my face, and I'm sure she notices the cut above my left eye, but I've already treated it. "You sure you didn't want to show me off, too?"

Zahra's gaze never leaves mine, and I feel the heat from her knee on my fingers, even through her thermal leggings and jeans. I want to kiss her, but I'm not sure of myself right now. I wish she'd give me a not-so-subtle clue that she wants me to kiss her. For the sake of the gods, why am I torturing myself like this?

"Maybe I do want to show you off, but I wonder if I should invite some of the others to be there, too." Yeah, like it helps matters having Kendyl or Kyle there. She focuses on the image of Miles's face on my chest, but I don't want her to look away. I don't want the spell between us to fade, not yet. She lets me off the hook with her next breath. "I think we can survive without the audience, can't we?"

"I think so. I think my uncle and his girl will be audience enough." I roll my eyes and chuckle to myself. "He's gonna give me the business the minute you show up."

"He's got to be excited for you. Having a pretty girl come to the house to see about his nephew." She can't resist teasing me now. The lighthearted vibe feels good, and I don't want to let it go. "I can hear him now saying, 'Yo, I see you, nephew.'"

Yeah. I can't wait.

CHAPTER TWENTY

"Hey, come on in. We're just finishing up the menu now."
Nova-star-level heat nerves flow through me as I invite
Zahra to come through the door. I've been looking forward to this
all night, and I'm worried I've built things up to be more than what
it might be in reality. This step feels right, it cements things on a
different plane for me, and even though we aren't official, Kyle's
birthday party later today could change things. Today has "EPIC"
written all over it. I can feel it. The minute I kiss her cheek to say
hello, though, all my other thoughts disappear in a plume of smoke.

I escort Zahra into the dining area, where Unk and Lennox,
his new love, await. The food has been laid out buffet style, which
surprises me a bit. I thought we were sitting down to eat. Oh well, I
guess I'll shake that off to be the other host for this occasion. "Unk,
Ms. Lennox, I'd like to introduce my friend, Zahra Assante. Z, you
already know about my uncle, but Ms. Lennox was the other person
I told you about last night."

Unk rises from his seat at the head of the table and saunters
over to greet Zahra with a handshake. "I'm thrilled you could make
it. I know last night was particularly rough. Even Yasir looked like
he'd been through a fight or two, and he wasn't even on the field."

Zahra flashes a smile, looking over at me as if to ask if Unk
knows what happened last night after the game. I shrug; I didn't
plan to tell him much of anything…unless I had no other choice.
"Thank you for inviting me. I've heard a lot about you."

"And the feeling is mutual. He's been floating around here the
past few weeks." Unk chuckles. "Please, have a seat. Enjoy whatever

looks good to you. Ya-Ya and I have been at it all morning to make sure you all can enjoy."

I cringe at the mention of my nickname in Zahra's presence. No, he didn't just drop that in the middle of the conversation…*ugh*. "Yeah, I had a hand in the shrimp and grits and a few other things."

"You didn't say you could cook." Zahra cuts her eyes at me as she sits in the seat at the other end of the table. "You're just full of surprises…*Ya-Ya*."

"You're lucky I like you—only family calls me that," I correct her. I'm never gonna live that down. If she ever calls me that in school, there goes my rep. "I'm not gonna lie, though, it sounds good coming off your lips."

"Oh my God, you two are so freaking cute," Lennox gushes as she takes a bite of her pancakes. "You two are so connected. Don't ask me how I know. I just have a feeling when I see you together. You just…fit."

Unk pulls Lennox to him, placing a finger to his lips. "They're just *friends*, babe. I don't know what's the hold up, but that's their story, and they're sticking to it."

"I don't care what they're talking about. You two are absolutely stunning together. You are gorgeous, Zahra." Lennox sits down in the chair across from us, shaking her head as she gazes at us. "From what Xavion has told me, you've had a positive effect on his nephew. I can see why; there's a glow about you, young lady."

Zahra blushes and leans into me. "Thank you, Ms. Lennox, but I don't know if I've had as much influence as people think I have. We haven't been around each other that long, but I'll take it if you're saying it, too."

"You should take the compliment, I'm awesome like that, but you'll find out soon enough. Both of you will," Lennox quips. "Look, Yasir, I've grown to care for your uncle deeply, and I hope that we will have the chance to build a friendship, too. You're important to him, which means you're important to me, okay?"

Okay, she pulls that card on me real quick. She's right, though. I don't remember the last time he smiled like that. It's a good look.

"I hear you, Ms. Lennox. I look forward to it."

Unk does his best to cut the convo short and save me from a few more embarrassing moments. "Okay, I need to get you out of here before you really have my nephew regretting doing this get-together. Besides, they need some privacy, and we still have a series to finish streaming."

Lennox rises from her chair, grabbing some of the dishes as she makes her way into the kitchen with Unk. "Fine, since your uncle wants to leave you two to your privacy, I *guess* I can lay off the inquisition for now. Oh, and I'm really not buying that 'best friends' bit, okay? I'm just saying."

Zahra watches Lennox head outside, and once she closes the door, she lets a giggle escape her lips. "Are you sure your uncle is ready for all of that?"

"Yeah, I think he is, but it's going to be a wild ride, I can tell." I rise from the couch, offering my hand for her to stand. "Would you like to see the surprise I have for you?"

"Lead the way, handsome. I can't wait to see it."

"By Nyati, these paintings are beautiful," Zahra says. "It's like you captured the essence of my home country with each stroke and color. I almost feel like I can step inside and be right there. Are you sure you've never been there before?"

"No, I created them from a few pictures Unk had. Do you like them?" I roll up the most recent painting she viewed, moving to place it into the bin with the rest. "I think they still need a lot of work, but I've been studying some new techniques to try to give them a more hyper-realistic feel. I *want* people to feel like they can step inside them."

Zahra turns around and slips her hands around mine, gazing into my eyes. I want to turn away, but she's so captivated, I don't want to ruin the moment. "I could feel *everything*...the sun on my face, the ocean breeze, even the water near the river tribes. You made me miss home."

I smile, pressing my forehead against hers. "I was afraid to show them to you," I admit. "Outside of Unk, no one has seen my paintings before. I figured that I could trust you with some of the things that mean the most to me. I trust you, Z, for real."

"Ugh, if you wanted me to fall for you in one singular moment, this was that moment. I'm glad you can trust me. It means a lot to me."

I glance toward the ceiling before meeting her gaze again. I will the words to come out of my mouth and pray that they don't sound like something out of a sappy *Lifetime* movie. Nothing ventured, nothing gained, right? "I know we're supposed to just be friends and everything, but the weird part of it all…"

Zahra picks up on my voice trailing off. "Tell me."

"It feels like we were made for each other, as cliché as it sounds," I confess. "There's something that I feel deep in my core every time our eyes meet, like there's more between us, but I can't figure out what it is that connects us deeper."

Zahra looks away, so I don't force the issue. I want her to feel safe, but I have to get my thoughts out before they eat me alive. She focuses her gaze on a corner of a painting on the easel in the center of the studio. She breaks from our embrace to peek under the cloth that conceals the rest of the painting.

I grab for her hand in a knee-jerk response to not wanting her to see what lies beneath the cloth. "I'm sorry, it's just that…it's sort of a work in progress, and I don't know if I'm ready for you to see it yet."

"Too late to be shy now. What's the image of that has you so nervous?"

I know I said I trusted her, and now it's proving to be my downfall. Oh well, it's not like she won't see it eventually. "It's a painting…of you."

Zahra widens her eyes as her gaze falls back to the concealed painting, then shifts to my face before pivoting back to the painting. She turns to face me and slips close enough to tiptoe and brush her lips against my face. "I understand if you think it needs to be perfect, but I promise I'll love it regardless. I want to know how you see me."

I breathe deep, turning her around to face the painting. "Take off the cloth so you can see how I see you...well, at least one version of you."

She tugs on the paint-splattered cloth, watching it slide off the top of the easel. Everything seems to flow in slow motion as the painting reveals itself from top to bottom, uncovering a stunning, full-bodied portrait of Z in a formal dress and head wrap. She gasps as she sees her body adorned in golden arm cuffs wrapped around her biceps in a spiral, snake-like pattern, and rings on her index fingers and thumbs. A diamond- and amethyst-encrusted pendant rests against her chest, along with matching earrings that look like they drip from her earlobes.

She keeps turning her head back to me as though she can't believe what she sees. From the meticulous attention to detail around her eyes and the contouring of her cheekbones, to the way her lips are splashed in the black, gold, and purple color scheme of the Kindaran flag. She marvels at her portrait on the canvas. Her braids are swept up into a ponytail with a matching headwrap encased around her hair, giving a playful-but-serious look to her face.

Zahra covers her mouth with her hands as she stares at the dress, and I notice her fingers shake. A halter-neck maxi dress, also in the Kindaran flag colors, shows cut-out patterns on the sides of her waist, and from the slight side profile of the portrait, it's clear to see that the dress is backless, stopping a few inches below the middle of her back. From there, the dress flows down to about three inches from the ground, where diamond-encrusted strapped heels are on her feet.

Okay...she still hasn't said anything. "If you don't like it, I can start over and rip this one up."

Her hands are still covering her mouth, and I brace myself against the overwhelming emotions coursing through me. "By

Nyati," she says, "it's like you took my essence and captured everything I wanted to exude. I can't believe that's how you see me."

"So I don't need to change it, right?"

She turns around and faces me, wiping a tear from her cheek. "Don't you dare touch this painting. Please don't change anything. It's so vivid… I feel like I'm looking in the mirror."

I exhale, bringing her hands to my lips. "You had me worried for a minute. I spent the past few nights trying to get this right before I got up the nerve to show it to you."

Zahra wraps her arms around my neck, pressing her lips against mine so hard it blurs my vision. I don't know where this is coming from, but I'm quickly losing myself in the kiss between us. I pull away, but she holds me in place, almost like she's determined to keep me there in the moment with her. She deepens her kisses, taking steps with me as we move backward.

She giggles the moment we hit the wall, smiling as she encourages me to keep going. I slip my hands around her waist, the intoxicating scent of her perfume causing near-dizzy spells. She locks her fingers around the back of my neck as I lift her off the ground.

"Are you sure about this, Z?" I ask between kisses, shaking off the dizzy spells. By Nyati, her lips are so soft. "Should we be doing this? I mean…we can stop, this isn't …"

"Don't stop kissing me, Ya-Ya," Zahra whispers in my ear before caressing my neck to make a path back to my lips. "We're just kissing. *Friends* can kiss, remember?"

Before I lose my nerve, I pull Zahra closer, focusing on her lips before I close my eyes. I lose my breath all over again the second our lips touch and fight every instinct to pull away. Every nerve is on fire and getting hotter by the minute. Okay, so, um… I've never kissed a girl like *this* before, and the energy coursing through my body scares me beyond my capacity to understand what's happening.

I almost rip myself away, bringing my fingers to my lips in disbelief over what we'd done. I can't look up, can't handle her reaction. I vibrate from head to toe, willing the insecurities that want to rise to the surface to stay in the depths of my mind. I swear I feel hot to the touch, and I'm close to passing out.

When I finally get my nerves together to meet Zahra's gaze, I come face to face with a confused expression I hoped wouldn't be there. "Umm…Zahra, I…I wanted to…well, that is to say…"

Zahra grins at me, placing an index finger against my lips to quiet me mid-sentence. "It's okay, I liked it. Actually, I liked it a lot."

I let out a long exhale, placing her hand against my chest to try to slow my rapid heartbeat. "It's been a minute since… Let me stop lying… I've never kissed a girl before. I'm… Did I do it right? I don't know what to say right now."

Zahra leans in closer, purring in my ear, "Yasir…kiss me again."

I blink a few times. Is this actually happening? "Are you sure? Like, really?"

"Yes, silly… I can show you how I want you to kiss me, if you'd like?" Zahra gives a knowing wink. "Did you like kissing me?"

"Is that a trick question?"

Zahra rubs her nose against mine, coaxing me as she stares into my eyes. "Then kiss me, Yasir."

I cup my hands around her face this time, mimicking some movie scene I committed to memory or something. I stare into her eyes again, only this time I notice her studying them. "What's wrong? Is there something on my face or something?"

"Your eyes…they've turned colors," she says, her gaze never looking away from mine. "They're this shade of purple, like an amethyst gemstone… They're so beautiful, I can't stop staring."

The uncertainty washes over me like a waterfall. I have no idea what she's talking about. My eyes have always been a mix between amber gold and light brown. For her to say my eyes are on a whole other color spectrum has me a slight bit panicked.

I draw back again, but Zahra keeps me with her. I don't resist when she brushes her lips against mine, but I still have her last thoughts flowing through my head. What's happening to me? My eyes have never done that before. Was she playing with me?

She keeps at it, playfully kissing my chin, then my nose. "Oh, no, you're not getting away again. Kiss me... Yasir, kiss me."

Despite my best efforts, I can't concentrate on being in the moment with her. "Zahra, there might be something—"

"We can deal with that later... Kiss me."

I give in to her wishes—or at least my body does—slipping my hands around her waist and losing myself in the embrace. I retreat to the recesses of my mind, intent on traveling as we continue our interlude. I hope it will settle me down so I can enjoy this moment.

I conjure the first image that comes to mind, taking me across the Atlantic and to one of my favorite places on my bucket list, Victoria Falls in Zambia.

In a blink, I'm floating above the majestic beauty of the largest waterfall in the world, its size literally forming the border between Zambia and Zimbabwe. I gaze over the expansive curtain of falling water, marveling at the columns of spray rising from the falls, almost feeling the water against my skin, providing a refreshing reprieve from the heat of the day. I smile as I locate the Knife-Edge Bridge, setting down on the platform to take advantage of the special vantage point of the Eastern Cataract and the Main Falls and the area called the Boiling Pot, where the Zambezi River turns and heads down the Batoka Gorge. The awe-inspiring sight was exactly what I need to get in sync with Zahra.

I'm so taken with the view that I don't notice Zahra standing next to me with a stunned expression on her face. I struggle to understand how she's there, too, and can't find the words.

Let's be real. I'm at a loss for words to explain *how* she's here with me. How in the world is this even possible?

She grabs my arm, almost too scared to move. "How are we here, Yasir? We were just in your room, and now we're in...Africa? How are you doing this?"

I shrug at her questions, unsure how to answer them. How the hell am I supposed to know how she's here with me? I was in a zone, trying to balance my psyche, but I'm really worried over how I did this and how can I get us out of whatever I just did.

Even though I'm terrified and doing my best to keep Zahra from freaking out with me, I'm happy she's in the space with me. That's probably the only reason I'm not screaming right now. It's bad enough we're floating inside my head and can feel and see and hear everything surrounding us. What scares me the most is staring into the bottom of the falls and praying that I don't lose concentration and we end up falling out of the sky.

No point in arguing the why of it all. I'm content to enjoy the ride—even if I'm confuzzled as hell with no way to figure out how to get out of this conjured daydream. "Do you want to see more? I think we still have some time to kill."

"You still haven't explained how we're literally somewhere else other than back home in Oakwood Grove," Zahra insists as she grabbed my hand. "I feel like I should be freaking out, but I can't understand why I'm not freaking out. What's going on?"

"I have no idea how to answer your questions because this is the first time someone else has been in this space with me." But she seems to be okay. "Do you trust me?"

"Do I have a choice?" Zahra holds my hand tighter, wrapping her arm around mine. "I don't know if I'm dreaming or if this is real."

She's not the only one. I suppress the rising fear in my heart and keep moving forward, holding her tight around her waist as we lift from the bridge and take flight. In seconds, we land at the base of Mt. Kilimanjaro in Tanzania, taking in the snowcaps that adorn the three volcanic cones and the rest of the top of the mountain. The descending sun provides the backdrop to a tide of elephants making their way across the savanna outside of the massive mountain forest that encircles it. I smile wide as I observe the captivated look on Zahra's face. We take a few more seconds to enjoy one of the Seven Summits on the planet.

"Ready for the next stop, pretty girl?" I'm getting a little more comfortable with what's going on, and I begin to remember how I leave when I'm meditating. That calms me down a lot more and gives me more control over things.

Before she can answer, we fly in a flash farther north into the land of the pharaohs, arriving at a location that draws another confuzzled glance from Zahra. "Where are we now?"

"Abu Simbel. It's one of my favorite places in the world." I'm beaming as we gaze up at the statue of Rameses II and the smaller statues at his feet.

"Well, don't keep me in suspense. Why?"

"Because Rameses had a temple dedicated to his wife, Queen Nefertari, and the smaller statues that surround his feet are of her and their children, along with his mother." I guide her around the base of the statues, enjoying the monument all over again through her eyes. "Standing monuments to their love to last beyond their lifetimes. Who wouldn't want that?"

I stare into her eyes, smiling over the wonder in her expression. "What's on your mind, if you don't mind me asking?"

"Ask me when we get back," she says.

One last burst across the burning sands of the Sahara with what feels like light speed and we're back in my studio. We settle into our bodies again, breaking from our kiss and searching around to see if anything has changed around us. I hold her in my arms, waiting for her to get her bearings.

"Umm, that was one helluva kiss, boy. Are you sure that was your first time?" Zahra's trying to catch her breath, fanning herself the entire time. "What would you do for an encore? Good grief."

I chuckle, keeping my hands around her waist to keep her steady. "That depends on whether you want to stick around to find out."

Zahra looks at her watch, shocked that only five minutes have passed by while we were, quite literally, on the other side of the world. "Oh, I'm definitely sticking around, but... Wait, how in the world did you... Was any of that real? Our bodies were still right here and... Wow, all that from just a kiss?"

"I really have no clue, but it was all real," I reply. I'm serious, I really don't. "All I wanted to do was show you what was in my mind. Everything else is as surprising to me as it is to you."

Zahra plants a series of kisses across my lips over and over. "I only have one more question, in light of tonight's 'excursion,' Mr. Salah."

"Yes, Ms. Assante?"

"When can we do that again?"

I crack up laughing. "I don't have a problem with that at all."

"You know, we're going to have to talk about how you did all of that, right?" Zahra remarks. "My head is still spinning."

A knock on the door makes us jump.

"Ahem…Ya-Ya, I wanted to check on you two," Unk bellows through the door. "It's almost two in the afternoon. We have to get to it if we're gonna get this order to your friend's birthday party. You need time to get back, get ready, and not be late."

I break from our embrace, looking skyward, wanting to scream. "Gotcha, Unk. I'll be ready to roll in ten minutes."

"All right, bet, kiddo. Wheels spin in ten."

Zahra buries her face in my chest, shaking her head. "Do you think he heard?"

"I know he heard us, but I'll deal with that during the delivery," I counter. "Am I wrong for thinking that everything around us completely disappeared while we were…well, you know?"

Zahra shuts her eyes as she taps her forehead against my chest a few times. "You're not wrong at all. I was in that space with you, and I didn't want to come out, period. I'm still feeling some kinda way about being ripped back to reality without my consent."

She blushes for a moment, pulling me over to a mirror on the other side of the studio. "Umm, we might need to not be so obvious."

I search for a napkin to wipe the traces of her lipstick from my face and lips. "I'm with you on the rip, that's for sure, but there's nothing we can do about that now. Come on, I'll walk you to your car."

Before we leave, I catch a glimpse of what Zahra tried to explain before we kissed. My eyes have a strong purple glow around my irises. I blink a few times, not believing what I'm seeing, and the glow seems to consume the whole of my irises now. *What's happening to me? This isn't normal.*

"Are you okay?" Zahra slips into my sight, moving her head so I don't have a choice but to face her. "Is it the thing with your eyes?"

I shake my head violently like I'm trying to get rid of whatever is happening. I breathe a sigh of relief when I look in the mirror and see my eyes have returned to their usual hue. "I think so, not sure what that was about. I guess it was some residual whatever from when we came back."

We walk downstairs, bypassing the adults as they continue chatting, stopping long enough to wave goodbye to Zahra before returning to their conversation. Once outside, the warmer-than-usual-for-fall South Georgia air hits us, which does nothing to quell the residual heat we tried to temper only minutes ago.

I kiss her lips once more before tucking her into the driver's seat. I wink, and she pushes the ignition to start the car. "You know we're gonna have to pick this up again soon, right? And I don't mean just the kiss, either."

"That's an understatement," she says, then motions for me to lean down to steal one more kiss. "Now, be a good boy and get things squared away with Unk. I need you freshly oiled and looking good enough to eat later tonight, okay? See you in a couple of hours."

CHAPTER TWENTY-ONE

I watch Kendyl's eyes as she gawks at Storm's interior, and I think it's safe to say that she's impressed with all the work Squad and I put in on the mods.

"Damn, boy, this is one of the nicest Jeeps I've ever seen!" she says as she continues to run her fingers along the seating and the doors.

With the deep-purple neon accents that match the undercarriage neon, she's a sight to behold. How can she not be? She's the one thing I get to brag about, and I do it at every opportunity.

The only reason Kendyl's able to get the full effect has everything to do with Kyle calling me to ask if I could pick his girl up and bring her to the party with us. That isn't even a question, especially when he's been true to his word about having my back. Besides, I knew it would put a smile on Zahra's face.

Now, if I can keep from being so obvious about it.

Zahra turns to face Kendyl, still smiling while the wind blows through her hair. It's a clear night, perfect for the top to be open. "Now you see why she's half mine, right?"

"Chica, like, this thang is pretty, pretty." She keeps playing with the neon on the door panels, then leans forward into the front seats, planting her elbows on the middle console. "You might have picked up some cool points with me, Yasir. How did you put all this together? It had to cost a few stacks, at least."

"Well, my Squad in the A helped with a lot of it," I tell them as I pull out of her subdivision. Okay, so I'm feeling a little showy tonight, and I'm in a good mood, so why not? That whole situation with Zahra earlier in my studio has me buzzing. "We learned from the boys at the customs shop my ace's uncle owns."

"Speaking of your Squad in the A, you haven't mentioned them much." Kendyl switches up the flow, ramping up her interrogation and cutting her eyes at Zahra the whole time. "Do you still talk to them? Do they know what you got going on down here?"

"Kenni," Zahra warns.

"I mean, come on, Z, you gotta admit it's the first time he's said anything about his life before he got to Oakwood." Kendyl turns toward me and jumps back into her bag of questions. "So what's good, bro? You gonna let me dig or nah?"

I tighten my grip on the steering wheel as I drive, tapping my thumb against the gearshift. Okay, so she wants to be the big bad bestie, huh? "I know why you're digging, but you wanna play, so let's play. Let's start with my ace, Dante. He's been like an older brother to me. Then there's Caleb, and his older brother, Malik, and, well, there's Alyssa and Dominique."

"Oh, now we're getting somewhere." Kendyl rubs her hands together like she's struck gold. "So what's up with the girls in the Squad? Anything we need to know about?"

"Okay, Kenni, you're getting a bit wild. What's up with you?" Zahra's trying to slow down the freight train before it starts to slide off the rails, but I'm with the shenanigans. "Are you kidding me with these questions? Like, for real?"

"He doesn't seem to have a problem with it, do you, Yasir?" Kendyl smirks as she looks into the rearview mirror, and she cracks up when she notices my face. "See, he's even trying not to laugh in the mirror. I'm doing you a favor, chica."

I'm having a ball watching them argue back and forth. Real talk, I've been waiting for Kendyl to bring the smoke. I glance over at Zahra, then back at Kendyl, and I pull the car over so I can really get the laughter out of my system. "Kenni, you're wild, I swear. Ally is bisexual, and Nique is a lesbian, for the record."

"TMI, my boy, TMI." Kendyl leans back in the seat, crossing her arms over her chest. "I didn't ask for all that."

"Nope, but you didn't ask for specifics, either, chica." My turn to apply some pressure. "Man, this is too funny. Do you want me to call Nique real quick? She loves girls who have a little fire."

Zahra bursts into laughter. "Aww, come on, babe, you know you belong to me. I'd never let anyone take you from me."

Kendyl takes her hand and pushes it off. "So I'm trying to protect my girl and I'm being treated like the bad guy? Mhm, I see how it is now."

"You're the one trying to find drama where it ain't. It's not my fault it backfired on you." I finally pull off and back on the road, shaking my head and chuckling while driving. "I get it, though. You're looking out for your ace, and you should. Hell, Dante's dying to figure out who I'm trying to holla at so he can give her the third degree. Squad takes care of its own."

"I'm glad you see things my way, unlike my bestie over there sitting in the *girlfriend's* perch," Kendyl teases as she lunges forward to kiss Zahra on the cheek. "You're all right with me, my boy, but you're not off the hook. I got a lot more questions to ask before we get to Kyle's house."

"I kinda figured as much, and you're about to find out I'm not as thin-skinned as you might have guessed," I warn her. "You might wanna prepare for the answers to those questions, too. I'm learning you just like you're learning me, as friends, girlie."

"Yeah, that reminds me." Kendyl taps against her temple as she ponders her next inquiry. "You've gone through a whole makeover from what we saw when you first got here. You're from the A, but the way you wear the oils and scents and the way you have your hair cut, it's screaming something from overseas. Where are you from, for real?"

Zahra almost queues the record scratch. "Wow, would you look at the time? We're almost to Kyle's anyway. I think we can pick this up another time, okay? Besides, I'm *supposed* to be the one asking these questions, remember?"

"Ugh, then you need to get to asking, chica, because if my inquiring mind wants to know, others are gonna want to know, too," she stresses. "He's a mystery to all of us, and you seem to be the only one he's willing to open up to, so yeah, I'm gonna need y'all to get that handled and soon, okay?"

"It'll get done when we say it gets done, sis." Zahra rolls her eyes over the hypocrisy of it all. I'm not gonna lie, she's being nosy for the sake of being nosy. "When did you become Oakwood's Tamron Hall?"

"There's a method to my madness, chica," Kendyl points out as I turn into Kyle's neighborhood. "First thing they taught us in the journalism club: if you can control the narrative, you do it before someone else does it for you."

"So pause, stop the presses, I'm confused." I slow down long enough to locate the street number of Kyle's house since the GPS says we're already there. "One minute, you're in protective mode over your bestie, and the next minute, you want to help me control the information that gets out to the school? What gives, shawty?"

Kendyl sighs as we finally arrive at the long driveway that leads to the estate. "Okay, here's the real, playa. My girl likes you, and you like her, too. I'm willing to give you the benefit of the doubt because you've opened up more in the past few days. If you were still the brooding loner, things would be way different, trust."

"Fair enough. I admit I could've been a bit more open with people, but everywhere I've gone to school, whatever I've told has been used against me." I put Storm in park, then open the door and hop out. I slip around to the passenger side and open the door for them to get out. "Since you're talking about controlling the narrative—I like that, by the way, I'm gonna have to borrow that— if anything comes up, I'll make sure you and Z know about it first. Sounds like a winner?"

"Deal, my guy. Now, let's see what's going on. I need to see about my baby before things get too wild around here."

CHAPTER TWENTY-TWO

"**T**hank you all for coming out for my son's seventeenth birthday!" Mr. Channing says through the microphone. "I have no doubt that you will enjoy yourselves." He steps off the stage to mix and mingle.

The Channing estate, in every sense of the word, personifies everything that anyone who likes to entertain would want to have in their home. The tree line alone boasts privacy on levels that even the most introverted personality would appreciate. The waterfront, resort-like style of the pool gives the adults something to enjoy and still be separate from the teenagers, while the covered verandas speckled about the ten-acre backyard allow us kids the ability to enjoy ourselves without the overbearing gaze and interference.

For me, the walk to and from the trucks earlier to get things into the home and the backyard almost wore me out, and I swear I'll never complain about Unk's five-bedroom house ever again. Thank the gods we didn't have to cater for the event; we only provided the seafood as part of the expansive menu that's housed inside of one of the larger verandas closest to the house.

I stroll with Zahra through the maze of tents that augment the verandas in search of the rest of the group. It isn't long before we find Kyle and Kendyl; they're in the eye of the storm, with Kyle soaking up every bit of the attention showered on him. Kendyl is posing and smiling for the cameras, too. Kyle's cousin, Quentin Channing, is standing beside him in the midst of the throng of people, gushing over his younger protégé, telling anyone who will listen that Kyle is the next college football phenom.

"If anyone needed a quick reminder of whose night this was, there should not be any doubts now," I remark, leading Zahra to the area where Kyle told me we would camp out for the rest of the night. "This is bananas. I would have never thought things could get this interesting down here."

"See, it's not as boring as you thought, huh?" Zahra's smile lights up the night sky. "It's nice to actually be able to just enjoy things, be Kenni's cheerleader, and let her step into the spotlight with Kyle. It's a beautiful thing."

"Yeah, I just hope that it stays that way." I keep my head on a swivel as we move through the crowd, and I'm fighting the nagging feeling that there could be someone here who doesn't belong. In the back of my mind, I'm still thinking about whether that viral video will come back on me tonight. I know it sounds a bit extreme, but nothing's happened yet, which means something can happen sooner or later. "It's nice to not be in the spotlight for a while."

"My mom loves to say, 'Don't borrow trouble.' Let's enjoy the night, okay? There's plenty of time to worry about things another day," Zahra points out. "We haven't had a chance to have a fun night. I'm gonna make sure you do."

I notice a group of people swirling around an elder gentleman and his family but can't make out who they are. "I don't recognize those people. Who are they?"

"That would be the mayor and Mrs. Lance." Zahra rolls her eyes. "That means Ian and Chrisette are around here somewhere. It looks like we're gonna have to do our best to make sure the plan is in motion and followed to the letter."

"I thought Mayor Lance was out of town. At least, that's what Unk told me when I asked about the VIP list."

"Yeah, so did I, but rumor has it Ian convinced him that Mr. Channing's party was the place to be this weekend," Zahra explains to me. "He's as much of an egomaniac as Ian is. Apple…tree."

"Okay, so we stick to the plan, then," I declare. "As soon as Kyle and Kenni get over here, we can figure out what needs to be done next and take it from there."

Before we settle into our seats and enjoy the music, the microphone screeches a couple of times, and a distinct voice sounds off through the air. I don't know who stepped up on stage, but I have a bad feeling the spotlight's gonna get shifted to someone against their will.

"Ladies and gentlemen, it is a pleasure to be here among you all to help celebrate the coming of age of one of our favorite sons of Oakwood Grove," Mayor Lance announces to the crowd. After the applause dies down, he continues as he motions for Kyle to join him and Ian. "Kyle Channing, we can't wait to see what you and my son, Ian, will accomplish during the rest of this magical undefeated season, and I will be in the stands cheering you on."

We look on, helpless, as Kyle tries to find the opening to take the microphone away from the mayor. He's sandwiched between Ian and Mayor Lance, and his distressed expression can be felt by everyone except for the Lance men.

"You know, I remember when you and Ian were in Little League, and the connection between you two as quarterback and tight end was evident back then." Mayor Lance continues to lavish praise on both Kyle and his son. "Who would have thought that all these years later, you two would be in a position to get Oakwood Grove another state title?"

"I'm going up there. I'm not leaving my boyfriend caught out there like that," Kendyl seethes as she attempts to get up from her chair.

Zahra grabs her arm as we watch Chrisette, Ian's girlfriend, saunter up on stage to join the group. "I know what you wanna do, babe, but it's gonna make things worse."

"How do you expect me to just—"

I tap Zahra's shoulder and smirk as I point toward the equalizer making his way through the crowd. "I have a pretty good feeling all this is about to get shut down in a few seconds."

As the crowd cheers and roars, Mr. Channing steps back on the stage. His face shows no emotion as he whispers something in his son's ear before stepping to the mayor. He holds out his hand, staring the mayor down for what seems like forever. I pump my fist in a silent show of solidarity, hoping the mayor gets the point.

Before long, Mayor Lance places the microphone in Mr. Channing's hand and gestures to him to take center stage. Mr. Channing then points toward the stairs, a not-so-subtle clue for the mayor and his family to step off the stage, and taps the microphone a few times to make sure he can be heard. "We would like to thank the mayor and his family for their gracious birthday wishes for our son. We know he can get a bit long-winded at times, so I wanted to make sure he kept things under the mandatory three minutes before the crowd turned on him."

Man, it's the low-key shade for me. I wanna be like him when I grow up.

The laughter radiates through the crowd at that backhanded remark, and I'm there for all of it as I see the scowl on Mayor Lance's face. Kyle and Kendyl have already made their way down to the lawn and are heading in our direction. I grin as I scope the relief on Kyle's face over being saved by his father.

"Man, that was too close, bro." I tap fists with Kyle as we slip inside the veranda. "Did anyone even know the mayor was gonna pull that stunt?"

"Bro, I know my dad, and he's gonna have words for the mayor at the next council meeting," Kyle explains to us. "He's constantly trying to keep the focus on him, no matter whose night it belongs to."

The glare in Kendyl's eyes is enough to melt steel. "He's lucky I'm not that chick, or I would have embarrassed him myself. How dare he bring his family up on stage like that, and that nonsense with Ian and Chrisette? What in the hell was that about?"

Zahra puts her hand up to settle everyone down. "Look, you said it yourself, chica, this is your boyfriend's night, and we're focused on that, okay? There is no need to bring the Lance family up or anything that has nothing to do with the fact that we should be partying with the birthday boy."

"You're right, Z, so let's see about doing exactly that," Kyle declares. "Now, I'm not saying I snuck wine coolers into the ice chest, but if you happen to lift the lid and find something to smooth things out a bit, have at it, you feel me?"

In the next few minutes, we're sipping and enjoying the live entertainment. For most of the night, everyone has a fun time mixing and mingling among themselves. I even manage to settle in and indulge a bit.

I place my drink on one of the side tables and kiss Zahra before heading out of the veranda. "I'll be back. I need to hit the restroom. Are there any on the main floor?"

"Yeah, soon as you hit the back door, turn to your left. It will be the first door on your right. You can't miss it," Kyle replies, turning his attention to his social media feed. "We'll keep up with Z for you, bro."

I saunter through the crowd, determined to avoid eye contact with anyone to keep my anxiety tamped down. Despite my newfound semi-celebrity status, I don't feel as safe and in control around large crowds yet. In fact, I'm low-key scanning the crowd for people who don't look familiar to me, allowing my imagination to run wild, fabricating all sorts of doomsday situations and what I might need to do to get out of here. While I'm able to keep it together while Zahra is with me, dealing with it on my own is a completely different circumstance.

Real talk, I'm so out of sorts that exiting out the front door is looking really good right now. Each step I take toward the house feels like my shoes are filled with concrete, and despite my best efforts, my anxiety is spiking beyond my ability to function.

I shouldn't have left the safety of the group, but I can't do anything about it now. I'm focusing on getting in and getting back, and not having a full-tilt panic attack.

I get to the restroom without incident, but once I find myself inside the house, I come face to face with Ian, who happens to be in a better mood than usual. I take one look at him, realizing that he's been drinking. A lot. His inability to stand up straight is a dead giveaway.

"Yasir, what's good, my dude?" Ian's speech slurs as he greets me. "This party is wild, bro. I couldn't have crashed a better situation."

I scratch my head, trying to understand the statement Ian has a hard time getting out. I play it like I'm not in the loop, but I figure he might not buy it. Like I care if he did or not. "Wait…you mean you weren't invited to the party? How did that happen? I thought you and Kyle were cool."

"Well, I figured that *you* had something to do with that." Ian steps into my personal space, his breath reeking of something a lot stronger than what we'd been enjoying inside Kyle's veranda.

"Bro, you're drunk, and I'm not having this conversation with you. You said you aren't supposed to be here, then do everyone a favor and ghost." I push past Ian to head for the back door when he grabs my arm.

"Who the hell died and made you the gatekeeper?" Ian scoffs as he continues to hold me hostage.

Someone has to be playing a joke and catching it on camera or something. He's acting mad weird right now, and I have no interest in playing along. "Look, I'm gonna slide out of your space and leave you to whatever dream world you're living in, because I'm not there."

"You aren't going anywhere until we get some things cleared up."

I glare at him. If there weren't people around, I would have shot a fade quick. "We are not even close to being cool enough for you to dictate what we need or do not need to do, partner."

Ian releases his grip, standing his ground for a few minutes. "Look, I'm not trying to be your enemy, bro. You bailed me out after the game that night, even when you could have left me to… God knows what would have happened."

I cross my arms over my chest, leaning against the wall. "Oh, this should be good. What are you trying to prove, coming for me? I'm at a loss, so maybe you can give me a clue or two, huh?"

"I don't know what it is about you, dude, but every time we're around each other, I have this deep need to either wring your neck or try to find some common ground so we can at least be cordial." Ian sits on the edge of one of the couches, waiting for other people to leave the area. "Right now, I have no animosity toward you. You haven't done anything to me. What I'm not about to do is pretend like we're friends, either, but that's what's making things complicated."

Before I jump in with my thoughts about what Ian wants to discuss, Mayor Lance shows up out of the blue. "Who's your friend, son? I don't believe I've met him before."

Ian rolls his eyes, taking another sip of his drink. "Dad, this is Yasir Salah, and he and I are not exactly friends, more like acquaintances. I was asking him about some things we needed to talk about."

My anxiety shoots through the roof. I take a few deep breaths to calm things down before extending my hand to greet the mayor. "Mayor Lance, it's good to meet you, sir."

"Is this true, Yasir? Are you two not friends?" Mayor Lance inquires, not offering his hand back.

"Sir, he is correct. We know each other from school, nothing much more than that." I narrow my gaze in Ian's direction, wondering how I managed to get caught up in this situation. "In fact, I was just about to leave and rejoin my friends, so if you'll excuse me…"

"Wait a moment, there's something about you." Mayor Lance takes a closer look at my face. He raises an eyebrow as though he recognizes something familiar. That alone makes me nervous. "Your father wouldn't happen to be Bakari Salah, would it? You favor him greatly."

I flinch. "How do you know that name?"

"Because your father was—" He stops himself from whatever he is going to say next. "I'm starting to figure out the simmering acrimony between you and my son now," Mayor Lance asserts. "Considering he told me that he helped you escape the fight with those Baytown kids, I would think you would show a little more appreciation."

"Okay, pause…he *helped* me keep from catching a beatdown with kids who didn't even know who I was? With all due respect, sir, but what alternate universe are you two living in?" Oh, no, what we're not gonna do is play stupid games right now. "I did what I could to get those kids off his back, and he all but pushed me into my car for me to split from the scene so he could handle the cops, whatever that meant. Your son was not the savior in that scenario."

"Look, it's cool, all right? I'm not sweating it, for real. I know it's rough, being the new kid in town and all," Ian jumps in to say. This Jekyll-and-Hyde routine is getting old really fast. "You don't have to make things up to make yourself look better. I mean, you might have been the one behind why I got jumped in the first place, for all I know."

I suppress my anger, but it overrules my ability to be logical. I flex my fingers, balling them into fists and releasing them to temper my annoyance over the revisionist recent history Ian's spinning. I know I won't get the upper hand if I continue to debate, but I'm not backing down, either.

"Oh, so why didn't anyone call and ask for a statement? My uncle didn't get a call, either, or he would have told me." Dammit. I should've known I would regret not being there to tell my side of the story. "Don't you get it, Mayor Lance? None of this makes any sense. Am I the only one seeing that?"

"Yasir! Bro, we've been looking everywhere for you," Kyle shouts as he and the rest of the group show up. Mr. Channing is in tow, following his son and our friends to the source of the minor commotion. "What's going on here? Why do you have my boy hemmed up like this?"

"That's what I would like to know, Robert," Mr. Channing asks of Mayor Lance. "From the looks of Yasir's body language and the irritation on his face, he's not exactly happy with the way his interactions with you are going."

Mayor Lance turns to Mr. Channing for a moment before focusing back on me. "Nothing for you to concern yourself with, Asa. It seems that Mr. Salah might have incriminated himself over an incident that happened a couple weeks ago, and we were having a chat about it."

What the hell is this man talking about? I didn't do a damned thing. The last thing he's gonna accuse me of is assault. "Let's call it what it is, Mr. Channing: the mayor and his son seem to think that I orchestrated a fight. I have no idea what would possess them to want to accuse me of such things, but I think I might need representation, in case he might get a bright idea and accuse me of something I didn't do."

Mr. Channing strokes his beard. "So you and your son decided to corner a friend of my son's, at his birthday party, that neither you nor he were invited to, and without a lawyer or his legal guardian present engaged in a 'discussion' where you admitted he might have incriminated himself. Is that right?" He pauses for a few moments before he continues. "If that is the case, Yasir, it is in your best interest to give me a dollar so that I may represent you in whatever nonsense the mayor is trying to bait you into."

Oh, say less, sir. I pull out my wallet without a moment's hesitation and place a folded one dollar bill in Mr. Channing's hand.

Mayor Lance flinches for a minute, forgetting that Mr. Channing happens to be one of the most celebrated and notorious defense attorneys in the Southeast. I didn't; I understood the assignment.

"Now, now, we don't have to go to such drastic measures."

"Oh, I believe that it has to, unfortunately," Mr. Channing counters. "And since you insist on disrupting this night with your son's petty grievances, I'm going to ask you to leave."

"Are you sure you want to do that, Asa?" Mayor Lance challenges, almost like he wants to make a scene.

"Be thankful I'm willing to politely request that you remove yourself, or would you rather I advise my client to file harassment charges against your son on Monday?" Mr. Channing answers. "I mean, you said it yourself…it doesn't need to get to such extreme measures."

Mayor Lance glares at his son, who tucks his head to keep from meeting his father's disapproving gaze. "You're right, I think we will take our leave. I apologize for any disruption we have caused tonight. I'll see you for the council meeting on Tuesday?"

"I'll look forward to it, as always, Robert." Mr. Channing sinks his hands in his pockets, nodding toward the front door. "Be safe on the way home, please."

I stare Ian down as we remain in each other's space. "Something's off with you, seriously. It might be in our mutual best interest to stay away from each other, or things could get wild."

Ian frowns as he walks away. "Honestly, you might be right, but we're gonna have to find a way to coexist, one way or the other. Even though this went a little…weird…my yacht party invitation is still good."

I wave him off, turning my attention to the stunning beauty by my side, meeting her curious gaze with a mischievous grin. "Do I want to know what's going through that pretty head of yours?"

"Do I want to know why the hell Ian was trying to rile you up?" Zahra queries. "He's almost laser focused on you now for some reason, and I have a bad feeling about this. Is there something I should know? What invitation was he talking about?"

I shoo away Zahra's concerns with a dismissive wave of my hand. "You know Ian better than me. He runs hot and cold; one minute, he's trying to catch me slipping so he can make me look bad, the next minute, he wants to figure out how we can coexist. Let him try to bring the smoke; he's on a blamestorm anyway, and it won't go anywhere. Now, can we get back to the party? I think we can finally enjoy it without all the negativity swirling around."

Even with the bravado to show her that I'm not concerned about Ian, the truth of the matter is harsher than I want to admit. Ian's gonna be a problem, and I know it. If I don't figure out why things are so tense between us, it could cause other issues that I don't have time to resolve.

I also have to face another unfortunate truth…that I might not survive the glare of the spotlight. For my sake, and everyone around me, I better find a way to survive.

Failure would undo everything I've tried to build.

CHAPTER TWENTY-THREE

"That was more fun than I thought it would be. Kyle and his folks really know how to throw a party," Zahra says as she settles into the passenger seat. I keep my hand on top of hers the entire way home. She indulged all night with Kendyl and some of the other girls, and although it wasn't heavy liquor, we had a blast. Since I knew I'd be driving home tonight, I stuck with the sodas.

The only problem was keeping my emotions in check, especially with all the flirting she insisted on doing. I can't be sure of what's going on in her head, and being in the car with her will test my ability to resist if she decides she wants to apply some pressure. The way she keeps eyeing me, I'm gonna be in big trouble if she makes a move.

The rest of the night went as smooth as silk, with Kendyl and Kyle assuming the spotlight again, despite the other distraction of his cousin mixing and mingling, too. Quentin did his best to deflect all attention in his younger cousin's direction, but the crowd gravitated toward him until he left. Kyle didn't seem to care too much, having his favorite brother-cousin in the mix with him and bragging about the different records he'd break.

"Yeah, it was fun, but I need a severe recharge from the energy drain tonight," I admit with a sigh. "I'm looking forward to resting as much as possible tomorrow before school on Monday."

"Speaking of draining…what was that about with Ian?"

I guess she wants to get whatever it is that's on her mind out and on the table.

"I don't know what you're talking about."

"Yasir, don't play dumb. I know he was a bit lit tonight, but—"

I already feel my temper flaring over the mere mention of his name. "But what, Z?"

There are a few moments of silence between us, but she's staring me down like she's not gonna let it go. My grip tightens around her hand, a clear sign that there are tensions that still exist between me and Ian. I slow Storm as the traffic light changes from yellow to red, then loosen my grip once we come to a stop. "I honestly thought after everything at the mall and that madness after the Baytown game that he would just roll with things for a bit. What I'm trying to figure out is why he wants me at one of his parties."

"Wait…what?" She sits up in the seat, surprised by my question. "Where did that come from and why does he want you there?"

I shrug as I accelerate through the intersection. "It doesn't make sense, for real. He came at me with Eric earlier in the week, wanting to relieve the pressure between us, and then he came out the blue with a party invitation. He even thanked me for bailing him out."

"So are you planning on going to whatever party he's talking about doing?" she continues. "What type of party is he throwing?"

The answer to her question comes in the form of a notification chiming from both our phones at the same time. Usually when that happens, it's a group message, especially if some of the same people are close by. She checks her IG, and just like that, a whole group message from Ian's IG handle pops up on her screen. "Well, that's interesting."

"What's going on?"

Zahra's scanning the list of people, and she wrinkles her nose as she continues to examine the message. "The number of people being invited isn't really large, maybe around thirty or so, but a lot of Ian's clique are on the list. I also see Kenni and Kyle on the list, along with some of our circles. We've all been invited."

"Doesn't sound like the odds are in our favor." I drum my thumbs against the steering wheel, and I'm playing chess in my head. Something's up. "Is this a good idea to go? I still don't know if I trust him yet."

"It would be a different story if it was a smaller party or something, but it looks like he now wants to go big for his birthday," she explains to me. "Considering what he just saw being done for Kyle, he wanted to try to do something bigger and different. Being out in the Atlantic for a few hours would pretty much do it."

"Outside of you, Kenni, and Kyle, I won't know anyone else at that party." Yeah, this is gonna be a thing. I don't wanna be around strangers where I have to step outside of my comfort zone more than usual. "Sure, I just got to know a few of the other boys, but I'm not sure how… I don't want to feel like I'm being clingy because I'll want to be with you."

Zahra blinks a few times, and she squeezes my hand, mumbling something under her breath that I can't make out. She sighs before she finally utters, "I want you, too. I won't be far from you during the party, I promise. I can barely let you out of my sight as it is."

"Um, Z…I can't…I can't trust what you're saying to me right now, especially when we've been a bit lit tonight." I'm almost grateful that we make it to her house. I'm conflicted over what I really wanna say to her. "I can't afford to, not when things are so confusing between us."

I want to smirk over the way she pushes her bottom lip out, and she's staring me down like that's gonna make me change my mind. She's so damn cute when she does that, but I'm not going for it. Nope. "But we said it was better to wait for now, right? We agreed it was best."

I offer up a half smile, putting Storm in park. "We can talk about it more once we've gotten some sleep. Now, get in the house so you can get settled in. I'll check in on you tomorrow."

"Fine. Can I at least have a kiss good night?" She's insistent, that's for sure. She starts batting her eyes, and I'm still gonna get my way, one way or another. "I'm not trying to confuse things, but I really just want a kiss, please?"

I want to stick to my guns, but I can't resist when she asks like that. I close my eyes as I give in to her request, giving her a few quick kisses across her lips before I get out to make sure she gets to the door in one piece.

"Thank you," she says out of nowhere. "I know I haven't been easy to deal with, but I'm not doing this on purpose, I promise."

I know she's still a little buzzed, so instead of saying anything more, I give her a hug and point her to the door. "I understand, but I don't understand. It's okay, though, I'm getting used to you, and as much as it drives me crazy, I like it a lot. I like *you* a lot."

Zahra gazes up into my eyes, and she nods as she places her hand against my cheek. "I like you a lot, too. So what do we do about this?"

I take her hand and place my lips against her wrist, staring into those beautiful hazel-green eyes, and I say something completely different from what's really in my heart. "Like you said, we like each other, and we want to see where this goes, so let's enjoy what happens, whatever that might be, okay?"

I hate it when this happens. Someone has to take the lead, and neither one of us wants to be the one to do it. This push and pull is wearing us both down, and eventually the dam will break and who knows what will happen after that? Maybe it will be okay, maybe it won't, but I'm too scared to find out.

CHAPTER TWENTY-FOUR

After the past few weekends, where there was always something going on, it's nice to have a chance to breathe and do nothing on a Sunday. Last night was a lot, and I need the break, at least for a few hours, anyway. I plan to catch up on some pleasure reading or maybe check out some shows I've been missing. I'm probably late to the game on some of them, but I've been keeping a pretty busy schedule.

Unk's at the shop, handling a large order for a client in Jacksonville, so having the house to myself is a rarity I don't want to waste. Junk food on deck, something I don't always get to do, since he's on a sugar-restriction kick. Not that I crave anything sweet on a regular basis, but it's nice to have that option from time to time.

I'm just getting the chance to sprawl out on the couch to binge-watch when my phone rings with a number I don't recognize. I grumble, then pick up the call. "Hello? Who's this?"

"Hi, Yasir, this is Ms. Lennox. I hope you don't mind the intrusion. Xavion gave me your number. I told him I wanted to talk with you, if that's okay?"

Now, I have no issues with Unk giving up my number, but he could've at least given me the head's up or something. It smells like a setup. "Sure, I'm game. What's on your mind?"

"Well, I'd prefer having this talk in person. Can you meet me at Fire Street Food in downtown Savannah?"

I pause for a minute, trying to figure out the angle.

She must have noticed my hesitation, because she clears her throat before she says, "It's my treat. I felt like we needed to get a chance to get to know each other a little better."

Yeah, it's a setup, but I don't feel like she's planned anything off-key. She likes Unk, and we've already had this convo. To be honest, she's good for him; the least I can do is find out more about her. It might give me a chance to pick her brain in the process.

So much for resting on a Sunday afternoon.

"Cool, I'll be there. I can't wait to chat."

The oranges and lighter colors inside the restaurant put me in a better mood than I thought I would be, despite the anxiety over talking with Lennox *alone*. So many ideas run through my head over who she is, what draws her to Unk. The possibilities make me dizzy.

I get there about fifteen minutes early so I don't feel rushed, sitting at one of the booths near the entrance, making sure I face the exit as I run through the menu. It's been a habit I picked up when Nana and I went out to dinner at times, and I feel like I need to know who's coming through the door. Nana always said it was the first time she realized that my desire to protect others shaped the person I would become.

I'm not a big sushi fan, but there's enough on the menu for me to eat and not be disrespectful of her choice of location. I don't have much of an appetite anyway, so I order a kiwi and strawberry smoothie. I spend the time waiting for Lennox by people watching, and there's a lot to watch. I settle on a family, a mother and father and their two boys. The way they interact with the small boys triggers a memory I didn't know existed.

I'm with Mommy and Daddy, and we're on a beach watching the tides roll onto the shoreline. I don't recognize it right away, but the feel of the memory…it feels like I'm home. There's someone else there, and I can't make out their face, but it's another boy… He's older than me, I think. We're all wearing a mix of purple, black, and gold clothing, and the smiles on my parents' faces warm me inside unlike anything else has in a long time.

Where did that come from? I don't have any memories of my parents. It doesn't make sense.

"Hi, Yasir, thank you for meeting up with me." Lennox stands just outside the booth, pulling me from my thoughts. "You're a bit early. Have you already ordered?"

I stand up from my seat and wait for her to take her seat before I sit down again. My uncle taught me better than to not stand when a lady needs to be seated. Once we settle in, the waitress takes her drink order as she places my smoothie in front of me. "Not really, I only ordered the smoothie for now. I wanted to have something to drink in case my throat got dry."

She tilts her head slightly to her left, mulling over my response. "Does this make you nervous? That's the last thing I wanted. Would it be better if your uncle was here with us, because I can call him…?"

"Nah, that's all right. He's still handling that Jax order, and I want him to be able to complete it. It's a huge boost for business," I reply, then sip my smoothie. "I'm not always socially adept at things when I'm in public, but it has nothing to do with you being here. Promise."

She smiles, disarming me in seconds. Lennox has that type of vibe that seems to put anyone at ease, whether they want to be or not. She reminds me a lot of Unk's favorite actress, Sanaa Lathan; it makes sense how she caught his attention so quick. I also know my uncle, and it'll take more than good looks to keep him enchanted.

"Good, I'm glad. I was worried I'd gotten off on the wrong foot already." She takes a breath, leaning forward over the table. "So I'm sure you have a ton of questions about me. I'm an open book. Fire away."

"Like that? Oh, say less, then." I grin as I rub my hands together. "How did you and Unk actually link up? I don't remember seeing you at the shop all that much."

"Actually, a friend of mine told me about his shop." She pauses for a moment as the waitress comes with her drink order. She sips a few times and nods before the waitress leaves, focusing her gaze on me again. Sheesh, she has such pretty eyes… Okay, let me stop right now. "I started coming through during my lunch hour a couple of times a week at first, and we traded glances and smiles a few times. Next thing I knew, I was there every day."

"So what do you do for a living?" I don't mean to sound so formal about it, but she said she was an open book, so… "Are you from Savannah?"

"Yeah, he told me once you had a chance to warm up, you'd be a bucket of questions." She giggles and takes another sip of her drink. Even her laugh is easy and light. "I'm an antiquities dealer, but I've been teaching college classes online as of lately, mostly in African Studies. And no, I'm not from Savannah. I was born in Barbados, but my parents moved to the States with my sister and me when I was young."

I study her face a little longer, listening to her voice a few more times in my head. Color me confused. "I never would have been able to tell. You sound like you're from the South, but another part of the South."

"Depends on who you ask. We moved to Miami. Ended up going to school at the University of Miami, too."

I crack up laughing. "Thank goodness I grew up a Bama fan."

"Oh, so you're one of those delusional Tide… You know what, I was just starting to like you."

"Hey, I can't help it if it's no longer 'all about the U' anymore. You need to get you a Nick Saban, ma'am."

"Yeah, I see football season is a laugh riot with you."

I flip the convo back to the original reason we're there. "So are you into Unk? Like, for real, for real? I'm not about to be that kid who gets all attached and then you're gone in less than sixty days."

She stares at me for a few moments, and I'm not sure if I overstepped or not. Yeah, I probably went too far. I withdraw a little bit, waiting for her to give me the "stay in a child's place" speech, bracing for the impact of the words.

Instead, she smirks at me, shaking her head a few times before she sips her drink again. "Yes, I'm very much into your uncle. There's something about him that has me completely enthralled with him. And I understand your need to protect him. He's probably had a lot of women fall for him."

"Umm, I can't speak to that. I've only spent the summers with him before moving down here over a month ago," I admit, sipping more of my smoothie as I choose my words carefully. "You're the first woman he's really had to talk to me about, which says a lot. For a minute, I thought he didn't have no game, but seeing how beautiful you— I'm sorry, should I be complimenting you like that? I mean, I don't want to… Ugh, now I'm overthinking."

Lennox covers my hands with hers, rubbing her thumbs over the backs of my hands. I pull away because I'm trembling so badly, but the warmth of her hands radiates through mine, up my arms to my shoulders, and then down my spine. How the hell is she able to calm me down without so much as a whisper, in a restaurant full of people? I have questions, dammit.

"Don't try to make every interaction with people feel like you have to be perfect or you have to say the right things," she advises, keeping her hands over mine. "Believe me, even adults get it wrong, and we have time and experience on our side."

I nod, not sure what else I can say without feeling like I'm putting my foot in my mouth again. I hate times like these when I want to sound like the silver-tongued devil my uncle is around people, but I end up sounding like I have no basic understanding of simple communication. "Thank you for that. I've been trying to not feel so awkward around girls and women. It seems like it's easier when I'm not trying, but I never know until it comes out of my mouth."

"What about Zahra? The way she was around you when I met her, I'd say you're doing pretty well."

"Yeah, about that." I slip my right hand from her grasp, rubbing the back of my neck to calm down the rising tension. "I don't know how to get out of the friend zone, which is where she seems to want me right now. I'm trying to be, but that's not what my heart wants."

She gives my left hand a gentle squeeze, nodding. "I'm sure it's a confusing time for her, too. I saw the way she looks at you, and

I'll admit I spied on you two when you walked her to the car. That's not how a 'friend' looks at you."

"But every time I try to say something about it, she's all, 'Be patient, I'm not playing games with you.'" I think about the incident with Amber and the way Zahra kissed me, and it irritates me all over again. "Then, if someone even breathes in my direction, she's staking her claim without staking her claim. I don't know whether I'm coming or going sometimes, and as much as it makes me miserable, I can't stop thinking about her."

"I get it, and I promise, it will work itself out, one way or another. She obviously likes you, Yasir, and she might be going through her own insecurities and 'what if' questions in her head, too."

Okay, she's turning into the auntie I never knew I needed. Unk had better keep her around. "I'll try to see things her way, but it hasn't been easy. Every time we're around each other, there's this pull, this connection I can't explain, and I don't want to ignore it when it feels like this."

She gives up that smile again, and I forget all about what I want to say next. Talking with her is the closest thing to talking about things with Mommy, and as selfish as it sounds, I don't want to give that up. "Can I, like, text you when I need to vent? Talking to Unk is one thing, but I don't really have that…how do I say this…I don't have a grown woman who's young enough to understand where I'm coming from, you know?"

She leans in close, close enough to whisper to me without anyone else hearing. "I'd be honored to help in any way I can. To have you want to trust me means more than you know."

Not as much as it means to me, that's for sure. "Good, because I might be leaning on you a lot sooner than you think. Thank you for the chat. I'll save the rest of the questions for another time."

"No worries at all, I'm looking forward to the next time we sit down to talk." She gets up from her chair, grinning when she notices me rise to my feet with her. We leave the money and tip for the bill, then I escort her out to her car. "I have a feeling we'll have more interesting things to discuss the next time around."

CHAPTER TWENTY-FIVE

I don't know what it is about the middle of the week, but it has become a bit of a pattern for us as a group to hook up in the courtyard to figure out what the weekend looks like. With the upcoming yacht party Ian has going this weekend, at least we don't have to worry about where we'll all be going. The unfortunate part is that Zahra and I aren't sure if we're still going or not.

We sit on the benches nearest to the gym, staying as far away from prying ears as possible. Zahra chooses to sit in my lap, a confusing move for me considering what was said the last time we talked. I notice a subtle wink between her and Kendyl, and I have a funny feeling they had a whole other convo that has her making this move. I don't wanna push her off because, well, she knows where I stand, and I can't ignore what my heart wants anymore.

What started out as a simple conversation over when to arrive to board the yacht turns into a whole debate over whether any of us are going at all.

Kyle scowls like the mere thought of being on the boat with Ian will knock his status down a few notches. "So we're gonna forget about the grandstanding at my party, right? Or what about the subtle shots at my ace at every given opportunity? He's flexing, and I'm not going for it like he's on my level."

Zahra chimes in, and I hear every drop of bias in her tone. "Ky, you're right, but he might just be trying to keep the spotlight on him more than anything. It's on brand for him, you know?"

"Yeah, but something's still not feeling right about any of this." Kyle takes a sip of his water bottle. Kendyl sits next to him, rubbing his shoulders. I can sense the tension in him, too, and I wonder if something else is going on that we don't know about. "If we do go," Kyle says, "I'm staying in the open areas on the boat. Rumors are already rocking about others who are supposed to be there that aren't from Oakwood Grove."

I nod. "I get that, but you're sounding paranoid. There's nothing happening at the party, just like no drama went down at yours."

"We kept the guest list tight and away from random folks, bestie," Kyle scoffs. "The wild part about all this is he's been real loose with the invites. He's trying to play himself like he's got reach."

Zahra goes silent for a moment, and I focus on her to make sure she's okay. She returns my gaze with a nod and a half smile, then whispers in my ear, "I need to talk to you when we're done with the crew."

I mouth, "I do, too," before I turn back to the debate. "Aye, look, a lot of this is still out of my depth, so I'm not gonna pretend that I know the best move to make here. Kyle's got a point, though—Ian's been a bit more hyper than usual. Maybe he's angling for something, maybe he's just trying to top what Kyle did for his birthday party, but it's obvi to me that he's intent on keeping the spotlight focused on him."

Kendyl turns to Kyle. "I get what you're saying, and we can still find a way to get what we want while keeping out of the drama. As long as we stay tight and among ourselves, we could survive this and have a whole reason to people watch and be nosy for the hell of it." She kisses Kyle across each cheek and his forehead, and I legit watch him soften up fast. "If one of us leaves the group while at the party, then a wingman goes with them. It will keep what happened to Yasir at your party from happening this weekend."

"I'm feeling that," I co-sign. "Although I know if any of the girls go, y'all are all going together. We're not that naive."

Kyle and I get a good chuckle out of that quip, but it's not like I'm wrong. Kyle taps my fist, dropping a peck on Kendyl's lips before he shifts back to the rest of us. "All right, let's run with that plan. I'm still not with going, but we can at least stay insulated and protected while we're there."

Zahra kisses me, then rises from my lap. "I need to talk to my girl for a minute. I'll meet up with you later?"

"Yeah, I need to drop by Unk's shop to see if there's anything he needs. Meet me there so we can talk?"

"I'll meet you there."

Zahra opts to leave Raiden in the parking lot in front of Unk's store, then jumps into Storm and settles in the passenger seat, directing me to a secluded spot so we can be alone. I don't want to sound nervous while we ride, but I can't stop trembling in anticipation of the conversation.

We stop at Prentiss Park, a location she says she uses whenever she wants to be alone to create music. We get out of the car and walk to one of the empty pavilions to sit and talk. I'm carrying one of my parkas with us, since we're in a wooded area in the park and the weather has turned cooler than expected.

She wraps herself inside the fabric and inhales, closing her eyes like she's being transported. She sighs as she exhales, turning her gaze to my curious stare.

"Look," she says. "After what happened last weekend, and before we go to Ian's party, we should be a united front, you know? I'm just gonna come out and say it before I lose my nerve—I'm ready to be your girlfriend, if you still want me to be."

Okay, so I was *not* prepared for that to come out of her mouth.

She takes my hand, and I know she can feel my heartbeat pulsing through my grip, which seems to sync with her own pulse's rapid pace. I'm trying to get the words to come out, but they're stuck in my throat.

"I—I mean, are you—yes, of course I want you to be my girlfriend." The way I stammer out the words before I finally smooth out my tone, by Nyati, I swear I sound like a whole sappy greeting card. "I'm serious. Are you sure, no cap?"

"No cap, cuteness." She leans in and kisses me deep and slow. "I want us to be together."

"Now I feel like what I needed to talk about kinda pales by comparison." I lick my lips to moisten them, pausing for a moment as I continue to stare into her eyes. "My nana wants to see me this weekend, and she's asked if you could come with me to visit."

She blinks more than a few times, and I almost wanna take back what I said. "Well, that was sudden. Why this weekend? What's the rush? Wait a minute, is she ready to have that talk about where you come from?"

"I understand if it's too soon. I can tell her we'll come up another time if you want." Yeah, I need to backtrack, although a little quicker than I wanted, but—yeah, I mean, we'd just solidified our relationship seconds ago. "I know you said you wanted to go when we were just friends, but this is something completely different now. You're my girl now."

She acts like she wants to take off my parka, fanning herself like she's gotten hot all of a sudden. She adjusts quicker than I expect, too. "I still wanna go, baby. I promised I would help you see this through. What time do you want to head up there?"

"I wanna make it a day trip, get down and back before nightfall so we have enough time to prep for the party on Sunday night," I tell her. I can't stop staring at her, making her blush and bury her face inside my coat. "You're my girl. You have no idea how long I've been waiting to say that."

"Well, get used to it, pretty boy, because I'm yours."

I don't want to sound like I'm all doom and gloom, but this is coming out of nowhere, and as much as I'm happy that we can finally define what we are now, I can't escape this nagging feeling in the pit of my stomach.

I just hope I'm wrong for a change.

CHAPTER TWENTY-SIX

I've only been gone from the A for six weeks.

Six weeks feels like years to me.

Everything in the A that I remember as we travel up I-75 to get to my nana's exit…well, it looks different for some reason. Maybe it has more to do with getting used to Oakwood Grove than anything. Still, by the time we exit and head up University Avenue to turn into her neighborhood—Pittsburgh community—I've settled back into my groove.

Paradise Drive is only a few turns away. The only place I've ever known and felt safe.

The row of houses on that dead-end street come with an interesting story I was told when I was younger. The houses used to occupy the land where the highway exists today. So the city and the state governments, according to Nana's neighbors, negotiated to have all the houses on the street relocated. The foundations were extracted, set up on blocks, moved to their new plots of land, and resettled.

I always thought it was a cool, but irritating, piece of history. Nana wasn't around for all of that, so she didn't quite share my irritation. Still, whether by divine invention or just the pure goodness of the people, that street managed to be a haven of sorts for anyone who lived there and for those who visited. Almost as though the minute you turn onto the street, it becomes a "fortress" of sorts, like nothing else matters, and you can leave your troubles at the corner. I don't know how else to explain it. Chaos may swirl in the rest of the Pittsburgh community, but it never touches "paradise."

Maybe that's what I miss most…feeling safe despite everything.

Zahra and I had been vibing the entire drive, stealing glances during the five-hour trip, stopping in Macon to grab some food and gas up. I make a mental note to grab the special fuel blend I have at Nana's when we get there, since I only run Storm's engine on ethanol blends when I don't have time to mix the fuel for longer road trips.

I keep glancing at her, grinning over the beauty who's making herself comfortable in the passenger seat, playing with the music selection that became the soundtrack for the trip. I can't believe she's here with me. I mean, yeah, she said she wanted to go a while ago, but this…this hits different.

"Your whole energy is different, baby." Zahra breaks through my thoughts as we make the final turn before hitting Nana's street. "It's aggressive, edgy."

"Oh, really? How do you mean?"

"It feels like you had to match the vibe surrounding us. I noticed you started scanning the area more, like you were putting your head on a swivel to see every angle you could." She keeps studying me like she's never seen me before a day in her life. It makes me a little uncomfortable, but I adjust quick. "I'm trying to decide if I like this look on you…ruffneck."

I hide my grin. Okay, let's stop playing, I can't hide my grin, and I don't want to, either. She has a point without realizing it. I kinda remade myself a little bit because I didn't want my past to follow me to Oakwood Grove. What I failed to account for was having to come back home, and with someone who never knew or had seen that other side of me.

I shrug off those thoughts as I wink at her. "I hope once you've seen this side of me, you don't go running for the hills."

She leans over and kisses my cheek, sending waves of heat down my spine. "I'm a big girl. I'd like to think I can handle a few things."

"You haven't met my nana yet."

We pull into the driveway, making sure to turn the music down low. While Zahra is confused over my insistence, she doesn't understand what the streets already know. If anyone came to Ms. Johari's house for anything, the music had to be turned down or turned off. She always said it upsets the ancestors who commune with her, but I know better.

I take a deep breath once I put the car in park, gripping the gearshift tighter than I planned. I've been asking, and asking, since I was thirteen, to find out about my family tree. Now that the moment is here, I want to back out. The unknown is freaking me out, and I fear whatever it is that she might have to tell me.

I feel a soft, soothing hand cover mine while it remains on the gearshift. When I shift my gaze, her eyes pierce through to the very core of my being. I can't tear myself away, even if I want to. "It will be okay, promise." She rubs her fingers across the back of my palm, sending shockwaves through my arm. "This was a long time coming, and you're ready for this."

I get out of the car, moving around the back to the passenger side to make sure Zahra hops out in one piece. Okay, so I want to sneak a kiss in before we walk up the stairs arm-in-arm to the front door. I'm gonna have to calm down. I'm about to introduce a girl to my grandmother for the *first time* in my life, on top of learning information that has the potential to shift my whole life.

Even though I have a key, I ring the doorbell and step back to wait for her to go through her usual routine. I look to my left, where I notice the familiar rustling of the curtains, suppressing a smirk because I know what comes next. I'm not prepared for how far she's about to go, though.

"Now, why would my grandson ring the doorbell when he knows he has a key?" she shouts through the heavy, lacquered, and polished oak door. Her accent comes through with all the richness of a thick batch of molasses. Man, I miss her so much in this moment. "I do not think I should open the door, since I was not expecting any strange visitors today."

"Nana, I would have used my key, but I have a special guest

with me." I chuckle, cutting my eyes at Zahra, who stifles a giggle of her own at the spectacle we're putting on in front of her. "I know my grandmother would prefer that I make formal introductions before she welcomed the special guest into the house."

"They had better be special, or I am giving them the business."

"Nana, come on. Why would I bring someone to the house if they weren't special?"

"You have a good point, grandson." Nana taps her knuckles against the other side of the door. "They had better be pretty, or I will disown you. And you better be wearing your necklace, or I will have another reason to cut you out of my will."

Zahra breaks out into laughter, bracing one hand against the wall and holding her stomach with the other. "I love her already. She got you shook."

"Nana, I would never go anywhere without my necklace." I roll my eyes, intent on breaking through the stonewall she insists on throwing in front of me. She knows I don't go anywhere without my amethyst teardrop necklace. That's a karma I don't want. "She's stunning, and she's also the one I told you about."

"Wait…what?" Zahra whispers in my ear. "You told her I was coming with you? I thought this was a surprise."

Nana opens the door in grand fashion, causing both of us to jump. She gives me the once-over, then throws a sideways glance at Zahra. "Oh well, since you put it that way, let me get a good look at her for myself, make sure you are not slipping."

"Nana!"

"What? I have to make sure that you have good taste in girls, Ya-Ya."

Zahra keeps laughing at the "show" my grandmother puts on, unable to stop, even with her standing in front of us on the other side of the wrought-iron outer door. I want to die on the spot. This is not the way I envisioned things to go at all. "Oh em gee," Zahra says. "This was worth the trip and then some. I can't wait to find out what happens next."

I clear my throat so I can get my life together. "Nana, I would like to introduce my girlfriend, Zahra Assante. Z, this is my Nana, Mrs. Johari Salah, known in the neighborhood as Ms. Johari or Mama Johari."

Zahra blushes for a moment, extending her hand out to shake. "It's a pleasure to meet you, Ms. Johari. Yasir has told me a lot about you."

Nana takes a long look at Zahra, and her eyes light up. In the next moment, she rushes us inside, taking Zahra by the shoulders and studying her like she's connecting the dots in her mind. This smile…I mean, this *smile*…shows up out of nowhere. I have no clue what to make of it, and Zahra looks a little uneasy the whole time.

Nana keeps going into this trance, like she's looking through her and off into the distance. Her hands start trembling, and I do what I can to calm her. I don't want Zahra completely freaking out. First impressions and all that.

By the time I get the chance to shake Nana out of whatever is happening to her, she just snaps right out of it. Her gaze is strange, like she doesn't want to say what she's seen, but there's no way I'm about to let that ride. In the next moment, her facial expression turns again, and this time she's all smiles again. "You are Kua tribe, aren't you, little one?"

Zahra's eyes flash, and I stand there confuzzled as all get out. "Yes, ma'am, I am. But how did…?"

"Yeah, Nana, how in the world could you have figured that out just by staring at her?" Why do I get the feeling this all ties into a lot of what she wants to talk about? "And what's that whole thing you just did where you blanked out on us? I think we need to sit down, for real for real."

She ushers us into the living room, moving with a sense of urgency that triggers my anxiety. She takes each of our hands in hers, grinning the whole time as she sees the two of us together. "Yes, baby, we do… I had no idea… Please, you two, make yourself comfortable on the couch. I will grab some sweet tea and lemon and explain as much as I can."

. . .

We've spent the last two hours talking about my life in Kindara, and I'm sitting here reacting like all the things that happened that night before I was brought to Nana were happening to someone else. Every word she speaks feels like I'm sinking deeper and deeper into a rabbit hole, with no chance of coming out of it as anywhere near the same person. Nana has been an oral storyteller her entire life, so everything that comes from her sounds like it was written for fiction.

Except not one word of it is fiction.

"You, your parents, and your older brother, were selected by the Kindaran Council to be a part of the Kindaran Nine families." Nana began weaving the next part of the fascinating tale that is my life. "You were charged with knowing the location of, and protecting, the sacred Kutokufa Scrolls, because the Vodaran priestesses who brought you into the world saw what the Divine Mother had gifted you."

My head is spinning, trying to make sense of everything she's told me and Zahra so far.

My parents were…*murdered*?

My bloodline is Kindaran, and I wasn't born in the States.

I have—or had—a big brother?

I was supposed to die that night during an invasion—the Bralba invasion.

"That night was one of the worst nights of my life," Nana continued, wiping tears from her eyes like it all happened last week, much less over ten years ago. "Hassan brought you to me and gave the devastating news that my son—your father—and your mother had been killed to protect you and get you out."

"What happened to my…my brother?" I ask her, doing my best to keep my hands from shaking. "Has anyone been able to find him?"

"No, my child, Bomani—your older brother—was a part of the Kindaran military at the time of the invasion," Nana answers as she continues to rock in her chair. "I fear he is dead, possibly killed during the invasion. When efforts were being made to identify the bodies in the aftermath, the only thing found was his identification tags around the neck of a body found outside of Drana Tirin."

Tears streak down my face, and I'm sad and confused at the same time. Somewhere deep in my core, I feel the loss of family, another person who could've helped me figure out who I am. I just can't figure out why I'm so distraught over it. I don't remember him—except for a memory triggered out of the blue before I met with Ms. Lennox for lunch a few days ago.

But she still doesn't explain why she blanked out into a trance when she held Zahra's hand. That's gonna bother me for a minute, but I'm in too much shock from the other revelations to pay any attention to it right now.

"I know that this is a lot for you to take in one day, but I promise, we will take everything one step at a time, one day at a time." Nana leans in, taking my hands in hers, focusing her gaze into my eyes. "I am sorry that I could not tell you before now, but there is a reason we had to keep the truth from you."

I force tears back as best I can. It's more than I thought I'd hear, and more than I can handle in one short burst. I wanted to know, but now I don't know what to do with it all.

"So I'm…Kindaran? Like, I'm from the same country as you, as Zahra?" I struggle to get the words out. It's not every day that your world, your history, is split into pieces and put back together again to look like a whole other picture you're struggling to understand. "So what Tribe… Is that right? What Tribe are we from?"

"We are Solara Tribe, my darling." She keeps rubbing my hands, but I can't stop shaking. "And unfortunately, we were ground zero for one of the worst atrocities in Kindaran history."

"By Nyati…Solara was where everything happened." Zahra gasps and clamps her hand over her mouth. I'd almost forgotten that Zahra sat right beside me while she listened to everything I heard coming from Nana. It doesn't even register for me over what she might be thinking right now. "My father is a Kindaran historian.

I've read about what happened, and I was a little girl when we were evacuated to the States, but I never thought I would ever meet anyone who survived the attacks. We were told that everyone was killed."

"Well, my dear girl, as you now realize, that was not the case." Nana nods as she glances at her. "I have a feeling your father and I may need to have a longer conversation. If for nothing else, we may need to update his recollection of historical data."

"So I have another question," I interject. My head is still spinning, and I try to find some way to balance. "What about what I told you about the way my eyes turned red? And Zahra said she saw my eyes turn purple when we were alone. What does that mean? Is there something wrong with me?"

"No, there is nothing wrong with you at all, of that I am certain." Nana's eyes smile before the rest of her face follows. She places her hand against my cheek. "Nyati has placed something special inside you. What that is, and why the Divine Mother chose you, even I do not know. But I do know how to find out. I will contact Hassan. He has been on a separate mission for the Kindaran Council."

"Who's Hassan? Is he part of…the Solara Tribe? Or was he part of another Tribe in Kindara?" It sounds so foreign to me, the way it's coming out of my mouth. I have to get used to saying it, though… It's my heritage now. "Does he know where our kin who survived might be? Does anyone else know if they are still alive and if they know my parents? I have so many questions."

Nana closes her eyes for a moment, clasping her hands together and mumbling something I can't make out. When she opens her eyes, I can tell it pains her to have to explain things. "We had to… tell a different story…for the Solara Tribe to have a chance to rebuild. The truth of what happened there could only be entrusted to the Kindaran Council and the elder Vodaran priestesses. Not even Hassan knows the whole truth. All he was told was to find you and get you somewhere safe. That's how you were brought to me that night."

"But if I lived there, how am I not able to remember? I keep having these strange dreams that don't make sense to me." I blink a few times to try to access some of the images to describe to her. "I mean, I kept seeing different parts of the island, and I thought I'd never been there before. I even told Zahra that I didn't know the island, and I still don't know if I do or don't."

"A priestess suppressed your memories. As I was told by Hassan, the man who brought you to me, you were in so much shock, you could not speak," she replies, wiping a tear from her eye. "She warned that you might still have nightmares of that night, but we had hoped that they would not happen at all, at least until we had time to prepare you for what I have told you today."

"How soon can he get here? It sounds like he holds the key to a lot of my past, and I need to know it ASAP."

"These things take time. I do not know where he is on the planet right now. If I can get him to come to Georgia, I will tell him to come as soon as possible," Nana says. She leans back in her chair, rubbing her hands together. "There was no way to know when your subconscious might awaken. Now that we know it has, we need to unlock what has been hidden from you."

"Did you or Unk know what's going on with me?" I narrow my gaze, unsure of what answer I'll get from her. "Did you know the truth and keep it from me?"

"Ya-Ya, baby, take a breath, okay?" Zahra rubs my shoulders. I knew I was tense, but considering the information being laid at my feet, I feel like exploding. "We will get you through this, but you need to breathe. Breathe with me, slow and steady."

"I need answers, that's what I need." I massage my temples, feeling Zahra's hands moving to my back. "I'm not sure why I'm even asking. Who knows how much more of this I can handle right now? Everywhere I've been, I've felt like I was out of place. Now, I kinda know why, but I don't know why."

I feel Zahra's lips against my cheek, and she hums a tune in my ear, pulling me closer to her so only I can hear it. It's so hypnotic, so soothing, I almost forget where we are. Our eyes meet when I turn to face her, and she doesn't speak a word; the only thing I hear is the tune she continues to hum. I take deeper breaths, falling into a Zen-like trance, concentrating on what I hear more than anything.

She smiles as she hums, her eyes darting back and forth. I wonder if she notices something in my eyes and pray they don't change colors again. I'm already hanging by a thread. The last thing I need is to have something else that I can't explain.

Zahra places an index finger against my lips, her silent cue to stop worrying over whatever is happening to me. It's easy for her to say. She's not the one whose eyes are glowing… Who knows what hue they are this time around?

The moment she stops singing, a cloud lifts from my mind. I grin at her, mouthing "thank you" as I caress her cheek. She whispers, "We'll handle this, I promise."

"Yes, that is what I thought." Nana claps softly over what she's witnessed. "The gods placed you where you needed to be for their own reasons, and this is one of them, Ya-Ya."

Zahra smirks a bit, shaking her head a few times as she waits for me to give her any idea that I'm okay. I nod, placing a small kiss across her lips. "I wouldn't exactly say the gods had anything to do with it, Ms. Johari. Your grandson is quite the charmer. He had my attention from the moment he stepped on campus."

Nana doesn't say anything. She just continues to stare at us, crossing her arms over her chest. "My dear girl, first, you no longer have to call me Ms. Johari. It's Nana. Second, there is a fine line between coincidence and fate. Only time will tell if the gods were right or not."

I check my watch, realizing we better head out and make a few more stops before we make the drive back to the Grove. More than likely, the streets have already caught wind that I'm back, and it's only a matter of time before certain people check in to make sure I know that they know.

I kiss Nana's cheek, giving her a long hug, smiling when she returns my hug and squeezes Zahra so tight, I think she won't be able to breathe. "Now, I expect for you to come back and see me sometime. There is so much more we need to discuss, you hear?"

"Yes, Nana, I hear you." Zahra giggles as she takes my hand to leave. "I promise, we will have more conversations soon. I have to find out more embarrassing stories about Ya-Ya, and you're the perfect person to get that from."

"Yeah, nah, it's time to go, for real." I pull her to the door, coming close to picking her off the ground to carry her to Storm. "We have some other things to do and people to see."

"Yes, you do, Ya-Ya. You've been gone too long, and you might need to get things back in balance." Nana winks as she sits in her favorite rocking chair on the porch. "Things have been a bit off for the past few weeks."

Zahra's ears perk up, turning her attention to my concerned expression. "What does she mean by that? Is there something you're not telling me?"

The distinctive rumble of several engines catches my ear. It's faint at first, but the sounds get louder within minutes. I can deal with them if I'm by myself, but having Zahra with me complicates things, and there's no way I can talk my way out of the situation. Not when *she's* with them.

A few minutes later, the line of muscle cars, a mix of Mustangs, Camaros, and Chargers, pop up in front of Nana's driveway. Zahra surprises me by stepping in front of me, almost like she wants to protect me. Nana notices it, too, but all she does is continue to rock in her chair. If she had access, I'm sure she would have a bowl of popcorn in her lap, ready to watch whatever is about to unfold.

Dante exits from his Charger, walks around the front, and leans against the hood. The rest of the Squad follow his lead, blocking the driveway—and our ability to leave.

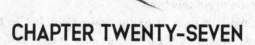

CHAPTER TWENTY-SEVEN

"**W**hat in the *Fast and the Furious* is going on out here?" Zahra remarks as they all leave their vehicles, crowding us while we lean against the front of Storm. "This is a little gaudy for my taste, but who am I to criticize?"

I wanna say she's biased because she's been around Storm for a while now, but the display of chrome, low-profile tires, and twenty-eight-inch rims can be a bit over the top for some. Judging from the unbothered expression on her face, it's safe to say she's not impressed.

Zahra's already in front of me before they come to a stop, and while I don't blame her for wanting to protect me, I think it's better if I deal with this head on. I like the ride-or-die side of her, but this ain't the time to be spoiling for a fight.

I'm trying to figure out why they look like they got pressure, though. Their collective expressions make it seem like I've done something to piss them all off. I have no idea what the hell that could've been. The only thing left is to let the convo play itself out, since it's obvious someone has something to get off their chest.

I wrap my arms around Zahra, inserting my thumbs inside her jean pockets. I feel a surge between us, and I'm not gonna lie, I don't want that to go away any time soon. She slips her hands over mine as I focus my attention on my Squad. "Dante, what's good, my boy? I told you I'd come holla when I was done visiting with Nana."

"Yeah, well, I figured we'd bring the party to you, in case you decided to, shall we say, take a few detours." Dante's sounding a lot more aggressive than usual, which has me a bit taken aback.

"Seeing the little baddie in front of you acting like she's gonna protect you, I guess that might explain why you've been MIA for the past few weeks."

I squeeze her a little tighter, a knee-jerk reaction to the agitation I feel coursing through me. A low growl escapes my throat, and I notice Zahra's caressing my hands to keep me calm. *Yeah, good luck with that.* "Forgive my manners. I'd planned on making more formal intros in a different way. Zahra, this is the Squad I told you about. The boys in the back are my brothers, Malik and Caleb; the girls in front of them are Dominique and Alyssa. And of course, my Day One, Dante."

I'm not feeling the way Malik and Caleb are eyeing me with every ounce of heat on them, but I'm keeping my temper in check. They know not to try me unless they just want to get put down. Alyssa catches my eye, and the malice in her stare is both confusing and concerning. She's the last person I expected to feel some type of way about anything.

Dante, as usual, takes the lead on how things are about to flow. He looks past us, waving toward Nana to acknowledge her. "Hi, Nana, how are you doing this afternoon?"

"Things are fine, baby. I am hoping that you and the Squad were coming by to have a civil conversation." I hear her still rocking in her chair, subtly setting the tone for how she expects everyone to act in front of her. Watching everyone straighten up when she speaks gives me a little hope that this can end without any animosity.

"Yes, ma'am, I guess the Squad and I wanted to make sure we didn't miss him this time. There's no telling when he might be able to come through again," Dante explains as he returns his glare in my direction.

"Okay, well, I will head back into the house. I have some other business to attend to," Nana says as she slowly rises from her rocker and shuffles inside. "Make sure you let me know when you leave, grandson."

The moment the iron door closes behind her, any hope I have goes up in smoke.

"When have I not been a man of my word, Te?" I still don't move, but I'm vibrating so intensely I feel a stronger squeeze against my hands to let me know Zahra's still with me. "I said what I said when I texted you. There were some things I needed to talk to Nana about, and it would take some time."

"Chalk it up to some within the circle who felt they wanted some sort of closure," Dante says to me. He turns around and looks at Alyssa—who still hasn't wiped the scowl off her face—in a not-so-subtle attempt to explain who has the most pressure to release. "Since you had to skip out of the city at a moment's notice, right?"

"So you wanna do this here, huh? Real classy, but I guess I shouldn't be surprised." I remove my hands from Zahra's waist, then step around to the passenger side of Storm and take her hand to follow me. I lean against the door, motioning the rest of the group to come closer. "So let's get this over with. I ain't got all day."

"Yasir, you don't have to do this right now, okay?" Zahra interrupts. "We've been through a lot over the last few hours, and you don't want to say anything that you'll regret."

"It's cool, baby, they have pressure they need to release, so we can get that handled and let the chips fall where they may." I keep my grip on her hand, pulling her closer to me. "I'd hoped to do this somewhere else, but here we are."

"Yeah, here we are, and from the looks of things, she doesn't look like much. I don't care what Te says." Alyssa frowns as she steps in front of Zahra. "Damn, Ya-Ya, I thought you had better taste than this."

"Ally, stop being salty for no reason," I retort. I follow Zahra's gaze, realizing she hasn't taken her eyes off Alyssa the whole time. She's flexing her fingers to keep from balling them up. Yeah, she's spoiling for a fight. "I told you before I left that we were better off as friends. Why are you popping off like this?"

"Is that what you're trying to convince yourself of what happened that night, bro?" Alyssa scoffs at me, which trips Zahra's triggers to respond in kind. "Don't flex in front of your 'girl,' playa. We know you better than she does, trust."

I take a sharp breath, tapping my fist against Storm's hood. "Whatever Ally told you about that night, I'm telling you right here and now, that's not what went down, all right?"

"Why don't you do us a favor and tell us what happened from your point of view, then, Diablo?" Dante spits out. "Because you know the drill, and you know how things rock within Squad, too."

"Wait a minute, what are they talking about, Yasir?" Zahra pipes up. *Dammit.* "What happened between you and Alyssa? She's looking like—"

"Oh, don't act like you're concerned now, shawty," Alyssa cuts her off. "But let me tell you about the boy you're dealing with so you can make up your own mind. Yasir—the boy we all lovingly know as Diablo—was willing to risk betraying Squad by getting with me before he had to leave, knowing it would screw things up."

"That's not what happened, and you know it, Ally." My pulse is racing, and I can feel my temper intensifying to a level I won't be able to control. "You pushed the issue while we were working on your ride. I never gave you any idea that I was interested in anything. That's bad for business."

"So you didn't try to stop me when we were kissing that night?" Alyssa throws in that tidbit, watching Zahra's reaction with a smirk. "You didn't tell me to put my clothes back on, either."

"Yes, I did. You were upset because I didn't tell you before I told Squad about what happened and that I had to leave ASAP." I keep my voice as even as I can, even though I'm raging inside. This is getting way out of hand, and I'm catching too much smoke. "You'd been drinking when you came over, and I even made you sleep in my room while I crashed on the couch because I was scared you weren't thinking clearly."

"You took advantage of my feelings for you and promised me once you got where you were going that you would come back for me!" Alyssa screams. "I was willing to be with you over Squad because you told me you loved me. And like a fool, I believed you."

"Wait…what the hell?" Zahra twists around and stares at me. She searches my eyes like she's looking for the truth. "Is any of what she's saying true? Do you have feelings for her?"

"No—"

Dante inserts himself into our exchange, leaning against the front of Storm's hood. "You're like a brother to me, Yasir, and even I had a hard time believing Ally for a minute, but it made sense when I thought back on it. You were gone only hours after you told me you had to jet. Then Nique called me, saying that Ally was at her house, crying her eyes out."

"You're bugging out, Te. I don't know what conclusion you think you've come to, but that's not what happened, dammit," I flat-out state. "She tried to kiss me, that part is true, but I smelled the alcohol on her breath, bro. I made her sleep it off, and then—"

"And then you were gone by morning, right? And you left her in Nana's house alone and confused," Dante points out, turning his attention to Zahra, who still looks confuzzled. "Real talk, I'm sorry you had to hear about your boy like this, but he's not who you think he is. He's just like me and the rest of the boys in the crew. We're players, which is why we all agreed that Nique and Ally were like sisters and off-limits."

"I didn't have a choice in the matter, don't you get that?" I insist as I rub the back of my neck. I silently count down from ten to get my life together. "I tried to stay until morning to make sure she'd sobered up, but Nana rushed me out the door because there were some— You know what? Never mind. Nothing I say will change your minds."

"You're right, and the fact that you're trying to drop Nana in the middle of your bullshit is low, even for you, especially when she isn't out here to speak for herself." Dante jumps in my face, but he forgets who I am. I don't even blink or flinch. My nickname is Diablo for a reason. "I don't know if you're even Squad anymore if you're gonna act like you didn't do anything."

"Then I guess I'm not Squad, but I'm not gonna sit here and cop to something I didn't do," I counter. I feel like things are slipping away from me, and I don't know how it's happening. "If you can't trust me as your Day One, big bro, then there's nothing more for us to say."

"Yeah, I can't trust you, and I expected more from you, to at least be a man so we can squash this and move on." Dante steps away from me, making the motion for everyone to get back to their cars. "When you're ready to come clean, shout and I'll listen. I owe you that much to hear you out as my Day One. Until then, don't holla."

They all get in their cars, leaving the front of the house one by one until the street is clear. Not one of them even bothers to say goodbye.

"Yasir, I-I need to know what happened. Are you willing to talk to me about it?" I hear Zahra's trembling voice, but I already know she's upset. I just don't know if there's anything I can do to ease her mind.

My eyes are closed so tightly I can almost see colors behind my eyelids. My jaw is clenched to the point that my muscles twitch. "I'll tell you everything you wanna know. It's not pretty, but it's the truth, I promise."

It takes me about an hour of driving before I can calm down long enough to say anything regarding that night. We're not entirely quiet during that time. I mean, we still talked about everything else that happened with Nana. Zahra's being patient with me, which I appreciate more than she knows, and I'm doing my best to figure out the best way to explain myself.

"Alyssa and I started out as friends. She became friends with me when I first got to Douglass, the last school I attended before I came to Oakwood," I begin, switching between glancing at her and keeping my eyes on the road. "I'd kept her at arm's length for nearly the entire semester, but she never gave up on trying to be my friend."

"Go on, baby," she encourages me.

"Once I got over my anxiety of dealing with anyone outside of

Squad, things took off fast between us. She became a best friend of sorts, helping me learn Doug and how things flowed, helping me with homework. We bonded over her Mustang and Storm. I learned how to work on her car, and she learned Storm." I breathe a sigh of relief, but my hands never leave the steering wheel. I'm still on edge because I don't know what she's thinking. "Eventually, I introduced her to Squad, and it actually felt good to have her there. Nique was already Squad, so having another girl for her to vibe with, it felt like a win-win, you know."

Zahra turns her body toward me as we cruise down the highway, her focus solely on me. She still isn't saying a lot, which ramps up my anxiety and then some.

"Before the school year started, Nana had been getting these strange calls, and she told me it was nothing at first, so I didn't pay any attention." I groan in frustration, irritated that my hindsight is kicking in long enough to let me know how stupid I had been. "Then I overheard a tense convo one night when she thought I was asleep. She was angry—like, white-hot angry—and told whoever was on the phone that it wasn't fair to put me through it again."

"Put you through what again?" she chimes in with the lead question.

"Before I finally settled at Doug, I had a history of temperamental outbursts, getting into fights, all that." I turn on the windshield wipers as we're riding through an unexpected rainstorm and tap the brakes to disengage the cruise control. "I'd moved through so many schools, I'd lost track over the years, but Nana managed to help me through it. I eventually found boxing through Unk, and I was starting to even out and not let my temper get the best of me. I was so angry about my parents and everything that came with it."

"What about the night that Ally was talking about, the night I assume you two had sex?" She sounds like she choked on those words, like it hurt to even say them out loud. "What really happened?"

"Ally and I never had sex, and that's the truth." The force of my words bounce off the windows in the cabin. "But thinking back on it now, I guess I see why she might have thought so."

"What do you mean?"

"That whole night was a nightmare," I recall as we weave through traffic. "Nana called me, panicked, and said that I needed to get some clothes together and be ready to leave at any moment. She was out of town, and I was home alone. When I asked her what was wrong, she wouldn't tell me anything, just that I needed to be ready to head down to Unk's when she called again. None of it made any sense."

She's completely enthralled with the story I'm spinning, and I promise, if I wasn't the main character, I'd be on the edge of my seat, too. "Keep going, baby. I'm still listening."

"I told her I had stuff to do the next morning, and she said that I had to cancel it all and tell whoever I needed that I had to leave the city. She hung up before I could ask anything further." I blink a few times, taking my right hand off the wheel. The rainstorm starts to let up, so I accelerate to keep up with the traffic around us. "I ended up calling Te, telling him that I had to leave town and that I couldn't explain right then. We had a tense exchange, but I stuck to my story and told him I'd explain when I got settled where I was headed."

Zahra nods, silently letting me know she's locked in.

"While I was getting some clothes together, thinking it would be nothing more than a weekend trip, someone was banging on the door. Not knowing who would be at the house after midnight, I grabbed the stun gun and headed for the door." I stare straight ahead, gritting my teeth. I don't want to remember the rest of this night. "I heard Ally's voice, yelling for me to let her in. Her eyes were red, and she looked like she'd been crying. I asked her what was wrong, and she yelled at me, asking me why I was leaving Squad—and leaving her."

"Did you kiss her?"

"She tried to kiss me, yes, but I smelled the alcohol on her breath. I assumed she'd gotten the call from Te and got upset. She kept yelling at me, telling me that I should have told her myself, that she shouldn't have heard it from him." I blow out a sharp breath, taking a few calming breaths where I can. "She started crying again, and I went to hug her to try and settle her down. I kept telling her that I couldn't explain what was going on but that I would tell her myself when I got where I was going. She had her arms wrapped around my neck, and when I tried to break from our embrace, she reached up and tried to kiss me."

"Okay, pause, baby, take a breath," Zahra says to me, but I wonder if *she* needs the break. "How did it go from her trying to kiss you to her saying that you didn't tell her to put her clothes back on?"

"When I made her sleep in my room, and I grabbed some blankets and a pillow to sleep in the living room, Nana called again. Ally was half naked by the time I got back to her," I utter. I'm getting exhausted reliving this whole thing. "I told her that Ally was there, and she said she would be there before Ally woke up, and she would explain everything to her after I left, but I needed to go right then and there because they had found me."

"Who's 'they'? Who found you?"

"Beats the hell out of me. It wasn't until I got to Unk's that I got part of the story that tied into the oils and scents I'd been mixing and that it was to keep whoever wanted me dead from finding me." I shrug, pausing for a few more seconds before I pick up where I left off. "When I tried to call Ally back to make sure she was okay, she said she hated me and didn't want to see me again. It wasn't until I called Te back to give him the update that he asked about what went down with me and Ally and said that she was upset about what happened at the house."

"So for the past few weeks, while you and I were trying to figure things out, you left all that going on without trying to make it right?" she asks me.

"She wouldn't take my calls, Z."

"What about Te?"

"He told me to give it time to blow over and that he would work on Ally to get her to at least hear me out."

"So that means you never tried after she stopped taking your calls."

I snap my head in her direction, my eyes widening as I notice her irritation. "What could I have done? I can't force someone to talk to me, baby."

"Would you have given up on me so easily?"

"No, I would have tried to get to you no matter what."

"Because you have feelings for me, and not her, right?" She crosses her arms over her chest, turning her gaze toward the road. "How do I know that you won't do the same thing to me if these 'people' who are trying to do you harm find you again and you have to move to who knows where?"

"I don't know what I can say that will convince you," I reply. "Yes, I have feelings for you."

"I don't know if there is anything you can say right now." She shakes her head, wiping a tear from her eye as she considers her next words. "I think it's best if we just stay friends for now and we can see what happens down the road. I can't go through what she went through, even if you didn't encourage anything."

"Zahra, please." My heart is on the verge of breaking. After everything I've gone through today, this is the one L I can't take. I reach out to take her hand, but she pushes it away. "I tried to reach her. She blocked me in every way possible. I didn't have a choice."

"Yasir, just take me home. I need time to think. Give me the space to do that, okay?" She still won't look at me as she speaks. "I promise, we will talk about it once I've had some sleep, but right now, it's hard to understand your side of things."

"But what about the yacht party tomorrow?"

"I'll ride with Kenni and Kyle. I'll understand if you're not okay with that."

I don't try to argue, as I'm giving in to exhaustion. I don't have any more energy to burn to put up another debate. I just focus on the road, not even bothering to look in her direction until we get to her house.

She attempts to say something when she gets out of the car, but by now, I don't want to look at her. I can't. It will hurt too much. Surprisingly, she doesn't try to force me to. She simply closes the door and trudges into the house, and I watch with tears streaming down my face as I pull out of the driveway and go back to Unk's house.

CHAPTER TWENTY-EIGHT

So remember a while back when I said I'll never figure girls out? Add today's unexpected series of events to that list.

I awake to a series of messages from Zahra, saying that she overreacted in the moment, and she really would rather ride with me to the party. The other messages are a string of "I didn't mean what I said," and "We need to talk this through," among other things I'd rather not talk about because it's liable to make my head hurt and my heart ache.

The minute I finish reading the texts, I almost throw my phone against the wall.

Between the lack of sleep from feeling disconnected from her all night and making a surprise run with Unk to pick up some extra inventory for the shop because it's a holiday weekend, I'm completely exhausted before noon.

Oh, and *of course* it's a holiday weekend, which makes all the sense on the planet over why Ian would throw a party on a Sunday night. No school on Monday, which means all types of shenanigans are possible, with enough time to recover before school on Tuesday.

Now, I have to balance whether I want to ask for… What the hell am I asking for? To be forgiven? I didn't do anything. One minute, she wants to be friends because she's scared of how she feels, and the next minute, she's not scared and wants to find a way to figure things out.

Just throw the whole damn weekend away.

I still don't have a clue over what to do about my—former?—Squad in the A. Dante wants to act like I'm the bad guy when I know for a fact that Ally twisted the whole situation to keep from going out bad. She caught feelings, I didn't do anything for her to get caught up, and because I didn't handle things well—yeah, that's on me, real talk—I get labeled a traitor.

I'll have to deal with that later.

The more important matter at hand stands about five foot six with hazel-green eyes that take me prisoner every single time I gaze into them.

My challenge…resisting her charms. She's the one who needs to get back on my good side, not the other way around. I gave her my truth, and she chose to break things off.

My other challenge? Trying my best to not make it easy for her. Yeah, I want us to be together, but she doesn't need to know all that so soon. If the roles were reversed, she'd be putting me through it.

I step out of the shower, then towel off so I can get my oils rubbed into my skin. I think about what I want to put on for tonight. The petty in me rages to the surface, and I remind myself that, while Zahra and I are trying to figure out where we stand, she and I aren't together, together. She made that decision for the both of us.

Laid out on my bed are two distinctly different outfits, and as I consider my options, I have a YOLO moment. I put away the hoodie and jeans I planned to rock, choosing to go with a two-toned, black-and-gold turtleneck sweater to pair with relaxed black jeans and matching Timbs. This feels like a bold look that would get the attention I'm in the mood to command tonight. The bomber jacket completes the combination, and I can't resist pulling out a gold curb chain necklace and my prized black-and-gold-trimmed Black Panther helmet pendant.

I check things over in the mirror once again, and I have to admit, I look good, if I do say so myself.

Unk and Lennox are downstairs in the living room, watching some movie I'm not interested in.

I hear a whistle from Lennox, and I'm blushing in seconds. "Well, well, well, look at you, handsome. I like that outfit; it looks really good on you. Zahra's a lucky girl."

I bypass part of her compliment, smiling over the fact that a grown woman thought I put together a look that looks good to her. I hit the remote to ignite Storm's engine, then slip the jacket over my outfit. Even though it's still a bit mild out, once we are on the water, the temperature drops a good ten degrees, easy.

"Have fun tonight, kiddo," Unk says as Lennox snuggles back in the crook of his hip. "We won't wait up, but don't get home too late."

I pull into the driveway of Zahra's house, taking a deep breath before I get out of the car. My nerves are on edge, despite all that big talk earlier. I have no idea what to expect, which adds to my urge to go back and wait for her to come out. I've run through at least three different speeches I've rehearsed in my head as I take my time ringing the doorbell.

She opens the door before I have a chance to press the button. Dammit.

I should've stayed in the car. I'm not ready.

The sweater dress she's wearing compliments her body so well, I wonder if someone knitted it just for her. We didn't have the chance to really talk about what we were planning to wear, but it's scary seeing the golden speckles woven into the black fabric. She finishes the outfit with a pair of black leggings and matching, knee-length, faux-fur-trimmed boots.

Whether we meant to or not, we synced up our outfits.

I don't know how to feel about that.

She glances up into my eyes, and as much as I want to be mad at her, by the gods, why can't I stay mad at her? She comes close to breaking my heart, and all I can do in that moment is take away the pain I see in her eyes. What the hell is wrong with me?

Zahra must have sensed the conflict in me because she slides her fingers against my cheek, her eyes never leaving mine. She whispers, "I'm sorry," with the familiar trembling of her lower lip.

I hate repeating myself, but I'll forgive her anything as long as

I see her smile.

We stand there for what feels like hours, stuck in the moment, each of us waiting on the other to say something. I'm sticking to my vow of silence for now, even though she apologized first. I can't take my eyes off her, reacting to every movement, every embrace, every time my lips caressed hers, as though I met her for the first time. She already has me captivated, no matter what I do to keep it from happening.

I smile, extending my arm for her to take as I escort her to the passenger side of the car.

Once she settles inside the warmer interior, I lean in—I don't know why I do, it feels good—coming close to kissing her. "Why can't I stay mad at you?"

She gives up a slight grin. "The same reason I couldn't stay mad at you."

"So what are we gonna do about this thing between us?"

"Can we talk about it after the party? I'm sure the others are waiting for us."

I close the door and rush around to hop in the driver's seat, stirring through mixed emotions over having her in an enclosed area. I'm still mad at her, but we have to figure out how to deal with the tension between us. I feel it on her, too, but I don't understand how that's even possible. Nana sort of explained things, but she didn't explain everything.

First things first, though… Deal with the tension after the party.

I guess I can cross being on a mega yacht off my bucket list.

The sheer size of this boat is enough to make me wonder *how* Mayor Lance is able to afford something like this, much less allow his son to just take it without parental supervision.

I'm not complaining, though. Outside of the crew members to make sure this two hundred–foot monstrosity is traveling safely, I'm good with no adults being on board.

We step onto the aft landing, and it's like we've entered another world. Hardwood floors as far as I can see toward the bow of the ship. Enough lighting around the railing to make it look like it's daylight. The buffet table looks like it's at least a good twenty feet in length, loaded with everything: fruits and cheeses, seafood and chicken, chips and dips.

And that's just the *first* floor.

I take in all the kids that are on the yacht, and my anxiety kicks into high gear. I make a mental note not to bother with being on the bridge on the top level. Nope. I'm good. The amount of people I'd have to walk through is more than I'm willing to deal with tonight.

Not like I'm gonna have to worry about doing that. Our crew has already spotted me and Zahra, and from the expressions on their faces, I already know we're gonna catch all the jokes.

"Oh, you two decided you had to take the spotlight from the rest of us, huh?"

Kyle's giving me the business, but not in a bad way. I'd been trying to catch up to his fit game for a few weeks, and to get the seal of approval from him, and the rest of the boys in the clique, makes all the difference for me.

From the moment we step on the yacht, it feels like all eyes are on us, but I don't see a specific reason why. Everyone on board is playing the time-honored game of "can you top this?" when it comes to what they wear. There has to be others who have us beat, especially when they have deeper pockets.

"Aye, you got room to talk, my boy," I say. I do a head-to-toe scan of Kyle's fit, realizing that he wants to make sure his physique and height are on full display. "You pulled out the hoodie game tonight. I see the logo work. Starting the branding already?"

"Yeah, Quentin made it clear now that the NIL endorsement deals are out there, it helps to already have the following," Kyle replies as we tap fists. I turn to get a tap from Taylor, one of the other boys hanging with us tonight. "Me and TK hooked up with this graphic artist, and he got us right. We might need to get you to him soon, see if we can't turn you into a walking billboard."

"I'll leave that to the ballers, bro. I'm but a humble fan and supporter." My laughter is born more from nerves than anything else. "Besides, I probably look better promoting y'all than I would myself, anyway."

"Sooner or later, bro, you're gonna realize that you've got juice, too. Your ride speaks to that," Taylor points out as the boat rocks, letting us know we're in motion. "And don't think you haven't been getting attention, either. Eyes have been on you and Z the whole damn time."

Kendyl saunters into the space we carved out near the back of the yacht. She makes herself comfortable quick, dropping into Kyle's lap, while Tania, another girl who's tight with Zahra and Kendyl, finds her spot next to Taylor as he leans against the railing. She's a cutie, with her bisque skin and slender-but-athletic build due to her position as a setter on the volleyball team, wavy auburn red hair framing her heart-shaped face and high cheekbones, and a pair of light brown eyes that has Taylor's undivided attention.

Kendyl cuts her eyes in Zahra's direction, huffing like we missed an appointed time or something. "You two were supposed to be here a half hour ago. You're lucky Ian has a tendency to start things late."

Zahra blushes, glancing at me for a few moments while she plays with her hair. "Well, Ya-Ya and I, we…we had some things to handle."

Yeah, she gave a good cover excuse, but I don't have the energy to play make believe. "Yeah, some things went down in the A with my grandmother, and I'm still trying to sort through that information."

"Whoa, sounds intense," Kyle muses. He gives me a curious glance, then taps Kendyl on her thigh. When she pops up from his lap, he nods toward Taylor before he heads for the bar. "Yo, we're gonna grab something to drink real quick. Do you ladies need anything?"

"Wait, we're not about to bypass the fact that Z just called Yasir by a nickname we hadn't heard before, are we?" Kendyl snaps her gaze in my direction. "When did my bestie learn that, and when did you plan on telling us, *Ya-Ya*?"

"Okay, first, yes, that's a nickname my fam gave me when I was younger." I feel my temper boiling to the surface, and I'm ready to find somewhere else to be with the quickness. "Can we talk about that after we get the drinks, please? There's a lot going on that we need to let y'all in on, for real."

Tania kinda takes the hint, but I get the feeling from her body language that she doesn't want to be separated from Taylor for a long period of time. I don't care either way. I'm focused on putting some space between me and Zahra right now. "Yeah, just a water for me, thanks. I'm sure we can find something to do while you're… at the bar."

We finally get out of earshot of the girls, and Kyle cuts to the white meat before I have a chance to react. "So what's up with you and Z, bro? And don't say nothing; she's tiptoeing just like you are. Talk."

Well, since he wants to keep it a buck, let's keep it a whole buck. "She's in her feelings because when we got to Atlanta, there was a mess I thought I'd handled that blew back on me. A girl who… We were friends, and she wanted to be more, but we had rules in the crew we were in about coupling up. She got salty about me being with Z and got in her head about us being together."

Kyle frowns, and I prepare to catch a fade. After all, she is his best friend. "There's something you're not saying, my boy, so come with it, or you will catch smoke."

"Are you sure you want it all? I'm still trying to sort it out."

"If it means we don't get to scrapping on this boat, yep."

"All right, here's the rest… My grandmother dropped bomb that I'm not from Atlanta. I was actually born in Kindara."

Kyle's eyes light up, realizing the significance of what I'd just said. "Pause, so that means…"

"Yeah, it means that Z and I are from the same country. Born in different tribes within the country, but we're both Kindaran." I rub the back of my neck a few times, the weight of the information still sitting on my shoulders. "That was already hard enough to deal with, and then she went and told me that I've had heat on me since I was younger, but she won't say what that means right now. All she said was it was the reason why I had to move around a lot and deal with so many different schools."

"And now, Z's thinking you might get snatched up again, and she's pulling away." Kyle puts on the detective hat, drawing the conclusion before I can say anything. "Whew, that's a lot. No wonder she's so off-balance."

"She's not the only one, bro." We finally get to the bar to order the non-alcoholic cocktails… I'm not about to get caught up, nope. "I don't know what to say to her to tell her that she doesn't have to worry about that. If Unk gets a call and I have to jet ASAP, it's out of my control."

"Maybe we need to get her head right," Taylor says. "I mean, we're getting to the point where we can insulate a little bit. Our girls are starting to get along. Maybe between Kenni and Nia, it might keep her hopeful for the time being."

"I hear you, bro, and for now, I'm content with trying anything." I look at Kyle. "I'm really feeling her, and I can't see being able to exist at Oakwood if we're not together."

"No cap?"

"No cap. I've been off-balance and low-key hurting all day."

"Then let's see what we can do to get you two back in sync. It's obvi by the fits you wore that you're already in each other's heads." Kyle chuckles as we grab the drinks and head back to where we left the girls.

Until we see Zahra talking with some random dude who's trying to flirt.

All I can see is black. Deadass.

"Yo, ease back a bit. Don't overreact," Kyle advises as he presses his palm against my chest. "This is a party; I can't have you going off script because things aren't back in the flow with you two."

He's right. It's a party, and if she's good with idle chit-chat, then

I can do the same thing. "Look, I hear you, but if I go over there, it won't be pretty. I'll be back when I clear my head," I say as I break from Taylor and Kyle and head to the front of the yacht.

I take a few sips of the drink in my hand, wondering when the anger in my heart would calm down. I've only been in this section of the boat for a few quick moments, but I can't settle down. My instinct is to drop ol' boy overboard and deal with the consequences, but I don't want to let my temper and anger rule me.

The events of the past day-plus have me in a tailspin. I thought I had things on lock, only to find out how sloppy I let things get. As I slow my breathing and think things through, I realize that the whole thing with Alyssa was a bad look...I mean, a *bad* look. Would I have even given her a shot to explain herself if the roles were reversed?

I turn to walk to the back of the boat, when Chrisette and Amber startle me, stepping into my path. From the look in Amber's eyes, she's already had more than a few *real* drinks tonight. Chrisette's lit, too, but she's hiding it well...or so she thinks. "Um, excuse me, ladies, I need to get back to my group."

"What's your rush, Yasir? I know Z is a little occupied at the moment. I'm sure she won't mind if we're talking, right?"

Amber slips into my personal space, and to be real, I don't push her away this time. It's a party, right?

"I'm sure we can find a way to entertain each other until she's done with her convo."

"Yeah, but I don't know if that convo needs to happen between us, especially when Chrisette is here to stir up a mess." I glare at Chrisette, hoping she gets the point. "Where's your man at, anyway? I thought he'd be helping to steer the boat or something."

"Yeah, he's handling all that up there, but why does it matter?" Chrisette puts her hands in the air in mock surrender. "Fine, maybe I need to see what my baby is up to. I'll check up on you two in a bit."

I lean against the wall, almost finished with my drink, and Amber takes the glass from my hand. She examines the half-empty glass and stares at me with this slick grin on her face. "I think you need another one, don't you?"

What does she take me for? "I'm not done with the one I have right now, thanks, but no thanks. Besides, I need to get back to my folk, for real. Z and I have some things to talk about."

She gives the glass back to me, standing against the open doorway as I down the rest of the drink. I don't have time to really worry about whether I hurt her feelings. I need to get back before someone sees something that could make me look bad.

I turn to make my way back toward the area Zahra and the crew are when I start to feel dizzy. I attempt to take another step, and things start spinning.

"Are you okay, Yasir? You don't look so good." Amber props me up against the railing, her eyes roaming all over me as I struggle to maintain eye contact. "Maybe I need to tell Ian to take the boat back to shore so someone can check you over."

I hold my hand up in protest, insisting that nothing is wrong. If I paid attention to my body, "fine" is the last thing I can profess to be right now. "I'm all right, for real. I just need to sit down and clear my head."

"Here, let me get you into one of the rooms so you can lie down."

That's not an option. I don't care if things are iffy between me and Zahra. I'll go out bad if I get caught up with Amber on this boat. I can't allow that to happen. Even in my compromised state, I know who I want, and she needs to know.

I have to find a way to make things right, so we can get back to being together, the way we want to be. If I could simply apologize, have the type of convo that will clear everything, and kiss and make up…

Amber tries to pull me into the room, but I refuse to go. There's no way she can overpower me, regardless of how weak I feel. We're fighting when I sense us moving backward. My head is still swirling, so I can't tell which way is up. I fade in and out during the scuffle, and when I finally have a clear moment, I see the concern on her face, but it doesn't quite register over the why of it all.

"Yasir, stop fighting me, you're gonna... Oh my God!"

I'm not sure what happens next, because everything moves in slow motion, but the only thing I hear is Amber screaming, which I find odd when I haven't touched her. Before everything fades to black, I swear my mind is playing tricks on me, because I'm falling, and the darkness of the water greets me in seconds.

CHAPTER TWENTY-NINE

I'm in and out of consciousness, and everything feels like a dream. I hear voices around me, all of them panicked, but I can't really see anything. It's like I'm stuck in the darkness, with no real way to escape.

I hear monitors, and I feel something being stuck in my arm. I'm trying to ask questions, but even though I can hear myself, it doesn't sound like anyone can hear me. I'm almost yelling into the ether while trying not to panic at the same time.

What in the world is going on?

"Yasir, come back to me, please!" I hear Zahra yelling at me. "Don't leave me. I need you to fight!"

I muster as much strength as I can to push through and get to a small light that looks like it's miles away. As I get closer, the light gets bigger, and I see a doorway, and the light shines through the cracks around it. The closer I get, the farther away it moves, frustrating me the entire time.

I don't understand what's happening, and I'm legit freaking out that I can't find a way out of whatever this is surrounding me. I have to get back to Zahra, no matter what it takes.

Out of nowhere, all of these memories start flashing in front of me, almost like I'm playing a highlight reel of my life, but the things that I see are confusing me, to the point where I feel like they're someone else's memories. They can't be mine, can they?

"Let's get him into triage and get him stable while we still can," I hear one of the medics explain as I watch the scenery change from the top of the ambulance to the blinding lights of the hospital hallways. "Zahra, sweetie, we're going to need you to wait in the reception area until one of the doctors can update you."

No, I want her here with me. *Don't take her away from me, please!*

I fight with everything I have to get back to the doorway, but my energy is completely spent, and I feel myself falling into the darkness again.

But not before I hear a voice I don't recognize calling out for me.

"It is not your time, Yasir."

Who in the world is that?

I have no idea who the hell decided to make such a statement, but whoever they are, they need to keep their opinions to themselves.

And how are they able to speak to me when I'm stuck in literal darkness?

"I know you can hear me, Ya-Ya." The accent is thick, but I can still make out what they're trying to say. Not that I want to listen, anyway. *"Ignoring me will not help matters. I am here now, and there are some things we will need to discuss once we get you out of here."*

Yeah, I'm ignoring him. This is unreal.

I'm not sure what sounds more unbelievable, though…hearing another voice in my head or having a full-blown convo with that voice. I have to get a grip on things, for real. It's obvious he wants my attention.

The sooner I can deal with him, the sooner I can dismiss him and move on.

"I'm trying to figure out how you're so familiar with me and how you know my nickname, my guy. Who are you?"

"We can have that conversation soon. Right now, you need to wake up."

"And how do I do that, huh?" I shout back, but the voice doesn't respond right away. *"Oh, nothing to say when I need something useful, huh? Typical."*

I continue to wander in the darkness, not knowing which way

is up, trying not to freak out. The isolation I feel…this ain't it. For the first time in my short life, the concept doesn't work out so well in its actual application. I'm getting out of here, and right now isn't soon enough.

"Wake up, Yasir." The voice returns, repeating the command.

"How?!" Frustration makes itself clear and present, and fear begins to take up residence. *"How in the hell do you expect me to just wake up like I'm in a dream that I can control or something?"*

"Trust me, Ya-Ya. Just wake up," the voice insists. *"Just follow my voice. We need to get you out of here."*

Out of nowhere, a door opens, and an ambient light illuminates the doorway. The warm glow is soothing, and I hear Zahra's voice as I move closer. I feel itchy, like I'm shedding an old skin and slipping into a new body.

The light flashes as I step through, bringing a sharp pain with it. It only lasts a few moments, and I'm grateful for that because… whew. It takes a few more minutes to open my eyes and adjust to the brightness in a…a hospital room?

How in the fraggernackle hell—Unk's phrase, not mine—did I get here? I was on the boat with Zahra and the crew and… How long have I been here?

Where's Zahra?

The next thing I hear while I sift through the myriad questions in my mind is the answer to one of them. "Yasir? Baby?"

I swear those are the…Best. Words. Ever.

Anger's gone. Yep. Iced. Over with.

The fact that she's here tells me everything I need to know.

But what's the answer to the million-dollar question? A little help, please? "Hi, Z. How did I end up in the hospital?"

Zahra gives me this look like I'm supposed to know the answer to my own question. I return her confused expression with one of my own, and I do my best to suppress the growing fear rising deep within. "Do you remember anything before you fell overboard?"

Wait…pause. *What?* "What are you talking about? Is that how I got here?"

Nana slides out from behind Zahra and into my field of vision. How is she here? She's supposed to be in Atlanta. Zahra and I were on a boat earlier tonight before... Wait, I was arguing with Amber when I started feeling dizzy.

It's coming back to me now.

Events come flooding back, almost overwhelming my senses. Amber's attempts to coerce me into a private area while on board. Her taking my glass to try to get me another drink. Trying to get back to Zahra and having her block me. "The last thing I remember was getting away from Amber."

"Baby, you fell overboard, and we heard Amber screaming. Kyle and I jumped in to get you." Zahra wipes tears away as she attempts to fill in the gaps. "We almost lost you twice on the way to the hospital. You almost drowned."

That hits me hard.

Puzzle pieces start to come into focus. So that's why I was stuck in the dark? I don't know how to process that information, but seeing Nana struggle to hold back tears of her own almost shatters my soul. Being in that void inside my mind, with no way out, comes close to the scariest thing I've ever experienced in my life.

I glance at the clock on the wall across from my bed, and while it reads that it's a few minutes before midnight, I can't get a quick gauge of whether today is still Sunday. "How long have I been out?"

"That is what does not make sense, Ya-Ya," Nana speaks up for the first time. "The doctor told us that it would be another day or two before we had any idea that you would awaken. It has only been a few hours. How do you feel, grandson?"

I must have really taken a few hits while I was in the water. "I feel fine. I don't have any headaches or anything like that." I check my wrinkled fingertips, the only real indication that what they're telling me actually happened. "I feel like I've been in a long-distance swim event, but that's about it."

"I'm going to get your uncle and let him know what's going on," Nana tells us before she steps out into the hallway. "I will also tell the nurses to go get Dr. Forrester. She is liable to be in as much shock as we are right now."

Nana disappears in seconds, leaving me and Zahra alone in the room. We stare at each other like we haven't seen each other in… like, ever. I ache…really ache for her to come closer. I'm desperate to feel her fingers on my skin.

Whether she senses my urgency or not, I don't care anymore, but in moments she's at my bedside. The anticipation kills me, dying with every second she takes to grab my hand, caress my arm, anything to put me out of my misery. The moment her fingertips trace a line from my ear and across my cheek to my lips, I want to combust right there on the spot. It feels so electric, like I've been awakened. I mean, I'm awake, but something else inside me senses her and reacts to her.

Reacts to her touch. Her scent.

What in Nyati's name is happening to me? And…why am I speaking of the Divine Mother like it's second nature?

"You gave me quite a scare, pretty boy." She cuts through my thoughts, keeping her hand on my cheek the entire time. "If you wanted my attention, all you had to do was ask me."

Even the sound of her voice enchants me. "I did ask you…but you took your time answering me."

"Well, then, ask me again."

"Are you sure? I mean, I probably look like I feel right now, and I feel like I've been hit with a steel beam. By Nyati, I probably look like pure trash."

"Okay, I'm gonna have to get used to you saying that," she confesses as she slides her hand from my cheek to interlace her fingers inside mine. Damn, I feel better already. I only hope she doesn't let go. "Trust me, Ya-Ya, you're still my sexy one."

My eyes grow wide. "I'm…*yours*?"

The grin on her face triggers all types of thoughts I shouldn't be having…especially when I'm wearing a whole hospital gown and very little else. "Yes, you're mine, Mr. Salah, if you still want to be."

"Keep playing with me if you want to." I pull her down to steal a kiss or a dozen. I want to hold on to this moment for as long as

I can in case I'm dreaming. "You've been mine, well, in my head you've been mine since the first time we met."

Zahra blushes, and I swear I see her eye color change from their usual hazel-green hue to the most stunning shade of platinum and a smoky white color. I couldn't explain it if I tried, but I don't want to take my eyes off them.

When did she have the ability to do *that*?

She catches me gawking at her, blinking the entire time. "Baby, are you okay? You're... By Nyati, stop staring at me like that. I shouldn't be thinking what I'm thinking when you stare at me like *that*."

"Ahem—I would say he's better than okay." Dr. Forrester interrupts our moment. Ughhhhh, I want to scream. Doesn't she know how epic this was about to get? "Mr. Salah, I don't know how you managed it, but welcome back, young man."

"Thanks, Doc, I appreciate it." I keep Zahra close so I can prepare for my next question. "So when can I leave? I really would like to get out of here."

Dr. Forrester gives me a curious look, and I've already braced myself for the "medical speak" over why I have to stay. "I wish that were possible, but there are some abnormal results in your bloodwork that we need to understand before we release you. Not to mention your CT scan came back with no damage. After the fall you took, and the concussion the paramedics reported when you arrived, in addition to the bruises and lacerations you suffered... nothing's adding up."

Nana and Unk come in with one of the nurses as Dr. Forrester explains things to me and Zahra. The worry on Nana's face gives me chills. "What was that you were explaining to my grandson about his bloodwork without either of his guardians present?"

Dr. Forrester clears her throat, turning to face them. "As I was telling Yasir, Mrs. Salah, we found some abnormal markers in his bloodwork, and we need to run some more tests, just to make sure things are okay. I also want to order a follow up CT scan. I can't make sense over how he has no head trauma."

Nana winks at us before she switches her attention back to the good doctor. She stares into Dr. Forrester's eyes for a few moments, and Dr. Forrester adjusts the collar on her shirt. "I do not believe more tests are needed, Doctor. In fact, the blood needs to be discarded. Yasir can be released tonight."

Dr. Forrester nods, confusing everyone in the room. "Yes, I believe Yasir can go home. Just make sure that he gets plenty of rest and that he hydrates properly. And have him follow up with his primary doctor within the week. There's no need for the blood to be retained."

What in the Jedi Mind Trick just happened?

"We will do just that, Dr. Forrester, thank you." Nana shakes her hand as she instructs Zahra to grab the bag with my clothes so I can get dressed. "We will make sure Yasir is properly cared for."

Nope, what we're not gonna do... Did my nana just... Come on, now?

Nana slides over to the other side of the bed, plants a kiss across my forehead, and gives a knowing wink. "Nana has a few tricks up her sleeve when the occasion calls for it. Now, you get dressed so we can get you home."

"I'll make sure that the paperwork is handled and Zahra gets to her car in one piece." Unk ushers them out of the room. "The nurses will probably wheel you out instead of letting you walk on your own."

Zahra stops Unk for a few seconds, skipping back to my bedside to steal another kiss. She stares long...longer than I think she would, and I'm here for all of it. "Please take care of yourself tonight. I'll be back in the morning to see about you. We still have things to talk about."

I take a few moments after they leave to get my head together. I start to get different pieces of what happened to me earlier in the evening, and I don't know whether to be angry about what Amber tried to do to me or if I should be upset with myself. Being in the room gives me a little too much time to think, but at least I can be alone for a few minutes.

Or so I thought. *"I like her. We should definitely keep her."*

I snap my head in the direction of where I thought I heard the voice. There's no way I could be hearing voices in my head right now.

"Yes, you are hearing what you think you are hearing, Yasir."

I flinch, covering my ears with my hands, willing the noises away. I can't be hearing things. I'm not going crazy.

"No, kiddo, you are not going crazy. There is a conversation we need to have, and soon."

"Who are you? What do you want?" I shout to the empty room. "Where did you come from and why are you here?"

"Go look in the mirror, and I'll show you who we are. Once you see for yourself, then we can go and have that conversation. Do you have somewhere that we can go?"

"If…and that's a big *if*…I see what I see, and it's something we need to convo over, then yeah, I got somewhere we can go."

"As you kids love to say, say less."

I'm completely out of my skull, listening to a voice in my head. I have to be dreaming or hallucinating or something. I didn't hear whoever this was before. Why am I hearing him now?

Wait…pause a moment. *Think, Ya-Ya, think on it.*

I *have* heard him before; I just ignored him.

And I heard him before I woke up from my concussion, but it takes a minute to connect those dots and figure it out.

It's obvious to me he wants my attention for real, for real.

So he wants me to see who "we" are, whatever that means. Okay, let's see what he's talking about.

I go back to the mirror, and at first, I don't see anything that would freak me out.

Until I open my mouth and notice—wait a minute. Are those *fangs*?

Nope. I'm not seeing this right now. My mind's playing tricks on me. The doctor said I had a concussion, remember? Yeah, that's what we're gonna blame this on, right now.

I rub my fingers over my eyes, try to focus, and take another look in the mirror. Instead of seeing my face, there's a combination of my face and that of a beast, almost like a split screen right down the middle. The black fur and the pointed ear adorned with an earring, the snout jutted out just enough for me to be able to tell the difference between its features and mine. The fangs are fully out of my mouth, and the eyes are wide open, like it can see beyond just what we're looking at in the mirror.

I stifle a scream to keep anyone from coming into the room to see why I'm legit freaking out. Make no mistake, I. Am. Freaking. Out! How in the hell is this happening? This isn't possible. There's no way.

His eyes glow bright purple, almost like a pure amethyst stone. In the calmest voice that doesn't sound like mine but is coming from my lips, he introduces himself with two simple words.

"Hi, kiddo."

CHAPTER THIRTY

I manage to sneak out of the house once I was discharged from the hospital. Unk is so consumed with making sure that Nana is comfortable in one of the spare bedrooms that I could easily slip out. I have to handle this alone anyway.

I pull into the parking area at Wright Square in the heart of downtown Savannah. I figure it'll provide the best possible hiding place on such short notice. I would've preferred to head down to Driftwood Beach, but that might have been pushing things a bit too far. We don't have that kinda time anyway, and the way this day has been going, I don't want to compound the issues I'm already facing. This…whatever the hell this is I'm having to deal with at the moment…needs to be sorted out before I can move forward.

I send a text to Zahra to let her know I got home in one piece and that I'm gonna crash soon. I hit Kyle to tell him the same thing, hoping I get some privacy to hash this out. With those bases covered, I beeline to the first location I can think of that'll provide the type of isolation needed: the granite stone of Tomo-Chi-Chi, the leader of the Yamacraw Tribe. He's the man responsible for negotiating the treaty that gave General Oglethorpe the land that would eventually become the city of Savannah.

Hey, I happen to be a history buff, all right?

The spot I choose has a tinge of mystery and a haunting beauty, much like the rest of the city. Considering we're under the cover of night, this would be the perfect location for me to have what might be one of the scariest convos of my life with an entity I had no idea resides inside me.

I mean, how the hell am I supposed to react, huh? One minute, I'm a normal kid, and after a wild accident and almost dying…well, the doctors told Zahra and Nana that I died *twice*…I come out of it feeling like Bruce Banner when he first found out about the "other guy" and had to learn how to deal with him. Thank Nyati I read comic books.

I don't bother to scan around me. No one's around this time of night to listen in on me, for all intents and purposes, having a whole convo with myself.

Not that the spot isn't already an odd choice to begin with. The large granite stone…a chunk that was taken from Stone Mountain decades ago…has its own superstition attached to it. As the legend goes, if a person runs around the stone while chanting Tomo-Chi-Chi's name, his ghost will appear. His remains were not relocated with the memorial, which gave rise to the urban legend.

While I didn't exactly buy into the ghost stories that surrounded the memorial stone, in light of what's happening to me real-time, I'm willing to make a huge exception over my initial skepticism. The fine line between coincidence and truth can be blurred at any time; all someone has to do is read deep enough between the romanticized lines of history to find what they want to see.

The lightning bugs flicker against the darkness, their bioelectrical impulses seeming to sync with one another. The light show, using the trees surrounding me as a backdrop, helps soothe the uneasy thoughts roiling through my mind. I can't resist focusing on the captivating display, as dozens of the fascinating insects keep things appealing.

I take a deep breath and let out a long sigh, bracing myself against whatever happens next. I close my eyes and allow my body to relax. "Okay, we're alone now. Show yourself."

For a few moments, nothing happens, and I sit for a few more moments, wondering if I should try it again or just pack it up and head home. I make another attempt, closing my eyes tighter to concentrate and remember what I did to bring the voice to life in my head. "Show yourself. I don't have the time for the grandiose entrance or anything like that. That time has passed, for real."

Again, silence.

"Look, if you don't show yourself, you disrespectful son of a bitch, I'm heading home and ignoring you until I feel like dealing with you," I yell into the air. "If you think this is some type of joke, I'm not the one for it tonight. Show yourself, dammit!"

After a few more moments, the voice roars to life, making itself known. *"I can only imagine the questions you have right now, Yasir. I can sense the anxiety and confusion in you. Let's get to it."*

I let out a mock chuckle. "Yeah, that's putting it mildly. I'm still trying to understand who, or what, you are, for starters. And how in the world are you in my head is at the top of the list. How was I not aware of you before?"

The voice bellows out a laugh of its own, causing me to roll my eyes, annoyed that I wasn't in on whatever the inside joke might have been at the moment. *"Okay, let's see if we can get the important questions out of the way. I just wish there was a Vodaran priestess to assist with the transition, but we will have to figure things out as we go along."*

"Vodaran priestess? What are you talking about?"

"Are you not Kindaran? I would have thought you would be versed in the traditions," the voice questions.

"I just found out I was Kindaran a couple of days ago."

"Hmm, interesting." The voice begins knocking on different walls inside my mind, which only confuses me further over what it's trying to find. *"Hmm, it looks like a priestess has conjured a barrier from your memories. We're going to need to do something about that soon."*

I still have no clue what he's talking about. I shrug, moving back to my original questions. "So out with it, mystery being. Who are you, how are you here with me inside my head, and why are you here now?"

"My name is Gamba. It is the Kindaran name that means 'warrior.' I was hoping to make a more formal introduction when you were ready to acknowledge my presence."

I rub my hand over my face. These answers are leading to more questions, and I can barely understand the answers he's giving. "So when was that supposed to happen? Considering my parents have been dead for a full decade now, would this conversation have ever happened? And who's to say I'm ready to acknowledge it now?"

"Yes, it would have happened, but it should have happened by now, considering the trauma of your parents' deaths," Gamba explains to me. *"If I did not believe you were ready, I would not be here right now. I would have stayed in the recesses of your mind until I was brought forth. This is why a priestess would have been a better medium for this conversation."*

"And why is this happening? No, pause, I need the other questions answered first, because I'm completely confused. What are you?"

Gamba continues with the rapid-fire responses like he's been waiting to drop all this on me for a minute. *"I am a nyxwraith, Ya-Ya. I'm a creature who is brought into existence to serve its owner, in whatever capacity that the owner needs."*

"And how did that happen? I don't think this is something I would have chosen to have happen."

Gamba sighs, a low growl escaping his lips. *"Nyxwraiths are conjured from the depths of their owner's psyche in times of great tragedy or loss. Even though your memories of your parents' deaths have been shielded from you, the trauma of your death and resurrection would qualify as the tragedy."*

"Yeah, you think?"

"I know this is a lot to take in, Ya-Ya."

"How long have you been rattling around in my head, Gamba? Only family knows my nickname."

"While I have just made myself known to you now, I have been around since you lost your parents," he replies. *"I was only in my infancy, too, so in a sense, I grew up with you, but I did not possess the strength to make myself available to you until now, although I was able to come when you needed me most."*

It takes less than a few seconds to put the puzzle pieces

together. "The ambush during the Beach Creek game...that was you."

"Yes, most of it was me. I only followed your lead, feeding from your instincts and emotions. It was life or death."

"The authorities said it was an animal attack, but it wasn't. I was...I was the animal. I'm a monster."

Gamba lets out a growl that shuts me down cold. *"We are not the monster, Yasir. They are all monsters. The reason you had to take up boxing had a lot to do with the bullying you endured growing up. Now that you have gained the ability to fight back and defend yourself, and others, you are the monster? I do not think so."*

"How else would you describe it, Gamba? Those boys I decimated at that game, they could've been killed," I scoff. "All I saw were bodies on the ground. I didn't know if they were hurt bad or worse, and you were nowhere to be found to help me make sense of it all."

Gamba tempers his growl to a low rumble this time around, and I take some comfort in that small victory. He at least understands my point. *"I am learning how, and when, to appear so I can keep you out of harm's way, Yasir. That time at the game, you were in danger of being badly hurt. It was either going to be them or us... and it was not going to be us. My function, my purpose, is to protect you from harm."*

I take deep breaths, trying to focus on the questions in my mind, but my emotions are on tilt, and I really want to scream instead. All of this is happening too fast and bordering on overwhelming. "So how are you doing this? Is this, like, Bruce Banner and the Incredible Hulk? I need a frame of reference to wrap my head around what's happening to me."

Gamba steps from the shadows, making his human form visible to me. He bears a striking resemblance to Aldis Hodge, the actor who played Hawkman in the *Black Adam* movie. I'd almost swear that he can be his father. He's wearing a black button-down shirt and matching slacks, making his salt-and-pepper goatee stand out that much more. He has a bald head, which is a good look for him, no cap. *"Considering you read a ton of comic books, I would imagine that seeing me as a human is not a total shock to the system. But this is what we will look like when you allow us to change into our nonhuman form."*

Gamba stretches as he gives me an idea of what my body will look like, his arms and legs growing to their fullest length. His fangs jut from his mouth as his snout makes room for the rest of his teeth. His mane grows from the top of his head, falling to just above his waist in its jet-black magnificence. His hands are twice their normal size, their razor-sharp claws gleam against the darkness that enshrouds them. Earrings that adorn Gamba's ears sparkle in the darkness, along with golden bracelets around his wrists, and a golden necklace that seems to be embedded in his fur.

By the time the transformation is complete, Gamba has to be standing something like nine feet tall, and despite his undeniable mass, I swear Gamba's floating above the ground, or he at least barely leaves any sort of footprints.

"So what do you think?" he says.

Man, listen.

I take one look at Gamba, and for the first time in our convo, I give up the most mischievous smile possible. All the lycanthrope comics I've ever read, combined with my love for the "other guy" and all things Wakanda...the Jabari Tribe and M'Baku, to be exact, but T'Challa's right there as one-with-an-asterisk...it all manifests itself into the most fearsome creature I could've ever imagined.

And I can imagine a lot!

"What do I think? By Nyati, I don't know whether I should have a fit that I can become this magnificent creature or be scared out of my mind that I can become this magnificent creature." I can't stop staring. Like, I'm legit scared and excited at the same time. "How the hell am I... There's no way I can tell anyone about this. My uncle? Nana? By the gods...how will Zahra react to this?"

Gamba radiates a warm, orange glow that puts me at ease. I have to get used to it now that I know where it's coming from finally. *"I know it might not feel like it right now, but I promise you, it will all work itself out. If you want to go fast, go alone. If you want to go far, go together. You're not alone, kiddo, and there's a pretty girl at the end of this journey. We need not disappoint her."*

Oh, wait, we're playing those games? "Since when did we start worrying about pretty girls? And how did you know about Zahra to begin with? By your admission, you've been around for the last day or so. She's been around since I got down here a few weeks ago."

Gamba emits a satisfied snarl. *"When that pretty girl managed to calm the storm inside you, for starters. And she did save your life before I had a chance to step in and do something. There is something there, and we need to see what it is."*

"I can see already that this is going to be a challenging relationship between us, Gamba."

"It doesn't have to be," Gamba insists. *"Sure, there will be growing pains, but there are some advantages to being a nyxwraith."*

"Oh yeah? Like what?" I challenge.

"Look through my eyes and take a glimpse skyward. The night sky is crystal clear, and you might be surprised at what you find."

I hesitate for a moment, then peer through Gamba's eyes, staring out into the night sky and marveling at the constellations, recognizing Ikba Scales, named for the Vodaran God of Justice, within the batch of stars just south of Ursa Major. Another glance to the east, and I locate the form of Nyati, the Divine Mother, looking down over her beloved Kindara. To the west, the distinct wildfire constellation of Nahara, its flames pointed toward the sun. I remember the last time I went stargazing, but they were never *this* clear and bright as when I look through Gamba's eyes. I even search for Adin's Bow again, marveling at how brilliant it looks this time around.

Now, if I could just figure out how I know where to look for constellations I've never studied, much less recognized, that would be great.

All of it stuns me into silence. The further I peer into the night sky, the more I see, beyond what I thought I would observe through a telescope. It throws me into a state of disbelief that I have vision beyond the naked eye. "What else am I—are we—able to do? There's so much I need to know."

"What did I tell you? Beautiful sight, is it not?" Gamba grins as I look like a whole kid playing with a new toy.

"I swear, I didn't know how beautiful things could be through your eyes. We have to do this more often," I declare. "Real talk, what else can we do? I have so many more questions now."

Gamba shakes his head, changing back to his human form. *"I think that is enough for tonight. There is a lot to take in as it is, and we need to figure out how this all works. We do not have much time. For now, I am content that you are not having a whole meltdown right now. We can have another conversation as soon as possible, but we do need to have a Vodaran priestess to help with the full transition so we can realize everything you have at your disposal."*

In a snap, I remember that Nana has already said someone would be informed of my "awakening."

At the same time, I'm trying to wrap my head around something Gamba just said. "What do you mean, we don't have much time? Is there something happening that I don't know about?"

"Yes. Now that you have been awakened, we have to get you ready."

"Ready for, what, exactly?" The riddles are killing me, and I'm not in the mood to decipher. "If I'm in danger, then I need to know so I can figure out my next moves."

"We are in danger, which is why we need to have a Vodaran priestess to assist," Gamba stresses. *"There is a lot to do in a short period of time, but I have watched from the shadows as you have grown. You will be ready when it is time."*

"I think I can arrange for a priestess, but I'm going to have to tell someone about you in order to get him to bring who we need. It's a risk; he's not family, but he's the only one who can do it. My nana trusts him, so I think we can trust him, too."

Gamba nods. *"If that is what we have to do, then we need to get it done. The priestesses can unlock everything within us, and that is important for whatever we might have to face down the road. We will have to trust him until there's no other reason to trust him. Either way, my duty is always to protect you…no matter what."*

I open my eyes, getting my bearings after using Gamba's eyesight. I check the time, realizing I'd taken the past hour sorting through everything. I can see so much clearer now, more than I'd ever known before. I walk back to Storm, working through all the scenarios in my head over how I would explain this new revelation to Unk and Nana. Zahra will have to wait until later; things are still so new between us and I can't worry about that right now. I need more time to get her comfortable with the idea that I am—well, metahuman, or whatever the term is nowadays.

First things first. Get home before someone realizes I've been gone all this time.

CHAPTER THIRTY-ONE

'm grateful that Storm is a hybrid as I approach the driveway at a gods-awful time of morning. The whisper-quiet EV part of the engine comes in clutch when I need to not be noticed or caught. Normally, I park in the garage, but that's not a good look right now, considering I'm not supposed to be out of the house after suffering a concussion and all sorts of other bodily injuries.

I purposely disengaged the alarm before I left the house, praying that Unk or Nana didn't check on me while I was gone. The moment I slip in the back door and notice the main level is dark, I exhale with relief, then tiptoe upstairs to my room so I can rest as best as possible. My body is still sore and hurting, despite my need to converse with Gamba and make some sense of what's happening to me.

Instead of heading straight to my bed, I'm firing up my laptop, and Google is, hopefully, gonna be my friend for a few minutes. I'm trying to find as many keyword combinations as I can to figure out where I want to research, but the only thing that keeps coming up is Lycan and lycanthrope myths and legends. The problem with that is that's not what I saw in the mirror earlier tonight.

What in the world am I becoming?

I continue my deep-dive until exhaustion finally takes over, whether I want to stop or not. The deeper I go, the more I want to find out, and the more I need to understand so I don't feel so scared. I resign myself to the fact that if I don't get some rest, I'm not gonna be any good to anyone tomorrow, least of all myself, and there's a lot of questions I have to ask and answer.

I peel myself away from my desk and slog to my bed so I can stretch out and get as much sleep as my mind will allow. Easier said than done, especially when the lasting images I see before I close my eyes are glowing orbs staring back at me, and I hear a voice in the dark assuring me that everything is gonna be all right.

As much as I want to believe that, I don't know if I can right now.

Zahra has never been in my room before. Still, I can't think of a better place I'd rather have her this morning, even though she doesn't realize I know she's here.

My room isn't immaculate—there are clothes on the floor, but they're the ones I wore last night, and maybe a couple of other shirts. My L-shaped desk sits in the far right corner, where she notices papers spread out among the books on the desktop. My laptop screen displays a Google search that I forgot about—I was researching lycanthropes before I crashed out.

Above the short end of the desk sits a bookshelf that is built into the wall. She pads over to be nosy, wondering what books I have on the shelves. From *Black Sands* comic books to, of course, the Miles Morales arc in the *Spider-Man* comics, *Black Panther* comics, and she sees the *Ironheart* comics, too. Then she moves over to the hardcover books, reading the spines that catch her attention. *Percy Jackson. The Witcher. The Lord of the Rings. Children of Blood and Bone* and *Children of Virtue and Vengeance* by Tomi Adeyemi. *Beasts of Prey* and *Beasts of Ruin* by Ayanna Gray. There are even nonfiction books I've collected over the last few years. *Letters to a Young Brother* by Hill Harper. *The Mamba Mentality: How I Play* by Kobe Bryant. To top it off, there's a hardcover copy of *Native Son* by Richard Wright, *Between the World and Me* by Ta-Nehisi Coates, and *A Collection of Poems of Langston Hughes*, among other titles.

Because it's a good thing to be young, gifted, and intelligent.

On my closet door is a full-size poster of Chadwick Boseman as
T'Challa. The poster only shows his head and shoulders, split down
the middle, with one side showing his head encased in the Black
Panther mask and the other side showing his face. Underneath the
striking image are the familiar claws that made up the necklace
always worn by the warrior king.

That's not what has her clutching her chest, though.

Sitting in its own corner away from everything, propped up
on a stand against the wall, is a remote-controlled F-22 Raptor jet,
painted in all black with purple and gold accents throughout the
fuselage and wings. Considering it's nearly five feet long and the
wingspan looks around four feet long, and I have space to keep
this beast in my room, it's safe to say that, outside of Storm, this is
my pride and joy.

I know her STEM-girl heart is fluttering. I have to find some
time to teach her how to fly it.

She steps over my Timbs, still marveling over all the reminders
of Wakanda—including the life-size Panther mask on my nightstand.
She rolls the desk chair along with her, settling at the side of my
queen-size bed, watching me as I sleep. At least, she thinks I'm
asleep. I can't help peeking the entire time she's been moving
around, closing my eyes when she turns in my direction.

I overheard a convo between her and Unk where she basically
said she's coming by to see about me. My newly heightened hearing
has its benefits.

"You know," I say, opening my eyes, "when I imagined you
being in my bedroom for the first time, this wasn't what I had in
mind."

She jumps, rolling the chair a few inches away from the bed.
"By Nyati, you scared the hell out of me, boy."

I chuckle as I sit up in bed, but she doesn't find it all that funny.
"I'm sorry about that, I didn't mean to throw you off, but now I'm
trying to figure out why you're staring at me like I've grown a third
eye or something."

"There's a reason for that, baby." She pulls up the camera on her phone and places it in my hands. "Tell me what you see, because I'm literally trying to understand what I'm looking at when I see you."

It takes a few moments for it to register, but as my eyes widen with the revelation, she begins to freak out a bit with me. I drop her phone in my lap, leaning back to check other spots on my body. "Wait a damn minute, how in the—?"

"How in the world did you manage to heal almost overnight from bruises and cuts that would have taken weeks to heal?" she finishes the question for me, hesitating to touch my skin. "What's the last thing you remember from last night? Did Nana do something to you before you went to sleep?"

I try to think, and I can't really remember anything, which frustrates me. I shake my head a few times, and the voice—Gamba—shows up out of the blue.

"Go on, take her hand. Take it," he says.

I turn my attention back to Zahra.

"I-I'm not sure how to explain any of it right now. I remember coming home, and then Nana gave me something to drink to help me sleep. From there, everything feels like a dream, but it doesn't. I don't know if I'm making sense right now."

"Yeah, you're right, it doesn't make sense. How are you feeling? Are you hurting at all?" She leans toward me and feels my forehead. "I'm still trying to understand how you don't have any bruises or injuries from last night. I wish there was a way for you to know what happened. I mean, I watched you die—twice—and it's like you didn't go through any of it."

"There might be a way," I reply, taking her hands as Gamba told me. "Close your eyes and let me inside."

Zahra hesitates as she takes my hands. "Yasir, I—"

"Trust me, baby. I'm not gonna hurt you. You know that."

"Yeah, I know. I trust you."

Once we're comfortable, I start chanting, using the words and incantations Gamba explains to me, repeating the words as I hear them. *Si oken re. Si oken re.* I don't have a clue what it means, but in moments, I'm inside her mind with her, sitting in a recliner in a theater room—that's the best way I can explain it. On the screen are the events from last night, almost literally from her perspective, like we're running a role-player game. She's next to me, watching along while she hears herself giving the voiceover, explaining everything that's happening.

I don't remember saying if my phone works or not, but I give Kendyl my phone and race to the back of the boat. Since the engine isn't running, I have a chance to not get caught up in the current. I pray he cleared the hull, but there's no way of telling what condition he might be in if and when we get to him.

Not seeing his body at least float to the surface scares me the most.

I take my boots off and tie my hair back, with only one thing on my mind. I ignore Kyle's screams for me not to jump off the boat, diving in feet first and swimming in the opposite direction, away from the boat. I shorten my strokes, working with the current and using it to help conserve as much energy as possible. I stop every few seconds, hoping I can see anything resembling his body above the water line.

"Yasir! Baby, where are you?" I keep swimming in the direction I think the current might carry him. I fear he's unconscious, which would be all bad, especially if we don't hear him screaming for help or anything. "Come on, baby, tell me where you are."

I dive underwater, realizing that it would be foolish, since I don't have a flashlight or anything to see through the darkness. I have to try something; I can't let him die out here.

I rise to the surface to catch my breath, hearing someone splashing toward me. I wipe my eyes, hoping it's Yasir trying to swim toward me. I float in one spot as the splashing comes closer, and I start to yell out again, but I feel a strong pair of hands grab around my waist, holding me still.

"I should choke you, scaring us like that, girl," Kyle growls as we continue to bob above the water. "What the hell were you thinking? I know you can swim, but we can't possibly find him in dark water."

"We have to try, dammit." I'm trembling as the cold water begins to affect me, but I refuse to leave. "Help me, please. I'll never forgive myself if we don't try."

Kyle nods, keeping his arm around mine as we swim farther away from the boat. "Ian's keeping the boat in place until someone can get to us. We need to get to him quick. He could still drown even if he's unconscious."

I really don't want to hear that part, but it only increases the urgency to locate him before it's too late. We swim in as much of a straight line as the current will allow, shouting Yasir's name in hopes that he hears us. The longer we stay in the water, the more I try not to panic.

Frustration takes over, and I'm scared that we won't find him before more help shows up. I close my eyes to try to calm down and think, even for a few seconds. I start humming, although I don't know why or understand why I'm doing it, but I just keep humming, trying different frequencies, hoping to find something for him to hear.

"Yo, what are you doing, Z?" Kyle must have felt me vibrating, but I can't think about that now. I focus on finding the right pitch to reach Yasir. "Yo, Zahra, are you awake? Talk to me. Don't blank out on me."

I shut everything out, hearing a faint moaning in the distance. I can't be sure that it's Yasir, but I stroke in the direction of what I hear. His voice is faint and fading fast. "I can hear him, Ky. Follow the direction I'm swimming. We don't have much time."

"How in the hell are you—"

"Not now, Kyle, just trust me."

We quicken the pace of the strokes, and I hear his groans getting louder as we get closer to him. The sounds stop as soon as we're on top of where I heard his cries. "He's right here. I swear I heard him in this spot."

Kyle looks around, his eyes locking with mine in disbelief. "He's not here, Z. What did you hear?"

In that moment, I hear my name being called, and it's coming from directly under us. I don't have time to explain. I just dive down *and start reaching below me as I kick as far as I can go. In my mind, I scream for Yasir to reach for me, almost letting the air out of my lungs.*

I feel fingers, but they aren't grabbing mine, so I reach with both hands and grab his wrist, pulling with everything I have to get him to the surface. Another pair of hands snap around my ankles, and I know it's Kyle trying to pull me up. He clutches my waist, kicking toward the surface, while I hold on to Yasir like my life depends on it.

We finally break through the water, blinded by floodlights coming from the shoreline. Kyle takes Yasir from my grip, pulling him to the shore toward the lights. I hear men yelling out at us to keep going in the direction we were heading, thanking the gods that we were able to find him.

We get him to the paramedics waiting for us, taking as much care as possible to lift him onto the stretcher. I reach for him, but the medics block me, assuring me that they'll do everything they can to revive him.

As they continue working on Yasir, Kyle holds me tight, repeating that he'll be okay and that he will come back.

"He's not breathing. I couldn't feel a pulse when we got to him."

"He's strong, Z. He'll get through this. We have to believe he can."

I jump when I hear the buzzing of the defibrillator against his body, gasping at the way he jolts, pushing down the fear in my heart. So many things were left unsaid between us, and the regret threatens to send me into a tailspin.

They ask us if we want to ride with him to the hospital, but I've already climbed into the ambulance before they even get the question out. Kyle follows me in, grabbing the blankets offered to us while they load him inside. I don't realize the adrenaline had been keeping me warm the entire time, and when it subsides, my body feels ice cold, and I wrap the blanket tighter around me. My eyes never leave the scene unfolding in front of me. He never once opens his eyes during the entire ride. Not even a flicker or fluttering of his eyelids. I'd have been grateful for a grunt, anything to let me know he's still with us—with me.

I hear one of the medics say that Yasir is "coding," whatever the hell that means, but when the machine goes from rapid beats to one long signal, my heart stops. They charge up the defibrillator again, sending another jolt to restart his heart.

Nothing else matters until I know he's alive.

I need him to come back to me.

We break the connection, and she blinks as she stares at me. "That…that felt like when you kissed me in your studio. How in the world are you able to do that?"

"I'm still as confused as you are. I was just— You know what, never mind." I have so many of my own questions it's making my head swim. How am I able to do half of what I'm doing? Where does Gamba fit in? "I'm hoping to get the chance to talk to Nana to see if she can help make things make sense."

"I can offer a few ideas, but that might require explanations that you may or may not be ready for, grandson." Nana creaks the door open, holding a coffee mug. She smiles, but I see the sadness in her eyes. Things might have gotten a little bit more complicated. "How much are you prepared to learn?"

CHAPTER THIRTY-TWO

Nana brings me and Zahra down to the living room, where two strangers sit on the sectional, I would guess, to see me. Unk and Lennox are there, too, and he has as much of a confused expression on his face as I do. He shrugs when I stare him down, which doesn't help me out *at all*.

"Good afternoon, Yasir. I have been told a lot about you. I know my appearance might come as a shock to the system, but I promise, this meeting is long overdue."

Okay, so what in the unexpected intervention is this?

While the stunning woman wearing a purple sleeveless pant suit with a black-and-gold corset belt and absolutely flawless copper-bronze skin is not familiar to me in the slightest, the man wearing a black, two-buttoned suit to almost match his sable-toned skin and long, flowing dreadlocks sitting next to her is very familiar. He's been in different parts of my nightmares when I'm in Kindara.

Zahra pulls me down to whisper into my ear. "They're Kindaran, baby. Something's going on, for real, if they're here to see you."

I pretty much have to take her word for it. How the hell am I supposed to know who is who, and for what? I just found out I'm Kindaran a week ago, and suddenly folks come through and I'm supposed to do what exactly? "I wasn't expecting you. From the look on Unk's face, he didn't get the memo, either. So anyone wanna help me understand what's going on?"

Nana steps in front of me, taking my hands in hers. I search through her gaze to give me some sort of comfort. Having strangers around only amps up my anxiety. "Listen to me, Ya-Ya," she says. "This is the man who saved you from the invasion in Kindara. His name is Hassan, and he brought you to me when you were younger."

I flinch, shooting my eyes in his direction. "Is this true? You were the one who brought me to my nana? I vaguely remember your face."

"Yes, Yasir, I am." Hassan rises from his seat, then walks toward me until he stands a couple of feet from me. He studies my face, looking up at me as he gives a knowing smile. "It has been so long since I have seen you. You have grown so much over the years."

"That's funny, because I don't remember ever seeing you."

"Yasir."

I turn to my grandmother and take a deep breath. "Nana, I get it. I'm supposed to be in debt to this man for saving my life, but where has he been all these years? If he has been in contact with you, why couldn't you have at least put me in front of him so I can have an idea of who he is now?" I stare at him, frowning as I keep my emotions in check. "All I see is a stranger telling me about events that I have no way of remembering, and you're backing him up? I'm not feeling this, seriously."

The woman rises from her seat on the sectional, slipping into my field of vision and almost commanding my attention without saying a word…yet. "Please forgive the abrupt intrusion, Yasir. My name is Kynani. I am a Vodaran priestess, sent to help clear up some of the confusion that may be happening with you."

"Well, you'd probably be the first to try," I reply, releasing Nana's hands from my grip and turning my body toward her to give her my attention. "I'm doing my best to keep from sounding ungrateful or disrespectful, but if you think you can clear things up, I'm all ears."

Kynani extends her hand for me to shake. She…I don't know how to explain it, but she stares into my eyes, and every aggression inside of me melts away. "My apologies, Yasir, it is obvious that no advanced notification was sent to alert you to our arrival. However, upon learning of your recent awakening, time is of the essence, and

I am personally hopeful that you will be agreeable to setting up a time for the two of us to begin your acclimation process."

Despite her ability to calm me down, I'm wondering why the conversation between us has such an air of immediacy to it. "What I'm having a hard time understanding is why is everything being sped up? It's like everyone expects me to put my life on pause, but no one is giving me a reason."

"I assure you, Yasir, things will be revealed as quickly as possible." Kynani nods as she responds to me, keeping eye contact the entire time. "There is a lot to discuss, and I am hopeful that it can be done as soon as possible."

I shake my head, feeling like I'm in the middle of a bad movie. I turn to Zahra, matching her hesitant expression, feeling every bit of the chaotic energy that's suddenly swirling around us. "How soon are we talking? I mean, I was kinda in the middle of something before y'all showed up."

Kynani raises an eyebrow, switching her glance toward Zahra. "You have already found a suitable mate? Is she aware of your awakening?"

"Yasir, maybe we can talk after whatever is happening here is handled." Zahra squeezes my hand, taking her free hand to get me to look at her. "This is all a bit… We can find time to sort through things later, I promise."

"Um, nope, not when I literally went through hell to come back to you," I protest. "We need to talk now."

Kynani places a comforting hand over my forearm, looking into my eyes again before nodding. "This is an intricate process, Yasir, and we need to get to it as soon as possible. Allow me to ask this question: is this young lady standing next to you a fellow Kindaran? This is important information for me to help with the acclimation."

Zahra grins, blushing as she stands in front of me. "Yes, I am from the Kua Tribe, as is the rest of my family. My father, Kairo Assante, is a Kindaran historian. Are you familiar with him?"

Kynani smiles. "Yes, I am familiar with your father. If it is okay with him, I would like to reach out. There is much that I may need to discuss with him, too. The stars are aligning more than I ever imagined."

Hassan clears his throat to insert himself into the conversation. "I may need to be involved with these discussions, Kynani. In fact, Xavion and Mama Johari need to be involved also, as Xavion is Yasir's current legal guardian. Yasir is still a minor, and this is too important for it to be left up to him."

A minor? My dude, I'll be seventeen in February, and by certain American laws, I can declare independence and leave y'all in the dust. Who the hell does he think he is, trying to act like he has a say in what happens to me?

Kynani turns to Hassan, then glances at Unk. "You are correct, his legal guardian is needed for such matters, and as such, I will bring him up to speed. However, as you are aware when we spoke to the Kindaran Council, your presence is not required. You are needed in the field with the rest of the priestesses to continue with the primary objective of locating the remaining Kindaran Nine."

I focus on the irritated expression on Hassan's face, wondering why he now wants to be involved on such an intimate level when he hasn't been around in any capacity before. "I prefer my uncle be involved; he's been the one dealing with everything down here in Oakwood Grove. I can't see doing this without my family not being made aware of things."

Hassan shakes his head. "Come on, kiddo, there might be some things that I can help with during your acclimation. I'm sure the Council can find someone else to assist the priestesses. This is too important for me to remain in the field now."

Yeah, that's a no. "So for years, you've been in the field while Nana was going through a confusing time with me, and now, when you realize that whatever I'm about to go through is taking you out of the mix, you feel like being in the field isn't important anymore? Thanks for your concern, but I'm not feeling it. I don't know you."

Hassan protests further. "There's too much at stake for me not to be involved. Let me see what I can do on my end to get things worked out."

"How about this? Find out why I haven't been able to go back to Kindara after all these years, since you're so interested in helping *now*." I keep my rising anger in check, but his insistence to be involved and the timing of it all puts me on edge. "Since you've been so invested in the process this whole time, and I'm still not convinced of that, and you're supposed to have influence, find that out for the rest of us."

Hassan winces, but then he nods in agreement. "Fair enough, Yasir. You deserve answers to those questions."

Unk walks over to put his hand on my shoulder, giving a knowing wink as he turns his attention to Kynani. "I'm in. This will be a good thing for him. Everything will be opened up for him, and hopefully it will give us a clue of what's been going on all this time."

"Very well. We will get started as soon as possible." Kynani takes her seat on the sectional near Unk and Lennox. "Xavion, there are some things that we need to discuss, especially if Lennox will be a constant in your life. I will also need to secure a temporary location until Yasir's acclimation is complete, so I do not impose on your space."

Well, looks like my work here is done. "Good, now that things have been settled, Z and I have some things to work out. I'll leave you to all the details, and I'll catch up later. There's still a lot I need to know."

"Whatever you have to figure out, do it quick," Lennox opines as she slips her arm inside Unk's. "There's a glow, this aura that swirls around you when you're in each other's space. It's addictive, and I, for one, want to see more of it."

I notice Kynani's inquisitive stare as Lennox continues gushing over me and Zahra. Her eyes dart back and forth between the two of us and trigger my curiosity.

Zahra smirks as she taps my chest. "From what I've been told about Vodaran priestesses, once they began studying their subjects, it was only a matter of time before an interesting convo pops up.

I have a feeling that things are going to get a little more exciting around here."

"Yes, Zahra, Ms. Lennox is correct. There is something swirling around you two, something…ethereal." Kynani continues her assessment as we stand there looking all kinds of confused. "I feel the Divine Mother's eyes on you both. That has not happened in quite some time whenever I have observed Kindaran children or young adults."

I start tapping my watch, almost yanking Zahra out the door with me. "Whew, would you look at the time? Appreciate the extra pressure. We'll talk later, okay?"

I walk her to the car, my nerves completely frayed thanks to the added voices in the house throwing their collective energy behind us when we haven't had a chance to put our energy into each other fully. All I know is that I couldn't let her go without telling her how I really feel. Everything else would have to fall the way they would fall. I send up a silent prayer for strength for whatever would happen before I stop her at her car.

"Are you okay? I know things were a little intense in there."

"Intense isn't even the word, but I don't scare that easily. Why do you ask?"

"I feel like I have to apologize for what you had to see just now." I rub the back of my neck, feeling the anxiety tingling up my spine whenever I think something bad is about to happen. "I mean, I'm still trying to process all that in there. It's obvi that something big is happening, and I need to find out how deep this goes."

"Then let's find out, together," she replies. "I know you want to figure out what this thing is between us, but it feels like there are some other issues that might be more important."

"But we just got a chance to… Never mind." Who am I kidding? My life has gotten complicated in two seconds flat. "I understand if you still want to be just friends. That's a lot to deal with on top of everything else that's going on."

The look on her face throws me off-balance. "I said what I said. I'm yours. My soul has chosen you."

Hearing her say those words somehow makes all the clouds in my mind disappear. Here I am acting like the sky is falling—let's be real, it's still falling—and she's the one telling me she's ready to face down the apocalypse with me.

"And mine has chosen you." I kiss her slow, wrapping my arms tight around her, not wanting to let her go. "I want you with me when we figure this all out. Will you be there?"

"That's not even a question, baby." She kisses me a few more times before I tuck her into the driver's seat. "Whatever is going on with you, I'll understand."

"Call me later. You have a whole house to clear out." Zahra closes the door and starts Raiden's engine. "I'll be waiting for you. Promise."

CHAPTER THIRTY-THREE

From the moment I step on campus, I'm bombarded with all sorts of questions, and I already wanna turn around and go back home. Half of the people are asking about what happened this weekend, and the other half are asking about something I've put out of my mind. My nerves are on edge with each question being asked, because all this is doing is making things more difficult for me to stay out of the spotlight.

"Yo, Yasir, I didn't know you had hands like that. You should hit Michael B. Jordan up for *Creed IV*."

"You're blowing up on TikTok, bro! I heard a few Beach Creek girls been trying to see about you."

"Wow, we thought you were dead, my guy. We didn't hear anything from your circle the whole time you were down."

"Is there anything we can do for you? We heard you're still suffering some side effects from almost drowning."

"Man, Ian and Chris must be breathing a sigh of relief that you're alive. I'd be finding a way to sue, for real."

What in the entire hell did I just walk into this morning?

I don't wanna think about any of that nonsense, especially when there wasn't much of a reprisal after that. Disappointing. Probably would have had to keep my head on a swivel in the A, but then again, Squad had my back.

I almost wish they were here, or at least that they knew I almost died.

I shift those thoughts out of my head while dealing with another wave of people coming through to check on me. I've never had so much as a passing greeting with most of these kids, and now they feel the need to come through and... I mean, I'm trying to understand what half of them are so hyper about, while the other half are on some fake sympathy train.

I shoot a text at Kyle while in class, asking if he's seen or heard anything I don't know about, waiting for his response to be the usual benign-slash-nothing-to-see-here. What I get doesn't resemble the usual, not by a long shot, especially when he jumps me into the group chat with the rest of the clique.

Bro, I don't know how that managed to get bigger, but you're all over the net today, Kyle replies. *Can't get away with anything, since everyone is recording it all.*

Yasir, you good, bro? Taylor chimes in. *I know this ain't what you asked for, and hopefully we can find out who posted that out there. You got enough going on with the boat incident stuff floating around, too.*

Yeah, I wanna say I'm good, but that's a whole lie.

I get caught between wanting to burn everything to the ground and hiding inside the nearest ditch to escape everything. I text back, *Someone obviously wanted me to see that, and they wanted the world to see it, and it wasn't a good thing. I'll be all right for now, but nah, I'm not trying to get used to the spotlight.*

I feel that. Let me and TK get to work a bit and see what we can find out, Kyle responds. *I think I have a clue who might have done it, but I need to be sure.*

I avoid the stares that no longer have anything to do with the war that Ian used to wage when it came to my physical appearance and the scents I wear. That's dead now. Hell, I almost welcome that negativity over the adulation being heaped on because I helped handle some idiots from a rival school. And this BS about wanting to make sure I'm okay? Yeah, that needs to be deaded soon, too, because I'm not here for that, either.

"Is everything okay, kiddo? You feel a lot more agitated than usual."

I jump in my seat, but not enough to draw attention. I

completely forgot that Gamba's still roaming around in my head. I take a quick breath and scan around me to make sure everyone is still paying attention to the discussion on the book we'd read and retreat to the recesses of my mind. *"I got caught on camera when we were dealing with those jokers from Beach Creek."*

"So what is the problem? Any publicity is good publicity, right? Especially when Ian has been off your back for the past few days," Gamba points out. *"As I understand it, he has more important things to worry about, right?"*

I can't have a conversation with Gamba in the middle of class. I'll look like I'm completely spaced out. I ask Mr. Trice, our English teacher, if I can go to the restroom, making up an excuse that I'm not feeling well due to the side effects of the medication. Once I step out into the hallway, I search for the first empty classroom and duck inside. The minute I think I won't be interrupted, I sit in a chair and journey into the recesses of my mind.

We settle into a sitting room in my mind that I created whenever we need to have a convo, and I grab a lemon iced tea while Gamba drinks water. I take a sip or two first, working through the chess game in my head. *"Ian's found a new angle; I can feel it. We need to find out more about him, and I don't mean what the fluff pieces of the town newspaper do on him and his family."* As far as I'm concerned, the best defense is a good offense. *"From the day I hit Oakwood Grove, he's been trying to ruin whatever reputation he thought I had, and I haven't been here that long. It's become a borderline obsession. Not to mention how weird his dad acted when he learned who my father was…"*

Gamba strokes his beard, studying me. *"Let your new friends do the digging for you for now. There is no need to get caught up. Besides, if he is still on you, he will feel the counterattack coming and try to blame this on you."*

"You might be right. I have friends now. I should trust them to have my back."

"Yes, you should. No one can handle anything alone. It is a blessing that you have people around you to help." Gamba leans

back in his chair, chuckling. *"I know it isn't an easy time, there are so many questions that have yet to be answered, but until they are, just take things as they come."*

I offer a chuckle and a shrug. *"Every day might not always be good, but there is always something good in every day."*

Gamba smiles. *"I like that. You should keep that when you're feeling stressed, and I can't get to you quickly. It's perfect."*

I disengage and head back to my conscious mind, realizing that I have enough time to get back to class without causing a stir. I take my seat, breathing deeply before I find out where we are in the discussion.

"Mr. Salah, is everything okay?" Mr. Trice inquires with a furrowed brow.

"Yes, sir, I'm okay."

"Good, now that you're back with us, can you please explain the significance of *Black Boy* by Richard Wright? The first question from last night's discussion homework?" Mr. Trice states as he leans against the front of his desk.

So all eyes on me to answer the question, huh?

Okay, let's do this. I hear Gamba whispering in my mind, *"You've got this, kiddo. Blow them away."*

I give the question some thought, smiling as I feel Gamba sending a warm and comforting energy through me. Yeah, Mr. Trice wants my thoughts on the book, he should be careful what he wishes for. "Mr. Wright was convinced, through his fictional accounts, that the true problem of racism is not that it exists, but that it is woven so deeply inside the fabric of American life that it may take generations to extract its influence, but not without destroying American culture altogether. Is that what you were looking for, sir?"

The class erupts in oohs and ahhs over the response, and the smile I see coming from Mr. Trice shows I had gotten the answer to my question. I'm sitting at my desk, soaking in the appreciation for my words, and for the first time this school year, I actually smile.

There's always something good in every day.

• • •

It takes the rest of the school day for Kyle and the rest of the boys to find out who's behind the viral video, but the wild part is that Ian had nothing to do with it. It doesn't make sense. We've been on this whole frenemy arc since I got here, and he's been trying to pull me into a spotlight I didn't want to be bothered with, and he has every reason to do it. He needs the attention off his party debacle and what happened to me.

But the clique did find out that we weren't off the mark entirely… Eric put the video out there, not Ian. I guess he thought if it came from another school that it wouldn't come back to bite him. Yeah, right. But that's not the funny part about all of this.

That video managed to convert a few of Ian's crew into begrudged fans, each of them showing a tempered respect for my ability to hold my own against hated rivals. The boy that I put down had me by at least a hundred pounds, and the rumors flew around both schools. He ended up becoming the subject of memes and all kinds of other embarrassing status messages all around social media, adding fuel to a wildfire I had hoped to not have to handle.

It's one thing to be the hunter. It's quite another to be the hunted. After seeing what I can become and what I can do once Gamba and I are in sync, I prefer to be predator instead of prey.

Things hit a crazy pitch once I get to Zahra in the courtyard, and I've had about enough of the circus atmosphere that I didn't ask for. Several different "promoters" want to try to turn me into the next Jake Paul and put me up against the Beach Creek kid for a boxing match. I got hit up during class, and I've just told one more person that I'm not interested before I even get to our spot under the Oak.

Never mind the approving glances and comments from the girls around school. It will only be a matter of time before someone catches smoke from Zahra, and I don't need her to get suspended over nonsense. Kendyl turned into a whole bodyguard to keep her bestie from chopping anyone's head off.

"Z, baby, let them go. They're only seeing me because I'm the hot flavor of the day." I cup my hands around Zahra's face. "I'm not stupid. Half of these wannabes are doing nothing but developing selective amnesia right now."

"I don't care. They don't get to be all reckless and I can't do anything about it," Zahra counters. "I swear by Nahara, I'll set these little girls on fire if they even breathe in your direction."

"I love that you're territorial, I wouldn't expect anything less from a Kindaran girl, but I promise you, there's nothing any of them can do for me." I press my lips against her forehead, giving up a smile when I hear a soft moan escape from her mouth. "That's better. Now, we need to focus on more pressing matters, like why is Eric trying to raise my profile and what does he hope to gain from it?"

Kyle walks up with Kendyl in tow, tapping fists with me as the girls group together. The expression on Kyle's face worries me a bit more than I want to admit. "That had to be the worst bait-and-switch I'd ever seen in my life."

Kendyl shakes her head, adding to the lead-in from her boyfriend. "Ian was pulling the strings, trying to make it look like he had nothing to do with it. My friends in the IT club were able to figure it out within a couple of hours. It came from Eric's account, but it was done on Ian's phone."

"I'm getting tired of this game he's playing." I grit my teeth, almost vibrating as I try to keep it together. "I didn't ask for this zoo swirling around us, but he's insisting on making this all about me."

"He's trying to take the spotlight off him. What happened to you at the party was a bad look, and he knows it," Zahra points out. "He still thinks that he can't be touched, but maybe we need to find a way to put some cracks in that wall."

Kyle jumps in, "His father had to pull some major strings to keep the drugs that were found on board from getting into the press. Turns out there was some harder stuff being used outside of the Molly and marijuana that we avoided the whole night."

"Yeah, he's been real quiet most of the day, which is not like him.

He's rattled because he has no idea what you plan to do," Kendyl says. "A lawsuit would put a major crack in that Lance wall, for real."

"What y'all might need to worry about is making sure the new superstar on campus can handle the spotlight." Ian pops up, interrupting the conversation. Chrisette stands by his side, a smirk spread across her face. "I mean, by the time we get done with him, he'll be the hottest thing in town."

I take a step toward Ian, but Kyle steps in front of me. Kyle glances back at me and mouths, "We got you," before turning his attention to Ian. Kendyl stares Chrisette down, almost daring her to speak. Zahra makes herself the last line of defense, posturing in front of me with a scowl on her face.

Ian smirks over the show of solidarity. "What's all this for? I was simply stating the obvious. I mean, he can take anyone he wants in a fight, so it's not like he needs any of you to protect him. Isn't that right, killer?"

"That's funny, I was thinking the same about you, bro," Kyle interrupts. "Damn, I thought you were smarter than this, yo. My ace almost lost his life because of you and your clique, and you wanna act like you didn't do anything, right?"

"I didn't have anything to do with it, and you can't prove otherwise," Ian sneers. He tries to step to me again, only to get blocked by Kyle in the process. "Why don't you step from behind your muscle and holla at me, man to man? Show everyone in this courtyard who you really are."

"Nah, I'm good. Besides, it wouldn't be a fair fight for you. Haven't you seen the video *you* posted?" I crack up laughing for a minute as I watch his face contort. "I mean, you must be losing your grip on reality or something. I was good where I was, and you decided to pull me into the spotlight. This is what that comes with, remember?"

"You're supposed to be the baddest on the block, but you won't step to me?"

"You might wanna look around while you're busy trying to make me out to be some simp who can't handle himself." I smirk as I see the stares in our direction. The ones who are close enough for me to hear what they really thought almost have me feeling sorry for him. "Remember, I still have you over a barrel. It's only a matter of time before my toxicology screens come back. I wonder how much longer it will take before Amber cracks under the threat of a drug charge. You might wanna quit while I'm in a mood not to bury your football career."

Chrisette pulls on Ian's arm, trying to get his attention. She frowns as she stares me down. "So who's the bully now, Yasir? How does it feel to be the one causing the pain?"

"Are you really forming your mouth to say anything?" Zahra steps away from me and gets in her face. "You can't possibly be that brainwashed. There's just no way."

"I have a clarity that you could never understand, Z." Chrisette stands her ground, furrowing her brow as she keeps her gaze trained on Zahra. "If you actually took the time to understand the stress that he has been under this whole time, you wouldn't be so hostile toward him."

"And what stress would that be? He's been at the top of the food chain his entire life. His father has been mayor for as long as we can remember. Stop before you hurt yourself," Zahra deadpans.

Ian turns to quiet Chrisette, taking control of the conversation. "Let's be real, and you might want to let your new 'friends' know before it's too late. You're a menace and a monster, and the truth will come out sooner or later. I know about your rep in the A, 'Diablo.' You're gonna need the support around you when it does, playa."

"Thank you, but no thank you. I know you don't have my best interests at heart, so why should I take any advice off you, huh?" I wrap my arm around Zahra's waist to bring her close. "There's nothing you're gonna be able to do to rile me up, bro. You have to get close enough to do that, and why in the hell would I allow it?"

"Whatever, man, it's your funeral."

As Ian and Chrisette leave the group and the rest of the crowd disperses, Zahra turns to me, focusing her gaze into my eyes. "Are you okay, baby? I felt you vibrating when you pulled me to you.

How did he know about your nickname in Atlanta?"

Gamba chimes in, confusing me over the timing. *"Everything is okay for now, kiddo. I did what I could to keep things under control. There's something about Ian that is triggering something darker in us. Until we can figure it out, there's nothing to say to anyone."*

I stare into Zahra's eyes to reassure her. "I'm good, baby. I'm not about to concern myself with how he figured that out. It's been a weird day, and I may just need to take my mind off things for a bit."

"I can think of a few ways to make that happen," Zahra coos in my ear. "It is a bye-week, after all, so I'm sure we can find a few things to do."

"You two need to get a room," Kendyl chides, then plants a kiss on Kyle's cheek. "Seriously, though, Ian's becoming more of a problem than we thought, and now he's got Chrisette turning into a hype woman. And what's this 'Diablo' business that he was spitting?"

I grab Zahra's hand, making our way to the parking lot. I have other, more pleasant things to think about. "We'll figure them out later. Right now, Z and I need to get over to my uncle's shop to pick up something for dinner. He and Ms. Lennox are going out on a date tonight, and we'll have the house to ourselves for a few hours."

"Oooh, I think I like where this is going. Having a man cook for me sounds absolutely lovely." Zahra grins as she waves goodbye. "We'll catch up with y'all later."

As we head toward Storm and Raiden, I can't shake the feeling that Ian knows more than he's letting on. I just wish I knew who he found to give up that information. I tap on Gamba's door, letting him know we need to start digging into Ian's past and find something we can use for leverage. *"I'm gonna have to keep him at more than an arm's length. He's got it out for us, and everything in me is telling me he's playing a long game. We need to be prepared."*

"I'm with you, Ya-Ya, but that can wait until tomorrow." Gamba peers through my eyes and sees Zahra next to me. *"Right now, I need to make myself scarce. Based on the grin on your girlfriend's face, you will have a need for privacy tonight."*

CHAPTER THIRTY-FOUR

Zahra's eyes are on me almost the entire time I'm preparing the crab legs and fried shrimp we picked up from Unk's restaurant. Every time I glance in her direction, she has this slick smile on her face, and the only thing on my mind in that moment is Unk's advice on "catering to your girl." By the time I place the steaming-hot plate in front of her and wait for her approval, I finally understand what he meant.

She gives me this *look* like I've done the most wonderful thing for her tonight, and she can't wait to show her appreciation.

But for me, tonight feels like more. Despite the intimacy of the night, this has connectivity written all over it. We haven't had a chance to really learn each other and understand what it all means for us. She also wants to catch me up on Kindaran culture now that I know my true origin.

I wonder if she will have to teach me, to be honest. If what Nana told us is true, there's suppressed information and memories that I don't have access to. That may keep me from getting a grip on our shared culture. But what if I know more than she does about Kindara once my memories are unlocked?

So many questions, not enough answers.

I catch her staring off as she continues to consume her dinner. "Penny for your thoughts, pretty girl?"

She winks at me, popping a shrimp in her mouth, realizing she's been caught. "I have a few thoughts, but it may cost you more than a penny. Who taught you how to cook? The shrimp are to die for."

"Well, I mean, Unk is one of the best on the coast at what he does. I picked up a few things over the years, and between him and Nana, I had to learn quick." I pour some apple juice into a glass for her before I sit next to her at the dining room table. "I'm sure I'll figure some more things out as I continue to practice, but I'm glad you're enjoying it. I was low-key nervous. You're the first person I've cooked for outside of them."

"You keep cooking like this, and I'm gonna have to watch myself. If anything, I'll need to return the favor." She cracks open a crab leg to slide the meat from the shell. "How do you feel about what's happened so far? I know it has to be a lot to process."

I pop a piece of crab meat into my mouth as I ponder her question. It's a lot, that's for sure. "I'm still trying to get over the fact that I'm Kindaran. I've been processing the meaning of it all since Nana dropped everything on me."

"What do you remember about Kindara?" she asks, almost like she doesn't want to say the wrong thing. "I've read on people who have suppressed memories, and sometimes they manifest themselves in dreams. Have you had any dreams or anything?"

I tap my index finger against my left temple. I'm not sure how to explain what's been happening, except to say it. "I've been having, well, nightmares, I guess. It's hard to explain, but I travel to Kindara, and I see different aspects of the island. Then I—" I can't say anything more, and I almost shut down. The nightmares are way too intense to talk about.

She takes my hand in hers, placing her other hand against my cheek, and gently nudges me to meet her gaze. "We don't have to talk about that if you don't want to. My parents told me of your parents' bravery to help repel the Bralba invaders. Maybe that's what's been hidden from you. What I do want to talk about is how you were brought into this world by Vodaran priestesses—if what Nana's saying is true, that means your family was one of the Kindaran Nine."

I shrug. All I can do is take her word for it. "I still don't know what any of that means. I feel like I have so much to learn. Unk might know a lot, too, since he's my mom's brother. I don't even know what Tribe that side of the family is from, so I'll have to sit down with him to work through that lesson. And now I have Hassan to deal with, and he's supposed to be a friend of the family, but I have no idea what he's really about, either. Who knows what other family I might have and if they survived the invasion like I did?"

"Maybe Daddy can help with that," Zahra offers. "He's one of the foremost Kindaran historians in the world. There's nothing he doesn't know or can't find out."

"I don't know, Z. What if your father isn't too keen about me dating his daughter?" All of this is swirling around my head too fast. I don't know if I'm ready to even meet her parents or anything. I mean, I know I have to eventually, but this is a lot all at once. "Hell, maybe I'm overthinking all of this. I don't know how to act right now. All of this is just so amazing—and scary."

She smiles bright, causing me to smile with her. "My father will be thrilled that we're dating. He never liked any of the boys I might have been interested in because they weren't Kindaran. He almost came to blows with one boy I was dating and his father one time at a dinner at their house."

I grin as I think about it. "Maybe talking to your dad might help connect some of the dots in my mind. The gods know I need a basis of understanding. It might help with so much more."

"Well, now that we've gotten that out of the way." Her smile turns more suggestive, and I'm here for whatever is on her mind right now. "I'm still waiting for you to explain that kiss with the paintings and then that flashback of that horrible night. I know I have to be patient, but I don't think you realize how epic that was for me."

My cheeks heat up, and I look for anything to focus on instead of her stare. She giggles for a moment while I try to get my life together. "I guess it's my turn to keep from being so flushed that my skin feels like it's on fire. It was epic for me, too, and honestly, I don't know how to explain what happened. I was so nervous that I wasn't kissing you the right way that I did whatever I could to stay in the moment with you. I may need to reach out to Ms. Kynani so she can help explain how I did it."

She sighs, fanning herself as she takes a sip of her juice. "If that kiss was any clue of what's to come, I'm gonna need you to get with her as soon as possible. I'm completely floored that you even have access to the priestesses to begin with."

I tilt my head to the side. I'm genuinely confused. "Why is that? Doesn't everyone?"

Zahra laughs softly as she caresses the back of my hand. "Yeah, until we can unlock your memories, I have a lot to teach you. According to Daddy, there's never been anyone who wasn't already picked by the Kindaran Council to have that type of access to any of the Vodaran priestesses."

I scratch my head, trying to connect the dots the best I can. "Is that because my family is one of the Kindaran Nine? I'm still trying to figure all of this out, and I'm worried that I might be sounding dumb. I hope I'm not bending your ear off."

"No, not at all. I'm loving this, and you're not dumb," she assures me as she cracks open another crab leg. "There's so much we can learn together now, and learn about each other, too. I can't wait to find out."

"Neither can I. It feels so right when I'm around you." I'm smiling so wide I can feel my dimples deepening into my cheeks. "We need to finish things up so we can enjoy dessert before Unk and Ms. Lennox get home."

"Yes, absolutely. I'll be waiting in the living room." She kisses my lips soft and slow before she tips away. "You know, a girl could get used to being spoiled like this. I think I'll keep you around after all."

My cell phone rings, startling both of us. I pick it up, noticing Nana's number pop across the screen. I answer it and place it on speaker so we can both hear the call. "Hi, Nana, is everything okay?"

"Yes, grandson, everything is faring well." Her voice sounds soothing, steady. "I have been able to speak with Kynani at length since we arrived, and I was wondering if Zahra is with you."

"Yes, Nana, I'm here," Zahra chimes in.

"Wonderful. I have already contacted your uncle and his girlfriend. We would like to have you over to Kynani's rental property tomorrow night." We hear the smile in her voice, but the cryptic nature of her message throws us off. "It is time."

"Time for what exactly?" I ask.

"To show you who you are."

CHAPTER THIRTY-FIVE

Nervous doesn't even begin to describe my feelings as Kynani invites us inside. "Good evening, Yasir, Zahra. Please come in. I am pleased you could make time for tonight's occasion."

The heat we're generating might as well be calculated for nova-level radiance. I've been looking forward to this for so long, I'm a little worried that I've built things up too much. I squeeze Zahra's hand, tempering my emotions, realizing that I could bring Gamba to the surface before I'm ready to show him to the group.

That might be what Kynani and Nana have in mind, though.

I breathe a sigh of relief that everyone else who needs to be here has already arrived. That means more to me than anything, and it also means we won't have to wait around to do whatever it is that they need to do to bring everything out of me.

And that's the scary part: what the hell is inside of me?

Kynani escorts us into the dining area. Unk and Lennox sit at the table, along with Nana, who can't stop smiling when she sees us walk in.

"Just have a seat, enjoy, since we didn't have to cook today, and let's let Ms. Kynani and Mama Johari explain why we're all here," Unk says.

Since he puts it that way. "So why are we here, Ms. Kynani? Nana was a bit cryptic over the phone."

Kynani smiles as she sits at one head of the table, sharing a glance with Nana at the other head of the table. "The reason why we asked you and the women in your lives to be here has everything to do with what has happened to you over the past few days. It is time to bring things full circle, in a manner of speaking."

I rub the back of my neck, unsure how to elaborate what Kynani led with. "I assume you mean the *other presence*, right?"

Zahra snaps her head in my direction, along with Unk and Lennox. "Um, what *other presence* are you talking about?"

Nana interrupts Zahra before she can really crank up the interrogation. "We will explain things as best as we can and as quickly as we can, my child. Right now, we need to focus on Ya-Ya. Before the end of the night, a lot of things will change."

I squeeze her hand again, turning to kiss her lips. I whisper, "It'll be okay, promise," before I turn my attention to Kynani. "I trust her completely with whatever happens tonight. Now, what do you know about the *other* presence?"

Kynani nods, focusing her attention on me. "The other guy, as you are calling him for now, has already made up his mind about the persons in this room before I have had the chance to commune with him."

I raise an eyebrow, clueless over how she knows so much so soon. "How are you able to know that he's okay?"

"You have not had to retreat into yourself to calm him down. He always tries to make an appearance whenever there is a threat surrounding you." Kynani smiles as she peers over at Zahra and Lennox. "I believe he knows there are no threats here, especially when he has grown quite fond of Zahra. Not as fond as he is of you, of course, but fond enough to declare himself her protector. He has sensed something within her that he recognizes. What that is, I do not know at this moment."

Zahra takes a sip of the mimosa in front of her, then clears her throat. "Um, can I, and Ms. Lennox, get a clue of what you're talking about right now? What 'other' presence? Yasir, do you have Kindaran bodyguards following you in the shadows or something?"

Considering I had a convo with Gamba already—and he's being real obvious with his silence, now that I think about it—they all deserve some sort of answer.

"I think it's best if we have this conversation in the great room.

I think we will need to be comfortable for this part of the process. I can't really tell you… I kinda have to show you."

"I need you to relax, Yasir. Breathe…focus on my voice as we travel inside your mind."

I focus on the instructions Kynani gives me, but it becomes more difficult by the moment. It might have had something to do with the quick convo and Q&A we had before we started this part of the process. It didn't get worse as the layers were taken off the proverbial onion, but by the time we'd finished, the looks on Zahra's and Lennox's faces were a mix of shock and disbelief.

"You can't be serious," Lennox says as she sits with Unk. The confusion all over her face makes me chuckle, but that's more of a nervous laughter. "Are you telling us that there's some sort of monster inside of his nephew? And we're supposed to just accept it like monsters actually exist?"

Kynani is undeterred by the incredulous looks on their faces. "To take a quote from Mr. Spock: 'If you eliminate the impossible, whatever remains, however improbable, must be the truth.' Is it so hard to believe that there might be supernatural beings that walk among us on this planet?"

"Yes, yes, it is." Unk glances over at me, shaking his head in the process. "All this time, the information that Mama Johari tried to explain to me, the advice from the Kindaran Council on how to keep Yasir hidden from the world. All of this was real?"

I turn to face Zahra, desperate to get a gauge of how she feels about what she's hearing. I look into her eyes, searching for anything that'll keep me from regretting the decision to trust her with such a closely guarded secret. "Z, talk to me, please?"

Zahra caresses my face, tracing my eyes with her fingertips, biting her lip as she continues to move over my skin. "So this *other* guy… He's been in there this whole time?"

I shake my head, closing my eyes to lean into her touch. By

Nyati, she feels so damn good. "Kinda yes, but not really. I wasn't fully aware of him until after the boat accident. Why do you ask?"

"Your eyes… Every time they changed colors to match your emotions. I couldn't figure out what it meant." Zahra keeps staring, almost like she's waiting for them to turn another shade while we talk. "I was so hypnotized by them that I didn't think they could have meant something more…mystical."

I narrow my eyes and think back to the incident with Squad. Then again, when we first kissed in the studio after I showed her the portrait of her likeness. "So now that you're about to find out what I am—what I truly am—do you still want to be with me?"

Zahra grabs my hands and holds them in hers. "I guess I always knew what you were. I just didn't think it would be this beautiful. You might not know this about me, either, but I'm a Marvel girl, so I can't resist thinking that the boy that I've fallen for could be… Yeah, the whole 'Bruce Banner/Hulk' idea sort of intrigues me."

"Wait, you're into comics, too?" I wait as Zahra opens her phone and shows me the Marvel Comics app on her phone. "Okay, I'm officially in love, love with you right now. But wait a second… does that mean—?"

"Yes, baby, it means that whoever or whatever is inside of you doesn't scare me." Zahra kisses my cheek as she continues to trace my face with her fingers. "I don't know how else to explain it. The connection between us scares me more than anything else. It's like you were made for me."

Kynani clears her throat to interrupt our private side convo. "There may be something I can do to help clarify things in that manner, but right now, we need to focus on Yasir and his acclimation process."

I tremble as I shake off the chill racing down my spine. "We can talk about things after this is done. I want to get to know my nyxwraith, figure out where he came from and how we ended up together."

I sit in the middle of the living room floor opposite Kynani, crossing my legs to shrink the space I've taken. I close my eyes before the process begins, sending a silent prayer to the Divine Mother for strength through the process. *I know I'm not supposed to be afraid, but this whole process has me completely freaked out. Guide me through this as best you can, Divine One, and help me understand the importance of all of this.*

Kynani begins chanting in her Kindaran dialect, lighting candles that surround us. In the next breath, she closes her eyes, encouraging me to do the same. From there, her octave changes, the tone sounding like that of a soothing parental figure, coaxing whatever hesitant spirit lay in the depths.

"I can feel your presence within your owner. I encourage you to come forth. You are in a safe space here," Kynani declares, keeping the sing-song cadence in her tone to summon Gamba to the surface. "Yasir's uncle is here, and two new friends are here to speak with you. You can come out and say hello to them. They are a part of him. They are not threats to him."

I feel Gamba come through the darkness, taking his time to break through my conscious mind. Our eyes meet as Gamba gauges my approval over whether it indeed is a safe space to reveal himself. I nod, opening the "door" for Gamba to walk through. *"I don't think they're ready to see the full transformation, but I think seeing you through some subtle changes will be enough to convince them."*

Gamba grins, baring his fangs. *"Kynani and I are old friends. If she says it is safe, then it is safe. You can relax until it is time to complete the acclimation process."*

"Will I be able to see what's going on? Every time you fully take over, I'm stuck in the dark. I don't want that to happen while dealing with this process."

Gamba answers by giving a subtle and proverbial tip of the hat. *"After the process is complete, you will be able to sense everything. It will not harm too much if you keep an eye on the people around you. It might help once you come back."*

Gamba rises to the surface, taking over my physical body. He recognizes Kynani first, acknowledging her with a wry smile. "Good evening, Kynani. It has been a long time since we have last seen each other." He manipulates my voice so that everyone he introduces himself to would understand who's speaking to them.

Kynani returns Gamba's smile, a bit confused over why he regarded her with such familiarity. She doesn't overlook that he chooses to be agreeable for the process. "I apologize, you have me at a disadvantage. May I ask your name, nyxwraith? I recognize the cadence in your speech, but you still sound like Yasir, except for the deeper octave in his voice."

"Forgive me, my friend, I forget that it is difficult to manipulate his voice until the process is complete," he replies to her. "Allow me to refresh your memory of me before I give you my name... The last words I said to you at Solara were, 'The boy is the key to saving the Scrolls.' Do you recognize me now?"

"Gamba, by Nyati's grace, I had hoped..." Nana gasps as a tear falls. "If you're with my grandson, then that means..."

"Yes, the fates were not kind to me on that side of the veil." Gamba offers up a comforting gaze and smile. "But the Divine Mother saw fit for me to be of service in the most honorable way possible now."

I listen in on the conversation between them while keeping a sharp eye on the reactions from Unk, Lennox, and Zahra as things unfold in front of them. Unk looks like he's gonna have a million questions as everything is happening, and he's rubbing his hands over and over again, which is a dead giveaway that he's uncomfortable with what's happening, but he's helpless to intervene.

Lennox, on the other hand, gives the impression that she's taking mental notes, which has me wondering why she isn't completely flipping out. There's no way she's seen something like this before. I've never been through anything like this before, and I know I'm not calm. At. All.

I zero in on Zahra's surprised and inquisitive facial expressions and the wonder washing over her. I smile as I guess what could be going through her mind in the moment and can't wait to get her alone to find out what she's thinking.

My nana's reaction to Gamba raises more questions over who he was and why she regarded him with such...love?

Kynani smiles wide, recognizing him in an instant. "Gamba, I am elated that you are here. Your new owner is a strong one to be able to have you. How have you been able to survive for so long without communicating with him?"

Gamba lets a low growl escape from his lips, allowing the fangs to stick out from his lips. "It has not been easy, but he has had a lot of growing up to do, too. I had time to commune with our ancestors to assist me on how best to guide him. I am impressed with how he has handled everything he has endured all this time, despite what was hidden from him. I feel a shift in the winds."

"As do I, my friend, now that I see that you are here. For that shift to come full circle, it is time for you and Yasir to complete the acclimation process," Kynani stresses. She looks at Zahra, Unk, and Lennox and grins. "For the rest of you, this process will be foreign to you, but I promise I am not hurting him. I understand if there are concerns, but this will help him more than you know."

Unk grabs Lennox's hand to keep her close. "Yasir hasn't been in touch with his true roots and bloodline. If this helps him figure things out, then I'm staying with him to see it through."

"What does that mean?" I ask from the shadows. "No one really told me what this all means."

"Allow Kynani to come inside so we can explain it to you, kiddo. I promise, what comes after will be life-altering for the both of us."

Okay. I decide to trust the process despite the growing fear rising through me. "Then let's get to it."

Gamba turns to Kynani, giving the thumbs-up signal. "We are ready."

Kynani takes my hands in hers, coaxing me back to the surface. "Very well. Allow me access to your mind, Yasir. It is time to sync your essences to help you work better together."

Silence consumes all three of us. I wait for the next few minutes, wondering what's supposed to happen next. The shroud fades away, slow and easy, until I see Kynani and a man sitting in chairs in front of me, with an empty chair positioned to create a triangle between them. Gamba is nowhere to be found, which strikes me as odd.

I wanna say that the man in front of me is Gamba, but I can't be sure, either. "So I'm gonna need some quick questions answered before I even think about sitting down."

"To answer your immediate question, kiddo, this is what I looked like when I was human." Gamba stands. "I have not been able to assume my true human form in quite some time."

"Okay, pause, so when you presented yourself in your human form before, that wasn't the true you?" His facial features have changed a little, but everything else is the same. His cheekbones are more defined and chiseled, and his eyes are more oval-shaped than before. "I mean, your features aren't that different from when I first met you, but I can tell the difference."

Gamba smirks like I'm supposed to be in on whatever inside joke he has with himself. "I want to ensure that you understand that I am not trying to deceive you in any way, Yasir. You know me—well, your younger self knows me well."

I lean in closer, recognizing familiar features in Gamba's face. I can't quite place them, but I swear they resembled those of Dad. But my father's dead. "Who are you to me, Gamba? Are you a part of my bloodline?"

Gamba grins. "In a manner of speaking, yes and no, Ya-Ya."

"I don't like riddles all that much, even though I'm good at solving them when the occasion calls for it."

Gamba moves closer. "I am a close friend of your father, and I am also your godfather. He and I were best friends. He has spoken of you often and has kept watch over you this entire time."

I take a couple of steps back, reaching behind me for the back of the chair so I can sit down. I'm stuck between wanting to believe what Gamba is saying is true and writing it all off as one bad joke. "You knew my father? How is any of this even possible? I don't remember you... I don't remember anything from that time."

"I promise, we will sit down and have this conversation after we're done with the acclimation, kiddo," Gamba says. "I believe it will all come to you once Kynani is able to lift the suppression spells. I would never lie to you. I never did, even when you were smaller."

Kynani places her hand on my shoulder, giving it a gentle

squeeze. "There is much for you two to discuss, Yasir. As your priestess, it is my duty and honor to help along the way. Now that you have the one important answer, are you ready to continue?"

I remain fixated on Gamba, taking in every contour of his face, the same golden-amber color in his eyes, the way his lip curls on the left side when he smiles. I've been so detached from Kindara. And now, to find out that my protector—my nyxwraith—was my godfather?

I snap out of my musing long enough to acknowledge Kynani with a nod. "I'm ready. I've been waiting for this my whole life…at least, that's what it feels like, deep down."

Kynani claps her hands three times before rubbing them together to create a spark. When she separates them, we are consumed in an amethyst-hued flame that glows brilliantly against the darkness that surrounds us. She takes each of our hands, watching as the flames snake down our arms to where we connect, forming a triangle between us.

Seconds later, the flame consumes us all, but it doesn't burn us.

Kynani keeps her eyes closed to concentrate. "Gamba, do you pledge your life to your owner, to protect him from all enemies, foreign or friendly?"

"I pledge my life to my owner, my godson, and to protect him from all enemies, foreign or friendly," Gamba repeats.

Kynani continues. "Yasir, do you pledge to protect your nyxwraith from anyone who would try to do him harm, to ensure that you do not place yourself in any unnecessary peril, and when called upon, you both will do what is best for Kindara?"

"I pledge to protect my nyxwraith, my godfather, from anyone who would try to do him harm, to ensure I do not place myself in any unnecessary peril, and when called upon, to do what is best for Kindara," I repeat, just as Gamba had done.

Kynani focuses her energy among the three of us as the color of the flames changes to a brilliant crimson before dissipating. She opens her eyes and releases her grasp. "Yasir, Gamba, the acclimation has now taken hold, and the merge is complete. You should be able to move freely within Yasir's consciousness, but there are still limits as his nyxwraith. You cannot take over unless he is in severe distress, and he still can override if he sees fit. Any suggestions you make can be heeded or not."

I feel like I'm connected to something magical inside my own body. The rush of energy flowing through me—I swear I want to run for miles as fast as I can. And if we're connected, then that means I can view things the way Gamba does any time I want. It's like a whole different world has opened up for me, and I'm still scratching the surface of what we can do.

Gamba nods while I'm still scanning my subconscious like I've never been here before. "I understand. I know the limits of my power. My owner has the final say, regardless."

I give up a nervous grin. "How am I supposed to dictate to my godfather? I was always taught to defer to my elders."

Gamba claps his hand on my shoulder. "I am a guide and bound by Kindaran law to protect you, kiddo. It will be an adjustment, but we will be fine. It will give me a chance to learn this mature version of you."

"It is time to return, I imagine there are three people who are wondering what we have been up to this entire time," Kynani advises. "It has been my honor to facilitate this transition, and I look forward to guiding you further."

Kynani and I open our eyes, taking a moment to regain our bearings. I chuckle at the captive audience in front of us and their collective confusion. I turn to Zahra, who has the widest grin on her face, giving me a curious look that I keep a mental note to ask about later.

Unk stares at me, his gaze darting between me and Kynani as he holds Lennox closer. "I…I have no idea what to make of what I just saw. One minute, you both were covered in this…fire, but nothing was burning around you. The next minute, the fire is gone, and you two just wake up like nothing happened. Did it work or was that just a magic display?"

I share a knowing wink with Kynani, realizing the next half hour will be entertaining, to say the least.

CHAPTER THIRTY-SIX

"How long have you and Yasir been, shall we say, dating?" Kynani asks.

"Um, we've been, like, together for about a couple of weeks, so to speak, Ms. Kynani."

It's interesting that she's asking about how long we've been together, together, and I have a funny feeling she's digging for a specific reason. What that might be, I guess it'll reveal itself soon enough. All we can do is answer the questions and take things from there.

"There is something special I see between you two." Kynani observes us as we sit on the sectional. She nods. "While I was able to connect you with your nyxwraith, there is much work to be done to break through the spell that was cast to erase the traumatic experience from your memories."

Zahra and I sit across from Kynani as Lennox and Unk enjoy some time to themselves on the deck in the backyard. Nana has already retired for the night, so it leaves us and Kynani together to chat. Kynani explained after the acclimation was finished that she needed to sit down and get a gauge on how things have progressed between Zahra and me. The more she stares at us, the more her curiosity shows up in her facial expressions.

"I have a question, if I may ask." Zahra gazes into my eyes, grinning at me like she's picked up on some new things. "Now that the acclimation is complete, what happens to Yasir now? Do we just go back to our normal lives—if there is such a thing?"

Kynani giggles at the question, but I'm legit interested in the answer, too. "I understand why you would ask. The truth of the matter is that, in a manner of speaking, nothing will be normal for either of you from now on. It is my hope to help keep things as simple as possible, but there are things that you both will need to understand."

I interlace my fingers with Zahra's, taking a deep breath and exhaling slow and easy. "I think I remember this part from what I researched. There are *mwali duati*—metahumans—who are bound by Kindaran law and religion to protect the secrets hidden deep within Kindara itself. Is that what I have become? What does that mean for me and Z?"

Kynani offers a knowing grin, holding up her hand to slow the stream of questions. "I believe we need to have this conversation sooner rather than later. But I need to speak with your parents first, Zahra, and with Xavion and Lennox as well. This part is not something that should be kept from them."

"Is it too soon to bring my parents into things? I mean, I'm just now trying to wrap my head around what happened today. It's all so wonderful and confusing at the same time." Zahra tightens her grip on my hand, then smiles when I raise it to my lips to kiss. "I don't know that they will understand what happened, either. It might complicate things."

"Your father is a Kindaran historian. He understands more than you realize," Kynani says. "What he might not understand is the application of the history he has been researching this entire time. That will take time for us to help your parents work through their initial confusion."

"So how soon can we figure that out?" I ask her. "I don't want to sound selfish, but I just found Zahra, and for the first time in my life, things are starting to make sense. I would like to keep that ball rolling, after suffering for so long."

"I understand the need to speed ahead, young ones, but I must ask for as much patience as you can provide. All will be revealed in time." Kynani rises from her seat. "I will need to speak to your parental figures now, Yasir, since they are together at this moment."

She leans down, whispering low enough for us to hear her response. "Between you, me, and the gods, she is what your uncle has needed in his life this entire time. He has sacrificed a lot more than you realize. There is something swirling around Lennox, something that will be good for him, and for you."

She walks to the back door, leaving me and Zahra to have a moment to ourselves. Zahra turns to kiss my cheek, adjusting her body to face me, tucking her legs under her to get comfortable. "How do you feel about all of this? Do you trust me with what you are? I admit I don't know how to feel about everything, but I want you to know I'm not going anywhere."

I take her hands and kiss them over and over. She has no idea how badly I wanted to hear that from her. "I trust you completely. More than you know." I rise from the couch, offering my hand to help her stand. "I need to get you home. We do still have school in the morning."

"Lead the way, handsome. It will give us some more time to talk."

"Okay, so, outside of hearing Gamba's voice through you, I really don't know what that looks like, either. I mean, I've seen your eyes change at times, but you know about that."

We take the long way to Zahra's house so we can have some extra time to ourselves to vibe. Our phones are on vibrate, and the way they keep buzzing against the middle console, we'll have a lot of texts to deal with once I drop her off and head back home.

"Well, I kinda know what that looks like, but it's hard to explain." I give up a chuckle. "The first time it happened, I was literally left in the dark. Like, it feels like a dark shroud covering you, keeping you from seeing anything at all. It wasn't until Ms. Kynani finally merged our essences that I might get a chance to see what exactly has been manifesting itself through my body and mind."

"Well, it can't be that weird, right?" she questions. "I mean, is it like a lycanthropic change or something like that? Is there any way that we can get an idea from Gamba?"

"I don't know how to answer that question, baby. The thing that scares me the most is that you see what we look like in that form in real time, or Unk or Ms. Lennox." I grip the steering wheel tight this time, while trying to keep a comfortable grip on her hand. "Nyati forbid if it happens in a public space and people would rather kill something they don't understand or fear than try to ask questions to figure things out."

"You make it sound like...like..."

"Like, what, being a Black person in America?" I throw out the conclusion that she didn't want to voice out loud. It has to be said. "Not like it isn't already a struggle to go out into the world on that front, and now I have to worry about being a metahuman on top of that."

She massages my palm. The convo has gotten way too dark, that's for sure. "Then we'll do what we can to keep that from happening, okay? I meant what I said, I'm here, and I'm not afraid."

"Well, I don't know if I should be or not, but I guess I won't know until I know, right?"

"Okay, let's try to take this in a different direction, Ya-Ya." She moves up to my forearm to keep me in the moment with her. "Tell me about Gamba. Is he aware of what happens when you're dealing with other people?"

"Yes, he's told me as much, although he says he tries to avoid things and situations that are more...private for me," I explain. "In other instances, I can shut him out if the need arises."

"So that means he wasn't there when we almost...well." I can see the wheels turning in her head, and I have the same thoughts. That day in my studio almost triggers me, and not in a bad way, either. "I want to believe that moments like that belong to you and me."

"Yeah, those moments belong to us. There are no witnesses whatsoever." I feel her squeezing my hand, and I breathe a sigh of relief. "Like I said, I can shut him out if the need arises. It isn't complicated in that sense. Ms. Kynani made it clear that I can still live my life, but my nyxwraith is there when I'm stressed or in immediate danger."

"What else have you had the chance to chat with him about? Has he, like, talked to you about other things? Does he give advice at all?"

I grin at her, making her blush. "I found out that he was my godfather when he was alive and that by some form of Vodaran magick, or by Nyati's will, he was, I don't know, inserted in my psyche. I still don't know how it all works or what abilities we have."

"You keep saying *we*, Ya-Ya. I get a little confused when you say it like that," she confesses. "How will I know the difference between you two, besides the cadence and tone of your voice?"

I think on it for a moment, and then I snap my fingers. "Since he's not here to hear it, how about this: if you want to be sure it's me, we need to come up with a word or phrase that is unique to only me and you."

"Okay, so what word or phrase would we both know that will help me tell the difference?"

I mull over her question as I pull into her driveway. "If you ever need to bring me to the surface, no matter what is going on, get our attention and say the words '*karasu horo*.' It's a Kindaran phrase that, roughly translated, means 'return to me, my chosen.' If you have to repeat it, repeat it. It's something Gamba wouldn't know to respond to, and he'll have to bring me back."

"I love it, but I'm confused now. How did you learn that phrase?"

"Umm, so I've been learning a few words and phrases ever since Nana told us that I'm Kindaran. I'll see you tomorrow at school." I reach over to softly kiss her. "I can't wait for Unk to meet your parents. It should be an entertaining night."

"Will Ms. Kynani be with you?" she asks. "I have a feeling Daddy won't want to pass up the chance to meet her. For that matter, I assume Ms. Lennox may be there, too. I like her. She's really good for your uncle, now that I think about it."

"Yeah, she's definitely had a positive influence on him, and that makes me happy." I smile as I put Storm back in gear. "Now, get in the house so you can get settled in."

"Bye, cuteness." She blows a kiss before getting out of the car. "You're lucky I love you, or I'd have to do something about the bossy tone in your voice."

"Mhm, no you won't. You like it too much to make me stop. Now, off to bed, young lady. See you in the morning."

I pull out of the driveway, feeling the smile on my face and the starlit night overhead through the sunroof. I can't remember the last time I felt so at ease and calm, and I want to ride this out for as long as I can.

My phone rings, and I quickly glance and notice it's an unknown number calling. I don't think anything of it; it's probably Hassan calling to give me an update or something. "Hello?"

There's silence on the line, and I'm confused over why the person won't respond to my greeting. "Hello? Is anyone there?"

"I know who you are, and I know where you are." The voice on the phone sounds distorted, like someone is purposely trying to disguise themselves. "I'm coming for you, and I'm going to destroy you."

Before I can respond to the threat, the call disconnects.

CHAPTER THIRTY-SEVEN

I stare at the planes as they touch down at Drana Tirin Airport, confused over how I managed to arrive here. I scan the area, not really sure what I'm searching for, until I find a placard being held by a driver who has my name scrawled across it. I've been used to arriving on the island through the usual route, so coming through the capital city presents a new set of challenges.

Or maybe it might provide an opportunity to find a different clue to help me unravel the puzzle that, through these dreams, I guess I'm meant to solve.

The driver recognizes me, shakes my hand, and signals for me to accompany him to the idling Jeep Gladiator truck awaiting us in the staging area. As with my other dreams, no one really speaks, but I can't figure out if it disturbs me or if I prefer they not speak. If we are heading toward Solara, I need to brace myself for the emotional turmoil that'll greet me once we reach the gates to my home.

I keep my wits about me as I survey the landscape from this new angle. Even in my dream state, the chance still exists that I can be killed. Sure, it might be a remote possibility, but I've watched enough of the *Matrix* movies to know better than to tempt the theory that Morpheus made famous: that the body cannot live without the mind and that the mind makes the dreams real.

The Jeep makes its trek over the hills, coming in from the north side of the island, the driver making the approach with skill and care as the vehicle begins to traverse across the cobblestone roadway. The move is necessary; this time, storms sweep over the landscape, making the stones slippery. Kindara is "enjoying" its annual rainy season, and though it's on the tail end where the storms aren't as prominent or frequent, what does show up comes with its own wallop.

I hope I'm able to see something new during this recent sequence. I've made this normal trek from the south, so I take the new trajectory as a reason to scribble as many notes as possible on my notepad. Something has to happen during this ride that'll trigger something new for me to research. The winds shift the storm to a diagonal downpour, and if I concentrate hard enough, I can see the turtles slip-sliding their way through the grasslands.

The moment arrives when I normally witness the smoke pluming from behind the gates, but the storm has all but suppressed the fires from the battle. I notice a shadowy figure, something that I didn't notice during the last sequence. What I also haven't experienced from the last time is the torrential downpour that further obscures the person from my view. I can't make out the features of the person, which is frustrating me. There are only so many of these I can take before it leaves me hesitant to bother anymore. I'm not ready to give up, as I'm more concerned over figuring out who this person is and why they are so important.

I get out of the Jeep and climb the first hill that leads into the village, hearing the commotion that I've grown so familiar with as the rainstorm calms to a drizzle. I can tell how heated the fighting is just by the pitch and the cadence. I steel myself against the oncoming battle and its inevitable conclusion, although I have to admit that it never gets easier, no matter how many times I've gone through the torturous event.

I watch my younger self being led away from the fight, but I also notice something I don't expect. "I" am fighting against Hassan, almost like I'm fighting for my life on a different front. Hassan eventually picks me up from the ground and runs to safety, ignoring my cries that I don't want to leave the fight. I wonder why I would fight Hassan when I needed to be brought to safety.

I awake with a scream, slapping my hand over my mouth to keep from waking up the house yet again. I sit up in bed, taking a hand towel to wipe the sweat from my forehead and the back of my neck. I have a hard time understanding the new clue I didn't expect to find, but I tuck it away in my journal for later to compare what I've found in earlier trips. There has to be a connection.

I text Zahra good morning, grinning when the text comes back a few minutes later, the heart emoji conveying more than any words are needed. I send a few emojis back before I switch gears to text Kynani, asking for her counsel for the nightmares I'm suffering from, hoping she'll have the ability to help me either control what I'm witnessing or at least develop a deeper insight into what I find.

I receive a text back from Kynani, requesting a time to visit and assist. I glance at the time on my phone and realize it isn't quite seven a.m. yet. Fuck. I didn't pay attention to the time; she could've been resting... I apologize for texting so early, asking for her to come over after school. She mentions something about being up since before dawn to confer with someone on the Kindaran Council before she confirms that she will come and see me.

Now that I've gotten through that minor embarrassment, I switch gears again to check in with the boys when a call comes through, interrupting my messaging.

I recognize Hassan's number and freeze. Not because he has my number, but because he is calling so early in the morning. And after the last dream sequence that revealed him struggling to take me away from the battle scene, it now has me questioning everything about him. "What's up, Hassan? Is there something I can do for you?"

He chuckles, although I can't understand what's so funny. "I wanted to make sure everything has gone smoothly with Kynani. She requested to assist, so I wanted to make sure she is handling things properly."

I start to answer Hassan when Gamba slips into my ear. *"Something isn't right, Ya-Ya. He's a little too interested in what's going on with you."*

I pause for a moment, checking with my nyxwraith to figure things out. *"He's been dealing with other issues that took precedence.*

He had one of the priestesses come down when Nana asked at a moment's notice. Why are you telling me we shouldn't say anything to him now?"

"Everything okay, Yasir?" Hassan inquires. "I want to make sure the connection is still solid. We're out in the Mediterranean."

"His motives are not pure right now, Yasir," Gamba insists. *"He's fishing to find out what you know and what has been brought to the surface. Feed him something that will keep him happy for now until we can find out more."*

"He's not a threat, Gamba."

"I cannot say that for sure. I can only tell you what I feel. He is not a threat, but he does not have your best interests right now."

I clear my throat before I offer a response. I have to think quickly; Gamba hasn't been this agitated since we became aware of each other. "Yeah, things are fine, Hassan. Ms. Kynani has been great so far. I've been learning a lot from her, including more on Kindaran culture and tradition."

"That's great. I'm very glad to hear it." Hassan's tone remains upbeat, but I detect something underneath—it sounds like annoyance—that makes me wonder if Gamba is on to something. "Was she able to help with the more pressing issue you needed handled?"

I exhale slow, doing my best to measure my words. I'm not sure if it's factual or not, but it sounds good to try out. "Ms. Kynani made it clear that anything that I discuss with her can only be divulged to the Kindaran Council so they can figure out who else needs to know what's going on with me. I can't even tell Unk right now."

"Sure, I understand." Hassan sighs. I feel like he's trying to placate me, but I'm hopeful the paper-thin explanation will work for now. "I had hoped that more would have developed, but I will abide by the Council's order. Let me know when they reach out to you or Kynani."

"Will do." I disconnect the call, tapping my knuckle against my right temple. "Gamba, we need to have a chat. I need to understand why I can't trust the person who got me out of Solara and was able to get me to my grandmother when I was little."

Gamba steps out from the shadows of my psyche in his human form, sitting in a chair as he offers for me to sit in the chair next to him. "First things first, kiddo, we need to make sure there are no interruptions."

I open my eyes for a moment to step out of my subconscious, sending a text to Unk to let him know I'm up and getting ready for school, and about the meet with Kynani later today. I enter inside again, getting comfortable for the chat at hand. "Okay, we should be good for an hour. Do you want to explain what's going on?"

"As much as I respect what Hassan did for you, there's a story you should know," Gamba says.

"Well, we've got time, so let's get this done."

Gamba takes a deep breath like the story he's about to recount will hurt him as much as it might hurt me. "Before you were born, your father and Hassan were friends and rivals. It was a difficult space to build a relationship, but somehow, they made it work. That all changed when your mother came along."

I nod, acknowledging the story as it unfolds in front of me.

"We were all friends, your mother, your father, Hassan, and me. Your uncle was much younger, which is why he didn't immediately recognize my name. As we got older, the rivalry between your father and Hassan intensified." Gamba sighs as he continues to recount the memories. "Your mother was deemed the prize at the center of it all, but after a while, your father won your mother's favor and attention, much to Hassan's irritation."

I feel like I already know the punchline. "So let me guess, Hassan did what he could to make things difficult, right?"

"Well, not exactly." Gamba shakes his head. "Your mother enjoyed the attention she got, so she asked your father if Hassan could be extended family along with me. Since your father and I were best friends growing up, it caused a bit of tension...until your mother became pregnant with you."

"And that calmed things down? That's a bit convenient, isn't it?" I scratch my head, trying to understand the why of it all. "So let's skip the details that will make things a bit boring for me. Why are you skeptical of Hassan's motives? My parents are dead, and from what I'm gathering, you also perished, and he got away from the invasion to get me to my nana."

Gamba pauses again, regarding my skepticism. "You pose a fair question, and at the moment, I cannot provide a real answer that will make sense. I would never steer you wrong, kiddo. I want you to understand that."

"Could it be that you're salty because he's still alive?"

"That is not fair, Yasir. I chose this path on purpose. I was the one who was made your godfather, and I promised to protect you, whatever it took, even if it meant my life."

I wipe a tear from my cheek as I take Gamba's words to heart. "A lot of what has happened has left me here on this side of the veil damn near all by myself. Unk and Nana are the only family I have to see about me on this side, and I still don't know how he managed to get evacuated, but everyone else had to die. I understand the sacrifices you all made for me, but I don't know why you did it, and the only other person who can is Hassan."

Gamba leans forward, tapping my fists, offering up a sympathetic smile. "Your parents loved you more than anything in this world. If there was any way they could have escaped with you, they would have, but there was something else that was just as important as making sure you lived, even at the expense of their lives."

"What? What was more important than their sons?" I'm getting sick of this same narrative of "my parents had to make a choice." It's gotten old and tired, and I'm not with this nonsense anymore. "I have almost no memory of them, and the little that I do have is locked away from me. How am I supposed to be okay with all of this, huh? Tell me."

"Okay, let us take a beat for a moment, kiddo. I think there is a way to answer your question and help fill in some of the blanks." Gamba takes a deep breath, nodding to himself. "Can you wait until Kynani arrives? She has access to the Kindaran archives and information that very few people can get. I promise I am not stalling, just try to be patient."

"Easy for you to say. You have information that I don't."

Gamba claps his hand on my shoulder, staring into my eyes. "You have had information withheld for a long time, kiddo. I promise, between Kynani and I, we will get you straight."

I open my eyes, shutting Gamba out for the moment. My temper's flaring, and I need the time away from him so I can get my head together, since the night terrors manage to mess with me, too. I look skyward, praying to Nyati for strength to temper the anger in my heart. I've got to get a grip before all of this consumes me. If I don't, things could get much worse.

CHAPTER THIRTY-EIGHT

We're at lunch with the crew, going through the usual convo and planning for the next few weeks. Halloween is coming up, and I can't wait. Zahra and I put rush orders on the Black Panther suit and Storm's matching black cutout jumpsuit and thigh-high boots. When she showed me the white wig she'd found and ordered to contrast with the black suit... Yeah, I can't wait!

Still, there's something that I can't shake, and I'm doing my best to not spoil the excitement that swirls around all of us. I keep my eyes closed for a few moments, retreating into my subconscious mind, hoping I can settle whatever anxiety trying to creep to the surface.

Gamba notices it, too. *"What are you anticipating, kiddo? I thought this was supposed to be the fun part of the year."*

"I'm not sure, and that's what worries me," I reply. *"Whatever is scratching at my subconscious, it doesn't feel right."*

Zahra gently pulls at my forearm, which brings me out of my meditative state. "Are you okay, baby? You're on edge. I can feel it on you."

"I'll explain later, when we have a chance to be alone."

We are intent on outshining everyone during the costume party that weekend, but the girls are more hyper about something else entirely. From the annoyed looks on my boy's face, I have reason to be worried.

"I can't wait for the Bicentennial Ball." Kendyl's bouncing in her seat like she's won the lottery as she stares at Kyle from head to toe. "I get to see you in a tux, looking all... Whew, let me calm down."

Did she say *tuxedo*?

Man, is it too late to get off this train before it leaves the station?

The dreamy stare Zahra gives me answers my question before I can get it out of my mouth. By the gods, why? "I haven't had the chance to see you cleaned up yet, baby. The ball is the perfect time."

"Um, prom, anyone?" I protest. "Where does it say in the rule book that I have to wear a tux twice a year?"

"Bro, don't. Resistance is futile," Kyle groans as he shows his outward disgust. "Just accept that you're going to be assimilated into the Borg and get in line to get your tux like the rest of us."

Kendyl punches his arm, giving me a glare that has me put my hands up in surrender. Nope, I'm not about to get caught up in that power struggle. "We don't ask that much of y'all, and you get to see us at our sexiest, too? Win-win."

"Listen, bro, I'm feeling it at prom time, but I don't know about this." I'm still in protest mode, and I'm not about to back down, either. "Is this one of those Oakwood Grove things that I should've been warned about way before now?"

"Look, as much stress that Z and I are gonna be under getting things planned out for Anniversary Week, the least you two can do is get your lives together and be the eye candy we need you to be," Kendyl huffs, which completely throws me off.

Did I miss the memo or something? "What stress are you talking about? All you're doing is coordinating outfits, right? Okay, I get that, but what exactly are the events for Anniversary Week? Can the uninitiated get an entry-level information packet or something?" I'm disturbed by the "thought you knew by now" glances from everyone around me, and I drop my head and bang it against the table top a few times to get my life together. "So what's this madness with Anniversary Week anyway?"

Kendyl pipes up quick like this whole week has been her idea the whole time. "This is the week when the Founding Families came and settled Oakwood Grove two hundred years ago. We rock all kinds of events, but the one that means the most is the Anniversary Ball."

"So what has you and Z tripping right now, though? It sounds like y'all got caught up, and I'm trying to figure out who needs to bleed."

Zahra sighs, gritting her teeth as she glares at Kendyl. "Mayor Lance blindsided me earlier in the week. He wanted Oakwood Grove student participation in planning the Anniversary Week festivities. I got Kenni to tag along with me to see about the details, and as it turned out, it was an ambush. Chrisette was there, all smiles and whatever, and Mayor Lance asked the three of us to coordinate other events."

"Wait, he has to know that you aren't vibing with Chris like that," Kyle jumps in, with a concerned expression splashed all over his face. "That's a recipe for disaster, that's for sure."

"I want the record to reflect that I warned her that Chris was behind this setup," Kendyl announces. "Out of all the kids at school, and he singles you out? Come on, babe, we willingly walked right into that buzzsaw."

"And it was worth it, if I remember correctly," Zahra claps back as she pulls out her phone. "Let's see, we managed to get a large budget to get all the events we wanted to have completed, including the parade, the carnival, and Theater in the Park, something we'd been wanting in the town square for a while now, and we got him to make calls to Atlanta to get first-run advanced copies of *Dune Part 2*, *Aquaman and the Lost Kingdom*, and *The Marvels* before they hit in theaters to show for the Theater in the Park idea you and I came up with on the fly."

"Okay, okay, okay, you got what you wanted, but so did he. We still have to work with that twit," Kendyl points out. "My pimp hand is already twitching at the first sign of her slick shading anything we do."

"We can handle her, trust. She's outnumbered, and she can't run back to 'Dad' because she can't get what she wants. Eww, it still makes my skin crawl when she called him that," Zahra mentions, gagging at the mention of Mayor Lance. "We have to suck it up for the ball, and we get to do what we want in the park.

Gotta give to get."

"Remind me to hire you as my agent when I'm ready to go to the pros." Kyle's in shock, and so am I. I never realized how ruthless she could be. "You'll have these GMs shook."

"Yeah, yeah, enough of all that. I still haven't gotten what I want for the ball, so I'm about to correct that right now." Zahra leans in close, cooing in my ear low enough for the rest of them not to hear. "If you're a good boy, I promise I'll let you see what's underneath the dress I'm wearing after the ball."

I close my eyes tight, shivering when she kisses my earlobe. She ramps up her attack, like she has to convince me further. "Nod so I know you'll get your tuxedo for the ball, pretty please?"

Kyle lets out an exaggerated grunt when I comply without hesitation. "See? No fair, Z. I had a shot to at least get an honest protest from my ace."

That quip earns another punch from Kendyl. "Keep it up, and I'll change my choice of Halloween costume from Wonder Woman to the Wicked Witch of the West."

"Okay, damn, you don't have to play so rough."

"So, now that that's been settled, I need to know what your color schemes will be, so Ky and I don't clash or copycat." Kendyl pulls out her phone to jot down notes. "And I'm deadass, too. I'm not about to get dragged. Nope."

Zahra pipes up for the both of us before I have a chance to say anything. "Black, gold, purple. We're Kindaran, girl. Anything less would be blasphemous."

Kendyl glares at Zahra, irritated over her choices. My baby's right, though. Anything other than those colors, and there would be hell to pay. "I hate you, chica. Fine. Crimson and silver. You're lucky I love you, sis."

Zahra sticks her tongue out at Kendyl, putting her head on my shoulder. "You'll be all right, promise. Besides, I didn't get to show up and show out last year because my date flaked on me. I'm flossing this year, and it's gonna be in home country colors."

"I hope you're able to find a corsage in those colors, bro," Kyle points out. "Otherwise, you may have to go outside the city to get what you want. The last thing you wanna do is have the parents give you the business because you screwed up tradition."

"Yeah, first impressions are everything, pretty boy," Zahra stresses to me like I don't already know the drill. "Although I've been told that you'll be getting that out of the way this weekend."

"Uh oh, you get to meet Mr. and Mrs. Assante?" Kyle leans back in his chair. "May the gods have mercy on your soul."

"Stop it, Ky. My parents are not that bad."

"If you say so, Z." Kyle focuses on me, his expression turning serious. "Don't listen to her. Be on point from the jump, my boy. Her father makes my father nervous every time they're in each other's space."

Yeah, that makes me feel *much* better.

"Don't let Ky put crazy thoughts in your head, baby. I promise, my dad is hard on everyone...who *isn't* Kindaran."

"That's that BS, for real." Kyle scoffs. "We've been best friends for years, and that's the reason he gave me hell when we were growing up?"

"Sorry, bestie, but you survived it, right? Did you die? You're still alive."

"That's cold, girl. I'm heading to class before I get abused again." Kyle kisses Kendyl before he leaves the table. "I'll get with you and TK to set up the tux-fitting time. Holla."

Heading to our next class, Zahra pulls me into a cleared hallway, pinning me against the wall, studying my facial expressions. "Don't let Ky get in your head, okay? I'm serious."

"That's not freaking me out." I'm lying, but I find the convenient excuse to throw her off the trail. "I had another nightmare last night. I'm not sure why they're happening more frequently, but I've been distracted all day."

She caresses my face, massaging my neck to relieve some of the tension. "Have you told Ms. Kynani?"

"She's supposed to be heading over after school."

"Okay, I have volleyball practice. Playoffs are coming, and we need to be ready." She kisses my lips before she trots off toward her class. "Call me after you're done so I can prep you for dinner this weekend?"

"Yeah, hopefully Ms. Kynani doesn't take too long."

"Thank you for coming by, Ms. Kynani. Unk and I wanted to ensure you were with us before we headed over to my girlfriend's home to visit with her parents this weekend."

My anxiety levels spike the moment those words are uttered. By Nyati, I'm gonna meet her parents! I'm not ready for anything like this yet. We've only been together for a short time. No matter how I try to spin it, I can't avoid working through the worst-case possibilities in my head. I'm coming close to getting physically ill, and the dinner isn't for a few days.

Not gonna lie, Unk kept the conversation between us light, explaining that everyone has gone through the "meeting the parents" phase at one time or another. After a few minutes of conversing, even he's convinced that I've built things well beyond the realm of it turning out positive. Gamba did what he could to emanate as much energy from within to help balance me, but nothing's working. At. All.

Kynani's become the last-ditch effort to settle things down before we make the trip. I'm probably asking a lot, considering the original reason she's supposed to be here, but I can't worry about that. Getting through the dinner is more important to me.

"Yasir, I want you to sit down with me for a few moments." Kynani escorts me to the couch, motioning for Unk and Lennox to step out of the room. "Now, why are you building this meeting up in your mind as though it was going to make or break your relationship?"

"I mean, put yourself in my shoes… If I was your child, wouldn't you be skeptical of the girl I was dating?" I flip the situation, playing a real-life version of devil's advocate. "He's a Kindaran historian,

among other things. I did my homework on him; he's one of the
most well-respected professors in the world. I have no idea how
I'm supposed to hang in a conversation with him."

"Have you had a conversation with him?"

"Well, no, but—"

"Then, until you have a conversation with him, how will you
know if you can keep up with whatever subject matter he may bring
up at dinner?" Kynani invited an alternate version that somewhat
settles me down. "You have yet to meet the man, and you have
him built up like he is going to take one look at you and deem you
unworthy. What if he likes you immediately? Have you thought
about that?"

I open my mouth to form a response, but then I sit with her
last words. "Well, maybe you're right, Ms. Kynani. All of this is new
to me. I just don't want to mess things up. I really like her a lot…
and that's probably the first time I've said that out loud to anyone."

"Listen to me, Yasir. You are a son of Kindara, you are a newly
realized *mwali duati*, and you have the support of an uncle who has
helped raise a well-adjusted young man," Kynani asserts. "Not to
mention you have a Vodaran priestess who can help you realize your
true purpose in this world. He cannot possibly deny the greatness
in you."

I blink a few times, absorbing every word she's saying, and my
energy shifts in the moment. Confidence courses through me like an
electrical current, and it removes all the doubt I had before. I don't
know how she's managed to do it, but I'm grateful on several levels.

"See, I already sense the shift in you, young one. Now, when we
meet your girlfriend's family"—Kynani extends her hand, taking
my hands and squeezing them—"I am sure they will be very
pleased to meet you."

I breathe a sigh of relief, feeling my heartbeat slow down. "Yes,
I'm ready. I just hope they're ready for me."

"Good, now let us see what we can do about those nightmares."

CHAPTER THIRTY-NINE

"Mommy, Daddy," Zahra says, "I would like you to meet my boyfriend, Yasir. This is his uncle, Xavion Okafor, and his girlfriend, Lennox Alvarez. And this is Ms. Kynani, the Vodaran priestess who has been helping Yasir with some things."

Those words sound so gooey coming out of her mouth, like she's been melting chocolate off her tongue. I don't know how to really react to it, or if I should, while in the presence of her parents. I give up a smile anyway, because I can.

"Yasir, it is a pleasure to meet you and your uncle as well," Kairo, Zahra's father, states as he extends his hand to Unk. As they regard each other, I can't help but see how similar they look to each other. I mean, Unk's Kindaran, too, but it's like they're from the same area. Kairo has a low-cut fade and a well-kempt beard, and he's a little bit smaller than Unk in size, even though they're the same height at six feet tall. "I'm looking forward to finding out more about you all, including the young woman who I didn't expect to see outside of Kindara."

She grins as she motions for Kynani to stand next to her. "Ms. Kynani has told us a lot about what's going on with Yasir, and she's hopeful she can provide more insight."

Kairo takes Kynani's hand and politely kisses it before switching his attention to me. "And, if I may ask, what are you here to provide insight on, Kynani? I'm a bit confused over why a Vodaran priestess is away from our home country. Has the Council even verified Yasir's identity to warrant such attention?"

His thinly veiled questions put me on edge, and I understand what Kyle said about her father being hard on anyone he suspects isn't Kindaran. I'm not in the mood to play games or answer unnecessary questions to prove what has already been proven through my bloodline.

Kynani flashes a small smile, but in a blink, her eyes change from their hazel-brown hue to an amethyst tone that Zahra says happens to me when I'm a little agitated. "Mr. Assante, I understand your apprehension due to others you have encountered who provided false witness to our shared bloodlines, but I *assure* you I am not here on some whim or an unchecked rumor."

Kairo raises an eyebrow before his whole demeanor changes. He drops his head in reverence to Kynani, allowing a moment of quiet between them. In the next breath, his tone changes quickly. "Priestess, I apologize for my misstep. I do not mean to question your presence here. There is a reason why I am hesitant."

Kesi, Zahra's mother, holds her hand up, interrupting Kairo's further attempts to speak. She walks over to me, giving me a warm and inviting hug that catches me off guard. "I apologize for my husband, everyone. Yasir, Zahra, and I have had a few conversations about you, and while we did not find out your last name until a few days ago, I am happy to see that the young man in front of me has the aura that I expected to see around him. It has been such a long time, child, and you have no idea how much we prayed to the Divine Mother that you survived and were safe."

Umm, that escalated quickly. How did they know about me? *What* do they know about me? I have so many questions.

Apparently, so does my girlfriend. She switches her gaze between her mother and father so fast it's making me dizzy. "Wait a minute, you both knew about Yasir? What in the world is happening?"

"I'd love to know the answer to that question myself. How do you know about my nephew, Mr. Assante?" Unk hardens his stance. "I was under the impression from the Kindaran Council that Yasir's whereabouts and identity were kept under the strictest of confidence."

Kairo takes a closer look, glancing into my eyes while ignoring Unk's question. He studies my face, and a tear rolls down his cheek. He shakes his head over and over again, wiping more tears as they continue to fall. "I…I can't believe it. We searched for you for years. No one knew where you'd turned up. We feared the worst. You look so much like Bakari. By Nyati, you're alive."

Zahra pulls me away from her father, stepping in front of me as she regards him. "Daddy, what are you talking about? You searched for Yasir for what reason? You've got everyone, including me, confused and then some. What's going on? And I think I deserve the truth this time."

Kynani places a comforting hand against her arm. "What your father is trying to explain is that there is a connection between you and Yasir that neither of you were made aware of. Your father's knowledge of it is based only on historical reference, but even he could not be informed of what would happen once you were connected. Until now."

Zahra closes her eyes and starts vibrating in place like she's on the verge of exploding. "I'm as good at riddles as the next person, but this one's so embedded that I'm gonna need heavy equipment to extract the meaning. Can you dumb it down for the uninitiated, Ms. Kynani?"

"Well, to 'dumb it down,' as you say, the short version of what I mean is that you and Yasir are connected in more ways than the romantic relationship that you two have forged. Ashanti, the Goddess of Love, foresaw your link many moons ago, and Nahara forged your bond in fire, as Nyati, the Divine Mother, decreed."

Zahra grins at the confused expression on my face, and I'm really trying to get on the same page with her and Kynani. I'm even more confused when Kynani pulls Zahra over to whisper something that I can't make out. She turns to her father to continue the convo. "Um, Daddy, you never did explain things about Yasir."

Kairo regards Unk's body language, rubbing his goatee as he considers his words. "We were approached by the Kindaran Council while Kesi was pregnant with you, baby girl. They told us about

Bakari and Nasira, Yasir's parents, in Solara and our connection
to them. They were vague on the details until you kids were born."

Kynani chimes in, helping to fill in the blanks. "You both have
a tattoo on the inside of your left wrist. Yasir, yours is in the form
of a wind image, specifically a hurricane symbol, as you were born
under the viewing of Ubaka, the Vodaran God of Air. Zahra, yours
is a fire symbol, a phoenix to be exact, as you were born under
the viewing of Nahara, the Vodaran Goddess of Fire. The balance
between you is based on Yasir's ability to feed your energy and vice
versa, and for one *specific* purpose once you have reached maturity."

"The protection of the Kutokufa Scrolls," we utter in unison,
as though someone—or something—embedded the phrase inside
our minds.

I tilt my head to the side for a moment, wondering how I've
recited something I've never heard of before in my life. I can tell
Zahra's confused, too, and I'm asking the question for the both of
us. "Wait a minute, how did Zahra and I remember that phrase and
know to recite it at the same time?"

Kairo stares at me again, his eyes still wide with shock. "Yasir…
by Nyati, I still cannot believe it. I have so many questions to ask."

Kesi shakes her head, matching Kairo's incredulous expression.
"When we couldn't find you, and we feared you were dead…there
was no reason to believe… We should have continued looking for
you, Yasir."

"Okay, pause. Can we get in on what the hell is going on right
now?" Unk trades concerned glances with Lennox before he
focuses his gaze on Kairo. "As his legal guardian, I deserve to be
involved in the conversation as much as they are."

"You are correct, and you will all be involved. It is very
important that you are," Kynani offers. "For now, there will be some
conversations I need to have with the kids separate from you. Once
they have a full understanding of things, then they can bring you
into the larger conversation so that you can comprehend the depth
of their journey together."

"May we ask when we will have the opportunity to know?" Kesi inquires. "I am sure Xavion and Lennox will need to know how to support Yasir as we will need to understand how to help Zahra through this next phase. If my husband's research is accurate, there is a lot more to absorb."

"I think this would be a good time to have dinner, so we can continue this conversation with good food and new friends," Kairo announces. "I believe that things will clear themselves up once we have had a chance to eat."

I'm sitting outside with Kynani and Zahra after dinner is over, inside of the gazebo that's out of earshot of the main house. There's a certain Zen that I guess I shouldn't be surprised to notice when it comes to her or my nana. Zahra's almost bubbling over in anticipation of whatever Kynani has to say to us, and I'm low-key nervous. I have no idea what's about to be discussed, and all I can do is let things flow and see where I fit in.

The clouds above us provide a captivating backdrop, projecting a brewing storm on the horizon, but I refuse to believe that whatever Kynani brings to light will be anything short of game changing. Ever since she showed up, it's like different layers have been peeled off, revealing a different truth each time.

I guess today is no different, as Kynani's first question throws us off. "I know you both have questions for me, but for now, I will be concentrating on Zahra. My first question is simple, but not quite so simple: have you sensed another presence within your mind?"

Zahra snaps her gaze in my direction, and all I see are question marks in her eyes. She turns her attention back to Kynani as she takes my hand in her grip. "Um, no, should I have sensed a presence? I'm not quite sure what you mean."

Kynani studies Zahra and ponders her words. "Okay, let me try a different question: do you realize how influential your singing ability is over others? How soothing it can be or how you're able to have an audience bend to your will at any time?"

Zahra's quiet for a few moments, squeezing my hand as our shared incident comes to mind. "Yes, I think I do. I even have moments where I just whisper into the air when I want someone to do something, and they seem to listen to me."

Kynani taps her index finger against her cheek as she regards her answer. "Indeed. There is a reason for that, my child. Your parents would have been told, and they might have been told, but they could not know the depth of the meaning of it all. That is where I come in."

"I know this sounds like I'm being impatient, Ms. Kynani, but... what am I?" she asks. I admit, I'm trying to understand where this is all going myself. "You were cryptic before dinner, and it's been on my mind for the past couple of hours. Can we get to the heart of the matter, please?"

Kynani smiles as she pulls a stray hair from her face. "Your generation, always in a rush. But I understand your desire to be given all the information needed to make sound decisions. Allow me to accommodate your request: you are a *mwali duati*, Zahra. You are metahuman, too. Your abilities unlocked the moment," and Kynani stares directly at me, her eyes seeming to bore into my soul, "your betrothed's abilities began to fully manifest."

My mouth drops as I grasp the meaning of Kynani's words.
Zahra's metahuman, too?

Okay, I need a moment to make sense of all of this, seriously.

"Wait...so how was I supposed to know about my powers?" The elevated pitch in her tone is a combination of confusion and excitement. "And...*betrothed*? I mean, I like Yasir a lot, a lot, but I wouldn't say it's gotten that deep between us yet."

"You were able to sense your betrothed's scent, almost entranced by it when others were repelled by it," Kynani explains, smiling at us the entire time. "You have had a deep-seated need to have him close and want to keep him safe as of late. You even risked your life to save him, as I was told by Mama Johari. According to the sacred temple texts, once a nyxwraith is born, a trillsage is born as its mate."

My mind is swirling. "Pause, time out. A trillsage? Another kind of metahuman?"

Zahra gives up a nervous giggle. "Okay, so things have been a bit intense between me and Ya-Ya lately."

"Um, you think?" I can't avoid blurting out. "Okay, this is a lot to take in right now."

"That is one way of seeing things." Kynani giggles at the banter between us. "Nyati, Ashanti, and Nahara…the Divine Mother and both Vodaran goddesses placed this in motion long before you were both born. You are fated in this life to be together and in the next life. It is the reason why no other girls have been able to capture his attention and no other boys have been able to, shall we say, stay on your level."

"Whew, okay. That makes sense. So now that we've gotten that out of the way, what are my abilities, exactly?" The questions are coming rapid-fire now, and I can't say I blame her. I got questions, too. "I kinda knew about my voice, so does that mean I'm, like, a siren? There's so much in my head right now."

Kynani strokes her chin. "There is more to your voice, child… If ever you were in extreme danger, you have the ability to emit a scream that produces a miniature shockwave that keeps your attackers from advancing any further."

"Um, I've never had the—"

Kynani pats her hand, keeping her gaze focused on her. "We can get to your powers soon, but I need to make you both aware of what you are to each other. You are a trillsage, Zahra. It is written in Kindaran mythology that every few generations, a *mwali duati* pair are born—a trillsage and a nyxwraith—and while they are made aware of each other as small children, once they reach puberty, they are betrothed, as willed by Ashanti, to each other and to their shared purpose and responsibility to the Divine Mother: protecting the sacred Kutokufa Scrolls of Kindara."

Zahra switches her gaze back to me, caressing my cheek as she stares into my eyes like it's the first time she's laid her eyes on me. "So Yasir's a nyxwraith, and the whole acclimation ritual we witnessed…is that what I'll be going through, too?"

"I know this is a lot to take in, and I promise I will be here to help you both work through all the questions you have," Kynani advises. "If I need assistance from another priestess, then I will make the request of the Council. They will be more than accommodating once they have been advised that you both have been made aware of your other selves."

"But I have not been made aware of anything, or anyone, at least, not that I know of," she responds. "You're making it sound like I have a mental illness or something, or Yasir, for that matter."

Kynani raises an eyebrow. "I assure you, you do not have a mental illness, but I will advise that if you both have trusted friends, you will need to take great care explaining to them what is going on with you," Kynani cautions us, leaning in to keep our attention. "This is not an easy path to travel, and this is the first time that *mwali duati* will be guided away from the confines of Kindara, and we may have to adjust protocol as we progress."

Zahra's trembling in my grip, and I give a reassuring squeeze to let her know I'm right here with her. "Will I get the chance to tell my parents?"

"Soon, my child, but first things first, we need to set up another time so that I can facilitate the introduction to your other self… the physical manifestation of your trillsage, much like I did with Yasir. And quickly."

"Are you saying I'm a monster, too? Like Yasir's Lycan thing?"

A growl rumbles from me, unexpectedly shutting her down. "We are not monsters, baby. That's something Gamba made clear to me when I said it."

"Well, what would you call it, Ya-Ya?" Zahra's eyes widen as I watch the fear seep into her stare. Her bottom lip trembles as the reality of the situation sinks in. "This is something that we're gonna have to prep Ky and Kenni and the rest of our circle for, because if either of us—"

"I see you and your betrothed consume a great deal of comic books and graphic novels," Kynani smirks as she shakes her head at us. "This is not like the lycanthropes that you might have read about or the *Incredible Hulk* or *She-Hulk* that everyone here in the States is so enamored with lately. Neither you nor Yasir will turn into a mindless beast. Your trillsage's primary directive is to protect you and to protect your betrothed from harm, much like Yasir's nyxwraith's primary directive is to protect him and you from harm."

"Sheesh. This is a lot," she admits while she plays with a braid. "So what happens now?"

"Difficult to say at this point, but until I have a chance to get your trillsage merged within your psyche, helping Yasir through his acclimation process is priority," Kynani instructs us, although she's focused on Zahra. "He has a lot that he is working through, so the learning curve is a bit deeper, at least, until we're able to unlock his memories. I am hopeful that you can help, so that when the time comes, he will be able to help you through your own acclimation."

Kynani rises from her chair, opening her arms to offer a hug, grinning when Zahra and I embrace her tightly. As we trek back to the house, she continues to look at us, her smile maintaining its energy until we make it to the front door. "I have a good feeling that you two are bound for extraordinary things. I look forward to watching it all unfold."

CHAPTER FORTY

"**M**r. Assante, can I talk to you for a moment?" I ask, peeking into his office.

Finding out the truth about what happened to my parents during the Bralba invasion is an important piece that's missing from my memory. He is the closest credible source, and until I can get Kynani to unlock that part of my mind, he can fill in the blanks.

He's opened a few books on his massive desk, writing something down and then checking the information in the book, switching up every few seconds. He barely acknowledges me as he continues his work. "Sure, Yasir, what is on your mind?"

I don't feel like beating around the bush. Here goes nothing. "The Bralba Invasion."

He stops writing, looking up at me like speaking that into existence sends a shock through his body. He removes his glasses and motions for me to take a seat. "I guess, sooner or later, you would want to find out more about that time. Are you sure you want to hear about what happened? I do not want to dredge up any bad memories for you."

"Well, I've been told that my memories were suppressed and that it'll take a Vodaran priestess to unlock them, so I think we might be safe." I'm doing my best to keep my rising fear at bay, but the closer I get to hearing about it, the more I don't want to move forward. "No one will tell me what happened to my parents. I don't know if they were heroes, or victims, or anything."

"I don't know if I'm the right person to…"

"Sir, with respect, you're probably the best person to tell me what happened. You knew my parents, and you know all things related to Kindara…" I rub the back of my neck, hoping I can handle whatever he has to say. "It will help me connect with them, if that makes sense."

Kairo gets up from behind his desk, then ambles over to the bookshelf on the left side of the office. He thumbs through the spines of each book on the shelves, sliding from left to right until he finds what he's looking for. "Here it is, the Bralba Invasion, including timelines, major figures involved, everything you need to know."

He has to be kidding, right?

I almost throw the book against the wall. I don't care if Gamba awakens; this is an insult to my intelligence. "Mr. Assante, I can do a Google search and find what I need if I had to do a social science project. Had the invasion never happened, you would've been the closest person outside of my father as any man in my life. I need your help…please."

Kairo sighs, sitting in the chair next to me, resting a comforting hand on my shoulder. "I do not mean to be dismissive, Yasir. That day…it is still hard for many of us to talk about. It was hard for me to compile the information you have in your hands. I can promise you that you cannot find what I have learned in a Google search."

"But I lost almost everyone I loved. My culture, our culture, was hidden from me for reasons that still don't make sense." My voice cracks, and I feel small for letting it happen. "This is another piece to a puzzle that might help me learn more about myself."

Kairo leans back in the chair, exhaling sharply. "Okay, I still feel like this might not be the best idea, but ask whatever questions you have in your head."

"Okay, thank you." I pause for a moment to figure out where to begin. "Why was Solara chosen as a target during the invasion?"

"Your village, as we found out after the fact, held one of the Kindaran Nine families. Your family, Yasir." Kairo sighs again as he takes his time to find the words. "Each of the Kindaran Nine had a responsibility to protect the location of the Kutokufa Scrolls, sacred scrolls hidden on the island that hold the secrets to immortality and resurrection."

"But why are people invading Kindara? Are the Scrolls public knowledge or something?" I'm trying to make sense of why my world has been turned upside down.

"Several different countries have tried over the years, but one in particular—Bralba—has been a centuries-old enemy of Kindara," Kairo replies as he leans forward in his chair to maintain eye contact. "The rest of the world thinks the Scrolls are nothing more than a myth, but Bralba has been after them based on information they believe is true."

"And that is?"

"That the Scrolls belonged to them," Kairo flatly tells me. "And to answer the next possible question in your head, the Scrolls have always belonged to Kindara, but the Bralbans stole them three centuries ago. We were eventually able to get them back, but it took almost another century to do so. By then, Bralba had falsely claimed that the Scrolls were theirs. That's what started the ongoing conflicts between our nations."

I have other questions, but I don't want to overwhelm myself. A lot of this is making my head hurt. "Okay. So back to my family being a part of this Kindaran Nine. How did we get chosen?"

"It was because of your bloodline, Yasir," Kairo answers. "There are nine bloodlines that are direct descendants of the original nine *mwali duati*…these metahumans…who helped colonize this island with the humans. Over time, due to the intermingling of the two species, the abilities of the *mwali duati* began to lessen over the generations."

"And you're saying that my family line was targeted because of this gene?" I have to be careful with what I say. I feel like I'm in the middle of a legend being told to me, except I'm the legend, and I didn't even know it. "This gene comes from which line? Was it my father? My mother?"

"Hmmm, the last one we knew of that openly carried this gene was more likely your grandfather, or perhaps his father before him,"

Kairo continues with the information dump, and frankly speaking, I'm here for all of it, no matter how much it scares me. "What happened to you is a result of the gene that your bloodline has carried for generations. The nyxwraith gene. But it can only trigger during a tragedy or great loss."

"So is it possible that the priestess who suppressed my memories tried to keep the gene from being activated because of my parents' deaths? The invasion?"

"Yes, it is possible."

"Well, there's no need to worry about that anymore." I chuckle, but I'm not sure if it's from being nervous or over the sardonic humor. "I wonder what else could possibly happen."

"What do you mean by that?"

Well, damn it. Cynicism clearly isn't his thing. "Um, forget I said anything, sir. Do you mind if I take this book home so I can continue my research? I promise I'll have it back in one piece."

Kairo scratches his head, and I know I've confused him, but now's not the time to tell him that it awakened anyway, despite what the priestesses did. That I'm a newly realized *mwali duati* with a nyxwraith buried inside my physiology. That *might* compromise my relationship with his daughter. Or maybe it won't, I don't know. "Okay, if you say so. Let me know if you need anything, or if you want to have a longer conversation, my door is always open."

CHAPTER FORTY-ONE

"That'll be $43.03," I say while prepping the card machine. "I hope you enjoy the crab, ma'am. I think you'll love the sweetness of the meat."

I always have a lot of fun whenever I work at Unk's seafood shop, being around customers and helping with their choice of meat. In a weird way, it helps me when it comes to being around people and managing my anxiety attacks. It's taking time away from being with Zahra, but in my mind, I'm doing this to help whenever we're out at different events or even when we're out on a date. She's influencing almost everything I want to change about myself, to be a better version.

Unk's shop is part of a series of niche stores in downtown Savannah. The way he has it set up, the brilliant black tables are combined with a darker wood, which contrast against the brick walls that frame the shop, giving it a classic feel that meshes with the rest of the shops and the collective vibe they've created. He completed the look with mosaic floors, and the counter space melds well with the tables, as he wanted those who prefer to eat at the shop. He hoped the clean but crude appearance would still give his customers the approachable ambiance that makes his shop popular. The way I figure it, the packed building on a Wednesday afternoon is proof positive that it worked.

The way we work is like a well-oiled machine. I charm the guests out front, which frees Unk to pick through the day's catch to make sure that customers get exactly what they're looking for, whether they plan to take their purchase home or dine in. He makes sure to play both host and business owner when I am in school, so to be able to help him when I can during breaks is a win for both of us.

It's Wednesday evening after everything that happened at Zahra's house. I'm still trying to make sense of everything. There are so many pieces to this confusing puzzle that is now my life. Talking with Zahra's father only made things even weirder than normal, and now I'm not sure what's normal anymore.

As I finish helping yet another happy patron, I notice a couple of Chatham County sheriffs come through the door. They have concerned looks on their faces, which triggers me, but I can't figure out why. I continue to work with the people in line, keeping an eye on them until the line thins out a bit so I can address the officers without drawing much of a crowd. Once everyone has been helped, I slide out from behind the counter to turn the sign from "open" to "closed."

"Good afternoon, officers. What can I get you today?" My tone stays as calm as possible, but inside, I'm a bundle of nerves. "We have a pretty good selection of shrimp I think you might like."

"Good afternoon, young man. I'm Deputy Wilford. We were told that we could find Yasir Salah here. Are you Yasir?"

"That depends on who's asking." Unk pops out from the back in response to the sheriff's request. "Xavion Okafor, I'm Yasir's uncle. May I ask what this is all about?"

Yeah, I'm not feeling this at all. I retreat inside myself for a brief moment or two so I can alert Gamba. He's gonna need to help keep my adrenaline from spiking too high. The last thing I need is to trigger the very thing they're probably coming to question me about.

At that moment, Mr. Channing saunters through the door, giving a wave to Unk and glancing at the officers before heading in my direction.

Gamba perks up at Mr. Channing's presence, giving a quick prod inside my conscious mind. I'm so distracted by everything that I don't notice him making his presence known.

"Don't say anything for now. This could get interesting really quick."

I wave to Mr. Channing, walking over to the other end of the counter to assist, but before I do, I kick myself for forgetting to lock the door when I turned the sign. I quickly correct that problem before someone else comes through, wanting to be nosy. "What can I get you this afternoon, Mr. Channing? How's Kyle doing?"

"Kyle's good. His team should be back in town within the hour, I suspect," Mr. Channing replies. "Before we get into my order, do you have change for a five-dollar bill?"

Okay, he confuses me with that strange request, but I reach in my pocket and produce five single dollar bills to give to him. "Here you go, sir. Now, do you want a specific meat? Cod, or mahi perhaps?"

"We can talk about that in a minute, but for now, let me have those singles."

I hand the money over to Mr. Channing, getting the bill from him in exchange. I still think it's odd that he asks for the change, but I dismiss it and go back to what I'm doing while the conversation between Unk and the sheriff continues.

Deputy Wilford regards Unk with a handshake before replying, "Mr. Okafor, we have reason to declare your nephew as a person of interest in a couple of incidents that have happened over the past few weeks. We would like to bring him to the station to ask a few questions, just to ensure we can exclude him from further investigation."

Unk shoots a concerned gaze in my direction. My palms are sweaty in seconds, and I give up a weak shrug. I don't know what to tell him, but the first thing on my mind is whether or not the sheriffs have something on me. I'm not stupid, though; I have no intention of making it easy for them to figure out what they think they know. If they don't know, then I don't know, either.

Unk returns his attention toward Deputy Wilford, shaking his head in the process. "I'm afraid that's not gonna happen. He's a minor, and I do not consent as his legal guardian to any questioning without an attorney present."

"Sir, we simply want to ask some questions to exclude him as a potential suspect, nothing more," the sheriff repeats. "There's no need to make this difficult."

"It may have to be difficult. If you haven't Mirandized him, then he's not under arrest," Unk counters. "And if he's not under arrest, then he's staying right where he is. Your move."

"I didn't want things to get to that point, Mr. Okafor. If you want to do this the hard way, that can be arranged."

I suppress my rising panic, but it's becoming more difficult with each passing word between the two men.

"Well, until we can secure an attorney for him, and unless you're arresting him, which you must not be able to do, since you're only considering him as a person of interest, I'll suggest that you have a good afternoon," Unk advises the deputy sheriff.

"Mr. Okafor, if I may intrude," Mr. Channing says. "I would advise Mr. Salah to submit for questioning so that we can get this matter out of the way."

"Mr. Channing, I'm not comfortable with that advice," Unk retorts. "I can't be assured that they won't try to pull something during questioning."

"Considering I'm his legal counsel, I need you to trust me on this, Xavion," Mr. Channing announces.

Unk flinches for a moment, trying to understand the gravity of the statement. He stifles a chuckle to keep the sheriffs off balance. "You are?"

"He is?" Gamba repeats Unk's question. *"When did Method Man's cousin become our legal counsel?"*

"What you know about Meth, though?" I snap my attention inside my head for the moment. *"Never mind that, you might have missed a few things a few seconds ago. I'll catch you up to speed later."*

"Yes, I am." Mr. Channing holds up a crisp, one-dollar bill, folding it before placing it in his pocket. "As of a couple minutes ago, Mr. Salah secured me as his representation."

"*I like him. He's a slick one.*" Gamba grins. "*Let's see how this plays out.*"

"*You ain't seen nothing yet.*" It takes me a minute to finally catch on. "*Enjoy the rest of the show.*"

"Mr. Channing, I'm sure we can come to some sort of arrangement," Deputy Wilford voices. "We simply want to clear the air a bit. I'm sure you understand."

Mr. Channing takes a few steps forward, mimicking the sheriffs' stance. "Here's how this is going to go: I will confer with my client and his legal guardian, and then I'll give you a call and inform you whether or not I will advise him to come in for questioning in twenty-four hours."

"Very well, Mr. Channing. I'll expect your call soon." The sheriffs walk out of the shop, leaving Unk and Mr. Channing with me and a whole host of questions. "Now, gentlemen, would you be so kind as to meet me in my office when you close up in a few minutes?"

"I've still got another hour before I can shut down my shop, Robert, but you and Yasir can have a conversation until I get there, since he's retained you." Unk smirks. "Nice trick with the dollar bill. I saw that while I was dealing with the sheriffs, by the way."

I step into the convo with Unk and Mr. Channing, still trying to get an idea of what happened. "So when do either of you plan to let me in on the theater that just went down? We already put that one dollar show on at Kyle's party."

"Sorry, kiddo, we had to put on a show for the sheriffs, too," Unk says to me. He winks at Mr. Channing before he continues. "One of Mr. Channing's contacts inside the sheriff's office tipped him off that they would be coming for you. I asked him to show up to see what might have happened."

"Um, and now what? Like, I'm still expected to go down there and answer their questions, right?"

"Not until I prep you for your answers, no," Mr. Channing explains. He grabs a napkin from the dispenser to clean his lenses. "They're trying to box you in, to see if they can get you to answer the way they want you to, so they can fit the evidence they have collected against your narrative and then switch it to make you a suspect."

Unk slips behind the counter after he turns the sign back to "open" and busies himself before the next customers arrive. "I'm gonna let you two handle the particulars. I'll catch up after I've closed."

"Sounds like a plan. Let's go, Yasir. We've got a lot to discuss."

We step out of the shop, heading down the street to Mr. Channing's sprawling office a few blocks away. I retreat inside my head during the walk to have a quick conversation with Gamba before I deal with the issues at hand.

"What do you think?" I say as we sit down on a back patio I conjure up in my mind for the chat. *"Is there something you need to tell me before I go in?"*

Gamba takes a sip of water and places it on the table between us. *"We changed into our nonhuman form to take care of some trash that needed to be discarded. I did what was necessary to protect you back then."*

"What did you do to protect me, Gamba?" I fear the answer, but I can't act like I'm clueless, either. *"I need full disclosure, so I know what to tell and what not to tell."*

Gamba exhales slow and deep, turning his body to face me. *"One of the boys at the game had a weapon, and he intended to harm or kill you. I did what needed to be done to ensure your survival."*

I close my eyes for a moment, sitting with the new information. *"The other boys I saved Ian from had weapons that could have killed me, too. What was the difference?"*

"This one had a gun. Before I took him out, the gun went off, injuring one of the other kids badly. I do not know if he made it or not, but I had to take the one with the gun down no matter what." Gamba continues to sip as though the action was nothing more than a part of his primary directive. *"For now, find out what our lawyer knows before we offer anything. We can make a more informed decision after we know what we know."*

I slip out of the inside conversation with Gamba, focusing on heading into Mr. Channing's office to have an important conversation regarding my possible guilt or innocence. I greet Mr. Channing's executive assistant, Ms. Lynn, as we head to his corner office at the end of the hallway.

For a man whose family residence shows such extravagance, I'm shocked to see how plain and nondescript his office decor presents. I halfway expected the desk to be larger than life and every type of expensive art that could be purchased hanging on the walls. I remember seeing Mr. Channing's name on the marquee and the sign on the door into the office, so I'm at a loss for words over how my perception doesn't fit the reality of who's representing me.

"That look never gets old." Mr. Channing chuckles as he has a seat behind his desk, offering for me to sit down. "Now, let's get to the heart of it: the sheriff's office thinks they have something on you, and I need to know if they do or don't."

"I'm not sure what they're trying to find out from me, to be honest, Mr. Channing." I'm gonna stick to the "innocent until guilty" play until Mr. Channing comes up with something that makes me divulge any information. "The sheriffs coming down was a shock to me."

Mr. Channing strokes his goatee for a few moments, regarding my words. "Okay, let's put cards on the table, and then we can have a real conversation. In both incidents that the police have investigated, they have a partial print of a person who was at both locations, including a partial print on the weapons used to assault the persons involved. They will more than likely want you to submit your prints for a possible match."

I push down any outward emotional response, but inside, I'm cursing up a storm. "I see, and I'm failing to understand how I'm involved in any of this. I never put my hand on a weapon of any sort...well, except for the pipe that was used to try to hurt me in the first incident. I don't even remember seeing a gun when the other boys tried to rough me up at the other game at Beach Creek."

"And how did you know there was a gun at the scene of the

second incident?"

Fuck. Busted. "Okay, so I was there. Hell, they were trying to unalive me, all right?"

"Now we're getting somewhere. Well, the boys involved in the first incident were friends of Ian Lance, and they were vague about how they were assaulted," Mr. Channing says to me as he looks down at his notes. "It's no secret that Ian isn't your favorite person, and based on the incident at my son's birthday party, you have his full attention for whatever reason, so it leads me to believe that someone dropped a dime on you."

I clench my teeth, this time unable to resist allowing my anger to roar to the surface. "If he was the one to suggest I had anything to do with what happened to those boys in either of these incidents, I swear I'm gonna—"

"You're gonna do *nothing*, Yasir." Mr. Channing's tone shuts me down quick. "I would do my level best to avoid Ian and anyone he is associated with for as long as possible until we can get you cleared of this cloud hanging over you."

"There's no way I can do that once school starts back up next week, sir," I protest. "What you're asking is not anywhere near possible without the information going public. I would rather it not be public knowledge, to be honest. There will be too many questions that I don't have the capacity to answer."

"Then we will need to get this done as soon as possible. Considering we're still in the midst of the Bicentennial, we're gonna have to stall for time." Mr. Channing picks up his phone and scrolls for a few seconds before he presses his finger on the screen. "Deputy Wilford, please…Asa Channing, here. My client will submit himself to questioning after school on Monday. We have some affairs that need to be handled before we come down… Very good, sir, look forward to seeing you on Monday."

"So what do I do in the meantime? Monday's a few days away, and I still have to play keep-away until then." I lean back in the chair, ignoring Gamba's knocking on the proverbial door to get a thought in on the problem at hand. "My girlfriend already has me set up for my tuxedo fitting later tonight to prepare for the ball, and I can't stay away from the other festivities without arousing suspicion. It's a no-win scenario."

Mr. Channing acknowledges my dilemma. "I'm gonna trust you to exercise your best judgment, Yasir. For now, we'll keep this under wraps as best we can, and you'll be with Kyle and the rest of your circle, so they might be able to provide some buffers to keep things from getting crazy. Can you keep it together until Monday?"

"I'll do my best, sir. That's all I can promise at this point. Ian's father probably knows what's going on with the cases, and I wouldn't put it past him to leak information to his son," I concede. "He's gonna try to rile me up with what he knows, and I don't know what I can do to avoid that *when* it happens."

"Do what you can to avoid him at all costs," Mr. Channing repeats. "It could mean the difference between your guilt and innocence. Now, call your uncle and let him know I want the mahi and the crab, in lieu of payment, please, and thank you. It's my turn to cook tonight, and I want to impress my darling wife."

CHAPTER FORTY-TWO

We're sitting in one of Zahra's favorite large bean bag chairs in the loft on the second floor of her house, and Zahra's leaning against me as we're in a deep conversation with Kynani and Zahra's parents. It's been on my mind ever since my chosen said something about it at school earlier today. She was vague on the details, but something tells me I'm not the only one who may have their mind blown.

We spend a short time engaging in idle chatter, which does nothing but irritate her. Don't ask how I know, but I can feel it on her; that's the best way I can explain it. I'm trying to avoid her mood affecting my own, but I'm low-key feeling like I'm gonna explode if Kynani doesn't get everything out in space so everyone can digest and understand what's going on with us. I wish they would hurry up, though. This is turning into borderline torture.

Zahra jumps out of her spot next to me, nearly scaring everyone in the room to death. Her father pops into this stance like he's ready to go to battle in seconds. I instinctively pull her close, ignoring her father's glare, and she holds her hand up, nodding to let us know she's okay.

"What's going on? You reacted like something freaked you out." I remember that look on her face. It's the same one I had when… "Wait, did you hear—?"

"Zahra, are you sure you're okay, baby girl?" Kairo interrupts. "What is it? What's happening to you?"

"I believe I can explain. Once she has calmed down a bit, we can begin the conversation." Kynani moves toward us, placing her palm against Zahra's forehead before closing her eyes. "Sleep for now, warrior. We will call for you when it is time."

Zahra's shaking her head like she's trying to figure out what just happened. "I'm okay, Daddy, for real. I think there's something Ms. Kynani can help with to get that under control."

"If you say so, baby girl," he replies, switching his attention to Kynani. "Now, can we finally know the reason for the impromptu visit?"

Kynani shifts her focus toward Zahra again, smiling as she confirms that she's settled down. She then returns her attention to her parents, placing her hands in her lap. "Do either of you know what a trillsage is?"

Kesi shrugs, while Kairo nods his understanding. "Outside of what information is available in the Kindaran Archives and the Central Library, there is not much common knowledge on the subject. We know much more about nyxwraiths than we do trillsages."

Kynani nods as Zahra and I get comfortable with the history lesson that's coming. "The reason why there is not much knowledge is due to the fact that, except in very rare instances, nyxwraiths and trillsages do not venture far outside of the Temples inside of Mount Kindara."

"What information do you have on the subject, Ms. Kynani?" Zahra inquires, shifting her body forward to engage in the conversation. I match her body language, realizing that I'm more interested in the subject than I'd originally thought. "If nyxwraiths and trillsages are rarely away from the temples, what does this have to do with anything here in the States?"

"Before I answer that question, my child, I must provide a quick back story and history," Kynani expresses to everyone in the room. She leans back in her seat, waving her hands in a circular motion. In the next moment, images form out of thin air, begging our attention. "As your father knows, nyxwraiths can only be brought to the attention of their owners either through a traumatic event or by one of the Temple priestesses, when there is an imminent threat to the Temple. They come from specific bloodlines, which is how the Kindaran Nine families came into being."

"Yes, this is true, Kynani," Kairo confirms.

"What you may not know, Kairo, is that when a nyxwraith is realized, in a manner of speaking, a trillsage is realized at that same time," Kynani continues as she manipulates the images in the air. "A trillsage is, from birth, bound to their nyxwraith mate, by Ashanti's will and power. The trillsage becomes the guide, the nyxwraith its protector. And both are bound by the gods and Kindaran law to protect the sacred Kutokufa Scrolls of Kindara."

Kairo and Kesi gasp at the same time. He grabs her hand to pull her close. "I did not think that was possible. We would have been told by the priestess who helped bring Zahra into the world, right?"

"Sometimes the priestess who assists with the birth is not made aware of the *mwali duati* gene inside the baby when they are first born," Kynani explains further. "In your daughter's case, it lay dormant for some time because her mate had not yet realized his nyxwraith, until—"

"Until Yasir had to be revived during the incident at that boy's party," Kesi finishes the sentence. "It is almost like we are having to make up the rules as we go along. There is nothing in the texts that can even explain what is going on. We were told by one of the Vodaran priestesses a few weeks before the invasion that she had been having visions that Zahra's mate had been located," Kesi explains as she stares at Zahra. "We were to have made the trek from Kua to Solara to meet with Bakari and Nasira in person."

"Wait, what?" Zahra says, nervously playing with her hair.

Kairo turns to face Zahra, his gaze switching between me and her. "Baby girl, you were supposed to have met Yasir over a decade ago. When everything happened in Solara, we were forced to escape to the States while the Kindaran military and Mipaku Tribe—the border tribe—extinguished the Bralban threat. We did not know why we were singled out, but now it is starting to make sense."

"I am still trying to wrap my mind around our daughter being a trillsage," Kesi mentions out loud, incredulous over the revelation. "I mean, how would we even know if she were or not?"

Kynani turns to me, finishing the glass of water and placing the base of the glass on top of her palm. "Zahra, concentrate on this glass and sing. I believe high C should do the trick."

Kairo's confusion is written all over his face. "What are you talking about, Kynani? Zahra can sing, but that octave is Mariah Carey–level high."

While her parents continue protesting, Zahra takes my hand in hers, squeezing it a few times to keep my attention. I hear her vocalize a range of notes, working her way up the scales, her eyes focused only on the glass in Kynani's hand. I swoon as I listen to her find the right pitch, doing my best to not fall victim to her siren side.

In a voice I don't recognize, she gives everyone a bit of an advanced warning. "You might want to cover your ears. This could get a bit loud."

Zahra opens her mouth, unleashing a note and frequency that, at first, doesn't seem to cause the concern her warning advised. Soon, the volume rises, causing the windows in the loft area to vibrate. She's still focused on the glass, narrowing her eyes as the octave amplifies. The windows stop shaking as the glass in Kynani's hand becomes the sole focal point of her singing voice. Before long, the glass pulses, and a few seconds later, it shatters into several pieces onto the carpet.

Kynani maintains her grin, turning toward Kesi and Kairo. "And that's only one of the ways that you could tell that she is a trillsage."

Zahra's just sitting there, admiring her handiwork. I'm in shock over what I just witnessed. She can break glass! Now I'm wondering what else she can do.

She blushes as she meets the shocked expressions on her parents' faces. "So I've been practicing a bit."

• • •

Kynani is sitting in the backyard with us after finishing the conversation with Zahra's parents, and if we're being honest, there's gonna be several more conversations on the horizon.

I stay busy with Zahra as Kynani instructs us where to place the candles around the space we cleared out on the lawn, my mind traveling back to my introduction to Gamba. I never got the chance to really explain to her what happened, what I went through, but the way things are playing out in front of us, we'll be comparing notes soon.

"I heard a voice in my head earlier. Was that my trillsage trying to communicate with me?" Zahra asks as they close the circle around them. "It was the same voice I heard come out of my mouth before I started singing."

"Yes, that was her," Kynani answers. "We will be meeting her 'in the flesh' quite soon. I am pleased that she waited to reach out to you until it was time to complete the acclimation ritual."

"So will I have the same control over mine that Yasir has over his? This is all exciting and scary at the same time." Zahra places the final candle on the grass before meeting Kynani in the middle of the circle. "What does this mean for the future? I have so many questions."

"They will be answered in time, but for now, we need to get you comfortable with your trillsage." Kynani holds out her hands, nodding for her to take them. Seconds later, the candles catch fire in a circular sequence, the blaze surrounding them and almost shielding them from view. "Are you ready to meet her?"

"Yes, Ms. Kynani, I'm ready." She's saying the words, but I'm not sure she believes them. I know I didn't when I said them. "As ready as I'll ever be, anyway. One more thing: is it possible for Yasir to come with us? Is that allowed?"

Umm, I didn't see that coming.

"If your betrothed is willing to delve inside, if only as a silent and invisible spectator, then he is welcome to travel," Kynani states as she glances in my direction. "It is by her wish, but this is an intimate ritual, as you are well aware."

"I understand, and I will find a quiet corner and watch." Who's she kidding? It's one thing to be in the middle of it all. It's a whole other thing to watch from the outside. "I'm hoping not to freak out."

"That makes two of us, baby." Zahra takes a deep breath and slowly exhales. "Okay, now I'm ready."

I take my place just outside of the circle at Kynani's direction, and I brace myself for what I'm about to witness.

"Now, take a walk with me, deeper inside your mind, so that we can meet your trillsage," Kynani directs. She chants a few more words in her Kindaran dialect, and I grin as I finally understand what's being asked. "You have the control to create the outward surroundings in which we can meet her. Whatever you create, it will manifest itself in a space inside your mind."

Zahra nods, and it doesn't take long for her to create the space. In a flash, they're sitting under the Live Oak on Oakwood's campus, on top of an oversize blanket in the colors of the Kindaran flag. They're sipping on strawberry lemonade slushies as we all enjoy the late afternoon sun. Kynani looks around at the serenity of the scene and smiles as she spots a figure in the distance walking toward them.

"This is quite the backdrop for your first meeting, dear girl," Kynani opines. "I believe this will be more than suitable, and she is arriving as we speak."

I notice the woman, too, stunned at her striking features as she draws closer. In fact, they are as familiar as they are striking, so much so that I swear she and Zahra are sisters—except she told me she is an only child. I continue to study the young woman's face, and the moment she smiles, something clicks in my head, at least for a split second. I stay in the background as I watch the scene unfold in front of me.

"I know you, don't I?" Zahra remarks as she makes space on the blanket for the woman to sit. "You look so familiar to me, but I can't place your face."

"You do know me, little one. I used to babysit you when you were a little girl," the woman replies. "You've grown up to be such a strong, beautiful young woman. Your parents should be proud of you."

"Imara?" She clasps her hand over her mouth as she recognizes the woman in front of her. "You're my older cousin. You were my favorite cousin. I was so heartbroken when my parents told me you died while fighting off the Bralba invasion."

"I know, but the strangest and most wonderful thing happened. Nyati deemed me worthy to be your trillsage because I protected you in life…at least, to some degree." Imara moves closer, giving her the tightest hug, wiping the tears streaming down her face. "I didn't want to leave you, and I think it was that desire to find a way back to my favorite little cousin that had the gods smile on me and bring me back to you."

"I can't believe you're here." Zahra's voice breaks as she continues to hold Imara close. "I still don't understand, but I don't care right now. To have you here with me…I don't have the words to say how happy I am."

"Not as happy as I am. The gods are smiling on us both, baby girl."

Kynani smiles, watching as Imara and Zahra continue to banter, making the necessary preparations for the final step in the process. "It is time, ladies. Are you ready?"

"I'm ready. At least, I hope so," she tells her.

"I am ready, Kynani. I have been waiting for this for a long time," Imara answers. "We will have time to catch up on everything once the merge and acclimation has been completed."

Kynani claps her hands three times, repeating the same movements that began my process. She rubs them together, creating a spark. When she separates them, each hand is consumed in a crimson-hued flame this time, its brilliance cutting through the darkness. She takes each of their hands, watching as the flames consume the connection, then encourages them to complete the triangle by grasping hands.

As the fire rages, I notice as Zahra tries to resist playing with the flames as they flicker against her body. I don't dare interrupt, as I'm only there to watch it all, but I love the way she plays in her favorite element.

Kynani keeps her eyes closed to concentrate. "Imara, do you pledge your life to your owner, to protect her from all threats, foreign or friendly?"

"I pledge my life to my owner, my cousin, and to protect her from all threats, foreign or friendly," Imara repeats.

Kynani continues. "Zahra, do you pledge to protect your trillsage from anyone who would try to do her harm, to ensure that you do not place yourself in any unnecessary peril, and when called upon, you both will do what is best for Kindara?"

"I pledge to protect my trillsage, my cousin, from anyone who would try to do her harm, to ensure I do not place myself in any unnecessary peril, and when called upon, to do what is best for Kindara," she replies.

Kynani focuses her energy among the three of them as the color of the flames changes to a brilliant sapphire before dissipating. Satisfied that the process is complete, she opens her eyes and releases her grip. "Zahra, Imara, the acclimation has now taken hold, and the merge is complete. Imara, you should be able to move freely within Zahra's consciousness, but there are still limits as her trillsage. You cannot take over unless she is in severe distress, and she still can override if she sees fit. Any suggestions you make can be heeded or not."

Imara nods. "I understand. I know the limits of my power. My owner has the final say, regardless, unless it causes her harm."

Zahra flashes a mischievous smirk. "Ooh, I get to boss her around? You have no idea how much fun this is going to be for me."

Imara shakes her head, giggling along. "I see now that this is going to be an interesting time for the two of us, baby girl. I am your guide and bound by Kindaran law to protect you. I am looking forward to catching up with all the things that make up who you are, including…the young man in your life, as I understand?"

"It is time to return, as Zahra's parents will need to be informed of tonight's revelations," Kynani advises. "It has been my honor to facilitate this transition, and I look forward to guiding you further."

Once we come out of the depths of Zahra's subconscious, Kynani extinguishes the candles with a swipe of her hands. She glances at her, nodding at her new body language and the aura surrounding her. "There is one more thing that I will need to prepare you to deal with, in due time."

"What else is there, Ms. Kynani? You have already done so much at this point."

Kynani gazes into her eyes to express the importance of the words in her mind. She pulls me into the conversation to make sure she doesn't have to repeat herself. "You and Yasir will be tested. There is a storm on the horizon, and you cannot give up. That storm will be relentless, and it will do everything it can to make you submit."

I recognize the severity of her words. "If that's the case…we're gonna need backup."

"I would not have it any other way. You will need every resource at your disposal to get you through. But make no mistake; before this is all over…it may take a monster to save us all."

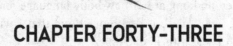

CHAPTER FORTY-THREE

Why in the name of Nyati and her children did I agree to get a tuxedo for this madness that's about to happen this weekend? I must be out of my mind to think— On second thought, let's get this done before I change my mind.

I make it into the town square, heading toward the tuxedo shop. The store is part of a line of essential businesses—Oakwood Pub & Grille, Ogletree's Drug Store, Feelin' Saucy Pizza, among others—that make up the heart of downtown Oakwood Grove. I park in the diagonal spaces just off the street, getting out of Storm to get this out of the way as soon as possible.

I greet all the boys who are on the way out with their suit bags, channeling the energy I feel as I wait outside for a few moments to get inside. I'd gotten about halfway through the line when I hear a voice that pretty much has the potential to undo all the positive vibes I've gathered.

"Just when I thought my day couldn't get any stranger, I had to run into you." Ian's hostile tone throws me off, and I struggle to understand what I did to tick him off this time. He's been gone the whole week. "I figured you were too bougie to hang with the townies."

"Bro, I swear, not today. I was having a great week. Let's not spoil it with some nonsense, okay?"

"It looks to me like someone's in a bit of a predicament. The last place I expected to see you showing your face would be at a shop renting a tuxedo," Ian says. "I wonder if you're just a glutton for punishment or something."

I wonder sometimes whether Ian has a GPS tracker on me, so it'll tell him to be in the same place at the same time so he can start some drama. If it's not for the fact that I dropped a non-refundable deposit on the tux I need to be fitted for so I can look presentable at the anniversary ball, I would turn on my heels and find another location.

Who am I kidding? It's Thursday night, and the ball is Saturday. I don't have the luxury of switching up so late in the game. I'm gonna have to grin and bear it, no matter what he may throw in my direction.

The team has been back from the by-week minicamp since yesterday, but I can't get around how he knew I would be here at this moment. A quick snap of my fingers triggers my memory; Kyle's appointment is thirty minutes behind mine, which means most of the team may have scheduled theirs around the same time frame. If I can tolerate Ian for the next twenty minutes or so, backup will be here to help me deal.

I agreed to keep my distance as a promise to Mr. Channing, but I should've known better than to think that would have been an easy task to maintain. There are only three decent shops to rent tuxedos, and two of them were marginal, which left K. Tyler Ltd. as the go-to for the cutting-edge fashion. If anyone wants to be seen, Mr. Tyler is the man to help them be *seen*.

Oh well, I'll just have to roll with it. "I'm not in the mood for your nonsense today, bro. Let's just get these rental fittings over with and let it be at that, feel me?"

"Man, there's no need to be all amped up, yo. I was simply pointing out that maybe you had more pressing matters that required your attention." Ian spreads his arms out as the tailor continues to work through his measurements. "I mean, I know I wouldn't want to act like nothing's popping off soon."

Gamba stirs awake, recognizing my spiking irritability. *"We have got to move to a bigger town or something. Is there anywhere that this man does not turn up?"*

I smirk at Gamba's comment as I take a step onto the platform to be measured. "I'm gonna break this down for you real quick. Whatever drama that you've created, it ain't gonna stick, all right?"

"I've no idea what you're talking about, playa," Ian responds. "Are you projecting your troubles or something? I mean, you look a bit disturbed right now."

"You know exactly what the hell I'm talking about," I remark. "Keep playing dumb. It suits you, for real. Did that take a few years to perfect, or did that come naturally to you?"

"Damn, you got all this energy, I see. They say a dog barks when they sense a threat, so what you barking for?" Ian chuckles. "What's the matter? Do I make you nervous?"

Gamba growls from behind the door to my conscious mind. *Why did we agree not to drop this idiot where he stands? It's like he knows we can't lay a finger on him or something.*

"Times change, and your time is up, my boy." I focus on the image in the mirror as the tailor makes sure the measurements are true to fit. "You're about to find out what it's like when you're not on that pedestal you love so much."

"I don't know, bro. The way those charges sound, from what I've heard anyway, you might be looking at getting off that pedestal before you got a chance to get it warmed up." Ian stifles more laughter. "You're looking at real time, for real."

"And I won't see a day of it, trust." I tilt my head toward the ceiling to give the tailor a chance to get the neck size correct. "Witnesses tend to be so damn unreliable."

"Yeah, and so are defense attorneys." Ian stares me down. "Don't trust the wrong one, and I'm sure the right one will run you something serious. If you want, I can take that Jeep off your hands if you can't afford the retainer."

I wait for the tailors to head to the back as I glare at Ian. The moment they disappear into the warehouse part of the store, I grab Ian by the throat and slam him against the wall.

Ian can't stop smiling. I know he's baiting me, but I don't care right now. "Woo, I think I hit a nerve."

Gamba tries to rein me in, but every nerve he soothes is white hot to the touch. *"Ya-Ya, I need you to settle down, okay? This isn't going to help matters at all. Step away from the wannabe pro athlete and be smart about things."*

"What the hell is your problem, huh? You've been riding me since I got here, and I don't remember doing anything to warrant the bullshit." I've reached the point where all I want is to shut Ian up. "You got something against folks who ain't from Oakwood? Is that it?"

"I'm not from here, either," Ian corrects me. "Just like you, I'm from another country."

I release my grip on Ian, taking a step back, regarding his facial features. "Wait a minute… How did you know I was from another country? And for that matter, you're from what country, exactly? I know you're not Kindaran. You're not built for that life."

"I'm not from your wannabe utopia, but you'll be okay." Ian frowns as he adjusts his shirt. "Not everyone wants to be a part of your island paradise, even if you keep wearing it like some badge of honor."

"So where are you from, then?" I repeat. "No need to keep the cheap seats in suspense, playboy. Speak your piece. It can't be that bad."

Ian closes his fists, almost ready to throw a punch. "My family is from Bralba. There, you happy now?"

I freeze, unsure which emotion would rise to the surface first: anger or shock. He's…from…where? "I stand corrected. It is that bad. All bad."

"I don't follow." Ian turns to face me, stepping down from the platform to take a seat. "What does where I'm from have to do with anything?"

"Damn, bro, you really don't know your country's history when it comes to mine, do you? You can't be that thick. I just found out, and I'm still trying to make sense of it." I'm fighting every urge I have to throttle Ian within an inch of his life. "You and your pops need to have a serious conversation. I have a sneaky suspicion he's got a lot of information that you need to be aware of."

"Are you suggesting that my father is hiding something from me?" Ian gets defensive, his anger rising by the second. "You seem to know a lot more than me about whatever you're spitting, so get it out. Tell me what you know."

"It's time to leave, now, kiddo," Gamba implores me. He notices the amethyst-hued flames rising around us, which isn't a good sign. *"He's trying to rile you up. We're too emotional after the bomb he just dropped on us. Let's go."*

"Ask your father about your country's history. I'm not doing that labor for you. If I do, I'm liable to say something I won't regret." I step back a few feet, keeping a close eye on Ian's movement within the store. "I think I'm gonna put some space between us. It's best for everyone."

"Nah, bro, we're gonna finish this right now." Ian grabs my arm, trying to hold me in place. "You're not about to drop something like that about my father and leave. I was seven when we left, and I still don't know why."

Kyle and a few of his teammates happen to slip into the store and witness the scene unfolding. Kyle makes a beeline for me, which makes Ian loosen his grip enough for me to slip away. Taylor keeps Ian occupied. Kyle has to pick me off the ground to remove me from the store as we hear Ian ranting to Taylor about needing to finish our conversation.

I'm literally vibrating, I'm raging so much, as I work hard to move around Kyle. "I can't even get a damn tuxedo without this fool coming in to gum up the works, bro."

Kyle waits for me to calm myself a bit before he says anything. "I just got off the phone with my dad before TK and I got here. This is definitely not the definition of 'stay as far away from Ian and crew as possible,' bro."

"So I'm the one who has to play keep away while he gets to trigger me at every possible corner? How the hell is that supposed to work?" I pose the question that I know has no logical answer. "We have things to do this weekend, and as much as I would love to be a hermit for my own sanity, I have a whole girlfriend that I can't let down."

"Believe me, I feel you, and I told Dad that, so we're gonna have to find a workaround so our girls don't kill us all." Kyle chuckles at the thought. "We got you, my boy. Let's get through this weekend, and then we can deal with the madness on Monday, cool?"

I'm already over it all, switching gears to the last thing Ian said to me before things went left. "I think I might have figured out why Ian has been so fixated on me for so long, but I don't think he even knows why."

"We can't worry about that now. What's more important is that TK and I and the rest of the boys get our measurements handled so the tuxedos can get back in time for the ball." Kyle taps my fists before heading back in the shop. "For now, let's focus on what's in front of us and take care of them as they come up. I'll hit you up after we're done."

I make it to Storm, shaking off the rising anger over Ian's offer to "take it off my hands" before settling into the driver's seat. I start the engine, closing my eyes for a moment to gather my thoughts. "Gamba, we're gonna be on high alert all weekend. You know that, right?"

"Yeah, kiddo, I did my best to keep the flames at bay. There's a lot more to this thing with Ian than we thought, and we might have to keep an eye out for anything and everything." He pauses for a moment to think on things. *"We will have to dig deeper, figure out if there is a connection we're not seeing, which means a conversation with both Kynani and the Kindaran Council."*

I agree, but unless it has anything to do with spending time with Zahra, I'm comfortable ignoring it. It can wait until after the weekend.

And speaking of spending time with Z, what we have to do later today isn't what I had in mind, but it's important.

We have some things to tell the rest of the clique, and I honestly don't know how they'll respond.

CHAPTER FORTY-FOUR

I have no intention of sounding any alarms, but after our conversation with Kynani, there's no choice but to lay all the cards on the table with the rest of the clique. I know Zahra's going through a lot of the same emotions I am, but she's got her best friends here to help her through it. As much as I would like to lean on my people—or at least my former people—that's no longer possible, not after everything that happened when I was up there last time.

Now I'm stuck trusting people on the strength of my girlfriend's connection to them. It's not exactly a bad thing, though. I've gotten attached to them, and some of the others in our circles at Oakwood, but there's something about that built-in trust that's always been there. But this is a huge bomb to drop, and we have no idea how they may react to it.

Zahra told me before everyone arrived that they might be a bit confused over where the chat would take place. Anytime something serious needed to be discussed, she and Kendyl would camp out in her bedroom, door locked, with the explicit request from her parents to not disturb them until they got whatever the crisis had been calmed down. If that's the case, Kyle and I being in the room will really throw Kendyl off.

Not to mention, we won't be in her bedroom to talk this time.

The minute Kyle and Kendyl walk through the door, all Zahra's concerns are realized. All we can do is get them where they need to be and try to keep them from freaking out.

We're camped out in the basement, with all sorts of pillows and blanket pallets sprawled all over the floor. We even put the fruits and pastries that Zahra and I brought from the grocery store out on trays to cushion some of the blow of what we have to say.

Once everyone is settled in their spaces, my anxiety levels shoot through the roof.

I'm not ready. Nope. This is a bad idea.

As soon as I sense the hesitation in Zahra, I've completely forgotten about anything I'm going through, period. I whisper in her ear, "Are you okay? I can feel your hesitation. I'm here with you, baby."

"I was about to ask you the same thing," she utters in a low, hushed tone. "I understand if you're not ready to trust them. I can just tell them about what's going on with me."

I shake my head, letting her know we're in this together. "I'll be okay. I have to trust them sooner or later, right?"

Zahra kisses my lips and nods before she turns her attention toward Kendyl and Kyle, noticing the confuzzled expressions on their faces. "What?"

Kendyl's never one to beat around the subject. "Girl, get your life together and let us know why we're here and why it's not in the usual spot?"

Zahra exhales slowly, grabbing my hand as she braces herself. "Okay, so a lot has been going on that we haven't had a chance to tell y'all about. It's going to seem unbelievable, but you're my best friends, so there's no way we could hide this from you. And I'm hoping Yasir can trust you with this, too."

"You're starting one of your famous rants, chica. Just spit it out," Kendyl says. "I promise, we can handle whatever it is that you're dealing with. What's going on with you two, and why are you both looking like it's the end of the world?"

"Yeah, when we got done with our tuxedo fittings, I'd never seen him so focused on making sure Anniversary Week goes great for you," Kyle chimes in. He glances at Kendyl, then back to us again, confusion spread all over his face. "So what's really good, and why are we just now hearing about it?"

Zahra flinches for a moment, placing her hands over her ears to calm herself. She murmurs to herself, and I recognize that she's having a conversation with her trillsage. Is that what I look like when I'm talking to Gamba? I make a mental note to figure out a way to not look like I'm spaced out when those convos need to happen.

She pops out of it seconds later, and she focuses her gaze on Kendyl. "Kenni, remember that situation at the mall with those Beach Creek boys, when I tried to get Yasir's attention?"

Kendyl nods, looking up at Kyle before she turns her attention back to me. "I remember. We always knew you could sing."

Zahra sighs, offering a small smile. "Yeah, but I didn't know how to answer your questions back then. I know now, and I'm scared that you'll see me differently once I tell you."

Kendyl reaches over and pulls us to where she and Kyle are to join in a tight group hug. If they keep this up, I'm gonna have to take back everything I said about not trusting them. "Z, we've been damn near blood for over a decade. You are my sister. We love you too much to worry about what you're having a hard time telling us. And Yasir...I know I gave you the business when we first met, but you mean the world to my girl, which means you're my people, too."

"You know you're my ace, bro, so you know I got your back, whatever it is," Kyle adds his piece. "You're my dawg. We might not be Day Ones, but it's felt like it since we had a chance to really hang."

I'm gonna need them to stop making this so damned easy.

"If you tell me that you've developed superpowers, I'm gonna scream," Kendyl interrupts me. "Just get it out. I wanna be right, so spit it out, sis."

"Okay, okay, okay, sheesh. Yes, Yasir and I are metahuman. Happy now?"

Kendyl just smirks like she unlocked the cryptex from *The Da Vinci Code*. "Yes, I'm happy now. You made it sound like it was something we needed to be afraid to know."

Zahra smiles big and breathes out a sigh of relief. "I'm so glad you're my aces. You have no idea how much I stressed over telling you about any of this."

"Of course, only you would have best friends who could, and would, understand any of this and not run for the hills," Kendyl expresses as we burst into laughter. "But now the question is how do we keep this under wraps with the rest of the cliques we run in, and what does this mean for all the Anniversary Week shenanigans? I mean, you're both whole enhanced beings now. Doesn't that come with a secret identity or some other nonsense that we're supposed to keep hidden?"

"Yeah, we've really been reading too many comic books." Kyle breaks out into more laughter. "I mean, it's obvious that you both have abilities. When will you find out what Yasir's are?"

"Hopefully soon, but we'll have that conversation with someone who can help with those answers. But considering that he is supposed to be the bodyguard-slash-beast in the equation, I am wondering what that might look like," she continues. "I do have a thing for boys who know how to handle themselves and take the lead."

"Yeah, it's the reason Ian got to you freshman year before it all fell apart," Kendyl points out. I give her a hard glare, and she simply shrugs. "What, you know it's true. I'm just glad you came to your senses before things got out of hand."

It gets *quiet* in seconds.

The cliché of being able to hear a pin drop on a hardwood floor doesn't cover how quiet it is right now. I shift my gaze between the three of them, and they're all having a hard time maintaining eye contact.

This can't be life right now.

"Wait, what was that?" Yeah, she can't just drop a bomb like that and I'm supposed to act like it didn't hit. "Is that the reason why Ian's still so fixated on me? Y'all used to go out?"

I shudder at that hard truth as the silence gives me all the answers I want. Leave it to Kendyl to be her blunt-force-trauma self at the wrong damn time.

"Damn, Kenni, did you have to drop the anvil on my head like that?" Zahra says. "I'm still trying to get that idiot out of my atmosphere, and he still manages to show up like a bad rash. His fixation with Yasir is just begging for more drama."

"It's begging for more than that, baby. He's trying to get me locked up," I growl, doing my best to keep Gamba at bay. He's been pretty quiet during this whole bit, which makes me wonder if he's just waiting for the perfect time to show himself. "I would've been able to at least sidestep a lot of this craziness if I'd known."

"Speaking of bad rashes, how are we supposed to deal with him and his girl Chrisette tomorrow night at the Theater in the Park event?" Kyle asks.

"She will be with Ian the rest of the night anyway, and as long as they're boo'd up, that will be less stress on all of us," Zahra replies. "What we need to do is let them pick a spot and then pitch our spot way away from them instead of the other way around. The minute they see us camped out, it gives them control."

"Say less, I'm with that plan." Kyle grabs a donut. "Any other drama that we need to see about? I'm sure that we can't be the only ones going through it."

Zahra nods at Kendyl. "I have one thing on my mind, considering the ball is a couple of days away now. What we need to talk about is how we better outclass the entire town at the ball. The dresses we finally were able to pick up from the seamstress are fire. And what about the tuxedos that the boys ordered, though? Let's talk about that for a minute."

Kyle quickly kisses Kendyl and rises from their spot. "Yep, I'm about to head out. This is not the part of the convo that I signed up for. Until you say it's cool, I'm leaving my boys out of the mix, but no cap, I'm gonna end up looking at my dawg a little differently from now on."

"I'm still the same, my boy, but yeah, I get what you're saying," I reply, tapping fists before I kiss Zahra and follow him out the door. "We're gonna let you ladies hash out whatever you need to for the ball. All we need to do is show up and look boss."

Zahra stands to give Kyle a hug, laughing at his impromptu exit just when things are getting interesting, and she encourages Kendyl to escort him out while she takes my hand to head up the stairs. "Believe me, things are going to be a lot different from now on. There's no such thing as normal anymore."

CHAPTER FORTY-FIVE

Being inside Carrington Park and witnessing the spectacle of the Theater in the Park event, I have to admit, this is fire. The girls did their thing with all the decorations and other pieces speckled throughout the park. I wonder what other talents my girlfriend has in her tool bag to be able to put something this large together.

I remember the conversations after Zahra and the rest of the girls handled different tasks to get things completed, and I had to do my best to calm her down. Chrisette whittled her nerves raw, and it doesn't take a genius to figure out that Zahra needed a break from her and, by indirect extension, Ian.

My creator's eye absorbs every aspect of the location, and I beam with pride over her attention to detail. From the various large movie screens that are showing at least five different movies to the marked rows and the specific spaces that were created to protect each viewer's line of sight, I couldn't find anything I would alter to improve the atmosphere. How in the world they pulled this together in such a short period of time, I'll never know.

Zahra and I stroll arm-in-arm through the park, waving to familiar faces, stopping to speak to others as they're all jockeying for a position in front of whatever screen shows the movie they want to see. The concession stands have a relative number of people in line, the volunteers coming from Oakwood Grove High, and, in a surprise move, Baytown High also came through to pitch in for the special occasion. The proceeds from the event, as agreed upon by Mayor Lance, will benefit both schools to improve their respective campuses.

All in all, everything is running with an efficiency that keeps the adults quiet and happy.

"So, do you like?" Zahra asks as she wraps her arm around mine, leaning over close enough to sneak a kiss on my cheek. "I know you have something that you would change."

"Nope, I'm not changing anything at all." I scan over the entire landscape, smiling at everything they've created. "It all looks so good. I could stay here all night."

Zahra taps my chin to get my undivided attention. "Are you sure you want to be here all night, my handsome one?"

I blush at the not-so-subtle hint. We really haven't had a moment to ourselves in a while. "Well, not *all night*, all night, but you get what I mean. We can at least stick around long enough for one movie. This is your pride and joy of an event, you know."

"Good recovery. Besides, I've had enough of people this whole week." Zahra kisses my cheek again, then we continue our walk-through. "Specific people especially. Ugh."

"I thought that was supposed to be my thing. You know, not wanting to be around a lot of people?" I chuckle at her smirk.

"After dealing with Chrisette over the past couple of days, I really don't want to have to deal with her tonight." Zahra looks more fatigued than usual, and that worries me. Maybe we should head home so we can both recharge. "I almost wanted to choke her out last night because we couldn't agree on the final movie listing. Between that, getting ambushed into working with her in the first place, and enduring her passive-aggressive shots at me the entire time, if she so much as looks in my direction, it's gonna be a problem."

"You said it yourself, baby, all we have to do is stay out of their way, and we can get through the night in one piece." I return her kiss on my cheek with a kiss across her lips. "Now, let's find the rest of the crew and camp out so we can have some fun tonight."

We meander through the crowds, bypassing the screens playing movies we want to watch later, spotting our group in the area where we preplanned to meet up. There are others around them, but I don't mind the extra company tonight. I feel good about the way things are going, so much so that I tell Gamba to keep a minimal watch over things in the background.

"There are too many people around, and we still have unresolved issues with Ian that have not been handled. I cannot see taking the night off. Having you defenseless is not what is warranted," Gamba says.

"I understand, but I have to be able to have fun sometimes. I can't be in a constant state of emergency."

Gamba moves from the shadows and into my sight. *"You can have fun, but I will keep an eye out for other threats. I have a feeling that things are not entirely safe here. There are too many spaces where people can cause problems. I'll be right here if you need me."*

"Okay, old man, I hope you're wrong, but I can't tell you to stand down."

We finally find our spot already laid out for us where we're greeted by Kendyl and Kyle first, dropping into the space between them and our other friend Taylor and his date, Tania.

"Has anyone been able to track where Ian and his crew has settled?" I ask the group. "We want to stick to the plan to keep things peaceful tonight."

"I saw them a while ago outside one of the other movies," Taylor says as he settles back in place with Tania. "They're chilling out over there, so we have a couple of hours at least to enjoy the rest of this movie before we move to another screen."

"That sounds like a plan to me." I welcome Zahra to sit in my lap as the movie continues. "What else have we missed?"

"Thankfully, nothing," Kendyl tells us. "It's been pretty smooth for the most part. Even the adults have been relaxed. Kyle's dad and Mayor Lance, though…they've been eyeballing each other all night, but I think that has a lot to do with the constant power struggle."

"Yeah, they don't like each other. That's never been a secret in this town," Kyle adds as he sneaks a glance in his father's direction. "It's like my dad has something on him that he can use at any given moment. I'd love to know what that is so I can hang it over Ian's head. He's gotten bolder since we got back from minicamp."

That part has my attention. "What's going on, bro? I don't want it to sound like it's all about me all the time when it comes to that dude, but I don't have a choice but to wonder."

"My uncle is one of the sheriffs working the case of those boys who got assaulted at the game against Beach Creek," Taylor says. "They're comparing notes with some claw marks the Oakwood sheriffs found when those Baytown boys got hurt. They still think it's an animal attack of some sort, but they can't figure out what type of animal fits the claw marks."

I tense up, causing Zahra to turn to face me. I give her a subtle shake of my head, silencing her before she can ask a question. "So they still don't really know what's going on at this point, got it. What does this have to do with Ian?"

"He's still on you, thinking that you're the one responsible for the attacks," Taylor told him. "The reports from the victims said they saw a flash of light before whatever attacked them showed up. They still don't know what happened to them. All they know is that when they finally woke up, you were nowhere to be found, and they were in the hospital."

"Which reminds me, no one's still not saying much of anything about that night to anyone," Kyle recalls. "Do you know what happened or what they were talking about? I mean, they were trying to hurt you bad, they were wrong as fuck for that, but something saved your ass."

Gamba stirs while in his nonhuman form, scratching against my conscious mind. *"The less they know, the better, Ya-Ya. This isn't the time or place to have that conversation. We can sit them down after we have a conversation with Zahra."*

"She deserved to know long before now, Gamba," I scoff at him, kneeling as I scan over his paws and teeth. I feel the aggression, but it's not needed. Not tonight. *"We need to tell her later tonight. Keeping her and Imara in the dark is a bad move."*

I turn my attention back to Kyle. "The last thing I remember was blacking out. One of them had a lead pipe in his hand, so I can only assume that I got hit over the head or something," I explain away as much of my appearance as possible, even if it does sound thin as hell. "When I woke up, I saw them on the ground and bugged out of there. You know how this town is, bro. I would have gotten blamed for whatever happened because I was the one standing and they were the ones hurt instead of me."

"Yo, no need to get defensive, Yasir, for real. We're on your side." Kyle holds up his hands. "My dad is repping you against anything they might be trying to pull, so that's gotta mean something, right?"

I move my gaze from Kyle to Taylor, trying to get a gauge of their expressions, unsure of what to believe. Even the comforting glances from Kendyl and Tania aren't enough to assure me that I'm not being ganged up on.

Kendyl adds to the supportive voices to keep me calm. "Yasir, look, we know you were the victim. There's no doubt about that. You're right, this town is screwed up with the way it treats certain people. We got you, but more importantly, my best friend has you. That's all that matters right now."

I'm breathing a bit slower now. I check my watch and then up toward the screen before I tap Zahra's shoulder. "I'm gonna get some drinks, baby. Do you want anything else while I'm up?"

Zahra grabs my hand, stopping me before I can get to my feet. "Do you think it's a good idea for you to roll around like nothing has happened? What about what Mr. Channing told you? You're taking a chance of dealing with Ian and something going wrong."

The answer to her question comes in the form of a voice I never expected to hear nor faces I expected to see at all. "Don't worry, Zahra, he's still got Squad, and Squad takes care of its own."

Hearing Dante's voice freezes me in seconds. They couldn't have possibly dropped into town without a heads-up. "Whiskey. Tango. Foxtrot!" I shout more out of reflex than anything, but I have more profane words that threaten to flow out of my mouth.

I rise to my feet so fast it almost makes me dizzy. Kyle and

Taylor are on their feet, too, not recognizing the group of people who just pop into our area without much of an invitation.

But my Day One never needs an invitation, not when it comes to his "little brother."

I stare him down, noticing Malik and Caleb in the background, standing behind Alyssa and Dominique. I notice the formation they're in, and I don't know whether to add fuel to the tension or to defuse the situation. I choose the latter, wondering why he's down here in the first place. "Long time, no hear from, big bro. I thought you were waiting for me to call you when I wanted to talk."

"That was before Nana told us you were almost murked before we had a chance to make things right." Dante moves in close enough to tap fists and give me a hug. "I wouldn't have been good with you being gone and saying what I needed to say to a gravestone."

Kyle steps in, glaring at Dante, waving a finger at Malik and Caleb when they try to move in to protect him. "Yo, Yasir, are these your folk from the A who turned their backs on you?"

Dante frowns, switching his gaze between me and Kyle. "I have a feeling you've been hilariously misinformed. We never turned our backs on him, but there were some things that needed to be cleared up."

"I'm never misinformed when it comes to my boys," Kyle barks as he moves closer to Dante. I don't want to get between them, and I plan to let things play out, but if I need to get a little rough and tumble, neither one of them will be left standing. "And how do you think you know me, playa?"

"Because my Day One told me about all of you," Dante announces. "He told me that you've been his aces down here. On the real, you've had his back, and I appreciate you looking out."

"It's obvi we've been looking out better than *you* have." Kyle focuses on Malik and Caleb the whole time. "Enough with the pleasantries. Why are you here?"

"I wanted to come and apologize," Alyssa steps in front of

Dante, causing Zahra to stand up to slow her approach into my personal space. "I was so pissed at you, and when I saw Zahra, I saw red. That's not fair to you when you tried to do everything in your power to keep things as friends between us. And after we heard what happened with the boat—I just couldn't have that on my conscience."

Is she serious right now? Things have been icy for weeks, and *now* she wants to clear things up? A piece of me considers hauling off and cracking all three boys' jaws for playing me like I allowed Alyssa or myself to be compromised. The other pieces of me are relieved that they even took the effort to come down here and find me.

"I appreciate that, real talk. I'm still salty that it took y'all this long to get at me." I sigh, battling my conflicted emotions, badly wanting to choose violence. Doing it in public, though…not a good look at all. "You're still like family to me, and I'd never turn my back on family. But since you're here, you might as well have a seat and get to know my folk down here."

"You're right, Ya-Ya. And yeah, we're cool with doing that, if your people don't mind?"

"Yeah, have a seat. If Yasir says you're cool, then you're good with us." Kyle and Taylor make some space for them to sit down. "This is my girl, Kendyl, and TK's girl, Tania."

"Okay, so now that that's settled, I'm going to go grab those drinks."

"Baby, I'd feel better if one of us was with you." Zahra presses the issue. "For real, we don't know what to expect right now."

"I'll be okay, I promise," I repeat, pointing at the concession stand. "See, direct line to the spot and back. You can keep an eye on me the entire time, but Ian's not stupid enough to start something with all these witnesses around."

I kiss Zahra's lips and hop up before she can offer up another protest. In the next minute, I'm already in line to grab the bottled drinks.

"You know, she was right. We are taking a risk without backup."

Gamba peeks through my eyes, scanning through to ensure no continuous threats surround us.

"We're good, godfather. I made sure to keep things on a swivel the entire way here. There are two other people in front of us, and we'll be back before we know it." I wonder why my nyxwraith insists on creating trouble where none exists. *"What's with the heightened alarms all of a sudden? Besides, my Squad is here, too. There's nothing to worry about."*

"Because you were right; things got out of hand during that incident in the parking lot. We have to be more careful and keep a cooler head."

"Well, we can keep the cooler head, starting Monday. We still have other events to attend, and things will be okay." I approach the window to place the drink order and pay. I turn for a minute to check on Zahra and the rest of the crew before I circle back to get the bottles, realizing they're back to the movie. *"Which reminds me, I'll probably need you to make yourself scarce later tonight. I'll need privacy until morning, once we're safe at home."*

I turn to walk back to the movie when I bump into someone and drop the bottles to the ground. I frown as the person I collided with remains in my personal space. Anger radiates through me. "Yo, you didn't see me... Damn, I'm not in the mood for you or any of your clique, my boy."

When I look up, I take in his school colors and realize I'm in trouble. Jordin stands mere inches from my face with his hands balled tight. "Well, whether you're in the mood or not, you're about to deal. You can bet that, playa."

Before I can find a way around Jordin and clear out, the other boys from that first encounter, Mark and Reggie, show up quick and close out my escape routes. I size up yet another potential situation that I'm probably not gonna get out of, and the only option I have available would expose me.

Gamba springs to life, trying to get through to me. *"Don't let them bait you, kiddo. We have to find a way out of this mess ASAP before something bad happens."*

"I'm open to ideas, and I don't wanna hear, 'I told you so,' either." I don't even bother to pick up the bottles I dropped. I can't afford to have either of them get the drop on me. If anything, I'm doing my level best to get anyone's attention. *"If we don't, I'm gonna have to make a scene."*

"Well, well, well, I didn't think you'd have been stupid enough to roll out in public knowing what you have over your head, Yasir," Jordin utters. "I guess you aren't as smart as I thought you were."

"What in the hell do you want now, my boy?" I keep my tone as even as possible, but I can't avoid the adrenaline spiking. It won't be long before Gamba makes his presence known to everyone around us. "Am I making you nervous now? You got all this backup like you're worried I might get the best of you… again."

"Don't antagonize them, Yasir. They may trigger something we can't control. We need to get your friends' attention."

Gamba's right, and I know it. While no one is looking, I press the preset button on my phone to call Zahra and pray she hears what's going on so she can get my boys over here ASAP. As soon as I hear her say hello through my ear buds, I'm back to being the eye of a storm that I didn't create. I know she'll sense my agitation. I just hope it's not too late.

"Man, you're really feeling yourself these days, I see." Jordin's smirk widens to a sinister smile. "That's okay, I actually want you to act up a bit tonight. All these people around, they'll get to see who you really are."

"Do us all a favor, bro, and split with your crew." I cut my eyes toward Zahra, and I see something that gives me the chance to stall these boys out just long enough to make things very interesting. "Oh, I get it, you want me to throw the first punch so you can say it was self-defense, right? Not gonna happen. I got better things to do than to get arrested over something else I didn't do."

Ian shows up with Eric and some of their teammates. Great. It's a party now, for real. "Yo, Yasir, what seems to be the trouble?"

I let out a growl that slows everyone down for a moment. My attention remains fixed on Ian. "Step away now. This one doesn't concern you."

"Nah, bro, these Baytown boys need to understand they're in hostile territory," Ian balks at my request. He's making things worse, and he doesn't even know it. "If these boys need to be reminded, we have no problems knocking it up across their heads."

"What, my guy? You're running your mouth when he had to bail your ass out. What are you gonna do?" Jordin taunts us as he moves into my personal space, close enough to point a finger in my face. "What can you do? You lay a finger on me and you're going to jail for assault."

I close my eyes, feeling the heat resonating through me, and I allow every ounce of fury to rise to the surface. I no longer care what happens; all I want is for everything to burn. When I open them, everything I see has a dark crimson hue. "I'll give you one last warning. Walk away. Go and enjoy the night. What happens next will be on your heads."

"Put this man out of his misery, boys," Jordin commands the other boys around him. "He wants the smoke."

"If you know Diablo like we know Diablo, you'd be thanking God for your life, playa. If he really wanted to choose violence, you wouldn't be standing right now," Dante chimes in as he, Kyle, Taylor, Caleb, and Malik all surround the Baytown crew. "Since you swear you know him as well as the information your plug provided, then you should know that you need to raise up before something bad happens to you."

When I say I'm grinning like I just won the light heavyweight boxing title right now?

I take a step in their direction, baring my teeth long enough to allow my fangs to jut out, watching as the group takes a collective step away from me. "I'd listen to my brother if I were you. He doesn't like repeating himself, and neither do I."

Jordin looks around him, realizing that the odds are no longer in his favor, along with the commotion that the scene has attracted, and he sneers at me with every bit of malice in his heart. He backs away from the rest of us. "Sooner or later, you're gonna get caught slipping, and I'm gonna be there when it happens."

They slink away before any of the security officers or the OGPD can come through and break things up. Not that there would be anything left for them to break up. Just saying.

I don't bother with a response. They're not worth it.

"You good, bro?" Dante taps fists with me as I nod toward the rest of the boys. "Do we need to do a sweep and make sure the place is sanitized?"

"Nah, I think they'll stay away from us for the rest of the night." I'm still trying to calm down. My body is vibrating and in fight mode, even though there is no threat. I quickly turn inward, assuring Gamba that I'm okay and that we'll talk about things once we get home. "They honestly thought they had the numbers on us. That's the only reason they came at me."

"Yeah, nah, something's off with them, and I'm not entirely sure Ian was there to have your back, either," Kyle says to me. "I'm really starting to wonder if we need to keep a sharper eye on things the rest of the weekend."

Before I can respond to Kyle's concerns, Zahra jumps into my arms, with the rest of the girls following her into the middle of the group. In the next minute, she punches my arm. "That's for not listening to me and almost getting yourself caught up and scaring me."

I rub the spot, even though she didn't hit me hard. "I promise, it wasn't on me this time. I didn't even know they were going to be here."

"I'm not worrying about that right now. We're still here to have fun for the rest of the night," Kendyl announces. She takes Kyle's hand and pulls him back in the direction of our area. "Get whatever you gotta get so we can make sure that happens, and the next time your girl says you need backup, listen to her, okay?"

Ugh, I'm not gonna live this one down at all. I turn my attention to Zahra, and I can't resist kissing her forehead and hugging her tight. "I'll do my best to keep something like this from happening any time soon. Forgive me?"

She kisses my lips a few times, caressing the spot she just hit with every bit of care she can muster. "You're forgiven. Now, can we get back to our spot so we can finish the movie? I was kinda enjoying *Kraven the Hunter* before you decided to get into trouble."

CHAPTER FORTY-SIX

I let Zahra drive Storm to her house tonight, giving me a chance to relax for a change. After the earlier incident, I need to decompress. Besides, she's been wanting to drive her, considering she's been allowing me to drive Raiden lately.

I'm drifting in and out of sleep while she's behind the wheel. Yeah, it's easy to trust her to handle my pride and joy enough to rest the entire ride. I'm still trying to process what all of this actually means for us, but I'm putting all that to the side—we're still in the middle of Anniversary Week.

I want to enjoy—and make sure she enjoys—everything that this week has to give.

Her phone starts buzzing in the holster, and I peek over for a brief moment as she tries to keep from waking me. She's whispering into her AirPods, but she might as well be speaking in her normal tone. My senses are so dialed up that I can hear her from a mile away. "You good, sis?"

I can hear Kendyl trying to speak in a hushed tone as she responds to her bestie through her pods. I'm legit starting to enjoy these abilities and then some. "I'm checking on you, chica. Wait, why are we whispering like we're about to commit a crime? Is there something you don't want your boyfriend to hear?"

She softly giggles. "Nah, tonight took a lot out of him, so I'm letting him sleep until I get home."

"Well, aren't you being the wonderful, doting *girlfriend*? That's sooo cute." Kendyl makes gagging noises over the phone, causing Zahra to laugh a little louder. "Did you two get a chance to talk about this ongoing beef with Baytown and what Ian has to do with it?"

"Nope, and I'm not going to, either," she states flatly. "We're all gonna have fun this weekend. I don't care if the rest of the world is burning to ashes."

"Oh, I'm with the shenanigans, trust, baby." Kendyl's voice kicks up a notch as her excitement builds to a fevered pitch. "I'm not trying to lower the temperature at all, know that."

"Good, then we can ignore all the adulting that we'll have to do once Anniversary Week is over. Sound like a plan?"

"Yep! So now that that's settled, did you two at least get some practice time in for the trap waltz that we're all supposed to be lighting up the ball with tomorrow?" Kendyl sounds ready to kill us both if Zahra says we didn't. "You know we gotta show up and show out, since it's the Bicentennial and everything. We get to really leave a mark and have the whole town talking for weeks."

Even though I've been working at Unk's almost all week, she still managed to sweet-talk me into practicing after work. It gave us a chance to bond and find out more about each other—at least as much as we can until my brain gets unlocked. I gave up everything I knew about my life in the A, and she taught me as much as she knew about Kindara as we perfected the steps of the waltz.

I had to let her lead for the bulk of the week, but before long, I was leading her, which put a smile on that pretty face. We even had a chance to create our own steps, just in case the spotlight found us during the waltz.

"Oh, I think we might surprise a few people tomorrow night," Zahra boasts as she accelerates through another intersection.

"Good, because I'll be damned if Chrisette and her clique try to make us look bad. She's already split the cheerleading squad because some of the girls wanna step with me," Kendyl huffs through the earpiece. "She swears that this week is only for her and the rest of the Founding Families. I wanna make sure she has no choice but to bow down to the real queen."

"I love it when you get like this. You get hyper when the lights are brightest."

I sit up in the seat, and she places her index finger to her lips to keep me quiet while she tries to finish her chat. Yeah, that's not gonna happen. This is too juicy not to take advantage.

"Tell her majesty we won't let her down," I say with a smirk. "The last thing we want is to make her look bad."

Kendyl gasps as Zahra puts her on speaker, causing my girl to crack up laughing as a result. "How in the world? What else did he hear?"

"I didn't hear anything you wouldn't say to me face-to-face," I respond, freaking her out even more than she is already. "Oh, and I'll deal with Ian once I'm out from under this mess from the Beach Creek game. I can't set another fire until I've put out the current one."

Zahra is having a hard time keeping Storm on the road, she's laughing so hard.

"I thought you said he was sleeping, sis?" Kendyl shrieks. "Did you have me on speaker the whole time, trick? Ugh!"

Okay, now I'm struggling to breathe, but I had to show off a bit. Thanks to Gamba, I have a whole other level to all my senses.

Zahra calms down long enough to answer Kendyl. "I promise, Yasir was asleep. I can't explain how he's been able to be engaged in our convo the whole time, but this is too funny."

"No the hell it ain't, girl. That's scary on so many levels. Can he read minds or something?" Kendyl's having a whole meltdown, and Zahra's trying to calm her down and not laugh at the same time. "Put him on speaker. I wanna know how he knew what we were talking about."

"I'm pretty much peopled out for today, Kenni," I say loud enough for her to hear. "You know, that whole introvert energy and everything? Today was a lot, for real, and I still have to get myself together for tomorrow night, you feel me?"

Zahra jumps in quick to keep things from getting too far out of hand. "Okay, bestie, I'll see you in the morning when we have to go grab our dresses. Love you, mean it, bye now."

"Love you, too, baby. See you in the morning, and get your life, *Ya-Ya*."

Zahra disconnects the call as we pull into her driveway, and she puts the car in park before she shifts her body in my direction. "So did you have fun freaking out my bestie, baby?"

I burst into laughter all over again, holding my stomach the entire time. "Yeah, I had a lot of fun. It took my mind off the emotional roller coaster I was on all night."

She caresses my cheek, pulling me in for a quick kiss. "Yeah, tonight wasn't supposed to go like that, but I'm glad that it ended well. Your Squad has your back again. That's gotta count for something, right?"

"Yeah, I'm happy about that, but Kenni's right. Sooner or later, I'm gonna have to deal with the smoke from the Baytown crew. I've made them look silly on two separate occasions." I stretch to really wake myself up, then slide out of the passenger seat and literally trudge around to meet her on the other side of the car. "If they're smart, they'll come for me when there's not so many people around."

"Shhh, no need to think about that right now, okay?" She wraps her arms around my neck, encouraging me to pull her up so she can stare into my eyes. "Your only job for the rest of this weekend is to keep a smile on your chosen's face. Can you do that for me?"

I slip soft kisses across her lips, then set her down on the ground and kiss her forehead. I move a stray hair from her face, watching her blush over the move. I flash my eyes at her, giving up a knowing grin and then exhaling slow. By Nyati, I love this girl. "Anything for you, my chosen. Anything for you."

My phone rings out of nowhere, taking us out of our moment. I lean in to see who it is, and the same "unknown number" pops up on my screen. I allow it to ring a few times, hoping that whoever it is gets the hint that I'm not gonna answer the call.

"What's that about, Yasir?" Zahra asks after I close the door and get my head together. "Is something wrong? Who was that?"

I blink a few times to buy myself some time to reassure her that there's nothing for her to worry about. "Dante's calling. I guess he's making sure I'm safe at home. I'll call him back after you're in the house."

"Are you sure? You look a little unnerved."

"I promise, I'm good. I'll call you once I'm home."

Zahra narrows her eyes like she doesn't believe a word I'm saying, but I don't want her to press the issue. At least, not yet. "Okay, I'll talk to you once you get home."

The phone rings again before Zahra gets in the house, and I realize I better answer it before it becomes a situation. I hop inside, accidentally hitting the speakerphone button as I answer the call, silently encouraging her inside the house. "Hello?"

"I bet you felt real safe having your crew around you to get you out of that situation you were in." The same distorted voice booms loud and clear across the speaker, causing a chill to creep up my spine. "It won't matter, though. No one will be able to keep me from ending you."

"Who the fuck is this, and how did you get my number?" I let out a frustrated growl, desperate to regain some control. "And why are you using an auto tune to hide your voice? Are you that scared of me?"

I don't understand why any of this is happening. What did I do to this person? I don't remember doing anything to anyone—I mean, not anyone who didn't deserve it.

I better figure it out fast before I fuck around and find out the hard way.

"Don't worry, Yasir, you'll find out everything in due time, and I fear no one, not after what I've been through." The voice lets out a chuckle that boils my blood. They're intentionally mocking me, and I don't like it. "I'll see you soon."

CHAPTER FORTY-SEVEN

I wake up the next morning with the biggest smile on my face. I can't remember the last time I've felt this good, and I don't want to lose this feeling at all. Even with everything that happened last night, the way it ended and all the good vibes that came through as the sun breaks through the clouds…it feels like it's gonna be a great day today.

I'm intent on putting that phone call out of my mind, too. I can't worry about things that I can't control. Whenever the person who's threatening to unalive me shows up, that's when I'll handle it. That's it, that's all.

Being in the middle of both of my cliques and having them getting along the rest of the night before they jetted back to the A had me beaming with pride. It couldn't have gone any better, and it's been a minute since I've had a chance to really feel like I'm at home and comfortable. I don't want to let it go.

Dante was true to his word, personally escorting Nana back and calling me to let me know she's safely tucked away and under constant watch. Having that off my mind helps more than I can even say.

I pop out of bed, connecting my phone to the speakers as I skip into the bathroom to shower. I have to head to the shop to pick up my tuxedo and then slide over to the flower shop in Savannah to get the corsage for Zahra that I had to special rush order in to have it ready in time for the ball tonight.

Even Gamba is in a whole good mood, which adds to my excitement.

"Today's gonna be a good day," I tell my nyxwraith as we vibe to Burna Boy. "I can't wait to cut loose a little bit and just be a kid for a while."

"It is gonna be lit, as you kids love to say." Okay, I'm enjoying the way Gamba's trying to get on my level with the slang and popular phrases. *"You are right; today should be fun and magical. I am looking forward to seeing you smile and enjoy life."*

I step into the shower, enjoying the heat of the water on my skin. I go through the to-do list in my head again to make sure that everything is covered. I'm not gonna lie, I'm legit nervous, and I can feel the rumblings of my anxiety threatening to push to the surface. This night has to go perfectly.

Steam fills the bathroom, adding to the mystical vibe I'm feeling right now. If I concentrate hard enough, I can peer through the fog and allow my mind to take me anywhere I want to go. I imagine being in either Ghana or Senegal, enjoying the landscape and the beauty of those countries, or even traveling north, across the Mediterranean Sea to check out Italy. I haven't had a chance to see the Leaning Tower of Pisa yet, and I can only imagine what it looks like in person.

And to have Zahra with me every step of the way? Pure bliss.

"I wish I could be there to help you with your first big function, my son."

I jump out of my skin, suppressing an audible gasp that makes me wonder if I'm hallucinating. *Dad?* I spin around in my shower like I expect to see him leaning against the counter. It's like when I first got to Oakwood Grove, and somehow Mom and Dad sat inside Storm with me, telling me that everything would be fine.

"Dad? Is that you?"

"Yes, my son, I am here."

I rub my eyes, blinking them several times over, almost wishing that I can see him as clear as the hand in front of my face. I turn off the shower and grab a towel to wrap around me. "How is this possible? Am I able to actually see you for a little longer this time?"

"I believe I have a theory." And sure enough, Dad's leaning

against the counter, a smile spreading across his lips. "I think that the days are getting closer to Fete Gede…the Festival of the Dead, celebrated in parts of the Caribbean, and in Kindara, too. As the holiday gets closer, the veil between the afterlife and the living world thins, and we are able to pass through, if only for brief moments, to visit those who are able to see."

"I don't care how it's possible. I'm just happy to see you, Dad." I sit in the chair believing what I see and grinning the whole time. He's actually here. "There's so much I want to talk to you about, including everything with Zahra. Have you and Mom been able to see what's going on from where you are?"

"Yes, we have, and we're so proud of what you're becoming." He pushes off from the counter, moving closer to where I'm sitting. "I am sorry that we can't be more help with the trials that you will go through. I can imagine you have a lot of questions, and perhaps we can have a longer conversation soon."

I slowly nod, realizing that we're on borrowed time, so I don't waste a second of it. "Do you know about Gamba? Is he able to communicate with you at all? You're right, I have a lot of questions."

"Save them for the next time your mother and I are able to see you together," he says to me, glancing over my face, another smile beaming through with all the pride I feel from him. "Tell me about Zahra. She seems like a wonderful girl. The gods are smiling on the two of you, pleased at their work."

"Dad, she's unlike any girl I've ever met." No cap. I'm serious when I say that. "She's as smart and as pretty as Mom, and she… By Nyati, she's all I can think about sometimes. I know it sounds ridiculous, but…"

"She fits you." Dad finishes my thought before I can say it out loud. "Ashanti and Nahara knew what they were doing when they paired you. You're meant to do great things together."

I switch the subject before time runs out on us. "Dad…I can't remember things about our life in Kindara. I mean, I see flashes of things when I was little, but it feels like there's so much more that's locked away."

"I understand, my son. All will be revealed soon. Trust your nana and the Vodaran priestess to help bring all of that back." Dad glances at his arms, and I notice that he's starting to fade away. "I have to go, but I promise we will try to see you soon. I love you, my son."

"I love you, too, Dad. Kiss Mom for me." I shed a tear as his form dissipates inside the fog, then a grin spreads across my face. I know I'll see them again; I just have to prepare for the next time.

I step out of Storm, enjoying the mild afternoon, marveling over the way the clouds move across the sky for a few moments. Yeah, today is a good day, and it's gonna continue to be a good day; I can feel it. The sun is peeking through long enough for me to stand and bask in the warmth before it ducks back behind the clouds. It isn't until then that I realize I can't remember the last time I sat down to ground myself with the earth.

Mental note: *get that done ASAP.*

I open the door to the tuxedo shop, observing all the activity going on around me. If I didn't know any better, I swear it's prom season instead of Anniversary Week festivities. All the boys are in full-blown showcase mode, dropping videos on TikTok left and right, running the poor employees through it with their last-minute changes to their accessories.

Nah, I'm good on all that. I'm sticking to my plan: get in, get my tux, and get out. Simple.

Kyle's already working his way in my direction, grinning ear to ear as he shows off the crimson and black tuxedo. "Yep, I'm gonna be ridiculous tonight, on God."

I burst into laughter, stopping long enough to give the consultant my name so he can grab my rental. "Oh, but you were giving me the business when Z was whispering in my ear about going all out for this ball. Now look at you."

Kyle stares me down, causing another hilarious outburst. I'm legit holding the wall to keep from falling on the floor. "Yo, we ain't gotta bring all that up, my boy."

"It's all good, for real, but as long as we can get up outta here so we can get ready for everything later, that'd be great." I shake my head, still holding my stomach from another fit of snickering. "I still got some other things I have to pick up so I don't rush."

"Yeah, and I see you got Storm looking shiny, shiny." Kyle whistles as we glance out in the parking lot. He's one to talk, though. His truck looks like it went through an extra coat of candy-coated paint. "You gonna light up the neon, too? Just show out, then."

The consultant finally returns with my tux, and the minute I pull it out of the covering, all eyes are on me. The next thing I know, there's this collective buzz swirling through the shop. A few of the boys are elbowing each other as they gawk at the black, purple, and gold pattern in the vest that peeks out from under the black suit coat.

"Wait, you mean we could've rocked something like that?" one of them remarks to the consultant standing next to him. "You got anything like that in the back? I wanna cop it if you got it."

Nope. I'm not stepping in the middle of any of that. "Time to raise up outta here, bro. I'm not about to get caught up in whatever is about to happen."

Kyle chucks up the deuces and follows me out of the store, weaving through the foot traffic still entering through the door. I breathe a sigh of relief, thankful that it didn't get any wilder than it could've been. I tap fists with my dawg, then carefully lay the garment bag on the back seat and reach for the remote so I can start the engine.

That is, until I get rudely interrupted by the usual suspects. "Looks like you got out without too much of an issue, Yasir. How wild is it in there?"

So let's figure this out, shall we?

Ian and Eric are standing in front of Storm when they should be trying to work their way into the store so they can get their tuxedos. They have these non-threatening expressions on their faces like they don't have an ounce of pressure to release toward me. And I'm not allowed to interact with them in any way because Mr. Channing said it would complicate things.

What am I supposed to do in this situation?

I can tell you what I'm gonna do: I'm opening the door, getting in Storm, and getting out of here before something goes left.

But Ian holds the driver's door open, preventing me from closing it.

Dammit.

I pull a little harder to get him to release his grip, but he's insistent on keeping me here for whatever reason. Yeah, this isn't gonna end well, and I better find a way out before something else happens and I get blamed for it.

"Dude, what's up with holding my door?"

Ian sort of shrugs, then he lets go of the door. "For real, I don't want any problems. Tonight is too important to my father for anything to go wrong, all right?"

I raise an eyebrow, still skeptical over what angle he's trying to come at me from. "Okay, so if that's the case, why are you in my space? This is the exact opposite of not wanting any problems."

"Yeah, I feel that, but I'm serious right now. I wanna call a truce, just for tonight," Ian says. "I need this to go smoothly. My dad's reelection campaign is riding on the success of Anniversary Week, no cap."

I want to believe him, but he's been coming for me at every opportunity, and now he wants to act like, what? Are we supposed to be cordial or something like that? That's just ghetto.

"Okay, say I believe you. That means no BS tonight, right?"

"Yep. No BS tonight."

"You'll forgive me if I'm looking for the trap door." I lean back in the seat, glaring at him with every bit of irritation I have in me. I'm keeping my temper in check, despite every fiber of my being telling me to act a fool.

Against my better judgment, and to stick to the "good vibes only" type of day I'm gonna have by any means necessary, I close my door and start up the engine. Before I leave, I tell him, "I feel like I'm gonna regret saying this, but I'm gonna hold you to it. I accept the truce. Be easy."

I know what he's saying, but actions speak louder.

If he's smart, he'll honor the truce.

And if he doesn't?

It won't end well for him, and that's a promise.

CHAPTER FORTY-EIGHT

I finally get home after picking up everything I need for the night, and to be real, I'm legit trying to find a way to summon some extra energy to handle people later. It isn't that I don't want to do people, but it's *certain* people I don't want to be around. I'm a bit wary of whether Ian can keep his word—all signs are pointing to *no*—but I'm not about to let that ruin my good mood.

If anything, I'm leaning toward the extrovert side of my personality tonight. It feels good, too, no cap.

I lay the garment bag with my tux on my bed, making a beeline to the bathroom so I can freshen up and get this fit together. There's a stunning beauty who's expecting me to flex so she can watch the other girls be high-key irritated that the spotlight will be focused on us. I even mixed a special batch of oils to have the desired effect.

Yes, I want her to swoon even more than she already does.

I check my phone before I jump in the shower, grinning as I see the text from Zahra. She leaves a series of flirty emojis and a "I can't wait for you to see what type of dime you have on your arm" message that has my imagination on tilt. She's been secretive all week, not even giving me a hint of what her dress looks like. All she would say when I asked was that I won't be able to wipe the smile off my face the minute she comes down the stairs.

She rarely disappoints, so there's no need for me to worry that it won't be something that's ripped off the runway. She's particular like that, and I love every bit of it.

I'm about to start getting ready when Unk knocks on the door. "You good, kiddo? I wanna make sure you don't rush out before I can get some pics for your nana and Lennox."

"Yeah, I'm good, but wait… Where's Ms. Lennox?" My senses are tingling. I smell a setup. "I thought she was already here to hang with you tonight."

When he opens the door, I shake my head in disbelief. He's in a pair of suit pants and a button-down dress shirt, and I already know where this is going before I can say another word. He leans against the doorframe with this smirk that lets me know the fix is in.

I groan as I continue to apply the oils on my skin. "Let me guess, y'all are chaperoning tonight at the ball. You couldn't give your nephew the heads-up or nothing, right?"

Unk chuckles as I pull my pants on and reach for my shirt. "Sorry, I had to keep this one under wraps until the last possible minute. We're not gonna be there the entire night, just long enough to see y'all rock this trap waltz I've been hearing about."

Man, the relief that comes over me when he says that… Yeah, I can roll with that part. "Okay, but I need y'all gone the minute it's over, real talk. I can deal with adults being there to make sure things are cool, but I need y'all to be somewhere else enjoying the night without worrying about me."

"I'm always gonna worry about you, Ya-Ya," Unk utters while helping me with the tie that I obviously don't know how to handle. "After what you told me happened at the park last night, I want to make sure that things go smoothly tonight. I don't need you getting caught up in any more drama that you didn't create."

"I feel that, but I got tonight on lock," I tell him, stepping in front of the full-length mirror on my closet door to make sure everything is in its place before I put on the coat. "I mean, there's nothing that could pop off with all the grown people around to keep us from really getting lit."

"That's a good thing, young'un, because I was concerned about whether to let you do this tonight." Unk sits on the bed, his solemn expression throwing me off a bit. "I mean, Ian and his crew are gonna be there tonight, too."

"And I got backup, so the odds are even," I counter, not really wanting to bring Ian's name into the mix. I'm in a good mood, and I'm not about to let that fact mess things up. "We've called a truce, so I'm not tripping about anything popping off."

"Do you think he's gonna keep his word?"

"If he doesn't, he won't like how that ends."

"Yeah, that's what has me worried," Unk remarks. His expression hasn't changed at all, which puts me on edge a bit. "Thanks to that TikTok, the Grove knows you got hands, and that isn't exactly a good thing."

At this point, I'm irritated, and I'm trying to keep Gamba on the low. "Unk, you know there are two ways I don't go with anyone, and that's back and forth. If he tries to start anything, I'm gonna end it. Self-defense is still a thing. Good vibes only, you know?"

Unk picks up the suit coat and helps me put it on, then looks at the finished product in the mirror with a satisfied grin. "Good vibes only, I feel that. But if you get to a point where you need to handle yourself, do what you have to do. I got your back regardless."

I smooth out the coat, taking a lint roller to get rid of any dust. I do a last-minute check of it all, and I like the way the suit hangs. Yeah, this will work. "I appreciate that, seriously. Now, I need to get on the road so I can pick Z up and set this night off right."

"Yo, I wasn't expecting to see you here," Kyle says, leaning against his truck with this perturbed expression on his face. I can relate; when Kendyl and Zahra get together, things tend to take a lot longer than they should. I don't know what happened, but it can't be good. Although I guess I can take it as a compliment... She must've really wanted to blow my mind if she asked for her best friend to come over at the last minute.

I tap fists with him and match his body language for a few moments. He's irritated, but I can tell he's not trying to look like it. "I don't know what you've done to my best friend, but she's literally frantic over the phone with my girl, getting her to sweet-talk me into coming over here to help her get ready."

I shrug. "I have no idea what I did, or if I even did anything. I haven't even talked to her today."

"Well, you're about to get the whole experience, that's for sure," Kyle says just as the door cracks open. Someone's hand motions for us to come inside the house, and I can only assume it's Kendyl because Zahra's mom wouldn't be that dramatic. "Yep, that's our cue. Time to check out the show."

I rub my hand over the length of my face as we trudge up the stairs. Only Nyati knows what's about to happen right now. If this is what I have to look forward to when prom season comes around, I'm in for a long night.

We slip into the foyer, and Kendyl stops us in our tracks. We're at the base of the staircase, and it's a curved descent from the upper floor to where we're standing. I can already feel the drama building as Kairo saunters in from the great room and acknowledges us with a handshake and a warm smile.

"Good evening, sir. I hope you've been doing well," I say to Kairo, trying to suppress my nervous energy. I know we've technically gotten all the pleasantries and "getting to know you" stuff out of the way a while back, but he is still her father. "I take it the ladies are upstairs handling last-minute preparations."

Kairo laughs as he leans against the wall, glancing up toward the second floor, and shakes his head. "Boys, you know how women are when it comes to gala events like this. Get used to it, because it does not get any better."

Great. Prom season is going to be a whole production if what he says is true. I'm all for getting dolled up and black carpet ready, but it's not like we're going to a celebrity-studded event or anything. Oh wait, maybe I shouldn't speak too soon.

"Yeah, Anniversary Week is huge for the town, bro," Kyle adds his perspective the best way he can. "The only reason that this year is so over the top is that it's the Bicentennial. Next year should be much less spectacular."

That's not making me feel better, bro. In fact, it's really giving me "you're doing the most for no damn reason" vibes, but I can't really say that out loud. "If they want us to get there on time, we'd better get rolling in the next ten minutes, or they'll be blaming us for not getting a good table."

Kesi appears out of nowhere while we're talking, clearing her throat as Kendyl seemingly glides down the stairs to join us at the base of the landing. She smiles at me and does this subtle wave before she checks behind her as though she were waiting for her cue to begin. "Ladies and gentlemen…*her*."

Okay, let me find out Mrs. Assante knows about some of these TikTok trends. But that's not what has my attention now.

The vision of pure, exquisite, radiant beauty descends the stairs, and I swear everything and everyone fades to black. The only thing I see…the only thing I *can* see…is as close to a real-time rendition of what I could've imagined Zahra to look like if I created a painting of her in the dress she's wearing.

My gaze never leaves hers, and I'm in complete swoon mode, almost forgetting to breathe. To say she looks stunning doesn't do her justice. I'm trying to find the words, and honestly, that's not gonna happen. Nope.

Even Gamba finds his way to my conscious mind to peek for himself. *"By Nyati, she is goddess-level gorgeous. It's like the goddesses put the finishing touches on her and allowed her to borrow their glow for the evening."*

Man, he takes the words right out of my mouth, and he's probably said it much better than I ever could. I've never seen her look more beautiful than in this moment, and I'm fumbling over every word that I want to speak for fear that it might insult her.

I'm so frozen in space and time that it takes a sharp elbow to my side from Kyle to shake me out of my daydream. He leans over and whispers, "This is the part where you take her arm and slip the corsage on her wrist, my boy."

I blink a few times to remind myself that I'm in the here and now, and I reach out to take her hand and lead her to me. I pull the corsage from its container and—I don't remember giving the box to Kyle, okay, but I think that's what happened—I stare into her eyes for what seems like an eternity. "You look… You've taken my breath away, Z. It's like Ashanti placed her touch against your skin and gave you her glow tonight."

"Did you really just steal one of my lines?" Gamba says with a laugh. *"What you know about that, godson?"*

"You're here to help me," I remind him. *"And that line was boss-level epic."*

Zahra blushes as I finally slide the corsage onto her left wrist, then offer the crook of my arm for her to take. "I was hoping you would approve of the final touches. I begged Kenni to get over here to help with that. It was a two-person job to get what I was looking for."

I kiss her cheek, still unable to tear my eyes away from her. "All I can say is thank Nyati for the both of them. I'm…I still have no words right now."

"Oh, I have a few words. Soooooo, now that you two have had your magical moment, can we get to the ball before all the good seats are taken?" Kendyl taps her foot against the hardwood floor, giving every bit of attitude she can, much to the amusement of everyone in the room. "Mama, come on down so we can get the pictures together and get up outta here, please?"

CHAPTER FORTY-NINE

The moment we step into the building, the whole room shifts in our direction. The pop of so many different colors from our clique's outfits start murmurs from the crowd, and with the way I've been feeling today, I soak up every ounce of energy. I glance down into Zahra's eyes, and I feel the excitement in the air.

I didn't realize how spacious the interior was, and I have to admit I'm shocked. There's room for everyone to maintain their own space, with a large buffet that includes four different punch bowls and a *lot* of food. Like, they "pulled out all the stops" type of menu. I hate to be biased, but me and Unk could've done better on the selection. We weren't working this event, though; someone else is in charge tonight. The seafood isn't up to par, the other meats are questionable, and even the vegan choices are lackluster.

Zahra cuts her eyes in Chrisette's direction, coming close to sticking her tongue out like she's ten years old or something. I can't help noticing the heated stare coming from Ian, but he's not gonna faze me tonight. He asked for a truce, so we're honoring the truce—at least, for the most part. There's nothing in the rule book that says we can't step into the spotlight and take the shine away from the competition.

Taylor and Tania, once they join us at our reserved table, can't stop laughing over the glares coming from the rest of the group surrounding the wannabe power couple of Oakwood Grove High. Taylor taps fists with me and Kyle before we take our seats, shaking his head as he continues to laugh out loud. "Did y'all have to break out the top-tier outfits, yo? People started buzzing before you came through the door."

"Good, because that's what I wanted to happen," Kendyl brags, smoothing out her dress so she can get comfortable. "I told you we needed to apply some pressure, and we did that."

Well, she's not wrong, and we aren't the only ones who notice Chrisette seething. As Zahra told me on the way here, Chrisette's family is one of the six Founding Families that settled in Oakwood Grove two centuries ago. I can imagine that comes with a bit of unreasonable expectations and a bit of entitlement, now that I think about it. The weird part is that none of the children of the other families have been as obnoxious about things, but that's not in my circle of concern.

We all turn toward the podium on stage as Mayor Lance taps the microphone to get everyone's attention. He clears his throat a couple of times before he takes the microphone off its stand. "Welcome to the Anniversary Ball, everyone. We are so glad you could all be here for the event. I'd be remiss if I didn't offer kudos to our talented Oakwood Grove High students for their efforts over the past couple of days."

Zahra rolls her eyes as the crowd erupts in applause, and I pull her close to kiss her cheek and try to fix the irritated expression on her face. I take my index finger and shift her eyes to meet mine, whispering, "You did that, baby. Take your bow."

"*We* did that, baby, but look at Chris trying to stand up like she spearheaded the whole thing," Zahra points out. "She only focused on the things that would make her look good. I'm over it, and I'm over her."

"Don't worry about all that," Kendyl says. "Once we put this trap waltz on them, they won't know what hit them." Kendyl gives up a smirk and a wink to both of us as she continues to clap with the rest of the crowd. "They're not ready for this smoke, I promise."

Kyle and I nod along with Taylor and a few of the other boys sitting at our table, which causes the girls to collectively raise their eyebrows. Zahra locks eyes with me, leaning in close so no one else can hear her. "I know that look, Ya-Ya. What do you have up your sleeve?"

Mayor Lance continues his announcements before he gets around to the part we've been waiting to hear. "And now, as part of the Anniversary Ball tradition, our young adults will show off their dance skills with the group waltz. I can't wait to see what they've come up with this year."

Zahra keeps me in my seat while the rest of our crew makes their way to the dance floor. "I'm serious, what are you up to, pretty boy? You've been riding high all day, and I can feel it on you. What do you have planned?"

I cup her face in my hands, leaning her forward to kiss her forehead, and shake my head before I place my fingers over her lips to keep her from asking any more questions. "Don't worry, what we have planned, Ian and his crew will never see coming. We can show you better than we can tell you."

"By Nyati, that was lit! How cool was that?" Zahra shouts.

Who knew putting together a waltz with our own spin on the steps would draw so much attention? I mean, there were only a dozen couples dancing, but the way we were able to stay in sync with each other kept the audience clapping and cheering us on.

And the sour expression on Chrisette and the rest of her group was so worth the effort we put in to get the routine done. I even came up with a few old school steps Unk taught me for the boys to perform that had our girls screaming in surprise. If she thinks that was something, she's really gonna burst when I spring my other surprise on her later.

The routine was only supposed to be ten minutes long, but the way we executed, it felt like we were only out there for a few seconds. By the time we glided off the dance floor, the roar of the crowd was overwhelming. And when I say we glided, I mean I couldn't feel the floor. It wasn't supposed to be a contest between the groups that danced, but the conservative versus contemporary style was on full display.

Zahra's sitting in a chair as I return with a drink for her, and she's glaring at Chrisette as she trudges over to our table. She gives her the quick head-to-toe glance, and I already know it's gonna be pressure the minute she opens her mouth to speak. "Is there something wrong?" Zahra says. "Are you lost, little girl?"

Chrisette huffs, stopping mid-stride as she regards Zahra's hostile body language. "I guess there's no truce tonight after all, huh?"

"There might be a truce between our boyfriends, but make no mistake, I don't need you in my space under any circumstances." Zahra grits her teeth, and I know she's trying to keep her temper under control. Imara doesn't need to rise to the surface any more than Gamba needs to if I'm in the same situation. "So move along, lick your wounds from the L you just took with the waltzes, and figure out what else you plan to do with the rest of your evening."

Ian rushes over to the table, and for a few seconds, I'm ready to react to whatever energy he's about to give off. He has a concerned expression on his face, like he didn't expect his girlfriend to come over. "Whoa, okay, there's no need to pull the claws out, right? What Chrissy meant was y'all did your thing with that trap waltz. Had we known it would've been approved, we could've come up with our own version."

"Nobody told her to come over like we're cool and everything, either." Zahra frowns as she stares Ian down. "I had to put up with her all week under protest, and I made the best of it."

Kendyl slips into a chair next to Zahra as she gives up her own menacing expression. "Let's make this loud and clear for the people in the back. She wants both of you—hell, we all do—to stay in your damn lane. The audacity you're coming with like we're supposed to be cordial is high comedy, I promise you."

Chrisette's about to respond to Kendyl, when she notices Zahra's index finger in the air. I don't know about anyone else, but this isn't gonna end well. "We're not friends anymore, and I'm able to tolerate you in small doses when we're in public spaces like this, but whatever redemption arc you think you're on, this ain't it. You're gonna have to come better than empty congratulations."

"Okay, fair enough, but you understand that things flow much more smoothly when Ian and I are at the top of the power structure."

Umm, what? She can't be serious right now.

"If we have to tolerate each other—your words, not mine—then we need to make sure the natural order of things is acknowledged."

Before Zahra can get up to take things up a notch, I hold my hand out to her, flashing the widest smile I can to distract her. It must've worked because she's caught in my stare, and it's like no one else is around us in that moment. "I know we just rocked the trap waltz and everything, but would you like to dance, my beautiful one?"

She doesn't say a single word. We're still staring at each other, and her eyes switch to this shade of red, and I know what's going through her mind now. Kendyl's tapping her left shoulder, but I don't think she's noticed at all. She finally manages a nod, wearing a smile on her face that threatens to melt me right there on the spot.

The music kicks in before she can get her bearings as I lead her out onto the middle of the dance floor. I take as much care as I can despite my body wanting to be much more aggressive. I place my other hand at the small of her back, holding her close to me, the jasmine-and-honeysuckle scent on her skin sending me deeper into the zone we're in.

I remain captive to her gaze, but she's literally spellbound by whatever I'm projecting to her. "What do you see?"

"Your eyes…they're this rich color of cobalt," she utters, reaching up to kiss my lips. "I can't stop staring. They remind me of the Aegean Sea, like in the pictures I saw a few weeks ago."

"You're one to talk. Your eyes have a shade of red, like they've been replaced by garnets," I remark, still unable to break from our shared gaze. "I guess I should be asking what you're thinking instead of what you're seeing."

I pull her closer, staying in the moment with her, not wanting to leave for anything on the planet. I can't resist asking the question in my mind, but it begs the ask. "I have a feeling I was saving you from killing Chrisette when I came back. You know she's trying to fight for power, and she knows she's losing."

"What is it your uncle loves to say? 'Not my monkey, not my circus.'" She leans against my chest, listening to the music swirl as we sway with the rhythm. "She's trying her best to stay on top of a hill that means nothing to me."

We spin slow and easy; each move feels effortless even though we've never had the chance to dance this closely before. I release my grip on her hand, slipping it on my shoulder so she can clasp her fingers around my neck while I lock mine around her waist. We fall in step with each other, letting the flow of the songs control our movements. It feels so perfect being in this space with her, creating the energy between us.

"Tonight is not about anyone but you and me," I declare. I study her face, and I can't avoid the smirk spreading across my lips. "And I'm looking forward to creating some more magic with you tonight with no distractions, no interruptions."

"I love the sound of that." She raises her left eyebrow, curious about the tone in my voice. "So what's the surprise?"

I shake my head, removing one of my hands from her waist to lift her chin, and I lean down to press my lips against hers. It's soft at first, my silent request for permission. She smiles through the series of kisses, nodding her approval for me to kiss her the way I really want.

We deepen our embrace, and for a few minutes, the landscape changes the same way it did when we were in my studio. I have a little better control over things this time around, and from the grin on her face, she looks like she's ready for the trip this time.

I watch as she wiggles her toes against the cobblestone beneath our feet, and I smell the salt in the air and the heat on my skin as we notice the sunset from the top of the island. She casts her gaze toward the buildings as they slope down the hillside and lead out to the beach.

The surprise in her voice is worth the trip. "Wait a minute, how did you—?"

"Do you know where we are?" I ask as I press my lips against the nape of her neck. "Surprise."

"We're in Santorini, Greece. I'd know this place anywhere. I was just thinking about it when I— Oh, you're gonna get it when we get back." She leans her head back on my chest, tapping her hand against my arm as we take in the picturesque scenery. "How in the world did you pull from my thoughts and bring us here when we're supposed to be back in the Grove? All I did was look into your eyes and the color reminded me of this place."

"A magician never reveals their tricks—at least, not yet." I spin her around to face me, and her smile melts me in seconds. "I wanted tonight to be *special*, special, and I actually have one more surprise when we get back."

We travel back, finding ourselves still on the dance floor, among the crowd as the music continues to flow. I offer the crook of my arm for her to take as I escort her to our table, where Kendyl, Kyle, and the rest of our group are staring at us like we made a whole spectacle of ourselves.

"So you two had one of your moments again, huh, sis?" Kendyl's the first one ready to act up. "I'm gonna need y'all to keep all that to yourselves, please and thank you. Ain't nobody got time for you two to create whatever you just had out there so we can sit back and be jealous and stuff."

"Yeah, I could've sworn there was this purple glow around y'all while you were dancing, like you were the only ones on the floor," Tania remarks as she takes a fan to cool herself down. "I don't know what y'all got going on, but I'm low-key jealous that we can't get in on whatever you're doing."

Zahra can't stop laughing, giving me a sideways glance the whole time. I shrug it off like it's nothing. Sounds like a personal problem to me, real talk. "I'm sorry, sis. The next time we decide to have our moment, we'll try to make sure you're not witnessing the magic."

"Yeah, yeah, whatever. So what else do we have left to do tonight?" Kendyl smirks like she's got something up her sleeve, and Zahra's glaring at her like she wants to wring her neck. "I know this food ain't it, so maybe we need to head into Savannah and grab something to eat."

Unk and Ms. Lennox stop by the table for a few moments, and Unk taps fists with the boys before offering his arm for Ms. Lennox to take. "Okay, so now that we've seen what we came to see, we're about to head out. I'm glad the steps I taught you boys flowed so well. You had the crowd shook."

"We appreciate the lessons, sir. It was a good look out there," Kyle says to him. "Maybe we'll cop a few more moves from you for next year so we'll have more time to put our own flavor on it."

"Bet. Ya-Ya, we'll see you at home later. Be safe out here, all right?" Unk advises before they pivot and stroll toward the exit. "And congratulations to you all. This week has been very entertaining and well organized. Proud of y'all."

Once they leave, Kyle and I share glances real quick, and I nod that now's the time to handle that last surprise I have in store for Zahra. We get up, kiss our girls on the cheek, and head toward the exit with all due haste. "We can roll up outta here, definitely, but there's something I gotta grab first, and I need my ace to help me with it. Be right back."

CHAPTER FIFTY

Kyle and I rush to Storm, and the first thing I do is open the cargo door and lift the secret compartment. Inside, I pull out a small box I've been hiding all week. It took forever to get here, but it's worth it on so many levels.

I turn to see my dawg furrow his brow, wondering if he missed something. "So what's this big surprise that you've been teasing all week?"

"My nana had been holding this for me since I was little." I smile as I hold up an obsidian pendant. "She always told me that I'd know when I wanted to place this around the neck of the girl I'd fall in love with."

Kyle gives me this confuzzled expression. "I'm not getting it. I mean, I know you and Z are into each other, but this looks like a regular onyx stone."

"Actually, it's an obsidian crystal mined from our native country," I explain to him. "It's been blessed and charged by a Kindaran priestess, and it protects its wearer from negative energy and physical harm."

"No cap?"

"No cap, bro. To most people, it sounds like an urban legend, but that's not how it works for us."

"But I thought you didn't know a lot of the customs. How do you know you're not proposing marriage or something?" Kyle poses. "I ain't ready to be your best man yet, playa."

We burst into laughter for a minute, but I get where he's coming from. "I trust my nana not to steer me wrong. This isn't a promise ring or an engagement ring, but it means a lot in our culture to place this crystal around those who mean the most to us."

"Okay, that's what's up, but are you *sure*, sure about this?" Kyle asks me. "I mean, this is next level, yo. Popping the 'L' word ain't something you just toss out in the air for no reason."

I don't know how to explain it to him without it sounding like I'm out of my mind. "I don't remember the last time I felt this deeply about anything or anyone. I wouldn't do this if I wasn't sure, sure. Trust."

We tap fists before I close the door. "Then let's make the grand entrance and gesture so the rest of the girls in the place can have something else to hate on your girl about."

Kyle sprints ahead of me to head into the building so he can get everything set up for the big reveal, and I lean against the back of my car and take in the moment. I'm not playing; I can't remember feeling this good about anything, ever.

Gamba pops up, like he does when I have nervous energy. *"Are you good, kiddo? Anything I can do to settle things down?"*

"We're good, godfather," I assure him. *"There's not much to worry over tonight. In fact, things couldn't be better. I'm feeling epic."*

I move from the car to walk back to the front entrance. I slip the box into my coat pocket, making sure it's safely tucked away. *"The only thing we need to prepare for is the screaming girls when I present the pendant to my chosen—"*

I get rushed from behind and pinned against a truck. I force my way to face my attacker, anger radiating through me. Jordin stands mere inches from my face with one hand balled tight and the other gripping my shirt.

"Yo, are you kidding me? You're not even supposed to be here. I don't have time to deal with your foolishness," I say, trying to struggle out of his grasp.

"Well, whether you're in the mood or not, you're about to deal. You can bet that, playa."

I look around and try to find a way around Jordin and clear out, but Mark shows up quick with Reggie, closing my escape routes.

"I guess I should thank Ian for getting you to drop your guard tonight," Jordin utters. "This beat down is gonna be easier than I thought."

Dammit. I should've known Ian would set me up.

"It's not gonna be as easy as you think."

Gamba senses my fear and anger and rushes toward the door to my conscious mind. *"Keep your calm as best you can until the security patrol comes. We have a couple of minutes. Just hang on, kiddo."*

"I don't know if I can hold out that long," I admit. I haven't been gone long enough for Kyle to think something's gone wrong, and the parking lot is empty. Everyone else is inside enjoying themselves. Unk and Lennox are already gone after watching the waltz we performed. I've got no help. "It's all on us if things go sideways. Are you with me?"

"Always, godson."

Despite the comfort his words bring, those couple of minutes might as well be hours, and I have no idea what they're prepared to do to me. I half expect Jordin to take whatever weapon he has and put me out of my misery quick.

"Man, you still talking bad, even when you're clearly done." Jordin punches me in my mouth before I have a chance to react, and I taste blood. He split my lip with ease. "Go ahead, yell for help. All these people inside can come out and witness your demise."

"Either get this over with or let me go. Time's running out." I'm doing everything I can to stall them out. I'm pinned and vulnerable. I need Kyle, my crew, and any others to help even the odds.

"Yeah, you don't know when to shut up." He punches me again, hard enough this time for me to realize he's done playing around. "I'm gonna enjoy silencing you for good."

Nope. I'm not going out bad without a fight.

Gamba feels the flames roaring around him, and he bangs against the door. *"Yasir, I need you to calm down. I cannot get to you. The angrier you get, the more intense the flames are. Please, I need you to settle yourself."*

Nah, there's another way to handle this, and I'm here for all of it. I unlock the door and let him in, hearing something growling in the darkness that catches our attention. *"What was that?"*

"It's something I had hoped to have a chance to explain to you, but it is too late for that now," Gamba replies as the growls grow closer to the door. *"The best way to keep it at bay is for you to calm down."*

"It's a little too late for that. We're in the middle of a fight, and I don't know what they might do to us."

"Then we better find a way to defend ourselves," Gamba says. *"I will need you to trust me if things get to be too much for us. We will need what exists behind the door to keep you alive."*

"You're not making any sense, Gamba." My mind is split between talking to him and dealing with the threats in front of me. I don't know how to react to what's happening to me. *"I can feel my rage building."*

"I understand, godson. Do you trust me?"

"Yes."

Gamba nods as we peer through my eyes to figure out how to get out of this mess. *"Then when it is time, we need to let go and allow things to happen as they are supposed to happen. I promise, I will explain it all."*

"But what if someone sees what we become?"

"We will handle it…together."

Jordin lets me go, but Reggie and Mark close in on me at the same time, Reggie from the front, Mark from behind. I get the drop on Reggie, landing a right cross to his ribcage, but Mark strikes my lower back near my kidneys, bringing me to my knees in seconds.

Mark and Jordin are on top of me before I can rise to my feet, raining elbows and fists down on me. The three of them find every inch of exposed bone and muscle that I can't protect. Every spot I cover after it's struck, they find three other spots to exploit and damage.

Then someone pops up that I don't expect to be there, and it only fuels my rage, knowing that he got the better of me, and

I allowed it to happen. He just stands there, watching me get pummeled within an inch of my life, and I can hear him laughing the whole time.

I try to keep blocking, but the pain's taking over.

"You really aren't as good as advertised, my guy. I expected you to at least fight back. I guess you're more like your folks than I thought," Ian taunts.

"Bro, what the fuck? You're gonna let these boys do this right here?" I can't hide my anger, and that dig at my parents was a low blow. "What happened to sticking up for the Grove?"

"Well, I mean, they have to get theirs, considering three of theirs were hurt, right?"

I yell out in pain, using my arms and hands to protect my head and face from the barrage of blows I take. The growling inside my head grows more intense, gets closer to my conscious mind, but it feels familiar, almost like I'm welcoming an old friend. My mind is having a hard time understanding it all, and it's confusing things.

"Now, Yasir! It is time!" Gamba screams out. I'm still trying to sort through my rage and fear, but letting him take control feels like the only option if we're gonna get through this alive.

Enough is enough.

I don't care who sees what happens next. I'm ready to jump off the edge and into the abyss. As far as I'm concerned, we can lay waste to everything and let Nyati sort it out. "I warned you, and now it's my turn!"

The next thing I see is a blinding flash of light, then I hear a blood-curdling roar I don't recognize from within it.

What comes next...legit scares the living hell out of me.

CHAPTER FIFTY-ONE

All I feel is darkness. And rage. And the desire for retribution. And for once, I don't care.

The shift happens quicker than the blink of an eye, and I'm so dialed up, I sense everything around me. My sight is nearly panoramic, and I hear things from so far away, I swear I can hear Unk and Lennox as they're just getting home from their night out.

I look down at my hands and see claws and how different my skin looks. It's literally a midnight black hue, and the thin layer of hair that covers my arms and the rest of my body makes me look absolutely menacing. I feel…taller? I don't know how to explain it, but my line of sight is so much different from up here. When I stretch my arms out to grab Mark and Reggie, I notice my limbs are *way* longer than I remember.

What in the world have I become?

All my senses are dialed up to a hundred. Everything, everywhere, all at once. It's coming close to overwhelming me, and I'm struggling to focus on anything when I know why my nonhuman form has risen to the surface.

I hear the screams from the boys, the abject horror fills their eyes. Instead of empathy, I'm licking my lips in anticipation of what I plan to do to them as soon as I get my claws into them. I let out a hair-raising growl, casting my eyes skyward to bay at the moon, then settle my attention back to them, taking delight in their fear, wishing they knew that it was *me* inside of this hulking creature.

While I enjoy the hunt for my prey, I can't help but feel a little distracted the moment I hear Zahra's voice cut through the noise.

She's trying to get to me, and Kendyl and the rest of the crew is trying to stop her.

"Yasir's in trouble. We need to get to him now!" I hear her say through the partying crowd around her.

"Z, what are you doing? We need to head that way, not toward whatever the hell is happening out there."

"You don't understand, Kenni. I have to get to him. Something's wrong. Something's really wrong."

"Yasir can take care of himself, baby. We have to get somewhere safe," I hear Kendyl yell out. "You can't possibly do anything that won't make things worse."

"I'm telling you right now, if you want to go, then go, but I've got to see what's going on. You can let me go, or I can force my way through. Your choice." I can hear it in her tone. She's gonna get her way, whether they like it or not. "I promise I'll be okay. I'll catch up with you in a bit."

While I'm distracted, Reggie and Mark manage to escape from where I cornered them. That's okay. I can catch them with ease. I spot Reggie first, trying to hide behind a car. He peeks over the hood, and before he knows it, I'm on top of him, ready to finish what I started. He screams again, running from the car just as I come close to snatching him mid-stride.

The cars are becoming a nuisance, and they need to be out of my way, so I lift and flip and toss everything in my path, not realizing the ease of how I'm able to do it. *The sheer strength I possess is unbelievable. I feel like I'm playing with Hot Wheels toy cars, and everything else that's in my path may as well be paper weights.*

The explosions from the leaking gas and engines don't faze me in the slightest. Metal is screeching and glass is shattering all around me, and I can't get enough of it. The carnage I'm leaving in my wake only fuels my desire to create even more chaos.

I let out another roar that echoes through the night air, and I feel like my anger and frustration, everything I've suppressed in an effort to behave and not cause trouble, is wrapped inside of that howl. Even the horrified screams from the onlookers cowering just inside the entrance to the hall don't affect me. I won't be satisfied until they're eliminated.

"Now this is what I'm talking about." I feel so powerful, like I can do anything I put my mind to. It feels too good to stop what I'm doing.

"Then let us handle this and be done with it," Gamba growls as we continue to pursue the boys. *"They need to know who they're dealing with."*

I finally track down and trap Mark against a car. There's nowhere for him to go without catching my claws, and the terror-filled look in his eyes makes me realize that he's figured it out, too. I stalk him slowly, my grin widening, and growl, showing my intention to end him where he stands.

"Please don't kill me, please!" he screams, but I'm fresh out of mercy. All I want is for him to suffer. "Oh my God, please, let me go!"

I can feel my feet clawing through the concrete, leaving prints behind as I continue to stalk my prey. Somehow, Mark manages to crawl under the vehicle, but he's still not safe from me. I grab the roof with both hands and throw the car over my shoulders, hearing it explode as it lands on top of the mangled heap of metal I've left in my wake.

I drop to all fours, using my agility to get ahead of Mark and trap him again. This time he's in a corner, and there's nowhere for him to escape. The flickering light from the damaged streetlamp above makes for the perfect backdrop for what's about to happen to him, the fear etched in his face leading to the fact that he knows his life is over.

I bare my teeth, moving closer and closer to dispatching Mark into permanent darkness.

It won't stop with him. The other two are still in the area. I can smell their distinctive scents. They won't be able to escape.

"Hey! Over here! Over here!" I hear a frantic voice trying to get my attention. The pitch sounds different, and I'm having a hard time making sure it is who I think it is, but after a few seconds, my senses sharpen, and I know who it is in a heartbeat.

Zahra.

I turn around, staring her down as I feel the heat swirling around me simmer down to a burn. I don't know how it's happening so fast, but I don't question it. Her eyes draw me in, even in my angered state of mind, and the strangest thing happens in that moment.

She closes her eyes, and while I don't see her lips moving, I hear what she's telling me loud and clear. "*Karasu horo.*"

Hearing it sounds like a thunderclap in my ears, snapping me to attention. I whip around to face her, and she's staring me down, almost commanding me when she repeats our phrase. "*Karasu horo.*"

In the next instant, my teeth withdraw into my mouth, my growl turns into a low mewl, and I drop to my knees. I still can't break through the anger I'm feeling, but it isn't as hard as before. I breathe deeply, allowing her voice, her energy, to seep into my pores, giving me every reason to settle down and take control again.

"*What is happening, Yasir?*" Gamba's confused over why we've stopped our rampage. "*Why are we stopping? We need to end this, now.*"

"*It's my turn to say I'll explain later, but you will have to trust me,*" I say. "*That's an order.*"

I turn my attention to Zahra, who hasn't moved an inch. "I hear you, my chosen. I'm here. I'm scared."

"I know, baby. I need you to calm down," she says. "I can sense your pain, but this isn't the way to deal with it. We'll figure this out together, I promise."

I'm at a loss over how we're communicating telepathically. I don't know how we're able to talk like this, but I'm grateful no one else can hear us.

Gamba grabs my arm, shaking me from the connection with Zahra. "*I understand now. We need to take control before the beast regains strength. Zahra has it distracted, so we need to concentrate*" *on putting it back in its cage."*

"It's not gonna want to go quietly. You know that, right?"

"Yes, I know, which is why we need to take advantage of the distraction before—"

"On my mark, unload it all." Lieutenant Greer, Sargent Bolton's superior officer, gives the order for the officers to fire on me. The fear in my heart that I might die is overwhelming me, and all I can think about is figuring out how quickly I can escape the bullets that are coming my way. "FIRE!"

I feel the first of them hit my hide, and I realize they're needles, not bullets. I knock them off as soon as they penetrate, and it hits me that they're using tranquilizer darts. I don't know how to feel about that. I don't want to be killed, but I don't want to be poked and prodded like an animal once I return to my human form, either. I can only hope that they don't take effect and I can get out of here.

The next thing I know, I hear the other officers yelling, "Where did it go? It just disappeared."

No, I haven't. I'm right here standing in front of them.

And then I start to rise, almost like I've taken flight. I feel light and airy, and when I look down at the group of officers, I realize I'm floating over and away from them. How in the hell am I able to do that?

The last thing I notice before it disappears from my view are all the vehicles that are overturned, most of them engulfed in flames, and a whole lot of confused people, including all the kids who have come out of the building to survey the damage. Zahra's being consoled by Sarge, and it almost breaks me that I can't be with her.

All I can do is try to find a space to land and get back to myself. I've left a complicated mess of a situation to explain.

CHAPTER FIFTY-TWO

My emotions shift between fear and anger as I sail through the forest outside of the building. I hope to find a safe space to return to my human form, and it better happen fast. There won't be much time; the police could be making the rounds to try and find me, and I can't get caught out in the open where I'm at my most vulnerable.

Soon, our incorporeal form solidifies, and we're able to touch the ground again in my human form. My clothes are gone, except for my tuxedo pants…or, at least, what's left of them. Panic rips through me as I figure out how I'm gonna be able to find some other clothes to cover myself. Indecent exposure is not the move after all the confusion tonight.

My next freak-out moment…the pendant I wanted to give to Zahra tonight. Before I shifted to my nonhuman form, it's a good bet that the jacket ripped apart. There's no telling what could've happened to it. By Nyati, I hope I can find it once this is all over.

I scan around again in search of anyone who may be in the area before I retreat inside my mind to have a convo. "What the hell happened back there? We could have killed someone. Seriously, Gamba, that was a populated area, and we were out in plain sight. I thought you had things handled."

Gamba shakes his head as I create a veranda on the shores of Kindara from one of my paintings for us to engage in a more civil discussion. "I did what I could, kiddo, but your rage took over and brought the beast from the depths. You both shut me out so you could satisfy your bloodlust. If it were not for Zahra distracting it, there is no telling what else would have happened tonight."

I tilt my head to the side, confused by the explanation. I ease into the lounger, taking a sip of water, considering Gamba's words. "So you mean to tell me that there's something else here with us? Where did it come from and how did it just show up out of nowhere?"

"Whether you want to believe it or not, everyone has a dark side," Gamba says as he joins me on the landing. "The problem is when you deny that it exists."

"Well, I'm not everyone." I stare off into the horizon. "What makes you think I want to indulge that side of myself? That I want to become the monster that Ian's trying to convince the whole town that I already am?"

Gamba exhales slow, and I feel the frustration rising inside him. "You are not a monster, my godson, but you cannot ignore that side of yourself. To become your truest self, you have to embrace the light…and the darkness. It is only then that you will be able to control the rage that is in all of us. No one is immune to it."

"Do you remember what happened a few minutes ago?" I ask, allowing the bluntness of my question to land between us. "Whether I'm a monster or not, damn near the entire town saw what we look like in nonhuman form. Nyati only knows how many took out their phones and recorded everything."

I hear a twig snap, jarring me from our conversation. My senses are still heightened from the transformation, so I focus my hearing to pick up where the activity is coming from. Gamba focuses on the sound as well, using the beast's energy to increase my hearing sensitivity. We hear the sheriffs cutting through the brush, realizing that they're still on the hunt. *"How far off do you think they are?"*

"Maybe a couple hundred feet, give or take," Gamba tells me. *"We will have to deal with the other issues later. Right now, we need to get to safety. Sounds like the sheriffs have picked up the trail."*

I hear voices bellowing through the night air, calling for me to let them know I'm okay. Part of me wants to yell out and put an end to the search, but something from deep within urges me to remain hidden. I keep moving, getting to the outer edge of the forest and into a clearing, heading toward another parking area. I find one of the vendor trucks, and the cargo area is wide open. I see some clothing left in plain sight, and I sprint over, praying something fits so I can concentrate on the more pressing issues at hand.

I hear the one voice I don't need, immediately wishing I stayed put within the tree line. Dammit.

"I was wondering if I would run into you again," Ian huffs as he leans against his Corvette. "You and I have an unfinished conversation to work through."

"Don't you have a curfew or something, my boy? I don't have time for games or bullshit conversation." I stand still, no longer bothering to hide my irritation. "It's been a long night. You tried for a second time to take me out and failed, okay? You were the one who riled up those Baytown kids. Let's just hit the reset button, go home, get some sleep, and try it again next week, huh?"

"Nah, we can do this right here and now." Ian steps in my direction. "And from the looks of your clothes, I'd say you have a lot of questions to answer. Let's see if I can rile you up again the way they did. Everyone's already seen what you can become. I just need the sheriffs to see for themselves and we can wrap this up, neat and clean."

Kyle and Taylor pop out of the tree line, along with Sarge and LT. LT steps in front of Ian while Sarge shadows me. Kyle and Taylor stand with me as I try, and fail, to step around Sarge to get to Ian.

"Your girl is worried sick about you, Yasir," Kyle announces. "We couldn't find you when those Baytown boys ganged up on you."

"That's because he and that thing that showed up might be one and the same, Kyle," Ian shouts. "He's a menace to this town, I'm telling you. You don't see his clothes right now?"

I'm desperate to find a plausible answer to throw everyone off the trail. The only people who saw me turn were Ian and Jordin and his crew, so I have a chance to still cast some doubt. "That thing was chasing me, and I barely got away from it. It managed to corner me, and in my haste to escape, it started clawing at my clothes. I was lucky one of the vendor trucks was still around, or I'd be half naked out here."

"All right, boys, let's settle it down a notch. We've found Yasir, and there doesn't seem to be any sign of the beast we saw earlier." Sarge jumps into the conversation to calm things down as best as possible.

"I told you before that you're off-key, all right?" Kyle demands as he focuses in on Ian. "You and these wild theories are getting really weak, for real. You have no proof and bad blood. Any idiot can tell you got pressure, my guy."

"I got pressure, all right, but that doesn't mean I'm wrong." Ian waves us off and opens the door to his car, then slides into the seat. "But as usual, Sarge and LT are here to save the damn day, so we'll have to pick this up another time."

LT inserts himself into the conversation. "What is Ian talking about, fellas? If you know something about what happened earlier tonight, you need to let us know. We'll have to keep searching for it until we get a positive ID."

That declaration sounds like a bad underground mixtape to my ears. This isn't going to go away anytime soon. I better find a way to spin this before it becomes a problem I can't solve. "It might have been a one and done, LT."

"I hear you, Yasir, but we have to make sure. The public that was here tonight will have their tongues wagging on social media by morning, and we need to be on top of things," LT says. "I'm gonna need you boys to scatter, get home. If we need you for anything else, we'll alert your parents."

Ian doesn't bother to stick around, slamming the door and screeching the tires while making his exit. The boys and I are left to deal with Sarge and LT, and that conversation seems to be long overdue.

"Yasir, what did we tell you about being the bigger man and keeping out of the mess you're already in right now?" Sarge closes his eyes for a few moments. "Thankfully, there were witnesses to your earlier incident and we know you weren't the aggressor, but you have to be smarter."

"Yeah, while the golden child gets off scot-free with everything he's done, right?" I counter. "Don't worry, I'll wait."

"Okay, you've made your point. We've been treating the family with kid gloves ever since they stepped into the mayor's office," Sarge admits. He glances at Kyle and Taylor, dropping a not-so-subtle clue on them. "And it's extended to people who shouldn't be putting themselves in the position to have to utilize that type of clout."

"So what happens now, Sarge? Do I get to go home, too?" I ask in earnest. I have to find Zahra. She's got to be worried sick, and she's driving my Storm, too. "Or is this gonna be one of those type of nights where paperwork is involved?"

Sarge cuts his eyes toward LT, getting a subtle nod from his superior officer. "You're good to go, Yasir, but be careful with anything you might be feeling as far as vengeance goes. We still have to follow social media buzz."

I simply nod and plod toward Kyle's truck to hop inside. As Kyle and Taylor slip inside, I wait for the engine to roar to life, content to get home as quickly as possible so I can put this nightmare of a night in the proverbial rear-view mirror.

"Yo, shouldn't you be getting with Z to let her know we found you? She's probably worried sick." Kyle turns to check on me in the back seat. "And what about your surprise gift? You still need to get that to her."

"I don't even know where it is," I reply. "I lost it, and my tux got ripped to shreds. For all I know, it's probably at the hall in the parking lot. Anyone could've found it."

"Then we need to head back there before they lock it down and see if we can find it," Kyle tells me, holding up his hand when I launch a protest. "We need to do this. I'm not gonna let you go out bad."

"Nah, bro, I'm gonna have to reevaluate some things, and I can't do that with her distracting me. I appreciate you looking out, but I need to hit the reset button." I slump in the seat, completely exhausted. "I don't care what you have to tell your girls. I just need to get home."

We pull up to the house after leaving the banquet hall (Kyle can be really persuasive when he wants to get his way), and I'm not gonna lie, I'm glad that we were able to find my pendant. I probably would've gone crazy if I'd lost it.

But that's not on my mind anymore.

The first thing I spot once I get out of the truck is Storm.

I don't know how Zahra could've known I was coming here. I made sure to tell my boys not to let anyone know I was heading home just yet, but here I am, trying to figure out what to say to Zahra before I'm ready to have the convo. My emotions are still all over the place.

The moment she exits the car, my heart skips a few beats. I'm happy to see her, but I hoped to get myself together first. I won't be able to tell her to go home, no matter how badly I want her to leave. Fear mixes in with confusion as she pads in my direction, flashing that smile that makes everything better, regardless of how bad I felt things had gotten.

"Are you okay? I was worried about you." She continues to check me over. "What happened to your clothes?"

"I'm still trying to figure out how to answer that question." I'm still reeling from everything I did to try to figure out what happened up to this point. "I woke up in the middle of the forest. The last thing I remembered before I blacked out was being damn near pummeled to death by a group of boys, and Ian led the charge."

My emotions explode, a violent storm that even Gamba can't settle down. While I'm rolling the film in my head to figure out what happened, and where things went left, at the center of it all is a simple, cold truth: I lost control...or maybe I just let myself go... and I don't know how to gain control over a beast I had no idea was there inside of me, too.

I lean against Storm's driver side, still trying to sort through my feelings, barely keeping eye contact with Zahra. I want to reach out to embrace her, but my thoughts are dominated by the images of the people who saw my nonhuman form and reacted with such fear and aggression. It's gonna be a minute before I forget how it made me feel.

I ignore Gamba as he tries to catch my attention. I'm not in the greatest headspace, and the overwhelming desire to isolate myself from everything and everyone races to the surface.

Zahra slips her fingers over mine, placing soft kisses across my lips. "I'm glad the boys found you. We'd been looking all over for you after…well, after all the confusion at the ball."

"Yeah, we managed to catch up to him without incident," Kyle mentions. "It's been a wild night, to say the least."

Taylor adds, "Bro, we've had wild nights before, but tonight was a whole level of weird. I'm still trying to wrap my head around what we saw tonight."

I drop my head, kissing Zahra's shoulder as I make every effort to calm down. "I had hoped to have a normal night with you, baby, but as usual, that jackass had to find a way to screw it all up. I'm beginning to wonder if there's a such thing as a normal night."

"What's important right now is that you're home safe," Zahra tells me. "And I'm sure we can find a way to salvage the night."

Kyle taps my fists as he and Taylor head back to his truck. "Kenni just hit me up. She's on the way to drop your car off before we jet, Z, so we'll stick around until she gets here."

"Yo, Kyle, TK, thanks for having my back. It means a lot to me, more than you know." I tap fists with Taylor, feeling the overwhelming urge to express my gratitude.

"That makes two of us, Yasir," Taylor utters.

"We'll leave you two to your privacy. I'm sure you have some catching up to do," Kyle says before they leave us alone. "And take care of that *other* thing you were planning, all right?"

"What's Ky talking about?" Zahra moves closer to me as the

others pull out of the driveway, finally leaving us in some peace and quiet.

I sigh as I consider my words. There's no easy way to say it, so I blurt them out before I lose my nerve. "I'm not safe to be around anymore."

Zahra raises an eyebrow. "What are you talking about? You're not making sense."

"You saw what happened earlier tonight, Z. Stop pretending that it didn't happen," I snap. I don't want to react that way, but the flood gates are open. "All that rage, all that anger, all because Ian triggered me."

Zahra grips my hands tight, pulling me closer. By Nyati, she feels so good in my arms. "We will figure this out, Ya-Ya. You're not alone in this. I'm right here. I already know what's going on with you, baby."

"Wait…what? How is that possible? You never got the chance to see what I can become before tonight."

"There's a longer conversation that we will need to have when we're with Ms. Kynani again, but I know what's going on with you, and I'm not afraid."

"No, I need to stay away from all of you until I can get a better grip on whatever *beast* keeps taking over me," I counter, struggling to keep my voice from cracking. "I'll never forgive myself if I hurt you."

"I'm a big girl, and I can handle whatever you think you have going on in there," Zahra shoots back as she taps her manicured finger against my temple. "Even when it was out and acting on all your rage and fear, the minute it saw me, it recognized me. Don't you dare push me away. We can get through this."

"Until I get triggered, right? I don't care that you were able to get it to settle down for a few seconds. You can't be everywhere, and if someone sets me off again, I can't be sure that I can calm down. It didn't even work earlier, or I would have had a chance to come to the surface. I was just that far gone." I tear up, and I'm no longer sure I can stop them from falling. "I can't take that chance. I've got to figure this out alone. It's better for everyone."

"It's better for me? Shouldn't I also have a say in this?" Zahra scoffs, shaking her head in defiance over what she's hearing. "You're giving up on us? Tell me that's not what you're saying."

"I don't have a choice, Z."

"You do have a choice, dammit. Do you love me?"

"Don't you hear what I'm telling you? I can't have someone's death on my hands," I tell her. I step away, creating space between us. "I'm scared of what's happening to me, but I need to get a handle on this."

Her eyes never leave mine. "Do…you…love…me? I know you do. There's nothing you can say that will convince me that you don't. Tell me you love me."

I take a breath. I gotta get my emotions under control, period. I don't mean what I am saying, but I can't have her harmed because of something I did. I cut out all the noise, searching for a voice of reason, anything to help me figure out what to do next. How am I supposed to explain to her the rage I'm feeling? She knows about Gamba, but this monster that dwells within me is another matter entirely.

"Yasir…do not let her go."

The voice shoots through me, stopping me cold. Hearing it unlocks something inside me, almost compelling me to listen. Even after all this time, it soothes me, its warmth feeling like a thick blanket. Mom. Like before.

I don't even question how she's able to reach me. I'm making sure I put her advice into action.

I reach out to pull Zahra closer without any hesitation, cupping her face in my hands and kissing her with every ounce of energy I have left. I pick her up and sit her on the hood, watching her eyes as they switch from a fiery red to a calming ice blue. I don't care about anything else; I just need her right there with me. I ignore the eye color changes for now; we'll have time to figure all of that out later.

Like she said, we have a different conversation to have with Ms. Kynani.

Without wasting another second, I pull out the box that holds the pendant, take it out, and drop the box on the ground. I'm holding it in my hands like my life depends on clasping it around her neck.

"I love you. I love you. I. *Love*. You." I keep kissing her lips, convincing myself that this isn't a dream. "Forget what I just said. I didn't mean any of it. I can't do this without you. You're my chosen. Please, say you won't leave me?"

"I never left, my chosen. I love you, too. I just found you, and you're not getting rid of me that easily." She wipes the tears rolling down her cheeks. "I know this is scary, but we'll figure this out… together. Promise. Now, what's this in your hand?"

I smile wide as I glance down at the small but significant piece of jewelry that has the power to change everything between us. "This was something Nana wanted me to give to the one who means the most to me in this world. *You* are that one."

She starts trembling the moment I place the necklace around her neck, pulling her hair up so I can connect the clip. "Is this what I think it is? Is this an obsidian stone from home?"

"Yes. Do you know what it means?"

She nods excitedly, planting more kisses across my lips. "I know what it means. Do *you* know what it means?"

Kendyl pulls into the driveway with Raiden before I can answer her. I keep Zahra right there on the hood, refusing to let her out of my sight.

Kendyl slows her pace, reading the body language between us. She gives Zahra a head-to-toe scan as she wipes her face, and her bestie is ready to read me up one side and down the other. "Is everything okay? Z, you look like — Yasir, what did you do?"

Zahra takes one look at me and closes her eyes. The smile she offers reflects the fatigue we both feel after such an emotionally exhaustive night. "It's been a long night, chica, but we are okay. We are better than okay. There's a lot that we have to explain, but it will have to wait until morning."

I don't have much else to add to that. I'm tired from everything over the past two nights. "Yeah, we'll see y'all in the morning. We can talk once we've had a decent night's sleep."

Zahra and I watch as Kendyl and Tania get into vehicles and pull out of the driveway. Then I escort her to Raiden, tucking her into the driver's seat, slipping a few more kisses before I wave and wait for her car to disappear around the corner.

I don't have it in me to explain to Unk and Lennox about what happened tonight. I'll have to deal with that in the morning. I take the remaining energy I have to climb to the studio window so I can avoid them altogether, thanking the gods that the alarm system only covers the first floor and the basement levels. I deftly slip inside and slowly descend the stairs, hoping I'm not making too much noise along the way.

When I make it to my bedroom, I plunge head-first onto the bed, screaming into the comforter and hoping neither Unk nor Lennox can hear me. So much has happened tonight, and there's no telling what tomorrow's convos will reveal. There's no way I can keep this from those I care about the most anymore. They need to know what they're getting themselves into and what we're asking of them.

No matter what happens, I have Zahra by my side. I can handle anything.

"It will be okay, kiddo. This is a bump in the road." Gamba cuts through the fog in my mind, trying to balance me as best he can. *"We will have the chance to sit down and talk things out with everyone in the morning. Just rest for now."*

"I will, but there's one more thing that I need to do."

In a last-ditch effort to grasp at whatever sanity I have left, I pull my phone from my pocket and tap on the number…outside of Gamba…with the one person who can possibly help me climb out of the darkness and unlock my memories so I can put everything together. With the threats from the mysterious caller to add to the chaos, it truly is a matter of life and death now.

My hands are shaking as the line trills, and the moment the call connects, my voice cracks. "Ms. Kynani? I'm scared. I really need your help."

ACKNOWLEDGMENTS

Happy 2023! Whew, this has been a journey!

When I first conceived Neverwraith, I immediately tabbed it as a promise fulfilled. A promise to my daughter and her third-grade classmates on a fateful Career Day way back in 2011. And a promise to my teenage self, who didn't see himself in the heroes he read about away from the comic book world. I was gonna get this book written for them, if for nothing else.

This has been a journey that has given me the ability to remember why I started writing in the first place. To be able to conjure new worlds, new characters, and see how far my imagination would take me. Only now, I get to employ a bit of #blackboymagic into the equation and create the type of young, gifted, and Black teenage boy that other Black boys would be able to see themselves in. It is my hope that I've done that for them.

And this is only the beginning!

Now, let's get to the standard issue part of the program where you get to know all the people who helped me get to the point to where you're reading right now, shall we?

To my parents, eternally, for your guidance, your love, and your support, for when you were here with me and from behind the veil, too. Mom, this is the first book I've released since you've been gone, and I can't wait to tell you and Dad about this whole journey as soon as I can.

To my sister, thank you for being in my corner, for being as much my hero as I hope I've been for you. I'm with you until the end of the line. Love you!

To my Beloved, for putting up with every peak, every valley of this rollercoaster ride, and handling it all every step of the way. I love you so much.

To my daughter… Daddy loves you, babygirl. Full stop. You've inspired me in ways I can't express, and I'm proud of the young woman you're becoming. I've got your back, no matter what.

To my extended family and friends, thank you for handling the hyperactive moments and not wringing my neck, for helping me through some of the more difficult parts of the book, and cheering me on every step of the way.

To my TRIBE, and the boss lady, Naleighna Kai … my other extended family, thank you all for getting your brother in the pen to the first checkpoint in this new journey. I can't wait for you to see what else I have in store! There's too many of y'all to call out, but you know who you are.

To my agent and "big sis," Lissa Woodson, this next phase of my career is all you. I'm blessed to have placed my trust in your vision for my brand and how you saw the way my literary universe would evolve. I'm calling it now; I'll be your first NYT bestselling client.

To my entire Entangled team: Liz Pelletier, Lydia, Rae, Riki, Meredith, Jessica, Bree, Curtis, Stacy, Hannah, and Brittany (I'm probably forgetting someone, so charge it to my head and not my heart), for all your efforts to help me bring my kids into the spotlight. This has been a wild ride, and I can't wait for you to see what happens next!

To my new besties, Tracy Wolff and Abigail Owen, thank you for putting up with my random texts and phone calls throughout this whole process. I appreciate you more than you know!

And to my readers, from my Day Ones to those new to my universe, I couldn't do any of this without your continued support. This "grateful prince" will do his level best to continue to create more worlds and characters and everything in between.

Neverwraith is a fun, action-packed book inspired by superhero origin stories. However, it contains some difficult themes and elements that might not be suitable for some readers. These include: Violence, blood, bullying, drowning, struggles with mental health, racial microagressions, mentions of war and genocide, alcohol and drug use, and mentions of parental death. Readers who may be sensitive to these, please take note.

Let's be friends!

🐦 @EntangledTeen

📷 @EntangledTeen

ⓕ @EntangledTeen

♪ @EntangledTeen

📰 bit.ly/TeenNewsletter

entangled teen

an imprint of Entangled Publishing LLC